MARKUS KANE

DAWN OF SHADOWS

ISAIAH BURCH JR

SILVERSMITH
PRESS

Published by Silversmith Press–Houston, Texas
www.silversmithpress.com

ISBN 978-1-967386-17-8 (Softcover Book)
ISBN 978-1-967386-18-5 (eBook)

To My Parents

CONTENTS

PART I:
DISCOVERY

PART II:
ALLIES AND ENEMIES

PART III:
TRIAL BY FIRE

Map of Aerias – Realms, Kingdoms & Territories

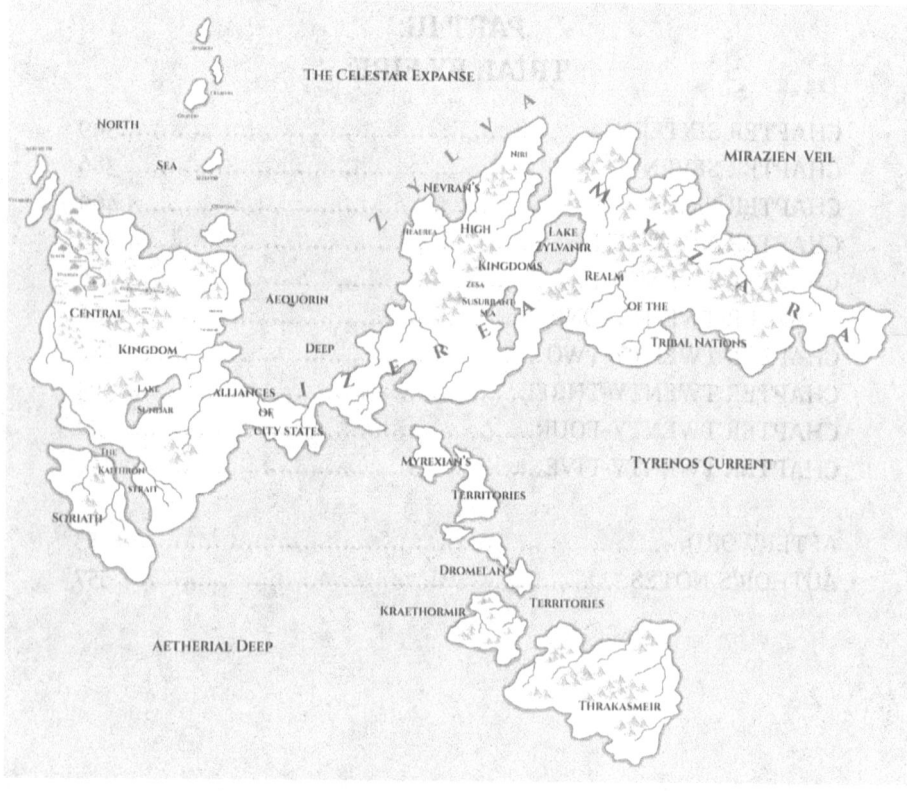

As charted by the Lorekeepers of Niri, 3rd Compilation Year

PART I:
DISCOVERY

CHAPTER ONE

The black scar from a wound carved down Markus' temple should have killed him. Some days he wished it had.

Tonight, it burned like a brand, throbbing in time with the neon signs that painted Vesper's skyline in artificial day.

As his fingers traced the familiar grip of his pulse pistol, he scanned the street through his binoculars. From his perch above the industrial district, he watched the city's nightly transformation: bright signs blazing for the highborn, while shadows claimed the alleys below. Steam vents hissed through cracked pavement where ancient stone met modern metal—a city that never quite decided what it wanted to be. Aerglides threaded between horse-drawn carriages, their antigrav hum mixing with the clatter of iron wheels on cobblestones. Three millennia of progress, and still the old ways refused to die.

At twenty-one, he'd learned to read these streets like others read books, knowing which shadows meant safety and which portended violence. Xara's intel never failed, but in this district, timing meant everything. He adjusted his binoculars, scanning.

A sleek, black aerglide pulled up across the street, incongruent in the rain-soaked grit of the neighborhood. Markus lifted his binoculars, shifting his gaze to the man stepping out—a tall figure in a tailored coat with the collar pulled up, the hem slick and uncreased from the ride. This had to be him. Markus caught a glint from the man's wrist—a heavy, custom gold watch Xara had warned him about, the kind usually reserved for business deals made in back rooms.

The man's hair was fair and neatly parted. But it was the smooth, rehearsed movements that marked him most: precise, like someone used to getting in and out of places without a glance from the crowd. As Markus studied him, he noted another touch Xara had pointed out—a signet ring flashing briefly as the man lowered the vehicle's door, a silent nod to an old, privileged family. Her client, right on time.

Markus' hand hovered over his pulse pistol—an M-12 "Stinger," fingers tense as he tracked his target through his binoculars. The man was crossing toward the east side of the district, slipping into the shadows where the neon signs faded and crystalline light-posts wavered, barely cutting through the dark. Indulgence and rot, Markus thought. He could feel the weight of it pressing down, heavy as the mist clinging to chrome railings and pooling in the alley gutters.

Just as Markus adjusted his binoculars, the man turned a corner and disappeared. Instinct firing through him, he moved fast, leaping to the ledge of the rooftop and scanning the alley below. In an instant, he vaulted over the edge, landing soundlessly on the top railing of the steel fire escape. Balancing there for a second, he gauged the distance, then sprang across a narrow alley, landing silently on the opposite rooftop.

From here, he had a better angle. Markus crouched low, his breathing controlled as his binoculars found his target again, the man's blond head bobbing through the thinning crowd. The city lights cast fragmented shadows on his face as he moved toward the red canopy of The Hive, where secrets and expensive contracts were hatched in silence. Markus' jaw tightened.

The silhouette vanished beneath the canopy—the kind that whispered you're seen by no one here. The Hive. A place that let people like him disappear, even the city's highest names with their blood ties and untouched reputations.

Markus caught his breath, forcing his heartbeat back to a steady rhythm. Every instinct urged him to move closer, to tail this man right into that den of indulgence and decay. But he held back. One wrong move and his target would be tipped off. Besides, he knew he didn't belong in a place like The Hive. Even dressed in his best black leather, sleek enough for the job, he'd stick out among the elite like grit in their wine. Watchmen were low on the Guild's list, barely good for more than temporary work when nothing better opened. The magistrate might bluff his way through those doors, but for the rest, entry cost more than a badge could buy.

Markus shrugged the thought off in disgust, keeping his focus sharp as the man disappeared beneath the crimson canopy. No, he'd stay right here, ready for Xara's signal, lurking in the shadows where he belonged.

* * *

The host's eyes flicked toward the door as the man entered with a measured stride. He wore a black suit tailored to perfection, contrasting with a crisp white shirt pristine against the haze of dim lights and lingering smoke. Golden hair slicked back and a neatly trimmed beard gave his features a sharp, almost cinematic quality. Every movement was deliberate, each gesture exuding a calm confidence that turned heads.

The gentleman paused, handing his coat to the host with a flick of his wrist. His gaze turned briefly to his own reflection in the foyer's ornate gilt mirror, a hint of satisfaction with a touch of vanity crossing his face as he adjusted his tie.

"Good evening, sir. May I have your name, please?" the host inquired.

A subtle nod. "Hans ... Lumen."

The high-end nightclub was a testament to the kingdom's heritage. Vintage crystal chandeliers hung from the ceiling, their light enhanced by Guild engineering to cast a flattering red glow over the room. The wealthy here preferred to conduct their schemes the old way—handwritten contracts and whispered deals, even though data tablets gleamed on their wrists. Some said it was tradition, others insisted Guild-enhanced paper couldn't be hacked like digital records.

Around them, bankers and smugglers moved through the space like pieces on a chess board, each step measured, each discussion weighted. Some wore the latest hover-tech accessories, while others displayed the traditional signet rings that had sealed deals for gen-erations. The grand setting exuded sophistication, yet its suave allure belied a darker, more dangerous edge.

Hans stepped into his reserved suite, a thrill coursing through him at the sight that awaited. Programmable crystals bathed the room in deep red wavelengths designed to flatter human skin tones. There, seated with the poise of a queen, was the most alluring crea-ture in the room. Her skin, the color of warm honey, seemed to absorb the light rather than reflect it. A del-icate silver chain rested against her collarbone, as its pendant—a winged Alq'arus—gleamed softly with each movement, an elegant contrast to her warm skin tones. She was indeed an untouchable thing of beauty.

Hans barely noticed the tray of appetizers glistening with sugars and syrup. His attention was entirely on her. Such a vision, this sensual and captivating creature, a woman who could stir chaos with a single glance!

"Quite the introduction to the main course," he said, eyes lingering on her as he took her gloved hand, bringing it to his lips with a gentle kiss. The brief contact sent a jolt through him; one he quickly masked with a suave smile.

"Lovely indeed."

Her lips curved into a knowing smile. "You're refer-ring to the menu, of course, Mr. Lumen."

He raised an eyebrow, intrigued. "Naturally. Xara, isn't it?"

"Much easier to pronounce than my full name," she replied, her voice a low velvet drawl. Her lips shaped each syllable of her Nevrish name with deliberate grace, every movement a calculated performance.

"A Nevrish name on an Earthen woman," he observed, his gaze lingering on her. "Quite the surprise."

"Expect many more tonight," she purred, leaning in slightly. "Shall we get down to business?"

The conversation flowed as smoothly as the wine. Each time Hans glanced up from a document, her eyes were already on him.

Her allure was undeniable, and Hans found it harder and harder to focus on the papers before him. He could feel the heat of her gaze, the way she toyed with him— her words laced with double entendre, her smile a delicate dance between invitation and warning.

"I must thank you for meeting me in person, Xara," Hans said, finally setting down the last document. "In an age of digital transactions, face-to-face meetings have become ... precious."

Her eyes, sharp as blades, held his. "You were quite persistent, Mr. Lumen. I usually don't comply with such ... requests." She paused, her gaze lingering on him a beat too long. "What exactly is your business, again?"

Hans leaned forward, his voice dropping to a conspiratorial whisper. "Acquisitions. Mining companies, for now. But I believe a woman with your skills shouldn't remain hidden in the underworld for much longer. I could offer you something far more ... lucrative."

Her lips curled in amusement. "More lucrative than counterfeiting and forgery?" Her voice dripped with skepticism, but the gleam in her eyes was playful. "I find that hard to believe."

He mirrored her look, their faces mere inches apart. "Perhaps we could discuss your role on my personal staff?"

Xara's eyes narrowed, a smirk playing on her lips. "How personal are we talking?"

Hans felt the heat rise between them; the air thick with innuendo. "That," he said smoothly, "depends entirely on you."

As she leaned in, the pendant on her necklace shifted, catching the light in a way that made it seem alive. The silver wings of the Alq'arus gleamed like embers, dangerously close to her skin. Hans found himself staring—at the delicate chain resting against the curve of her throat, at how the cool metal must have warmed to her heat. He imagined the first touch of it—how it would have been cold at first, before surrendering to her warmth, much like anything else in her presence.

His gaze flicked back up—and found hers already waiting.

Her silver eyes, as opaque and unreadable as the pendant itself, held him captive. There was something in the way she looked at him—a slow, knowing pull, like gravity itself had shifted in her favor. A silent dare. A quiet invitation. A trap?

His fingers curled around the stem of his glass, the smooth weight of it grounding him. He exhaled, a slow smile forming as he played off his momentary lapse. "Do you make all your associates this distracted, or am I just special?"

Her fingers brushed the pendant at her throat, her lips curving with lazy amusement. "Only the ones who are easily tempted, Mr. Lumen."

But just as Hans thought he had the upper hand, she leaned back, a calculated move that left him wanting more. "How about you lay all your cards on the table,

'Senator'?" Her voice was sharp, the playful tone gone.

Hans blinked, caught off guard. "I beg your pardon?"

She leaned in again, but this time, her voice was like ice. "I recognized your signature in that treaty you're hoping to pass off. You may be a senator, but I see through your games."

His smile didn't waver, but his mind raced. "That's merely a formality, my dear. Bureaucracy and politics— nothing you need to concern yourself with."

Her eyes glinted. "Perhaps. But I don't like to work for politicians. I find them ... untrustworthy. The price is now one-million crowns."

"And yet," he said, his voice softening, "I'm willing to offer you half a million crowns, and a second dinner date with a man who knows how to appreciate a woman of your caliber."

Her laugh was low and sultry. "Enticing. Let me know when he walks in."

She stood, graceful and untouchable. Hans felt a tinge of something unexpected—desire, yes, but also frustration. She was slipping through his fingers, just out of reach. He stood, and reached for her arm, but she turned and her eyes froze him in place.

"Mr. Lumen," she said softly, but with deadly precision. "May I remind you—you're not the only predator in this establishment."

For the first time, Hans felt the sting of being outplayed. He forced a smile while he adjusted his jacket. "Of course. I respect your ... talents. May I?"

He assisted her with her coat. Then his fingers slipped into his pocket to find his transmitter. One subtle click—that's all he needed. Let her think she'd won this round.

"Please. Allow me to reconvene with the mediator and work out the arrangements of meeting your price."

His voice remained smooth, practiced. "Till then, may I walk you to your 'chariot'?"

* * *

The side exit led them down a dimly lit alleyway, where two doormen offered polite farewells to the couple. Xara walked close beside Hans; her movements were graceful in her evening dress but her eyes were sharp as they catalogued every shadow. Hans' gaze darted to every corner, every dark crevice.

"Strange," Hans muttered, "that a place like this doesn't keep better lighting outside." From his post in the shadows, Markus observed them, noting details others might miss. He recognized Hans. His hand kept straying to an empty pocket—looking for a weapon that wasn't there. Xara's slight pause in step wasn't fear; it was recognition. They were being surrounded.

The first boy emerged from behind the crates, all skin and bone with a knife that caught what little light reached the alley. Markus recognized the setup—he'd run similar cons in his street days. The knife wasn't for using, just for scaring. The real threat would come from ...

"Nice suit, sir." The boy croaked with false bravado. "And you, miss—lovely dress. Could you spare a note or two? Maybe a few hundred crowns?"

Xara's fan snapped shut with a sharp click. "Isn't it

past your bedtime?" Her tone was aristocratic, bored even, but her grip on the metal fan shifted subtly—a weapon hidden in plain sight.

"Got a sharp mouth, miss. Pretty lips too—might cost you more for that insult."

"Get out of here, you filth!" Hans growled, playing right into their hands.

A second youth appeared behind them, tapping a wooden club against his palm. Markus counted the shadows—one more waiting, probably near the aerglides. Time to move.

He stepped out of the darkness, his mind already mapping the alley's weapons. Two rain barrels—perfect height for a stumble. Loose cobbles scattered like caltrops. Empty crates stacked against the wall—just enough space between them and the vehicles to trap someone. He'd fought in this alley before; its dangers were old friends.

The knife-wielder sneered. "Stay out of this, watchman. This is none of your ..."

The two teenagers paused, exchanging glances as they recognized Markus—who always left a violent taste of vigilante justice in his victim's mouth. He was the last watchman they wanted to tangle with.

"Please—do something stupid."

The boy with the knife lunged—predictable, amateur. Markus kicked one of the rain barrels, sending it rolling. Water sloshed out, slicking the cobbles. The boy's charge turned into a desperate scramble for balance. His knife clattered away.

The club-wielder came in swinging, but as he moved, Xara's fan flashed in the darkness. Metal ribs caught the boy's wrist with practiced precision. He yelped, club falling from numbed fingers. She stepped back smoothly, resuming her aristocratic pose as if she'd merely shooed away an insect.

Markus had already handled the second attacker, using the wet stones to his advantage. A third figure emerged, bigger than the others, moving toward the couple with purpose. Markus grabbed one of the fallen crates and hurled it between them. The wood splintered, forcing the man to dodge—right into the wall where he wanted him. Two quick strikes: one to the solar plexus, another to the back of the knee. The big man folded, gasping.

No blood spilled. Just efficiency born of desperate years on these same streets.

The first two boys scrambled up, dragging their larger friend as they fled into the darkness. Markus watched them go, counting heartbeats until he was sure they wouldn't double back.

"Get moving," he ordered, maintaining his official tone. His blood burned hot beneath his skin—too close to the surface. He needed them gone before the shaking started.

Hans nodded, still rattled, and offered his arm to Xara. Her composure never wavered as she accepted it, though her eyes pivoted briefly toward Markus—a look that contained volumes yet revealed nothing to anyone watching.

Their private aerglide hummed to life with the quiet precision of Guild engineering, while a more common public taxi—its older gravitic propulsion whining in protest—waited for the gentleman at the far end.

Through the taxi's fogged window, Hans studied

the watchman who'd intervened. Markus' expression revealed nothing—he'd learned long ago that the hardest fights were the ones you had to hide.

No applause, no thanks. Just bruises and silence. But that was fine. Markus didn't need to be seen—he just needed to keep the ugliness from reaching the people he loved. That had to be enough.

The taxi lifted into the rain-soaked night, its twin blades cutting through the darkness. Only when both vehicles had disappeared did Markus let out a slow breath, flexing his trembling hands. The familiar burn under his skin was rising—the price of even coming this close to combat. Another night, another fight avoided rather than won. He'd learned long ago that for him, victory meant no bloodshed, no evidence left, no questions asked.

* * *

Hans took another sip from his tin mug, the bitter black coffee doing little to warm him in the cold, damp COMM center. While the wealthy districts boasted crystal-powered heating and Guild-certified privacy screens, this public station made do with winking fluorescent and manual encryption machines that belonged in a museum. But a senator hadn't gotten where he was by being proud. Hans had climbed from district clerk to his current position, one compromised official at a time, and places like this, with their older tech and fewer records, served their own purpose.

He stood over the young technician, anxiously waiting for any incoming messages from his contacts on the other side of the kingdom.

"Still nothing, sir," the encryptor said, looking up. "I'll keep checking and let you know as soon as I receive messages."

Hans nodded but remained restless. Just as he was about to speak again, a fellow politician named Corregan entered. His tailored Capitol suit contrasted sharply with the station's worn interior. The man's silver hair and sharp features marked him as someone who'd survived decades of political warfare, though few knew exactly how.

Corregan leaned against the COMM center's window, casting a ghostly reflection in the evening gloom.

"So, she refused your offer."

It wasn't a question. Hans fought to keep his composure.

"She's demanding one million crowns."

"For forged documents?" Corregan's laugh was sharp.

"She knows their true worth then." He turned, studying Hans with newfound interest. "There's more at stake than just papers and seals, Hans. There're forces moving behind the scenes that would make your political ambitions seem ... quaint."

He reached into his coat, withdrawing a thin file. "The girl's forgeries are just one piece. Here's another—but this is all you get for now. Consider it ... insurance."

"Insurance?"

"Against what's coming." Corregan's smile was bitter. "You're not the first ambitious man I've seen climb these ranks. Most of them forgot to look down while reaching up."

He straightened his coat and moved to leave.

"Just remember—there are players in this game you

haven't met yet. Powerful ones. Don't let ambition blind you to the bigger picture."

Corregan's footsteps faded in the evening bustle.

Just as Hans tucked the file away in his coat, two men entered the room—dressed alike in blue shirts, trousers, and black jackets marked with gold-plated badges. Their sidearms and batons hung at their waists, giving them a stern, official air.

"Magistrates Dykes and Clovers," Hans said, rising. "Let's step outside for a word, shall we?"

He turned to the operator. "I'll be just outside. If anything comes through, let me know immediately."

In the hallway, the three men casually glanced over their shoulders, ensuring no one was paying them any attention.

The magistrates received separate vanilla-colored envelopes with the same practiced casualness they'd shown when he'd been nothing but a minor bureaucrat with ambitious dreams. Hans had kept their price steady over the years—it wasn't the money that bound them to him anymore, but the weight of all their previous deals.

Dykes squeezed his, patting it lightly, while Clovers peeked inside, seeing the currency.

"Careful," Dykes muttered, glancing around. "Show a little discretion."

"Right, right," Hans replied in a low voice. "There's more than enough for your usual share."

Clovers smirked. "Seems like a bit extra this time."

"That's for the others," Hans explained, lowering his voice further. "How many deputies can you guarantee?"

"A dozen for sure. Two more are on the fence," Clovers said, shrugging. "Not sure they can be bought."

Hans nodded. "Don't push them. Let them walk. Once I have the location, I'll call you both. Just remember—get in, get out, and hopefully, we'll catch some bigger fish while we're at it."

The conversation was interrupted by the creak of the front door as two teenagers walked in, their clothes damp from the lingering rain. Hans recognized them immediately and waved a quick farewell to the magistrates before addressing the boys.

"Can I help you two young men?" asked one of the officials, stepping forward.

"They're with me," Hans said, nodding. "I'll take it from here."

He led the bruised and scuffed teens over to a corner, handing them towels and a small kit of bandages.

"That was quite a scuffle," Hans said, his voice calm but pointed.

The taller of the two boys winced. "Yeah ... it didn't go so well."

"Why not?"

"That watchman," the boy muttered. "Appeared out of nowhere. Like a shadow! That—Kane fella."

Hans' eyes narrowed. "Kane? What did you call him?"

"Kane. But he goes by Markus. People avoid him like the plague."

Hans' mind raced, but he kept his voice steady. "Interesting. I had intel that the lady had backup watching her—but a watchman?"

"Makes sense," the first teen answered, "An unregistered watchman for hire."

"I see," Hans acknowledged, studying the boys' bruises. Something about this Kane character nagged at him—the way he'd fought in that alley had been too careful, too controlled for a simple street watchman.

"The Guild of watchmen wouldn't waste time keeping tabs on the bottom of their barrel. Perfect cover for her," he acknowledged.

The teens exchanged glances. "I doubt it. That's our first run-in with him."

"Pray it's our last," the second one added, "But in this district, you only have two kinds of contacts lookin' for runners to hire—Vitelli, and everyone else."

Hans' gaze sharpened. "That alley was supposed to be covered. Completely empty."

The boy shook his head. "He may have been lurking around. But watchmen never give us a second thought. They see us and keep walking."

"Perhaps she signaled for him," Hans mused aloud.

One of the boys scoffed. "She didn't look surprised at all when she saw us. It almost felt like she was expecting trouble."

"Or grown accustomed to it," Hans sighed, frustration mounting. "And the lady still has that satchel too."

"The lady? You mean 'Xara,'" one of the boys stated.

"You two know her?"

"We've heard of her. Her name gets around. She's quite the looker. Vitelli's been wooing her for months, to join his syndicate."

Hans chuckled darkly. "Small world. Tell me, does she ever meet with Vitelli?"

"Can't say," the taller one replied.

"We've never seen them together. But we've heard her name over the grapevine."

"Mr. Vitelli meets weekly at the warehouse with his

goons. She's not in the fold yet. But she might be there tomorrow."

"Same location?" Hans asked.

"Yeah—262 Browers Avenue. 8:00 p.m. sharp."

"You're certain this time?"

"We can't afford to slip up around Vitelli. He's made an example of someone who betrayed him once. That's why we covering our tracks—isn't that right?"

The other boy nodded, anxiously.

"He's right, Mr. Lumen. He doesn't suspect us! You gotta believe us."

Hans reached into the inner pocket of his suit, while observing the pair.

"Fortunately, I'm feeling generous tonight. Make sure I don't regret it."

Hans handed them both a few bills of currency, the same way he'd once handed out bribes when he was just starting out. "Stay clear tomorrow—for your own safety."

He'd learned long ago that concern for the welfare of underlings, real or feigned, bought more loyalty than threats. Even rats needed to feel valued.

They took the money, nodding eagerly. "Thanks! Be careful though, sir. That Xara's a serpent."

Hans smirked. "I'll keep that in mind."

Just then, the wire encryptor tapped him on the shoulder. "Sir? Mr. Lumen, I have your response from Arduiine."

Hans thanked the boys and moved to a private terminal, where the encryptor handed him the decoded message:

Good evening, Senator,
And greetings from the Council of Arduiine. We've ana-
lyzed the fingerprints and matched them with records the
from House of Lauvuine. The individual was using the alias
"Persia." Warrants are still in effect, and the bounty stands
at a million and a half crowns. However, thanks to con-
tributions from our backers within the National Separatist
Party, the bounty can be raised to five million if appre-
hended discreetly, outside of the district.
Funds will be transferred upon her capture.
Regards,
The Council of Arduiine

Hans quickly deleted the message, glancing over his shoulder to ensure no one had seen it. As he reached for the coffee kettle, he feigned a clumsy slip, knocking it over.

"Darn!" he muttered. "Guess I need more coffee."

"I can resend the message if—"

"No need," Hans interrupted, already picking up his satchel. "I'll be back in a few days."

But as he hefted the bag onto his shoulder, a strange realization hit him. He unzipped the satchel and quickly rummaged through its contents. It wasn't *his* satchel. It was Xara's. Somehow, between dinner and the staged alley mugging, she had switched them.

That damn watchman had ruined everything. Hans forced down his frustration—he'd been outmaneuvered, but he'd been outmaneuvered before. He hadn't gotten this far by giving up when things went wrong. There were always other angles, other pressure points to exploit.

If he couldn't buy or threaten his way to what he wanted, he'd find someone who could.

"Is something wrong, sir?" the encryptor asked, noticing his distraction.

Hans forced a smile. "No—everything is fine. Have a good evening."

And with that, he stepped out into the chilly night, his mind already racing to the next move.

* * *

The evening crowds parted around Markus as he made his way through the merchant district, the neon glow of Guild-certified signs casting harsh shadows across the worn cobblestones. His patrol route took him through the gray zones—streets where Guild authority mounted into something darker, where survival meant walking the line between law and necessity.

The subtle shift in the crowd's movement caught his attention first—the way people suddenly found reasons to be elsewhere, how conversations dropped to whispers. Then came the familiar hum of certified tech, the kind that cost more than he made in a year. Markus didn't need to turn to know what was approaching. Guild Engineers never patrolled these streets without reason.

The Engineer's uniform spoke of authority and precision—a high-collared navy coat with brass buttons and geometric trim. The Guild's winged insignia gleamed on his chest through a decorative working interface that glowed faintly as it processed data. His crisp white gloves and polished boots marked him as someone who supervised rather than serviced—a bureaucrat with technological teeth.

In stark contrast, Markus' worn black leather jacket told a different story—scuffed and patched but reinforced in vital places; it was chosen for survival and blending into places where even the local authorities feared to tread.

Two different worlds, meeting in the shadows between Guild authority and street justice.

The Guild Engineer sneered at Markus' makeshift pulse driver, the cobbled-together kind of weapon that kept street watchmen alive.

"Unauthorized modifications. That'll be a five hundred crown fine."

Markus bit back a bitter laugh. The fine cost more than three months' pay—about the same as getting Guild certification for the weapon. But certification meant paperwork, background checks, questions he couldn't answer, questions about his health.

"Your choice," the Engineer said, polishing his Guild badge. "Pay the fine or surrender the weapon."

This was how the Guild kept their power—not just through technology, but through the endless ways they made survival itself a crime.

Markus reached for his weapon in a slow and deliberate movement. "I don't suppose we could reach an understanding?"

The Engineer's eyes narrowed as they darted to the alley's shadows. His partner had conveniently wandered out of earshot. "Depends on the understanding."

A handful of crowns—barely a tenth of the official fine—disappeared into the Engineer's pocket. The man made a show of checking his datapad. "Seems I made a mistake. Your weapon's modifications appear ... minimal. Consider this a warning."

Not even Guild authority was immune to street economics. The Engineer would pocket the bribe, file no report, and they'd both pretend this interaction never happened. Tomorrow, they'd likely do the same dance with someone else.

This was Vesper's true currency: not Guild certifications or district permits, but the careful exchange of favors and silence that kept the city's rotors turning. Markus had learned long ago that survival meant knowing which rules to break and which bribes to pay.

He kept the weapon. The Engineer kept the crowns. And the gap between official power and street reality grew a little wider

The encounter left a familiar bitterness in his mouth as he continued his rounds. Street watchmen like him existed in the gap between Guild authority and criminal chaos—too useful to eliminate, too poor to properly license. They handled the messy work the Guild pretended didn't exist, keeping order in neighborhoods where certified peacekeepers feared to tread.

Markus checked his pulse pistol's charge—the power cell was starting to fade to a glow dimmer than Guild standard. Getting it recertified would cost three months' pay, assuming they didn't ask too many questions about his background. Better to trade with Xara's contacts for salvaged parts, even if it meant risking fines for unauthorized modifications. The Guild's rules weren't made for people like him.

His thoughts turned to home—or what passed for it

these days. Xara would be waiting, probably already plotting their next move. Sometimes he wondered if she understood just how precarious their position was, balanced between Guild law and street justice. But then again, she'd always been better at seeing opportunities where he saw only walls.

* * *

The overhead lamp cast a dim glow across the small table, the only light in the room at this late hour. Xara sat alone, carefully emptying the contents of her purse, moving her fingers with practiced precision.

From her updo-styled hair, she pulled out a pair of assassin's stilettos, Guild-crafted and disguised as hair-pins with fang-like tips coated with banned Alchemist's venom. One by one, she revealed her hidden arsenal—an ion pistol (old Kingdom tech, but reliable), a modified Guild silencer from beneath her skirt, and finally, her specialty—an X-27 'Whispershot' pulse pistol, its crystal core humming with stored energy. All of them clattered onto the table amidst a pile of currency, crowns, cards, and a tiny tube of lipstick resting atop the mess, a fleeting reminder of the dual life she led.

Xara's silvery eyes scanned the MEA's digital readout, humming steady beside her half-empty glass of ale. Her fingers traced the dual dating system required on official papers—Earthen dates alongside their Nevran counterparts, a reminder of how their worlds had both merged and diverged over three millennia. With deft hands, she slid cards beneath the analyzer's beam, reading both binary marks and subtle ink variations—details few could decipher in this blend of tech and artistry, but crucial in her line of work. At twenty, she should have been studying at the National Academy, not forging documents in back rooms. But the system had other plans for orphans like them.

Despite her usual exhaustion after a night like this, she was still wearing the high-collared evening dress, its clean lines and shimmering fabric clinging like a memory of the privilege she mimicked. The formality of it, still crisp against the grimy table, only amplified the divide between her two worlds.

Markus entered, damp and scuffed up from the night. He flexed his tired muscles, feeling older than his twenty-one years.

Without a word, Xara crossed to him with the same worried look she'd worn since they were kids—the look that had threatened anyone that dared mock her foster brother's scar. When she reached to push his wet hair back from his forehead, Markus jerked away, angling the scarred side of his face from her. But her fingers caught his chin, turning him back with the gentle firmness that had defined their bond since the day a scrappy eleven-year-old dragged him home from the streets and threatened to break his legs if he ever left.

He endured her fussing with an eye roll. It was a gentleness reserved for him alone—so different from the cold and calculating grace she brought to her illegal work. Four inches of blackened tissue ran down his left temple—an injury that should have killed him as a child, a mark that still made him feel like an outcast even before the very sister who claimed him as her own flesh and blood.

"I'm annoying you," she remarked, her voice carrying that rare warmth she showed no one else. Her eyes still carried that fierceness that once terrorized half the kids in Vesper, now layered beneath the sophisticated mask she wore for everyone else, where survival meant being smarter and tougher than anyone expected.

"No," he muttered. "You're procrastinating. How'd your 'date' go?"

"You're funny," she quipped, brushing him off with a grin. "Strictly business."

"And those 'runners' who jumped you?"

"I was covered," she teased, tapping his nose playfully.

But his gaze lingered on her dress, and he shook his head. For someone barely twenty, she rarely looked the part of a proper lady; usually preferring her sleek, practical travel wear. "Fancy look! Shame you're wasting it here!"

He turned away, his shoulders stiffening as he crossed the room. Her easy maneuvering through the circles of power always brought up something raw inside him—a quiet mix of admiration, protectiveness, and maybe, just maybe, a bitterness he didn't want to admit.

"How much did you get for your handiwork?"

Xara smirked. "It went south—he couldn't meet my standards."

Settling himself, Markus dropped into the chair beside her and pulled her leather satchel toward him. His tired, sideways glance stayed on her while his hands rifled through the haul she'd brought back. Without skipping a beat, he felt the weight of metallic account cards in between his fingers, the silver embossed crests of the Capitol's elite unmistakable. His jaw clenched as he held the valuable trinkets, feeling the braille-like markings used to decipher and access the funds.

She caressed and pried them from his fingers before he could crush them.

"How much did you say?" he asked softly before looking away. "Better yet—don't bother."

"Don't worry, luv," she said in a softer voice now, coaxing, as if reading his thoughts. "I know what I'm doing."

"Yeah? And what happens when you cross the wrong gentleman?"

He moved to the dartboard hanging on the far wall, casually flicking darts with precise accuracy.

"Or steal the wrong vehicle from the wrong owner? I'm sorry—'borrow' I meant."

His throws became harder, faster, embedding deep into the dartboard, then into the wall, finally puncturing a recruitment poster for the National Army, leaving it in tatters.

"What's on your mind?" Xara asked, her tone softening as she watched him.

"Just thinking," he said, eyes still on the dartboard. "Which prison camp will I be visiting you at?"

Her smile faded as she studied his broad back silhouetted against the dull light. "How encouraging!"

"You keep playing with fire, Xara. Find an honest living."

"Oh? You think what I'm doing isn't honest? Stealing dirty money and using it for good?"

He turned to face her, his frustration simmering. "You can't put those skills to better use?"

"Like what? You'd like me to take up a clerical job? Work at the comm center?" The bitterness in her twenty-year-old voice spoke of too many doors already closed. She gestured to her collection of forged Guild credentials scattered across the table. "It's slim pickings without the right papers, and connections."

She grabbed his hand, feeling the roughness of his calluses—not the hands a twenty-one-year-old should have. "And what does your line of work get you, Markus? A battered body, broken bones, and not enough sleep to last a night."

"Is that why you visit the physician every day?" Xara's voice was gentle, concerned. She'd noticed the tremors in his hands after fights, the way his scar seemed to pulse with an unnatural darkness in the dim light. It killed her that after all these years as siblings, he still wouldn't let her in completely.

He stiffened, the familiar guilt of keeping his blood condition secret from his foster sister twisting in his gut. But he thought it would be better if she suspected a simple injury than knew the truth.

"I don't know what you're talking about." He shrugged.

"You don't hide things well," she said, though her own conscience pricked at the documents hidden in her satchel—ones even her protective brother couldn't know about.

Markus turned away, staring out the window at the distant downtown square. Neon lights flashed in the black night, casting a garish glow over the rooftops, and the scent of alcohol from nearby breweries lingered in the air. The city felt like a prison, a maze of squares and shadows, a place where people merely survived.

"Home sweet home," he muttered. "What a life!"

"You're too young to be falling apart."

"Look—don't worry about me. Alright?"

"But it's okay for you to worry about me?"

"Yeah. That's how it works."

She sighed, standing beside him now. "How about you stay in one piece?"

"And how about *you* leave this behind—which includes saying 'No' to joining Vitelli's gang. Yeah, I know all about him. Your 'handiwork' has finally caught his attention."

Xara bit her lip. "Markus ... you are all the family I have left." The words carried the weight of their shared childhood, of all the years they'd protected each other.

"I'll look out for you," he said quietly. "But I'll be damned if you join up with those criminals."

He kissed her forehead, a silent plea for her to stay safe. The weight of unspoken words and the secrets they kept for each other hung in the air as he pulled back. The bond between them was unbreakable but strained by the paths they walked.

CHAPTER TWO

Havi nearly walked straight into Zeik's back when his brother stopped abruptly in the corridor. Knuevah, coming up behind them with armfuls of cleaning supplies, almost did the same.

"Look," Zeik whispered, nodding toward something that made Havi's breath catch.

The armory door—always locked, always forbidden—stood ever so slightly ajar. A sliver of morning light spilled through the gap, drawing their eyes like a beacon. The three boys exchanged glances, remembering years of stern warnings from Lord Nikel that warred with their burning curiosity.

"Lady Liyzia did say the east wing needed attention," Knuevah ventured carefully, though they all knew he was stretching her actual instructions about the guest quarters.

Havi shifted from foot to foot, torn between duty and desire. "If we're caught ..."

"We won't be," Zeik said, but his voice wavered.

"Besides, someone left it open. Maybe ... maybe we're meant to clean it?" Even he didn't sound convinced.

They stood frozen for several heartbeats, each waiting for the other to either advance or retreat. The morning sun crept higher, its rays reaching through the gap to paint golden stripes across the stone floor. Finally, drawn by a force stronger than caution, Havi took one step forward, then another.

The old armory opened before them like a page from one of Lord Nikel's tales. Its weathered stone walls rose three stories to meet carved wooden rafters—architecture grander than anything they'd seen in their young lives. Morning light filtered through tall, narrow windows, catching dust motes and illuminating treasures that, until now, they'd only heard about in stories. Their eyes were drawn to the distinctive, purple-toned figures in the ancestral portraits. These were Zylvan knights, whose lineage reached back to the first warriors who walked Aerias's soil in the dawn of the first age.

All thoughts of consequences faded in the face of such wonder. Zeik moved first, reaching out to touch an elaborate set of armor.

"We should be cleaning," he whispered, but his voice held more awe than duty. Soon they were all caught up in the magic of it—dropping their rags, trying on oversized helmets, straining to pull back heavy bowstrings, and pretending to duel with blades that had seen real battle. The weight of history disappeared in their childish delight.

They were too caught up in their mischief to notice the fourth shadow stretching across the floor.

A middle-aged man leaned to one side on his cane.

The three bowed with a hand to their chest, catching their breath.

"*Tarnüra*, Lord Nikel!"

"Good morning, Havi. Zeik. Knuevah. You know my armory is forbidden."

"The mistress asked us to clean it."

The older man raised an eyebrow and stepped forward to receive his longbow from one of them, examining it. "This is old and valuable. Handle it carefully." He spoke calmly to Havi, twelve, the youngest.

"Zeik has told me your tales," said Havi. "Many nights, I act as though I am 'you' with my own sword while listening to him."

"Good storyteller?" Nikel asked.

"Yes," Zeik answered.

"But we know we're not worthy of knighthood." Havi spoke, lowering his head. "Your tales are all we have."

Nikel glided his fingers over the weapon he named *Qirähnal*—the Sky Reacher, feeling its smooth curve as if sensing the many battles it had seen. The thick brass-covered riser with cryptic Nevrish markings was so tarnished that he could barely recognize the symbols, down to each flexible limb, tipped with gold plating where the string was attached.

High above, between the heavenly rays of light shining through the overhead windows, a legion of warriors watched over them. Every face of his ancestry decorated the walls in their proudest moment, each portrait capturing a Nevran warrior at the height of his service, cherished weapons held close to his heart. The collection encircled the armory, telling the story of generations who had maintained age-old traditions. The line descended through time until it reached Nikel's youthful image—painted before the injury that had ended his active service—and ended abruptly with an empty space beside it, marked only by scattered dust, cobwebs, and peeling paint.

"My Lord?" the youthful voice spoke, calling him for the third time.

The man returned his gaze back to Havi, handing him the bow.

"Continue with your chores. And remind me to pass my tales on to you in the evening light by the hearth."

He patted each one's shoulder and departed for the house.

Nikel found the kitchen already brimming with activity. The massive hearth, built in the old Nevran style with curved stones that trapped and circled heat, dominated the far wall. If the decadent aroma of cooking, sunlit windows, crackling fireplace, and endless chatter of three vibrant females didn't awaken him by now, then nothing would.

"*Tarnüra*, my Lord!" The two teenagers acknowledged him with quick bows.

It was then he noticed her presence at the carved preparation table, her hands moving over delicate tea vessels passed down through generations. Through the morning haze, her form seemed briefly luminous among the crystalline surfaces. She turned, meeting his gaze, and, for a heartbeat, the light around her transcended the ordinary. Then the moment passed as she approached.

The familiar ritual of their greeting followed—a kiss, then the tender press of right cheek to right, left to left.

"*Anusièri! Si ĩamar eliune.*"

His wife's native tongue was like a sweet melody to

his ears, the traditional morning greeting carrying all the love they'd shared across their years together.

"*Anusièri! Liyzia.*"

She sent the two girls off, leaving them alone.

"The boys were cleaning my armory this morning. It's been off limits for ages."

She didn't answer at first, her hands still moving methodically over the tea leaves.

He stepped closer, sensing the tension in her silence. "My dear..."

Her voice was soft. "I let you sleep for once without disturbing you."

He studied her face. "I see. Did you have another vision in the night?"

"Yes. That's two more visions I have seen this time." She murmured, her eyes drifted past him, seeming to look beyond the golden hue of dawn and into the unknown future she glimpsed in her dreams.

He wandered towards the large window, showering in the bright orange glow while lighting his pipe.

Through the glass, the garden appeared lush and vibrant, each leaf and petal catching the morning sun. But his eyes lingered on a single withered plant, stark against the greenery, whose faded petals bore a silent testament to their private grief.

"For a month now, these visions have troubled me," he said, his voice nearly swallowed by the silence that followed. "Each time, they grow stronger but remain 'blurry' to me. And now you have two more. Tell me."

"We will have guests soon," she began, evading the question. "We will need the extra furnishings when the time comes. The girls have begun polishing."

He tapped the tip of his cane against the stack of wooden chairs set aside for quests. His touch lingered as if sensing the weight of tradition pressing down, a reminder of legacies not yet fulfilled. "Guests are always welcome. What is the second vision?"

"I saw your armor in this vision. It will be needed again." Her words carried the weight of prophecy, and for a moment, Nikel thought of the troubling reports he'd heard from his contacts in the city—whispers of political unrest, of dangers that might soon reach even their quiet corner of the kingdom.

Now he looked at her with suspicion, tapping his knee with his cane, reminding her of his age-old limp. But to appease her, he stood upright, clicked his heels together, chest out, and shrank his gut in as long as possible until he finally exhaled, patting his stomach.

"I will need a custom tailor if I am to wear that armor again. Don't you think?"

She was clearly not amused. "That armor is to be passed down to continue the tradition."

He took hold of her hands. "Passed down ... to *whom*, my dear?"

Her lips parted slightly, as her eyes welled with a sadness that she quickly swallowed back. They stood in silence, bound together by the weight of the question suspended in the space between them. Then, from the hall, a burst of laughter and hurried footsteps to announce the arrival of the servants, jostling and chattering as they entered, dissolved the stillness that held them.

The moment broke. She was swept into the tide of their bustling energy, leaving him to the quiet echoes of their exchange. With a slow inhale, he settled the pipe back between his teeth as his gaze wandered briefly back to the untouched armor resting in the shadows. Tradition may clash with reality, he mused, but he wondered if her visions would bend fate's course.

One of the boys pulled him from his thoughts, and, with a final glance toward the eastern horizon, he joined them as they gathered for breakfast.

* * *

The merchant shop in Orwein stood as testament to traditional Nevran craft—high wooden beams carved with ancestral patterns, windows tall and narrow to catch the valley breeze. As Liyzia approached, she passed two elderly women, their seasonal shawls bearing the simple patterns of common folk, unlike the ancestral designs that marked Liyzia's as a keeper of older ways. The women fell silent at her approach.

Inside, dried herbs hung from the rafters in traditional bundles, their scent wafting in the crisp morning air. But today, that familiar comfort was broken by a whirlwind of voices—women chattering, laughing in that unmistakable tone of gossip. Her name floated out between the snickers, and her pulse quickened as it reached her ears.

She paused, hand hovering over the knob. For a moment, she considered turning away. But no—she was Liyzia, and she would not retreat from idle tongues. With a slow, deliberate twist of the knob, she eased the door open, her breath steady. The hinges creaked softly, but the effect was instant.

Like deer frozen in the path of a hunter's arrow, the women stopped, their giggling suppressed by awkward silence. Eyes darted. Smiles faded. Before her stood a small cluster of them, gathered like thieves caught in the act in front of high shelves stacked with rolls of linen and silk.

Liyzia offered a polite smile, though it barely masked the sting in her chest. One by one, the women peeled away from the counter. A half-hearted nod here, a clipped farewell there, and soon they slipped out the door like guilty children. It was as if her presence had soured their party.

The young clerk behind the counter, barely out of girlhood, brightened the moment she realized she was now alone with Liyzia. "Good day, *Anusièri*," she said warmly, which softened Liyzia's unease.

Liyzia nodded in greeting, about to place her order when the door swung open again. In walked a woman— Jetza, her wide eyes panning the empty shop to Liyzia. "Liyzia! My friend! What a pleasant surprise!" Jetza's voice, lively and strong, chased away the remnants of the earlier tension. She waved the girl at the counter away with a flick of her hand, and locked her gaze onto Liyzia. "Come now, how are you?"

"Well enough," Liyzia answered with a soft smile. "And your daughter? She grows more beautiful by the day."

Jetza beamed with pride. "*Märi Auni!* You are too kind. Vuchic and I keep a watchful eye—waiting for the right young man to swoop in and steal her heart. Though, I must say, I'm not sure any of these boys are worthy!" She threw a wink, then leaned in, lowering her voice conspiratorially. "And ignore those hens. They are not worth a second thought."

Liyzia could not help but chuckle, though the sound

felt hollow in her chest. Jetza, perceptive as ever, noticed the lack of sparkle in her friend's eyes as she unrolled a bolt of cloth. "What brings you to the shop today? Back to your sewing?" she asked, lifting the scissors to cut the fabric.

"I have a few things to make for the servants," Liyzia murmured, scanning the list she had written. "Knuevah's outgrown half his wardrobe, and the harvest ceremonies are coming."

Jetza hummed as she worked, talking about this and that—her daughter's latest suitor, the town's preparations for the harvest—but it soon became apparent that the conversation was one-sided. Liyzia was quieter than usual, her responses short, distant.

"Something's troubling you," Jetza finally said, setting down the scissors and turning fully to face her friend. "Tell me. I only confide in you and Nikel," she admitted quietly.

"My visions grow stronger with each passing season, far beyond what the ancient texts describe. Sometimes I wonder if that's why ..." she trailed off, one hand unconsciously moving to her shawl.

"Liyzia ..." Jetza's hand covered her friend's where it clutched the shawl, with a gentle but firm touch. Concern etched deep lines into her usually sunny face.

"Your secrets are safe with me. Is your 'gift' whispering to you again?" She kept her voice low, though they were alone.

"For you seem to be more inclined to this inner 'sense'—and more so than the knights. What does it say?"

Liyzia's gaze drifted to the rolls of cloth stacked high

on the shelves, lowering her voice to a near whisper. "A stranger will cross my path. An outsider."

"A warning, perhaps?"

"No ... no." Liyzia's fingers pressed against her chest. "There's peace in my heart. Great peace. But ... a fog's always there, hovering. It clears with time, but this one ..." She paused, searching for the right words. "He carries scars. Two of them. One I can see, and the other is buried so deep in shadow, no light will ever reach it. It comes to me, night after night, in my dreams."

Jetza's sharp intake of breath was the only sound between them for a moment. "Have you told Nikel?"

Liyzia shook her head. "He would question my sanity."

"He would not," Jetza protested as she gripped Liyzia's arm gently. "He trusts you more than anyone."

"Perhaps. But ... I haven't the courage to tell him fully. His life would have been smoother had he married a simpler woman."

Jetza's expression darkened, a rare sight. "Don't you dare say such things," she said firmly, with a voice like a blade cutting through the air. "For what it's worth, I believe you."

Liyzia blinked, her emotions oscillating between gratitude and sadness.

"Oh, Jetza ..." she sighed, shaking her head as if to clear away the cloud hanging over them. "Enough of this talk. How much do I owe you?"

Jetza waved her off with a laugh. "Told you before, your money's no good here. *Märi Auni!* You spoil us all."

"I'll send the boys to pick it up," Liyzia said with a soft smile, feeling a little lighter.

As Liyzia turned to leave, Jetza's daughter appeared in the doorway, just returning from an errand. She paused, glancing after Liyzia before leaning to whisper to her mother, "Is that the peculiar woman?"

Jetza's brows shot up. "Liyzia? Who calls her peculiar?"

"The women. They say she is ... different. Is she an Ilyrian?"

"An Ilyrian? You've been reading one too many bedtime tales! Their starlight would blind your eyes. Besides, no Ilyrian has walked these lands since the Great Sundering—ages ago."

"But Mother—last winter, during the frost, my friends and I swore we saw the petals of a lumidawn glowing one night on her property. An ethereal blue and silver glitter fell like dust upon the snow. Only their magic could coax such a bloom in the depths of winter."

Jetza's face darkened like a storm brewing. "Nonsense, child!" she snapped. "Don't make up such a ridiculous tale! She's mortal like the rest of us."

Her daughter hesitated, clearly ashamed. "She is the only woman I've noticed who wears her shawl daily. And clings to it. She speaks so ... strangely."

"Strangely?" Jetza's eyes softened for a moment, as she dropped her voice. "She is the kindest person I know, not strange. She's blessed with a rare gift."

The girl fidgeted. "If she's so blessed, then why does she have no ch...?"

Jetza's sunny demeanor vanished, and her expression hardened like stone. Her daughter froze, guilt flooding her face. "Never say such a thing again!" Jetza said, her voice cold as ice. "You're starting to sound like those gossiping hens."

The girl's face turned crimson. "I'm sorry, Mother. I didn't mean ..."

"See that you don't! Ever!"

"I won't; I swear it."

Jetza's eyes lingered on the door Liyzia had just left through, a shadow crossing her features. There were things even she could not explain, things she feared might be misunderstood—both by the town's busybodies and by her own daughter.

* * *

The crimson glow of the setting sun filtered russet hues through the twisted branches of the Shadowvein trees. Their pale striations seemed to pulse even in the dying light as Liyzia began the long journey back from Ninavey to Orwein. She sat at the front of the carriage, holding the reins while the three young servants sat behind her. The brick-laid road stretched ahead, winding through the rolling hills and past the forested edges of the Canivere Valley. The hushners, large, furry creatures pulling the carriage, moved steadily along in a slow, lumbering pace to a familiar rhythm.

A cool breeze stirred the Whisperleaf trees. Their distinctive rustle like distant whispered conversations made the boys shift uneasily in their seats. They rarely ventured this far, and the lush landscape beyond Orwein seemed like a different world.

As they traveled deeper into the woods, the familiar Shadowveins gave way to the older Songbarks, whose resonant trunks creaked softly in the wind. Knuevah, the eldest, noticed something. They had strayed from the main road, and Liyzia was leading them off the beaten path, deeper into Canivere Forest. His brow furrowed as the familiar paved road gave way to a narrow, dirt trail winding through the thick woods.

"Is she daydreaming again?" Zeik whispered, leaning toward Havi.

"Looks like it," Havi muttered back as his eyes followed the darkening trees.

The forest loomed around them, its shadows lengthening as the sun dipped lower in the sky. The boys exchanged nervous glances as the carriage slowed to a stop near a small clearing. Liyzia shifted in her posture and closed her eyes to listen, while facing the treeline. It was growing all the more foreboding by the moment. Without a word, rose from her seat and leapt down from the carriage before any of them could offer to help her.

"My Lady," Zeik called, hurrying after her, "where are you going?"

She didn't answer. Instead, she walked purposefully into the woods, her long skirts brushed against the undergrowth. Moisture dripped steadily from the overhanging branches of a massive Mistweep tree, the drops catching the last rays of sunlight. Zeik grabbed his hunting gear, motioning for Havi to follow. Knuevah stayed behind the hushners, glancing anxiously after them.

"Not safe out here," Havi muttered under his breath, quickening his pace to keep up with Liyzia.

Zeik glanced at him. "She's in one of her trances. It happens sometimes," remembering the whispered remarks he'd overheard in the marketplace. Some called her "touched by the old powers," while others said darker things about women who walked between two worlds. But Zeik had seen how she'd known exactly where to find him the day he'd gotten lost in the woods, how she somehow always knew when one of them was ill before the fever showed.

"Is it dangerous?" Havi asked, his voice tight with worry.

Zeik hesitated. "It depends on where it leads her—and us."

They followed her up a steep incline, fighting their way through tangled roots and branches. But from their view, the tangled limbs and branches almost appeared as though they were parting before her. No; it must surely be the evening wind, and not some will of her own. Either way, it only made the boys more nervous and superstitious with each step they took.

When they finally caught up, they stopped in disbelief.

Liyzia knelt by the large tree. Her movements were deliberately slow, almost ritualistic. The sacred shawl seemed to catch what little light remained, its threads shimmering with an inner luminescence that hadn't been visible in the merchant shop. As her fingers traced the ancient patterns, the boys could have sworn the air grew thick with anticipation. The image pierced through her mind again—those angry welts across young shoulders, eyes haunted by shadows too deep to name. The shawl exuded warmth beneath her touch, acknowledging its purpose just as it had done for generations of her kinswomen before.

Around her, the Songbark trees began to hum a low, mournful tone that made the boys' skin prickle. Even the hushners shifted restlessly, sensing something the boys couldn't quite see.

"What is she doing?" Havi whispered with wide eyes. Zeik shook his head. "That shawl was passed down through generations. It is a sacred heirloom. She was wrapped in it as a newborn." He hesitated, then added in an even lower voice, "They say it was woven by the Seers of the Valley, before the Great Sundering. The older women still tell stories of women who could read the threads of fate in such shawls."

Liyzia tied the shawl around the branch of the tree, letting it flutter in the breeze. The boys watched, bewildered, but Zeik dared not interfere. The shawl swayed gently, its silken threads catching the rough bark.

Before they could say anything, Liyzia turned and took their arms, guiding them back down the slope.

"She's lost her mind," Zeik spoke under his breath. "It's another one of her visions."

Havi nodded, glancing nervously around them.

But as they made their way back down the slope, the forest's usual evening clamor settled into something different—not the taut silence of approaching danger, but a gentle hush, like a shared secret. The last rays of sunlight filtered through the canopy in pools of honey-gold, warming the copper-bright leaves, as if the forest itself was acknowledging what had just transpired.

As Liyzia returned to the carriage, Havi tugged at her sleeve. "My Lady, it will be dark soon. Umbrahounds roam after dusk. I could fetch your shawl—it is still on the tree."

Liyzia smiled down at him with a serene expression. "Be at ease, child," she said, reaching out to brush a leaf from Havi's hair with the same gentle touch she used when he had a fever last winter. "All will be well."

The boys watched as she bundled herself up, her eyes fixed on the distant gates of Orwein. In the fading light, they could only wonder who the gifts were meant for, left behind in the cold, forgotten woods of Canivere.

CHAPTER THREE

The walk across town took over an hour. Worth it to avoid the hover-lanes where Xara might spot him. Markus paused outside the clinic, his hand hovering over the door handle. Even from here, he could smell that uniquely medical mix of disinfectants and recycled air that made his stomach clench.

Just another check-up, he told himself. Quick in, quick out. No one needs to know.

The moment he stepped inside, the familiar chill hit him. The dingy waiting room in lower Vesper was like most district medical offices—worn leather seats, a mix of data tablets and printed journals scattered across low tables. Guild-certified medical credentials hung slightly askew on water-stained walls. A basic bio-scanner buzzed in the corner, its antiquated display fluttering beneath the fluorescent lights.

His body tensed against the shock, unsure whether to give in to the panic rising in his chest or fight through it, hoping it would pass. Overhead, the buzz of the fluorescent lights drilled into his skull until ...

He wasn't twenty-one anymore. He was ten, sitting

in that damn waiting room, legs swinging off the too-tall chair with a black eye and a nose dripping blood. His cheek stung where gravel had embedded itself after the bullies had knocked him to the pavement.

He could still hear their taunts.

"Kane! How's that feel, 'Kane'?"

"Look at you, 'Kane'—your face keeps hittin' my fist!"

Each blow brought that name with it, pounding into his head as much as his body. *Kane.* The one name he'd never wanted, the name they'd latched onto like a weapon. He never understood why it stung so much; but it did. Every word, every punch made him feel like something inside him didn't belong.

The distant, echoing laughter of those boys rang in his ears, a ringing that only broke when ...

"Mr. Kane."

The voice shattered the memory. Markus blinked, catching his breath as he was jolted back to the reality of the cold floor beneath his boots and the fluorescent lights glaring down at him. His pulse still thrummed in his ears.

"Just call me Markus, Doc," he muttered in a voice rougher than intended. He shook his head, trying to push away the remnants of that memory.

The doctor stood in front of him, arms crossed, and eyebrows raised. "It's closing time. How'd you get in here?"

Markus glanced around, noticing how quiet the clinic was now. "Door's unlocked."

The doctor sighed, pinching the bridge of his nose. "I'll deal with Francis about that. But look, kid, I'm done for the day. You need to make an appointment."

"I've made several," Markus countered, his tone tightening.

The doctor frowned, shifting uncomfortably. "You still owe me for the last few visits and lab tests. Service isn't free. You know that. Try one of the other clinics in town."

Markus bit back a retort, keeping his voice steady. "But you're the best."

"And the costliest."

For a long moment, they locked eyes, the tension thick between them. Markus didn't look away, though he could tell the doctor wanted to. Eventually, the physician broke first, fumbling with his belongings on the counter, his hands awkwardly knocking his keys to the floor. He bent down to pick them up, trying to recover his composure.

"Look," Markus said, his voice low but firm. "I came up with five hundred crowns last month. I'll match that next week. I just want some answers. That's all."

The doctor glanced at him, taking in the weariness in Markus' features, the exhaustion behind his eyes. For a young man, he looked far too burdened. The doctor could not help but wonder why Markus hadn't enlisted in the National Forces or gone to the Academy like most his age. Watchmen did not make much—certainly not enough to cover the kind of bills Markus had been racking up. But he was trying.

"Look, kid," the doctor said again, though softer this time. "It's late. Come back tomorrow morning."

"I prefer the evenings," Markus interrupted, his jaw tight.

The doctor hesitated. "Fine. Six-thirty."

Markus nodded, a brief flash of relief crossing his face. "That's great. I'll bring what I can next time."

With that, he turned and walked out, footsteps echoing down the quiet hallway. The doctor watched him go, following Markus through the side window as he crossed the courtyard and disappeared into the night.

The doctor let out a long sigh, tossing his cap and keys onto the counter. He should have forgotten about Markus' bloodwork, written him off like any other patient who couldn't pay. But something nagged at him. Curiosity, or concern? With a resigned groan, he flipped through the medical records, finally pulling out Markus' file.

His examination room reflected the compromises of a district practice—modern diagnostic equipment crammed alongside traditional tools, a crystal-powered sanitizer next to worn anatomical charts. Like everything in Vesper, it straddled two worlds, neither fully modern nor completely outdated.

"Markus Kane, twenty-one, six feet, one hundred and seventy-five pounds, parents unknown, blood type ..." He trailed off, frowning as his eyes landed on the blood type section.

He grabbed a pair of surgical gloves and slid them on. Moving to the back, past the bio-metrics station and the softly vibrating vitals monitor, he sifted through the rack of samples until he found the one labeled "MK." His fingers wrapped around the tube—then froze.

The vial was half-shattered, the glass jagged and blackened as if it had been corroded by acid. The contents inside were charred, a thick, dark residue clinging to the inside of the container.

"What the hell ...?"

He slid the rack over and his breath caught in his throat. There, beneath where the vial had been, was a hand-sized black stain burned into the countertop. The surface, once smooth marble, was singed through, as though some chemical had eaten away at it. The acrid stench of sulfuric acid lingered in the air.

The doctor stepped back, staring at the damage in disbelief. He had never seen anything like this—not in all his years of handling blood samples. Something had gone terribly wrong, something that defied explanation.

His heartbeat quickened as he glanced back at the door Markus had left through. A cold chill crawled up his spine.

What had he just seen? Or worse—what *was* he dealing with?

* * *

That evening, Markus left the clinic courtyard with an unusual lightness in his step, ready to make the long trek back to the west side for his night shift. Through gaps between buildings, he could see Vesper's modest skyline—a jumble of old stone towers and newer constructions, whose windows created a scattered constellation of lights against the night sky. His mind was buzzing with the tension from the visit, but the cool night air helped.

The test results wouldn't tell him anything he didn't already feel in his bones. Something was wrong with him—had always been wrong. He just wanted a name for it. As if that might finally give him permission to exist.

Maybe this time would be different. He'd lost count of how many physicians he'd seen over the years—their reactions ranging from confusion to barely concealed horror when his blood samples ... changed. Some had thrown him out immediately. Others kept him at arm's length, treating him like a fascinating specimen rather than a person. The worst were the ones who'd seemed genuinely eager to help, right up until their tests started yielding impossible results. After that, they'd either disappeared or suddenly couldn't see him due to his mounting medical debt.

But this doctor ... something about his quiet determination felt different. He hadn't flinched or started spouting theories about genetic abnormalities. He had just listened, asked questions, and taken notes. For the first time in years, Markus dared to imagine a future where he wasn't constantly checking for cuts, wasn't living in terror of a simple nosebleed, wasn't carrying the weight of those two boys' screams in his nightmares ...

That is, until he stepped out of the gates and saw Xara standing there, her arms crossed, watching him like a hawk.

"Tell me you didn't follow me," Markus grumbled, rolling his eyes.

"Okay, I didn't follow you," she said, her voice dripping with sarcasm. "I just happened to be in the area where all the other *normal* watchmen use the clinics."

"What's that got to do with me?" he snapped, walking faster.

"You are right. I should expect nothing less from you—coming uptown, racking up medical debt like a lunatic."

He shot her a glare that would have made a lesser person back down. Not her. She met it with her usual calm, poker-faced mask, used to this dance.

"How much do you need?" Xara asked, her tone softening. "Tell me what's wrong, and I'll cover it."

Markus gritted his teeth. "It's nothing. Just a couple of blows to the head. I'm fine."

"Liar," she shot back, not missing a beat. "Why won't you tell me?"

"Why won't you tell me where you get all this money from?" Markus barked, stopping in his tracks to face her.

Xara's expression shifted slightly, but she kept her cool. "Can't."

"Why not?" he asked, his voice lower but more dangerous.

"It's to *protect* you, Markus."

"Exactly," he grunted, stepping closer, his face just inches from hers. "See how that works?"

They stood there, locked in a silent battle of wills. But as always, Xara was the first to change tactics. "Fine! Let's drop it. For now."

She reached out and stroked his arm as though he were a stray cat. "You catch the metro?"

"I don't mind walking," he muttered, already turning toward the street.

"Come on," she said, nodding toward the aerglide parked behind her. "I'll give you a ride."

Markus eyed the shiny vehicle suspiciously. It was one of those sleek models with twin turbines that roared like a predator waiting to pounce. Even at rest, the vehicle seemed to shift impatiently, the bottom thruster creating a subtle dance of shadows beneath its chassis.

"Don't worry, luv. I *borrowed* it," she said with a smirk, "from under the owner's nose." She ran her hand along the vehicle's sleek frame. "Plus, they left all the good mods on it. Custom turbine configuration, disabled proximity alerts ... amateur mistake."

He hesitated, glaring at her and then at the car, clearly annoyed. Finally, shaking his head, he climbed into the passenger seat. It wasn't just her constant thievery that got under his skin—it was her ease with it. Stealing these vehicles was no bigger deal than borrowing sugar from a neighbor. But there was something else, too, an uneasy feeling that always settled in whenever he rode in one of these.

As soon as he sat down, Markus buckled his seatbelt, watching as Xara expertly turned on the generator, revved the engine, and powered up the turbines. The heads-up display lit up, projecting warning symbols that she casually dismissed with a tap of her fingers. He gripped the door handle tightly, knuckles white as the vehicle lifted off the ground, wobbling slightly before stabilizing.

"Relax," Xara said, squeezing his knee. "I'm the best." Her fingers danced over the cyclic controller, adjusting the thrust ratios with practiced ease. The vehicle responded like it was an extension of her body.

He said nothing, but the death grip he had on the door suggested otherwise. The propellers vibrated beneath his seat, which Markus couldn't help but compare to sitting on a giant, angry hummingbird. The machine swayed back and forth, like it was constantly threatening to tip over. And, of course, Xara, always calm and annoyingly composed, drove with one hand on the cyclic control, the other lazily resting under her chin. She executed what she called a "Pendulum Swing" around a corner, with the side turbines working in perfect harmony to maintain their trajectory while the bottom thruster adjusted for stability.

"How are you not still on the racing circuit?" he asked, watching her weave through traffic like it was nothing. A proximity alert chimed as another hovering craft drew too close, but Xara had already anticipated it, seamlessly executing a lateral slide that left Markus' stomach somewhere behind.

She shot him a sidelong glance but said nothing. Her thumb absently traced the worn groove on the cyclic's grip—a telltale mark of an underground racing mod. He figured it had something to do with her complicated relationship with authority. She never lasted long anywhere.

"If I recall, you lasted what? Five minutes in Arduiine?" Markus teased, trying to distract himself from how she was threading between two cargo transporters with barely inches to spare. "Seemed like decent living."

"A dangerous sport in a dangerous district," she retorted, her eyes fixed on the road ahead while her free hand tapped a complex sequence on the thrust control panel. "I'll just leave it at that."

The vehicle dropped smoothly into a lower hover pattern, expertly compensating for the crosswind between buildings. Below them, the nightlife of Vesper's middle districts played out—street vendors with their illuminated carts, workers trudging home from late shifts, the occasional burst of laughter from neighborhood taverns.

Nothing like the gaudy entertainment zones uptown, but alive in its own way.

Markus rolled his eyes. "That's a convenient answer."

Moments later, their craft descended toward a curb, turbines whining as they powered down. The warehouse district lay before them like a different city entirely, the familiar glow of residential Vesper replaced by harsh security lights and long shadows, broken only by the occasional neon sign that marked some questionable establishment's entrance.

"What are we doing here?" he asked, his tone shifting.

"We're seeing Vinny Vitelli." Xara killed the power with a final twist of her wrist, as the vehicle settled onto its landing struts with barely a sound. The turbines spun down in a descending whine that echoed off the warehouse walls.

Markus shot her a look, watching as the HUD display blipped with one last warning before going dark. "I thought we talked about this."

"We did," Xara said casually, disengaging the security protocols with deft flicks across the control panel. She stepped out of the car to the sound of the door's hydraulics soft hissing. "But you're fully aware of my dinner with the senator. Besides, Vitelli paid me to pick up a few items."

"Then give it to the mediator." Markus' voice competed with the dying hums of the craft's systems.

"He wants to see me in person." She was already scanning the shadows between the warehouses, a habit he'd noticed long ago.

"So, send him a picture!" Markus snapped, exasperated.

"Markus, please."

"How often do you come here? His den of thieves?" His voice was sharp now in obvious annoyance. A hover transport passed overhead, its running lights cutting through the perpetual industrial haze.

"We've only met a couple of times. In daylight. At a café." She waved it off, but her hand instinctively brushed against the hidden pocket where Markus knew she kept her scrambler—a device that could disable any hover vehicle's systems within range. "He only invites his inner circle here."

"Well, congratulations! It looks like you've made quite the name for yourself in the black market." The words came out bitter, matching the acrid taste of the warehouse district's recycled air.

Markus turned away, staring out at the neon lights reflecting off the damp streets. The signs advertised legitimate businesses, but everyone knew they were fronts for Vitelli's operation. "It was only a matter of time before you caught the attention of this snake."

"Don't judge a book by its cover, Markus. He's a polished gentleman."

"And I'm sure he thinks of you as the perfect lady," Markus said dryly. Above them, cargo transporters cast moving shadows across the street, warning lights pulsing in rhythm with the district's antiquated steam vents.

"You're upset."

He reached over and squeezed her hand, a softness to the gesture that contrasted sharply with the hard look in his eyes—one Xara knew all too well. Their reflection was distorted in the aerglide's polished surface by the condensation from the district's atmospheric processors.

"We're getting the hell out of this town," Markus said, his voice low and steady.

"Where are we supposed to go? The east coast? The harbor towns?" Xara scoffed. "What jobs are we fit for out there?"

Markus leaned closer, his tone darkening. "I'm thinking we head to Arduiine. They'd love to meet you. Especially with that *bounty* on your head."

Xara tried to turn away, but Markus grabbed her face gently, holding her cheeks as she tried to avoid his gaze. The neon lights painted their faces in alternating shades of blue and red.

"How long have you known?" she whispered, ashamed.

"A watchman tipped me off. Heard your old alias—'Persia'—mentioned in a call. Your pretty little face is still circulating in their systems. Probably plastered on 'wanted' posters."

Her eyes darted, her mind raced. Markus could almost see her calculating, thinking of all the connections she might need to call in. Behind them, a massive cargo transport cast its shadow as it lumbered between the buildings with its anti-collision lights pulsing steadily.

"For once ... I don't know what I'm going to do," Xara said in a barely audible voice over the ambient hum of the city. A street vendor's call echoed from the corner, his cart's battered holo-sign blipping as he packed up for the night—another piece of Guild tech failing in the damp air of the warehouse district.

"Right now?" Markus replied in a firm voice. "You get in, you get out, and you cut ties with these people."

"You don't know Vicente Vitelli's reputation," Xara whispered.

"And he doesn't know mine," Markus shot back.

They locked eyes for a long moment, the weight of their secrets hanging between them, unspoken but understood.

* * *

The industrial district was alive with the grind of machines and the weary shuffle of workers, moving like ghosts under the dim orange glow of streetlamps. The air reeked of smoke and sweat, and even the few scattered stars seemed distant, as if choosing not to witness what happened here. Xara and Markus wove through the crowd, alert as always but playing it cool, just another tired pair among the throngs—while their sharp eyes scanned every shadow, every alley. They had to—especially in a place like this.

But even with their practiced caution, neither of them saw the eyes tracking them overhead. High on a rooftop overlooking the refinery maze, Hans Lumen leaned against a parapet. A sick smile curled on his lips as he watched the couple disappear into the refinery. The binoculars in his hand lowered slowly as he paid off two teenagers standing next to him, their nervous eyes flitting between the money in their hands and Lumen's shadowed face.

"Get lost. Don't show your faces around here again," he said, waving them off like insects.

Back on ground level, the rented facility Xara and Markus entered felt wrong the moment the door closed behind them. The oppressive silence wasn't the only thing off. It was the way the four men already knew their every move, standing in positions too deliberate to be random. No windows. No exit but the one they had just walked through. A fifth figure entered—suave, polished, with a woman clinging to his arm like an ornament.

"Good evening," the man said with a smile as sharp as a knife. "Mr. Vitelli is eager to meet you. Alone."

"Alone isn't in the cards tonight," Xara answered in a cold and firm voice.

The man's smile never faltered. "We'll see about that. Frisk them."

One of the goons stepped toward Markus, hand already reaching out. Before he even touched him, Markus' hand shot up, twisting the man's wrist until a crack sounded, followed by the man's yelp of pain.

"That's a 'no' from me," Markus growled.

Another rushed forward, but Markus met him with an uppercut so hard the man's head snapped back, blood pouring from his nose as he crumpled to the ground.

Two more lunged.

Xara had already drawn her pistol, but before she could fire, a voice cut through the room like a blade.

"Gentlemen!" It was too smooth, too calm. "Where are your manners?"

Vincent Vitelli entered the room with an air of relaxed control. He was older, cleaner than his associates, and carried himself with an unsettling grace. His eyes swept the room, taking in the bloodied men on the floor without a hint of concern.

"Xara, please excuse my men. Incompetence runs rampant, it seems." He reached for her gloved hand and pressed his lips against it.

Markus, standing taut beside her, only watched. He answered Vitelli's outward hand with a stony silence.

"Shall we?" Vitelli said, gesturing toward the inner office.

Markus felt the breeze from the open window behind him as they stepped further inside, but it did nothing to ease the tension in his gut. The room was too full of Vitelli's people, eyes that never left them, hands twitching near concealed weapons. He watched Xara take the two drinks Vitelli offered, handing one to him without hesitation. He knew she was playing the game—he never drank on the job.

"Let's make this quick," Xara said, her voice steady.

"Quick?" Vitelli smiled, swirling his glass. "But we've only just begun. You should hear me out."

"I won't be accepting any more of your 'offers,'" Xara replied smoothly. She reached into her satchel and pulled out a small, tightly wrapped bundle. "This is the intel you wanted from Lumen's files. Consider it delivered."

Vitelli's smile faded; it was replaced by a trace of intrigue. He unwrapped the bundle carefully, revealing two black, metallic cards. His eyes gleamed as he handed them to his accountant, who quickly placed them under a magnifying device.

Markus' jaw tightened. Every second spent in this room made his skin itch. He could feel Xara's fingers slip into his, a grounding presence as the accountant scanned the cards. It was taking too long.

"Twenty million crowns," the accountant finally said, nodding. "Authorized by Hans Lumen. It's legit."

Vitelli's face lit up with a satisfied grin. "Well done, Xara." He lifted his glass in a toast. "I always verify the work, you understand. Nothing personal."

The assistant handed Xara a briefcase of crowns. One million crowns. A fortune. Markus barely glanced at it. Stolen money, no matter how much they needed it, was a weight he didn't want on either of them. But that was the line they walked, wasn't it? The things they did to survive, to stay ahead.

"I am disappointed, though," Vitelli continued. "I had such high hopes for you. Joining my family—ah, the things we could accomplish together. But I suppose your ... 'friend' here doesn't fit the bill."

"I've got family already," Xara replied, ice in her voice.

Vitelli raised an eyebrow but said nothing, swirling the glass in his hand.

Suddenly, the assistant interrupted, eyes narrowing as she examined the cards again. "These feel ... scrubbed. Like there's more here, hidden."

Vitelli's smile vanished, eyes turning cold. "Twenty million crowns is a lot for a politician, even a crooked one like Lumen. But a scrubbed account?" His gaze switched to Xara. "Perhaps someone took a little extra."

"Or maybe they weren't his accounts to begin with," Xara replied, her voice casual but firm. "Who's to say Lumen didn't skim off the top?"

"True, but your sudden refusal of further jobs—it raises questions." Vitelli's voice had dropped a degree.

The room chilled. Xara's fingers tightened slightly in

Markus' as her other hand subtly shifted toward her sidearm.

"Are you accusing me of theft, Vitelli?" Xara asked, her tone as sharp as glass.

Silence followed. The kind that stretched, thick with unspoken threats.

Vitelli's fingers rubbed the edge of the card, eyes locked on Xara, weighing his options. It was clear she had stolen for Hans. What would stop her from stealing from him?

Markus' grip tightened on something hidden beneath his coat. His heartbeat thundered in his ears, the tension winding tighter like a clock ticking down.

Finally, Xara broke the standoff, her voice light but with an edge. "We're done here, luv."

As they turned to leave, Vitelli's voice cut in again. "I didn't say you could leave."

"And I didn't ask."

The air thickened. Chairs shifted; bodies moved—slowly revealing weapons. Knives, batons, but no guns. Not yet. Everyone held their breath, waiting for the first wrong move.

Through the window came the distant wail of security sirens. Vitelli's men tensed, then relaxed as the sound faded—just another night in the industrial district. But something else followed: the subtle vibration of multiple hover vehicles, the kind of synchronized movement that spoke of coordination rather than random traffic.

"Patrol glides," Xara whispered, her trained ear catching the difference. "Something's up."

One of Vitelli's men burst in, face pale. "Multiple

units approaching from the east and south. Guild-certified signatures."

The room erupted. Vitelli's carefully maintained control shattered as his men scrambled, shoving chairs aside, grabbing files, weapons, whatever they could.

Vitelli straightened his tie as the chaos erupted. "You know," he said, as if discussing a minor business transaction, "I've always believed that true value reveals itself over time."

His smile remained courteous, almost paternal, but his eyes measured them as if they were assets in a ledger. "We'll see what yours is worth."

He disappeared into the mayhem with the calm certainty of someone who always collects his debts.

The crowd outside was swelling, a cacophony of voices—some cheering, others shouting in fear or excitement. Through the open window, Xara and Markus watched as fists flew below, bodies crashing into the streets, the maelstrom of the brawl feeding the crowd's frenzy. It was a scene of pure mayhem, a twisted spectacle, and it was getting worse by the second.

Markus' heart pounded in his ears, his instincts screaming. "Let's go!" he ordered, taking charge. They bolted from the window and into the corridor, feet pounding on the creaky floorboards. Below, the sounds of ion blasts and gunfire erupted like a thunderstorm, rattling the walls. Screams, the splintering of wood, and the violent shattering of glass echoed upward.

A stray blast whizzed by, searing through the wall inches from them. Markus yanked Xara back, the sudden force sending them stumbling into a nearby table. The furniture crashed beneath their weight, but there was no time to dwell on it. The footsteps—heavy, relentless—were coming from the stairwell, the clatter of boots like a stampede.

"Get down!" Markus hissed, pushing Xara around the corner just as three lawmen stormed through the door.

Without hesitation, Markus lunged. His shoulder drove into the first man's gut, spearing him to the ground with a thud. The other two had barely time to react before they were on him, batons swinging. One cracked across his back, but it only fueled the rage boiling inside him. With a roar, he spun, unleashing a barrage of vicious punches. His fists connected with bone, leaving the men dazed, stumbling. Markus grabbed a fallen baton and finished them off with brutal efficiency, their bodies collapsing in heaps, broken and unmoving.

But the fight wasn't over.

A shrill sound tore the air—phaser blasts from the stairwell. Markus dived behind a stack of crates, barely avoiding the deadly beams. He crouched low, his breath steadying as he watched the boots of another figure step into view, the muzzle of a blaster pointed at the bodies of the downed men. The man was checking if they were still breathing.

Across the room, Markus caught sight of Xara, hidden behind a door. Their eyes met. They didn't need words, only the silent gestures of their hands, their unspoken plan forming between them in the tense silence. Markus began to move, ready to crawl away—

The rapid clatter of footsteps cut through the quiet. More men entered the room.

"Mr. Lumen—"

"Don't use my name!" Lumen snapped, his voice low and dangerous.

"We gotta fly! Who are you looking for?"

"They're still here. Search the place!"

"Who? The heat's closing in! We need to take what we've got!"

"Very well. Round them up!"

Markus stayed perfectly still, muscles coiled like a spring. He listened, heart pounding, as the men moved through the room, their voices growing more frantic with each second. The chaos outside was still building, and it was only a matter of time before everything exploded.

Minutes ticked by, excruciatingly slow. Every creak, every footstep sent a fresh wave of tension through his veins. Finally, the sounds faded, leaving only the distant echoes of the riot below.

Markus and Xara stayed hidden for another twenty minutes, neither daring to breathe too loudly. Only when the silence became unbearable did Markus signal her to move. They slipped out from their hiding spots, reuniting with a brief exchange of gestures.

"Hans," Xara whispered, her voice barely audible. "He's looking for us. How does he know?"

"Doesn't matter." Markus' gaze was hard, determined. "Stay low. Follow me."

And together, they moved, with the weight of the danger pressing down with every step.

* * *

The streets were still buzzing with the aftermath of the raid on Vitelli's gang, a violent clash between lawmen and outlaws that left onlookers in shock. Patrol cars and transports lifted off one by one, their lights flashing in the evening haze. As the commotion wound down, only a few deputies remained, cleaning up the aftermath, none paying attention to the lone officer emerging from the alleyway.

He moved with purpose, escorting a young woman, her head bowed, a cap pulled low. Just another prisoner, another criminal caught in the crossfire. It wasn't until a magistrate called out from the last departing transport that heads started to turn.

"Hey! The transport's this way!" The officer ignored him, quickening his pace, pulling the woman along.

Several men started moving towards them. "You gotta process her first," one said, stepping closer.

The lawman whipped off his cap, revealing Markus beneath it. His eyes locked Xara's, wide with shock.

"Like I said," Markus growled, "I can handle this one."

"Stop right there!" a voice barked from behind.

Hans Lumen stepped into the street, flanked by his corrupt officers. His eyes zeroed in on them, and a cold smile crossed his face.

Markus didn't wait. He smashed his fist into the nearest deputy's gut, grabbing his pistol in the same motion, and sprinted after Xara, who had already taken off.

"After them!" Hans roared, shoving his men forward. The motley crew of deputies—tall, short, slow, clumsy—scrambled into action, tripping over each other as they gave chase.

Markus tore through the crowd, struggling to keep up with Xara, who darted between people like a shadow.

They raced past the industrial sector's processing plants, where steam vents hissed beneath Guild-certified warning signs. Aerglides and speeders blazed past, their engines whining through streets that transformed from modern pavements to old cobblestones as they crossed into the older quarter.

"Damn it!" he muttered, scanning the crowd. He weaved through clusters of people, desperation building as the red and blue lights of a patrol glide bathed the street in frantic flashes.

The oncoming craft screeched around the corner, its high beams locking onto Markus. The engine roared as it barreled down the street, sending street vendors diving for cover. Factory workers scattered from their evening shifts, some cursing in multiple languages, others recording the mayhem on their data tablets. The craft smashed through trash cans, storefronts—anything in its path.

Markus bolted. He hurdled obstacles, adrenaline surging through him as the car's engine screamed behind him. He skidded over damp pavement, crashing into an outdoor diner. Tables flipped, food splattering as patrons scattered. Before he could catch his breath, the patrol glide hovered in front of him, turbines roaring, trash and debris swirling in the air.

Blinded by the high beams, Markus shielded his face, bracing for the worst. Two officers jumped out; weapons drawn.

Suddenly, another aerglide roared in from the side. It smashed into the patrol glide, sending it spinning out of control. The craft careened into a nearby building, erupting into flames.

Markus blinked, stunned. Through the smoke and fire, a figure emerged. Not a lawman.

Xara.

"Get in!" she shouted, throwing open the door. The craft's turbines were already spinning up to emergency power levels, the HUD flashing red with overload warnings she casually ignored.

Markus didn't hesitate. He dived in as Xara's fingers flew across the control panel, disabling every safety protocol and governor chip in seconds. They shot forward just as three patrol cars whipped around the corner in pursuit, their high-intensity plasma lights cutting through the smoke.

"Hang on, luv!" Xara yelled, executing what racers called a "Dead Drop"—killing power to the main thruster while reversing the side turbines. The vehicle dropped and rocketed backward, the sudden maneuver causing the pursuing vehicles' automated collision systems to frantically overcorrect. At the last second, the pursuers swerved, their own safety protocols fighting against their drivers' commands.

Xara spun the craft back around, rocketing down the main road. The three patrol cars followed, lights flashing, sirens wailing.

She pushed the vehicle to its design limits, sending the engine's core temperature into the red zone. She weaved through traffic with impossible precision, using the car's ability to shift laterally in ways that traditional ground vehicles never could. The pursuers and their vehicles, limited by their standard police protocols, couldn't match her raw skill and willingness to push the machine to its breaking point.

They zipped down alleyways, through industrial yards where automated loading docks stood beside manual labor crews, past the outskirts where steam-powered factories shared power grids with modern processing plants. The roads vanished, leading them into treacherous water ducts— remnants of the old city's infrastructure that even Guild engineers hadn't fully mapped.

"They're lighting us up!" Markus shouted, ducking as high-pitched phaser blasts tore through the air, scorching the rear of their vehicle.

"You think?" Xara yelled back, jerking the controls to avoid another round of shots. "You wanna ask if this thing can go any faster?"

She punched the throttle, cutting a sharp turn that sent them racing into the thick of the dark woodlands. The trees blurred past in a rush as ion blasts ripped through the canopy, branches and limbs falling like shrapnel.

Markus clung to his seat as they shot out of the woods, now hovering over a stretch of magnetic railway tracks. The speedometer climbed past one-hundred-and-thirty mph, with the patrol cars still closing in behind them.

Suddenly, a massive horn bellowed from behind.

The Levi train announced itself first through vibration—a deep thrumming that Markus felt in his bones before he heard the thunderous roar. The massive carriages seemed to slice through the air three feet above the tracks, their passage creating violent currents of displaced wind that buffeted their craft like a leaf in a storm.

Their aerglide bucked and swayed as competing

magnetic fields clashed—the tracks below trying to repel them, while the train's massive generators created a deadly corridor of electromagnetic force. Warning lights cascaded across the console as their stabilizers fought against forces they were never designed to handle.

"You still wanna catch the train?" Xara screamed; her voice barely audible over the roar of engines.

"Get over—onto the southbound lane!" Markus shouted, waving frantically.

Xara swerved, jerking the craft off the northbound line and onto the opposing track. She had to manually compensate for the magnetic field now, her hands dancing across the controls as she fought to keep them stable. The patrol cars remained hot on their tail, their standardized systems struggling even more against the magnetic interference. The Levi train now rumbled alongside them, passengers staring in disbelief from their windows.

For a fleeting moment, they were safe. But then a bright blue light appeared ahead, growing larger by the second—the horn of the southbound train shrieked, drowning the air.

Markus' heart slammed in his chest. "Punch it!" he shouted, shaking Xara's arm.

The southbound train roared into view. There was no time. No room. The northbound and southbound Levi trains thundered past each other with barely inches to spare—one beside them, one ahead. Their massive hulls created a lethal corridor of magnetic force between them.

Xara yanked the cyclic control while killing power to

the stabilizers—a suicidal move. The craft flipped sideways, its frame screaming as she threaded it through the knife's-edge gap between the rushing trains. Metal shrieked against metal as their vehicle's sides nearly brushed both trains simultaneously, the magnetic fields threatening to tear them apart. At these speeds, a fraction of an inch in either direction meant instant death.

Their pursuers, bound by their vehicles' safety protocols, never had a chance. The first patrol glide smashed head-on into the train, erupting in a fireball. The second and third followed, their remains disappearing in the inferno.

They emerged on the other side, but their victory was short-lived. The craft ricocheted off the southbound train like a pinball, systems failing as they spun wildly into the treeline. Everything became a blur of metal, trees, and screams as they tumbled through the forest, crashing to a violent halt.

The world went black.

CHAPTER FOUR

The world came back to Markus in fragments. Birdsong instead of hover engines, the sharp scent of pine replacing urban smoke, sunlight filtering through leaves rather than neon signs. For a moment, he couldn't reconcile this gentle awakening with his last memory of screaming metal and burning turbines.

The air smelled fresh of damp earth and pine. These were scents so foreign to their urban senses that Markus found himself taking deeper breaths, as if to verify they were real. A Mistweep tree loomed above them, its branches steadily dripping moisture onto their crashed vehicle despite the clear morning sky. Every muscle in his body screamed with the pain of their crash, but even the pain felt different here, cleaner somehow, away from Vesper's perpetual smog and steam.

He stared upward through the cracked windshield. Amber and gold leaves fluttered against the backdrop of the morning sky, colors that existed in their district only in the imported silks of wealthy merchants. Above him, the twisted branches of the primeval trees stretched like hands reaching for the heavens, their pale striations seeming to glimmer in the early light.

They were alive, yes, but in a world as alien to them as another planet.

Beside him, Xara stirred, her head still cradled on his chest. Her body was warm, but her breathing was shallow.

"Xara," he said, nudging her gently. "You alright?"

She mumbled, her voice muffled. "No ... I think my ankle's broken."

Markus closed his eyes briefly, grateful for the simplicity of a broken bone. "Anywhere else?"

"Just my pride," she grumbled. "First time I ever crashed."

He chuckled softly, the sound of it easing the tension between them for a fleeting moment. He kissed her forehead. "Crashed and lived to tell the tale. Lucky us!"

She gave a dry laugh. "Where are we?"

"Just outside Vesper, I think. Somewhere in the Canivere forest." He grimaced, remembering the drama of the chase. The familiar grid of city streets and the rumble of machinery were gone; they were replaced by wilderness that seemed to breathe around them. "We need to move, but first ... let's get you out of here."

The aerglide was beyond repair, its once sleek frame lay crumbled against a stout Mistweep tree. The emergency shields had deployed, sealing most of the windows except for the windshield, which Markus pried open, disengaging the locks with a hiss.

Climbing out wasn't the issue. Xara's injury was.

He set her ankle in a brace, using spare parts from the vehicle to make a makeshift splint. Each time she winced; his heart twisted. She handed him her pistol as he finished. "Just in case."

Once outside, he fashioned a pulley using rope from the trunk and hoisted Xara from the wreck. Every tug of rope echoed through the still forest as if the trees themselves were watching, waiting.

Finally, they sat side by side on a fallen log. Markus inspected her bandage, moving his hands with experienced gentleness.

"This is quite a pickle," Xara said through gritted teeth. "You sure you wouldn't be better off without me?"

"Now, where'd you get a stupid idea like that?" he scolded, tightening the wrap on her ankle.

She leaned back, letting her head rest against the tree. "My record. My past. It's catching up with me. And now, you know things I didn't want anyone to know."

Markus paused. His mind briefly wandered back to his own past, the medical results he'd never returned to check on. The clinic. The blood tests. He pushed the thought away and continued wrapping her foot. "We all have skeletons," he finally replied.

"Yours coming back to haunt you, too?"

The question was like a jab in the ribs. He shrugged but didn't answer. As she stroked his hair, her fingers were suddenly sticky with something. Blood.

"Markus," she gasped, her eyes widening.

He jerked back, grabbed her hand and wiped it clean. "Dammit, Xara, I told you! It's not healthy to touch it."

"It's only blood."

"It's ..."

She gave him a hard look. "Then tell me what's wrong."

"It's nothing."

"Which means it's something."

"For god's sake, are we doing this again?" He stood abruptly and scanned the trees as though the shadows held answers.

"We never finished it," she said calmly, her eyes fixed on his.

He sighed, defeated. "Can we agree on one thing? Vesper is behind us."

She smiled faintly, pulling two metallic cards from her pocket. "Well, at least I got something out of this. Lumen's money. Enough to start afresh."

Markus reached for the cards. "Seriously? Gimme those!"

Before she could respond, a distant rustling pulled them from their conversation. Instinctively, Markus reached for his weapon, while Xara's fingers tightened around her own.

"Is that the Levi train?" she whispered.

Markus shook his head. "No ... something else."

They stood quietly in the forest alive with its own secret rhythm. The rustling faded, but a pervasive tension remained.

"Come on," Markus said, turning northward. "We need to move."

With Xara hobbling beside him, they pressed deeper into the forest. Every snap of a twig, every flutter of leaves sent their hands to their holsters. The serenity of the woods only amplified their unease.

After what felt like hours of walking, they stopped to rest by a large fallen tree. The forest's silence pressed in on them. Markus left Xara with the pistol and ventured ahead to search for anything—food, shelter, a sign, anything that might ground them in this strange new world.

But the forest gave him nothing. No tracks. No berries. Just endless stretches of wilderness, broken only by the conversations of the Whisperleaf trees in the breeze.

Markus had heard stories about Canivere Forest— whispers that had reached him years ago during his stint in the perilous mines of the Bronze Hills. Tales of strange sounds and eerie, distant howls, of unnatural occurrences that sent shivers down the spines of even the stoutest of men. Old miners, veterans hardened by years underground, warned the younger workers never to stray too close to the forest edge. There were always sounds, they'd say—low, mournful hoots and shrieks rising from deep within the treacherous woods, just before daybreak, that seemed to proceed from the heart of darkness itself.

He could still remember those nights in the barracks, half-awake and listening to those eerie calls that played tricks on weary minds. The older miners would speak in hushed tones about ghosts, wandering spirits, and mysterious Nevran spirits of yore that were said to lure travelers deeper into the woods with their phantom melodies.

Old Man Thrace, the most seasoned of the mine foremen, once told Markus about the mysterious Nevran Seers who wandered the woodlands from the nearby Seven Villages to the northwest. Though Markus grew up with a fondness for the lores and legends of ancient cultures from the far east, his modern-day upbringing found it hard to believe that such beings could exist today.

But now, something was different. The Shadowvein trees shuddered unnaturally as he passed, their rhythm seeming to match his heartbeat. Whisperleaf branches, known for their constant murmur in the breeze, fell silent in his presence, only to resume their gossip once he moved past. Even the moisture dripping from the Mistweep trees seemed to pause when he walked beneath them, as if nature itself held its breath.

Since the crash, those old fears had stayed buried. Until now. Every rustle of leaves sounded like footsteps in a Vesper alley, every shadow between trees a potential ambush point. His street-trained instincts, so reliable in the urban maze, now betrayed him—seeing threats in natural movements, and turning wind through branches into whispered conversations.

A sudden crack of a branch sent him spinning, pulse pistol drawn. Through his sights, a small creature—something like the rats he knew from the city sewers but furrier—froze in its scamper, eyes reflecting an impossible iridescence among the Shimmer Maple leaves before it darted away. In Vesper, sudden sounds meant danger. Here, he was learning, they might mean recognition.

Standing in the forest's shadow heightened his senses, drawing forth the old dread. The air held that same electric quality he remembered from his childhood stories where reality wore thin and the impossible became mundane. His augmented senses, usually a source of confidence, now seemed to amplify every unsettling detail: the way the Songbark trees hummed a low, mournful tune he felt in his bones, the subtle wrongness in the patterns of shadow and light. When he passed near a cluster of Frostferns, their cool mist seemed to reach for him rather than away, leaving traces of frost on his skin that burned strangely instead of chilling him.

Maybe leaving Xara alone wasn't such a good idea after all. At least in her presence, the forest behaved as it should. But alone ... alone, the mysterious woods seemed to recognize something in him that he himself didn't understand.

* * *

Without hesitation, he turned back, heading back in the direction he had come, his pace quickening with every step. His thumb instinctively tightened on his weapon's grip, brushing against the familiar warmth of the M-12 'Stinger's' power cell. But the pulse driver's presence offered little comfort against the deep-seated fears stirring in his mind.

But along the way, something bright caught his eye—a flash of color between the twisted branches. He slowed, raising his weapon. For a moment, he thought it was fire. But there was no smoke, no heat—no burning branches. Just an unnatural stillness. The forest, once alive with rustling leaves and distant birdsong, seemed to hold its breath.

As he stepped closer, the object revealed itself—fabric, delicate and soft, caught on a low-hanging branch. But it didn't hang like ordinary cloth. It seemed to radiate with its own inner light—not bright, but aware. And a shimmer passed through the folds as sunlight brushed across it, like breath moving through old silk.

Nevrish designs matched those in the cryptic texts he'd glimpsed in the Archives—patterns that dated back to the First Age. Markings that predated the Kingdom's founding. Each step closer felt weighted with meaning.

He crouched beside it and paused. As his fingers hovered for a moment, a subtle warmth traveled up his arm—steady, rhythmic, like a second heartbeat. Time stretched thin. For an instant, he wasn't alone.

The sensation wasn't sight nor sound—but presence. Something pressed gently as the edge of his awareness, like a voice through mist, a name unspoken yet familiar.

The shawl carried her still—Liyzia. Not in body, but in trace. Memory woven into fiber. A mind once fierce and resolute now resting within the weave.

He bowed his head, breathing in its scent. Not incense or perfume, but mountain herbs, hand-blended oils, and the unmistakable weight of years. It smelled like something real—like someone who had walked where few dared, who had known both grief and grace.

When he opened his eyes, the forest remained dead still. From the Whisperleaf to the Autumn wind. This silence felt more like hesitation. Watching. Listening. And the chill in his spine was not cold—but from instinct.

Back Vesper, silence always meant danger. Here? He wasn't sure what it meant. Only that it was holding its breath for something more.

A Mirthenbunny stood just beyond the tree line, ears alert but unpanicked. It should've darted off the moment his boots shifted in the moss. Instead, it blinked—once, twice—then tilted its head, as if in quiet approval. Then, without a sound, it turned and slipped into the underbrush, vanishing like a dream that didn't want to be chased.

Markus watched it go, unsure whether he should feel unnerved or comforted. In the end, he simply stood there—shawl in hand, breath held—while the forest whispered nothing at all.

* * *

His feet moved before his mind could process why, every step carrying him faster through the twisted paths. Behind him, the forest seemed to wake, sounds returning in a rush that made his skin crawl. Was that the wind through branches, or whispered voices? Were those shadows moving, or just his paranoid imagination? The pulse pistol at his side felt suddenly inadequate against untold ancient forces he'd stumbled into.

When Markus returned with the shawl, he found Xara seated on a fallen log, gently stroking what at first glance appeared to be a woodland fawn. But as the creature lifted its delicate head, the patches along its flanks glowing with soft light—he recognized a Starfawn, rare even in these ancient woods. The moment Markus stepped closer, the creature's luminescence intensified to an almost painful brightness. But instead of bounding away, it stood perfectly still, fixing its eyes on him with unnatural curiosity. Other Starfawn were known to bolt at the slightest disturbance, yet this one seemed caught between fear and fascination, as if recognizing something both ancient and impossible.

Above them, the forest's usual symphony changed its tune. The Nightcallers, owl-like birds usually hidden in the highest branches, fell silent in the midst of their song. One by one, they began a different call— lower, older, in refrains he'd never heard before. In the lower branches, Duskweavers emerged from their silvery webs, their spider-like forms weaving patterns that seemed to point toward him.

Markus took a seat by her, clutching the strange, handwoven garment he had found tied to a tree limb together with berries he'd foraged along the way. Xara inspected the fabric.

"This has to be important," he said, running his fingers along the intricate patterns. "No one would leave something like this behind unless ..."

"Shh!" Xara hissed, holding up her hand. "Listen ... driftcycles!" her whisper was sharp, her pain forgotten. "Help me up!"

Markus hauled her to her feet, already scanning for cover. "Hans couldn't have ...?"

"He led the raid. He's got magistrate resources." Xara's breath hitched as pain shot through her leg. "Move!"

They scrambled downhill, Markus half-carrying, half-dragging Xara through the thick brush. Branches snapped at their faces, roots caught underfoot, and gravity sent them tumbling down in a cloud of dirt and leaves. Their hurried descent reverberated through the quiet forest like an avalanche hurtling toward the river below.

For a moment, only the sounds of their heavy breathing and the distant murmur of the river filled the air. The forest had grown too quiet—not the natural hush of wildlife sensing danger; no, something deeper. Even the wind seemed to hold its breath. The very air felt charged, like the moment before lightning strikes, and the shadows between the trees seemed to move with purpose rather than chance.

Markus had grown up reading the signs of city streets, learning which alleys meant danger and which promised escape. But here, every instinct he'd honed told him they'd stepped into something older than concrete and steel—something that made those urban survival skills feel inadequate.

"Hold on," Markus whispered, gently lowering Xara behind a thick patch of foliage. Something twitched in the corner of his eye. Movement—just a shadow between the trees. His hand covered her mouth, and his heart pounded as he watched a figure step into the clearing ahead.

A cloaked figure.

"Don't ... breathe" he whispered in Xara's ear, feeling that same foreboding that crept over him with the haunted tales of this old forest.

In the heavy stillness of autumn, nature awakened around the figure. Dead leaves spiraled in impossible patterns despite the windless air, while the massive Skytower tree's silvery bark caught and fractured the dawn light into ethereal beams that bent around their form.

The figure drew back their hood, revealing a Nevran woman haloed in light, her lavender skin shimmering with inner radiance. The forest responded to her movements—branches swayed in her wake, roots shifted beneath the soil, and the mighty Shadowvein trees were streaked with light where she passed. Even the birds suddenly fell silent.

Her deep blue eyes held Markus with an intensity that pierced through flesh and bone into his very soul. Every secret, every fear lay bare before that gaze. His mind screamed to look away, yet he remained transfixed— terrified and serene at once.

His street-honed instincts screamed danger, yet something deeper, something he thought he'd lost in the harsh years since childhood, reached toward her presence. The moment awakened memories of the old tales he'd heard in adolescence of beings who walked between worlds, who could breathe starlight and speak to the very essence of things. But such beings had vanished ages ago, hadn't they?

Yet here was this woman, shifting in form between solid and ethereal, leaving trails of soft light in her wake that danced like aurora through the morning mist.

And in an instant, she appeared right before them, the very air shimmering around her with an impossible light and warmth. Their weapons came up reflexively, trembling in their hands, but something deeper than fear made them hesitate.

When she tilted her head in curiosity, the morning light fractured around her like a as though reality itself seemed to bend. Each movement left ribbons of luminescence in the air, like strokes from an artist's brush painting with pure light.

A wave of calm radiated from her. Their weapons

lowered unbidden as fear dissolved like frost in sunlight. Above, the Mistweep branches wept droplets that vanished before touching the earth, forming a shimmering veil around them.

"Markus!" Xara's sharp whisper finally broke through his trance. He blinked, the spell partially broken, but the otherworldly sensations lingered. A glance at Xara confirmed he wasn't alone in what he'd witnessed—her wide eyes and pale face reflected the same mix of awe and disbelief he felt.

Markus fought to hold onto his skepticism, to focus on the practical threats of pursuit and survival. But each time he blinked, reality seemed to shift—one moment, she was solid, the next her edges blurred into light and shadow.

"What is this?" he thought, "some type of Nevran magic?"

When the woman's gaze met his, the walls he'd built over years of hard living started to sway like smoke in a strong wind.

Her slight smile suggested she had heard his thoughts as clearly as spoken words.

"For heaven's sake," Xara whispered, "She's a gentle Nevran woman." But even as she spoke the words, her mother's stories echoed in her mind—tales of the old bloodlines who could bend light like water and speak to the very soul of the forest. She'd always thought them bedtime fancies, meant to make a child feel less alone in a world that feared their kind. Yet here before them stood living proof of those ancient powers, and Xara felt a deep ancestral recognition, like remembering a song she'd never actually heard.

"*Vehl Rishnia! Zivo Nali?*" the woman spoke, her voice soft, lilting.

Xara, still catching her breath, hesitated before responding in kind. "*Zu tol, Eingiliaz?*

"I speak the common tongue," the woman replied with a light and unfamiliar cadence. Each word seemed to ripple through the air like stones dropped in still water. "Please, do not fear. I am unarmed."

As she spoke the morning mist curled around her, responding to her presence like a living thing.

Markus, still rattled, tried to focus on maintaining his glare, but the shifting patterns of light around her made it difficult to hold her gaze. "Lady, moving like that's a quick way to get yourself shot."

She smiled again, unfazed. "Why are you out here?" she asked gently.

Markus fought to keep his voice steady, to focus on the practical rather than the way shadows seemed to bend around her. "We're passing through. Why do you care?"

"These woods are dark and dangerous," she said, and for a moment, the forest itself seemed to echo her warning in the rustle of leaves.

"Safe enough for you to wander alone," Markus muttered.

"I am not alone," she says with a small, cryptic smile. "I am from Orwein. Close to here. You two ... you're from Vesper?" Her finger traced the air near the insignia on Markus' jacket—one he'd swiped off a dead deputy—and though she didn't touch it, he felt a whisper of warmth against his chest.

Xara slapped Markus on the cheek, out of his trance. "Snap out of it! Markus!"

The woman's gaze rested on Markus. Her eyes narrowed slightly as they traced the scar on his temple. She stepped closer, her expression thoughtful.

"You two are hurt. You won't get far like this," she says, stepping back slightly as if giving them space to breathe. "Let me help."

"We don't need your help," Markus growled, shooting Xara a look. But Xara was watching the woman intently, her guard visibly softening.

As they rose and proceeded along the path, the woman called after them. "Wait ... please! Have you come across a shawl? I lost it somewhere in these woods ... it's precious to me."

Markus slowed his pace, with Xara limping beside him. They exchanged glances, their expressions softening ever so slightly.

"You think it's hers?" Xara whispered.

Markus was torn between suspicion and sympathy. "Maybe. Maybe not. Something feels .... off. I don't trust her. I think she's one of those 'strange beings' — you remember the fantasies we read?"

"For heaven's sake," Xara whispered, "She's a gentle Nevran woman. We need help. And who better than her?"

He sighed; his mistrust gnawed at him. "Fine. Let's get this over with."

Xara turned back to the woman. "What name does it bear?"

"The house of Q'iirev," the woman said, hope in her voice. "It bears my name, Liyzia, daughter of Ruvira."

Markus sighed and reached inside his coat. "Here. This what you're looking for?"

The woman's face lit up as Markus handed her the folded garment. She clutched it to her chest with a gasp of relief, sinking to her knees. "Yes! Yes, this is mine! Blessings upon you both!"

Markus, not wanting to linger any longer, started to edge away, but the woman stopped them.

"I ... please, let me repay you. With food, shelter. You must rest."

Markus shifted uncomfortably, clearly still on edge. "That's not necessary"

"It *is* necessary," she interrupted, smiling. "Please, allow me to repay your kindness ... yes?"

Xara nodded compassionately.

Before Markus could argue, Liyzia let out a sharp whistle splitting the air like an arrow. The note seemed to linger impossibly long, making the leaves shiver. Within seconds, the scampering of footsteps startled the pair as they both reached for their weapons. But something about the sound wasn't quite right—it seemed to come from everywhere and nowhere at once, as if the forest itself was moving.

Xara was quick to lower Markus' weapon and hers, when a trio of boys burst from the cluster of trees, laughing, and carrying bundles of food and supplies.

"These are my servants," Liyzia explained with a nod to the boys. "They will assist."

When Markus opened his mouth to protest, she pressed a piece of bread to his lips. Warmth flooded through him—deeper than mere temperature, primal as breath. It tasted of hearth and home, impossibly fresh. His protest died in his throat as forgotten memories surfaced—not just of taste and smell, but of belonging, of a time before survival meant suspicion. His carefully shielded walls wavered, not from any mystical force, but from the simple power of remembered kindness.

She held his gaze for a moment longer, and there was something in her smile—knowing, yet gentle, teasing, yet kind—that lowered his defenses.

A servant handed Xara a crutch, and she gratefully leaned into it, taking a deep breath of relief. Unlike Markus, she accepted her piece of warm loaf with a slight bow—a proper Nevran gesture of gratitude that seemed to please Liyzia. The old tales of Nevran hospitality rang true; to refuse their kindness was to refuse their protection, and Xara knew better than to reject either. She caught Markus' eye and couldn't help but smile at his bewildered expression—it wasn't often she saw her hardened companion so thoroughly disarmed.

Markus tried to brush the strange feeling tugging at him ever since they stumbled upon this strange woman. It's easier to chalk it up to coincidence, he thought, watching Xara savor her bread with closed eyes. Right now, all that mattered was getting as far away from this forest as possible—however they could. Even if it meant accepting help from a stranger who somehow knew exactly when he would protest, and exactly how to silence him with a traditional gesture of hospitality that felt more binding than any contract. And perhaps, most unsettling of all, knew exactly how to make him question everything he thought he knew about trust.

The distant hum of driftcycles broke through the thick silence of the woods, fading in and out of the dense trees. Their mechanical whirring felt oddly out of place in the natural stillness.

Liyzia gathered the group and led them swiftly through the winding path back to the paved road, where they descended the hillside toward safer ground.

They soon arrived at a gravel road near the riverbank, where the hushners awaited—massive, patient, and unmistakable. Markus had only seen them in passing before, their enormous forms pulling merchant trailers through Vesper's crowded streets. But now, standing this close, he couldn't help but stare.

"They're bigger than I remember," he murmured, watching one lower its shaggy head toward him like a dog awaiting a pat.

The beast's fur rippled in the breeze, its bear-like face stretched in a lazy grin, tongue lolling. Despite their size, there was something disarmingly gentle about them—like oversized, fur-draped puppies who didn't know they could crush you.

Markus reached a tentative hand toward the nearest one. It rumbled happily and leaned in, nearly knocking him over. Xara smirked from the far side of the wagon. "Guess you made a friend."

Xara was helped into the rear of the carriage where she sat with the boys, while Liyzia lured Markus to sit beside her as she took the reins. They set off at a steady pace—slower than Markus would like, but faster than walking would ever have taken them.

The lumbering hushners kept them moving around twenty miles per hour along the gravel road. Though the hum of vehicles faded into the distance, Markus couldn't shake the uneasy feeling of being watched. Every time he glanced over his shoulder to check for lawmen, he'd catch Liyzia studying him with that unsettling gaze—as though she could see right through him. The forest shadows seemed to bend strangely around her profile, and when she adjusted the reins, he noticed the hushners responded before her hands even moved.

Like a veil being drawn back and forth across his vision, he kept catching glimpses of ... something else, something that made ancient Nevran legends stir in the back of his mind. He'd look away, check on Xara in the back of the carriage, scan the treeline for pursuit—but his attention kept being pulled back to Liyzia, as though she were a lodestone and his thoughts mere iron filings.

"You didn't have to help us," he said finally.

Liyzia's reply was soft but pointed. "And you didn't have to find my shawl."

"We'll pay you for the food and whatever else you can offer."

"Kindness costs nothing. It's freely given," Liyzia said, and the words seemed to carry timeless wisdom, like an echo of forgotten wisdom. The hushners' pace steadied without her touching the reins, as if they too felt the power in her voice.

"Nothing is free in this world, lady. You always help strangers?" Markus tried to focus on the practical con-cern but couldn't ignore how the morning light seemed to gather around her like a cloak.

She chuckled lightly, and the sound rippled through the air like music. "It's not every day I find strangers wandering in these woods. An odd pair, you two."

The shadows of passing trees danced unusually across her face, highlighting the knowing look in her eyes.

"Odd? Really? I mean you're the one who's actually ..."

Before he could finish, she did it again. That same hypnotic gaze froze him in his tracks as though she knew his thoughts. She squeezed his hand. "Relax! Rest your mind for now. The worst is behind you—a whole new world lies ahead." Liyzia's words carried that same mysterious certainty that seemed to wrap around her like a cloak.

They continued down the gravel road as the forest soon gave way to meadows and the rising sun in the east.

The distant whine of driftcycles cut through the morning air. But each time the sound grew closer, the forest seemed to respond to shield them; branches shifted to create deeper shadows, mist spread unnaturally to obscure their path. Markus noticed how the mechanical sounds became distorted, as if the ancient trees themselves were bending the noise around them. Even the gravel beneath the carriage wheels seemed to muffle their passage, while the pursuing vehicles' engines echoed misleadingly off the canopy above.

Another driftcycle roared in the distance, harsh, mechanical, out of place. But under Liyzia's guidance, their carriage moved with an older rhythm. The hushners' rhythmic trot and the wooden wheels' gentle crunch against gravel felt like they belonged to the forest's age-old song. Each time modern engines drew near, the contrast became sharper as if their pursuers' technology was fighting against the forest's will, while their own passage seemed blessed.

Xara watched Liyzia from the back of the carriage, as her own mother's stories stirred in her blood. All her life she'd dismissed tales of the old powers as mere fantasy, choosing instead to trust in modern skills—forgery, technology, cunning. But now, watching light bend around their mysterious protector, she felt an ancestral recognition, a deep knowing that transcended her upbringing. This was what her people had been before the cities claimed them, before they'd traded starlight for neon.

Markus caught Xara's eye in the back of the carriage—a look that acknowledged both residual fear and growing wonder. Something had shifted in their world, as surely as the shadows bent around their mysterious protector's form. The danger wasn't gone, but somehow, in this enigmatic woman's presence, it felt less absolute than it had mere hours ago.

* * *

The forest path began to widen, morning mist still clinging to the trees. Markus shifted in the carriage seat, watching the landscape transform from familiar urban sprawl to something wilder, more ancient.

"What lies ahead?" he asked, noting how the gravel road had begun to wind upward.

Liyzia's lips curved into a knowing smile. "The first of the Seven Villages—scattered like seeds flung from a farmer's careless hand, each grown in its own shape bound by a single purpose: to feed a kingdom that seldom finds the time to thank them."

"That is Orwein we're approaching?" he asked, skepticism edging his voice.

"Yes—both a breadbasket and a crossroad."

"For what?" Xara asked, curiosity sparking in her eyes.

Liyzia adjusted her cloak, her gaze fixed ahead.

"Trade, culture, history. Nevrans, Earthens, even the Skylanders to the north—all pass through here." She glanced at Markus.

"You'll find no sleek metal towers here, no hover-cars buzzing by. The people live as their ancestors did, rooted in the old ways."

Markus frowned. "Sounds like a museum."

Liyzia chuckled softly. "You'll see. Orwein isn't as quiet as it seems."

As the hushner-drawn carriage slowed, Markus squinted at the distant village in the ascending morning light. The jagged outline of rooftops blurred against the forest canopy, where massive stone buildings rose in elegant tiers that spoke of generations who had shaped this land. Unlike Vesper's metal towers and neon glare, Orwein seemed to grow from the earth itself—its walls alive with moss and flowering vines that the locals carefully tended.

Monumental pillars on either side welcomed them with their elaborate carvings. The hushners' steady trot matched the strange rhythm of this place, timeless and unhurried. And unlike the cold, glossy skyscrapers he was used to, the rustic buildings here seemed to breathe, their mossy walls alive in an unsettling way. Markus shifted in his seat, caught between fascination and unease, while Xara leaned forward eagerly, taking it all in.

While Xara tilted her head, marveling at the colorful fabrics fluttering from market stalls, each with a story woven in thread, Markus kept his collar high, conscious of every curious glance. The market buzzed like a hive at sunrise, never truly sleeping. Even in the dead of night, you'd hear dogs barking and coins clinking in shadow deals. Now, in full day, it assaulted Markus' senses—shouting voices and clucking hens blending with the sharp scent of fragrances into an overwhelming cacophony.

The air shimmered, thick with the scents of smoked herbs and baked bread. Even the stones seemed to resonate with quiet magic.

Spices burned bright as fireflies; their scents curled in the air, while merchants bickered with the intensity of rival songbirds defending their nests.

"Careful with that hushner!" a merchant yelled as a boy chased one through the crowd. Markus winced as the large strange furry creature brushed past his boots, and he nearly toppled into Liyzia's arms, much to Xara's amusement.

As they pulled into an open slot beneath the canopy's entrance, Xara's quiet warning set Markus on edge. His hand drifted to his weapon as a stranger approached.

The man was a middle-aged Nevran, scruffy yet not unpleasant—like a blend of hobo and hunter, with a peculiar air of purpose. Instead of the expected stench of the streets, he carried the scent of honey and wildflowers, as though he lived among the forests.

Markus was out of the carriage in an instant, his stance defensive, but Liyzia intercepted him, stepping between them with a disarming smile.

"*Tarnüra!* Finnor!" she greeted warmly, though her sharp eyes tracked his movements with careful precision.

Finnor tilted his head, studying them with an odd

intensity that felt both playful and probing. "Ah, Liyzia. New company, I see. Wanderers from the steel city ..." He paused, cocking his head as though listening to something unheard. Then, with a nod to no one in particular, he continued. "Yes, the steel city to the south. What brings you to our quiet corner? Might these two seekers be in search of something ... or perhaps, someone?"

His words hung in the air. Markus and Xara exchanged uneasy glances.

Finnor's attention shifted to Xara, his gaze fluttering over her like a curious bird. He chuckled softly, his eccentricity both endearing and unnerving. "Careful, young lady," he said with a teasing smile. "Your beauty might stir the dust of old paths best left untouched."

Xara met his gaze, unimpressed. "And what paths would those be?"

Instead of answering, he asked, "Tell me—what runs but never walks? Has a bed but never sleeps?"

Her answer was automatic. "A river."

"Ah, a quick mind!" Finnor's grin widened as he reached into his cloak and produced a small, vivid plant. "A gift for you—a Whisperleaf. Tiny guardians of the forest, ever watchful, ever alert. May it serve you well!"

Xara accepted the plant, her wariness tempered by curiosity.

When Finnor turned his attention to Markus, his playful air was replaced by something sharper, almost probing. "Tell me," he began, in a casual yet cutting tone, "why do you carry metal in your heart?"

Markus stiffened, his hand moving instinctively to his sidearm. Liyzia's gentle touch stopped him as her fingers rested lightly on his wrist.

Finnor's gaze bore into him, unblinking, as though he saw something beyond the surface. "Perhaps," he said, with a faint smile tugging at his lips, "it is the metal that carries you."

From his cloak, Finnor produced a fragile, withered flower. Its faded petals seemed to shimmer faintly, as though clinging to a forgotten light. "A lumidawn," Finnor explained, placing it carefully in Markus' hand. "In time, it will show you what lies beyond the veil. Things hidden, things you are not yet ready to see."

As Markus stared at the flower, a prickle of unease crept up his spine. The petals quivered slightly, or so it seemed. He glanced at Liyzia, who observed the gift with a guarded expression.

"*Ma'eth serai*," he mumbled, seemingly to himself, while Liyzia's slight nod acknowledged the traditional greeting.

With that, he bowed low and departed, light and jaunty, as though he danced to a tune only he could hear.

Liyzia watched him go, with an unreadable expression. "Finnor," she said as the boys assisted her with the empty baskets. "A friend to all. Harmless." Her eyes lingered on the path he'd taken.

Markus frowned, turning the lumidawn in his hand. "A quack."

"A fortune teller," Xara countered, her fingers brushing the Whisperleaf.

"You judge him after one meeting?" Liyzia asked softly, eyes glinting with challenge.

Markus hesitated, caught off guard by the question. He turned the flower over in his hand, tracing the edges of its brittle petals with a thumb. They shimmered faintly in the light, delicate yet strangely sharp, like they could cut if he pressed too hard. He didn't realize he'd been holding his breath until the sting reached his skin—

—a sudden pain, like a thorn prick.

Markus flinched. A hand touched his arm, grounding him. Liyzia was adjusting his tunic, but her eyes lingered briefly on the spot where the petal had touched his thumb, as if she had seen something he hadn't.

The two boys remained in the back of the carriage alongside Xara, who was now covered beneath a blanket, while Kneuvah took a seat up front.

Suddenly, a faint buzzing sound broke through beneath the subtle mixture of the crowds moving about. The sound grew louder with each passing second. Xara lifted her head, shooting a look at Markus.

"You hear that?"

"Multiple driftcycles," Xara muttered, her eyes narrowing.

"It could be anyone—couldn't it?"

"I know these machines" she stated, "They're coming in fast."

"Like they're ..." Markus paused, then moved his lips inaudibly, "looking for someone."

It was slow enough for Xara to lip read. Of all the tight spots they'd been in, this one was the tightest. Everything here was alien to them—the land, the language, and most unsettling of all, their newfound ally whose inexplicable powers made them feel even more adrift.

As Markus swiftly gestured in sign language, Liyzia

casually spoke to Xara, whose attention he couldn't snatch away from the Nevran woman. Whatever she said, quickly cut to the chase, and was convincing enough to force her to lie back down. Liyzia concealed her once more with the blanket, giving the boys a final command to keep watch.

Markus was caught between a rock and a hard place—confusion and panic overcame him. This was no time for niceties, even if it meant rudely grabbing Xara's light body in his arms and high tailing it out of there. Yet he couldn't afford to draw attention either. There was no telling who was on those approaching cycles. Hans' men? Vitelli's hitmen? Both?

He wondered what power or words in this woman's vocabulary could compel Xara—a woman who could be as vicious and desperate as a cornered alley cat! No way he'd be swayed so easily! Pacing back and forth, he watched Liyzia tighten her shawl about her waist followed by her outer cloak, as she confronted him.

"Is something wrong?"

His lips parted, and his eyes dodged between each of the boys, who were looking upon him with such curiosity and anticipation, then back to the woman. "No. It's just that—couldn't we just head to your place now?"

"Wouldn't that be suspicious?"

He could see Xara shifting beneath the blanket. "Suspicious?"

"Yes—to show my husband that I've brought two guests home by way of the market without more groceries."

Markus exhaled for a moment. "Of course! It's just that ..."

"You are nervous." She stepped forward and adjusted his cloak properly about him. "I understand."

"You do?"

"You will find the market here the most colorful. All sorts of colorful characters, from the sunniest smiles to warm your heart to the gloomiest growls attempting to swindle you. You needn't fear. Now come!"

The boys chuckled at him, as she escorted him out alongside her. With her arm wrapped around his elbow, she led him as a captain steering a ship in such a way that he couldn't resist.

"I would not worry about those driftcycles. They're not permitted without consent of local law." She squeezed his arm. "And our pleasant town is not an authorized transitional zone."

He was impressed by her knowledge of such things.

"We're not all neanderthals here," she winked.

"It's not the cycles that worry me, but the men on it."

"Of course. A dozen men are approaching as we speak."

In that moment, he could feel his adrenaline spike as his thoughts briefly took him back to the forest, and their encounter.

"They approach in great haste and despair—escorted by our most respectable Sheriff of Orwein. I believe they're looking for the most peculiar individuals."

"Yeah?" Markus asked as they began mingling in the multitude. "And who would that be?"

"Why—a young man and woman carrying secrets from Vesper. Who else?"

He took hold of her to stop as he looked back towards

the main cobblestone road they had entered. And like clockwork, a small band of men emerged, parting the crowd with their uniformed jackets that donned the official badges of the district magistrate's office. The local sheriff alongside them stood out as clear as day, and as clear as her own foresight she had just displayed moments earlier.

His thoughts were as scattered as the crowd wandering through the market's square. "Look! I'll make a deal with you. Help us? And we'll help you. Yeah?"

She readjusted his cloak one final time, concealing his face even more. Her smile suggested she'd already decided to help long before he offered.

"Come!" she said.

* * *

The market square of Orwein unfolded like a living tapestry of color and chaos. A maze of vendors and stalls crowded the narrow streets, their awnings creating a patchwork ceiling of faded reds and sun-bleached blues. The air was thick as the scents of spices mingled with those of livestock, and humanity.

Liyzia guided Markus with subtle touches—gentle pressure on his elbow, a light tap on his shoulder. Her movements were fluid, intentional, each step calculated yet appearing completely natural. Markus, despite the native cloak draped over his shoulders, felt exposed.

"Relax your shoulders," she murmured, barely moving her lips. "You're carrying tension like a banner."

Then a commotion erupted behind them—one of the Vesper lawmen stumbled into a cart of clay post. The merchant's angry tirade drew a crowd; his rapid-fire native tongue was completely lost on the red-faced official.

"Perfect timing," Markus acknowledged.

"Merchant Kaldo can argue for hours," she laughed, steering Markus down a narrow alley between stalls.

Next, they emerged into a section dedicated to textile vendors. Countless bolts of fabric created natural walls and corridors, while haggling customers provided ever-shifting cover. Through gaps in the crowd, Markus spotted another lawman, whose polished boots and rigid posture marked him.

"There!" the lawman shouted, pointing directly at him.

Markus turned. From several stalls away, the lawman moved in. He finally reached for the cloak, only to reveal someone who *wasn't* Markus, a head shorter, and engaged in a passionate kiss with his companion.

Liyzia stifled a laugh, pulling him along. "When I say 'Now,'" she whispered, her eyes taking on that authoritative look again, "step directly left behind the spice merchant's stall."

But Markus' attention had already wandered. A creature unlike anything he's ever seen scurried past his feet—a cross between a squirrel and a peacock, its iridescent tail fanning out as it scurried through the crowd. Without thinking, he took a step forward to get a better look.

"Markus, ..." Liyzia's warning came too late. The surging crowd had already separated them, sweeping Markus into a sea of unfamiliar faces. The stranger creature disappeared around a corner, and with it, Markus' bearings.

Panic rose in his throat as he spotted one of the law-men less than twenty paces away. Acting on instinct, Markus grabbed a nearby basket and held it like the other merchants and began a terrible attempt at a sales pitch. His mind went blank on what little Nevrish he knew.

"Fresh ... things!" he called out in what he hoped was a convincing local accent. "Very good ... local ... items. Yes! Best in all of ..." he realized he'd forgotten the town's name, "this place!"

A few locals stared at him with a mixture of confusion and concern. One elderly woman approached, speaking rapidly in her native tongue and pointing at this basket. Markus glanced down, realizing too late that he was trying to sell a customer's empty shopping basket.

Another lawman's head turned toward the commotion. Just as Markus prepared to bolt, a familiar hand caught his elbow. Liyzia appeared as if from nowhere, smoothly inserting herself between him and the approaching official.

"My apprentice," she explained to the confused elderly woman in her native tongue, barely containing her mirth. "Still learning. And basic words. And how to tell *merchandise* from customer's belongings." She steered Markus away, her shoulders shaking with silent laughter.

"That creature," Markus began defensively, "it was ..."

"A common market pest that the local children dye with berry juice to amuse tourists," Liyzia finished, finally letting her laughter bubble up. "Though I must say, your sales technique was ... unique."

They continued their dance through the marketplace, each near-miss building upon the last. The lawmen's frustration became increasingly evident—their composed façades cracking under the assault of persistent vendors, language barriers, and the general chaos of market day in Orwein.

They passed beneath strings of drying herbs that perfectly obscured them from a lawman's sweeping gaze. She paused, her eyes taking on a distant look. "Duck!"

Markus didn't hesitate this time, dropping into a crouch just as a merchant's assistant passed overhead with a long pole strung with dried fish. The lawman behind them wasn't so fortunate, taking a salted mackerel to the face.

The marketplace rang with laughter, the incident drawing every eye in the vicinity. Except for Liyzia and Markus, who slipped away like shadows, leaving chaos and confused officials in their wake.

They didn't stop until they finally reached a quiet courtyard several streets away, where flowering vines climbed the weathered stone walls and the market's clutter faded. Markus braced his hands on his knees, catching his breath, while Liyzia leaned against a sun-warmed wall, her eyes dancing with barely contained delight.

"So," she said, crossing her arms, "shall we add 'vendor' to your list of potential jobs here? I particularly enjoyed your passionate sales pitch for ... what was it again? 'Fresh things'?'"

Markus straightened, fighting back his own grin, "You didn't exactly jump in to help me out."

"Help? And rob everyone of such entertainment?" She

shook her head solemnly, though her lips twitched. "That would have been terribly selfish of me."

A breeze carried the fading sounds of the market their way—the chaos they'd left behind. Despite the ongoing adrenaline, he suddenly found himself feeling lighter than he had felt in days, and finally let the laughter bubble up. He tried to play it off and hide it, but it was too late by now.

"You know," she said, pushing off from the wall, "for someone who started the day getting distracted by a painted rodent, you didn't do half bad back there."

She started walking, clearly expecting him to follow. "Though next time, perhaps we'll work on your grasp of local commerce. I hear there's quite a market for empty baskets these days."

"What do you mean by 'next time'? Hey! Wait up!" Markus swiftly fell into step beside her, afraid of getting separated again.

CHAPTER FIVE

That evening, Liyzia led Markus and Xara toward her sprawling, multi-story stables, where the earthy scent of hay mingled with a faint musk of unfamiliar animals. As they approached, the distinctive sweet-sharp smell of Hornstriders reached them—like cattle yet with an undercurrent of something herbal, almost medicinal. The air carried a subtle warmth, stirred by the breaths of the creatures within.

A soft clicking sound drew their attention to a row of stalls where iridescent wool caught the fading light. It was the sound of Woolbacks shifting nervously, their fleece rippling with subtle color changes as they sensed strangers. In the center aisle, a six-legged Fieldrunner lifted its head, all three sets of paws tensing as if ready to round up the restless herd. Above in the hayloft, Xara caught glimpses of small, blue-shelled eggs nestled in straw—evidence of the Crownfeathers whose rustling plumage cast dancing shadows on the beams overhead.

As the strangers stepped closer, the animals began to shift uneasily, hooves scraping against the wooden floors. The Hornstriders lowered their four stubby horns, with low, guttural rumbling in protest. All eyes—glinting in the dim lantern light—were fixed on the newcomers, watchful and wary. One Woolback's fleece darkened noticeably in defense, making it almost vanish in the shadows.

But when Liyzia stepped over the threshold, her presence alone sent a ripple of calm through the space. Without a word from her, the animals quieted, their tension dissolving as if soothed by an unspoken bond. The Fieldrunner settled back on its haunches, folding its multi-jointed legs neatly beneath it. Turning back to her guests, Liyzia extended her hand and asked firmly for their weapons before they could proceed further.

Markus hesitated, tightening his grip momentarily before he handed over his pistol and the baton he had pilfered earlier. Xara, on her part, turned the moment into a theatrical performance, as she produced a seemingly endless cache of weapons from her clothing.

"One pulse pistol, a dagger, a pair of assassin's stilettos, two silencers ..." Markus counted aloud, eyebrows rising higher with each item.

"... my baton," Xara added, placing it atop the pile with a flourish, "and, of course, this," she said, holding up a pristine leather gauntlet like a prize.

Liyzia blinked at the arsenal. "Not proper items for a young lady to carry."

"They're gifts," Markus quipped, deadpan. "For her 'suitors.'"

Liyzia's eyebrows shot up. "Is courting that dangerous in Vesper?"

"I wouldn't know," Xara replied coolly, slipping the

gauntlet into Liyzia's hands. "Very few ever make it past *him*."

The tension dissolved into a chuckle from Liyzia as she separated the pair. She handed Xara customary attire to change into in one of the empty stables, then turned to Markus with a folded set of garments in hand.

"No thanks," Markus said flatly. "I'm good."

"Custom attire for you," Liyzia insisted, her tone unwavering. "As my guest. More comfortable you will be."

"I'm comfortable already. Thanks, though."

"Would you refuse and dishonor my family?"

Markus groaned inwardly. He'd assumed they would be grateful enough just to hide in some forgotten corner of the property. But no—she clearly intended to treat them as honored guests, even going so far as to carefully place a customary flower atop the garments. It was clear he wasn't getting out of this.

"Fine," he muttered, snatching the folded clothes. The fabric was soft, too soft compared to his worn leather and sturdy cotton—materials chosen for their ability to hide the occasional stain, to weather the consequences of his condition without raising questions. These new clothes felt like they'd hide or protect nothing.

"But if anyone asks, I was coerced by aggressive hospitality," he mumbled.

As he ducked into the nearest stable to change, Liyzia lingered nearby, waiting silently. The faint rustle of fabric was followed by Markus' voice. "That scarf—or shawl, or whatever you call it," he said, "does it belong to your family?"

"Yes," she replied. "As old as forty generations."

"This seems like a lot of trouble you're going through for us."

"My heart is grateful you found it."

Markus struggled in adjusting the unfamiliar fabric. "I need to warn you," he began, his tone grave. "I'm not really a 'people person.'"

"A 'people person'—a person made of people? This makes no sense."

"No, not a person who likes people. You know, like you."

"A people person is a person who likes people like me. So, you don't like me."

"Woah! I didn't say I didn't like you."

"But you said a people person is a person who likes people like me."

"No, I said you are *like* a people person."

"And a 'people person' would like people like me."

"Well, yeah."

"So, then you *are* a people person, since you said you liked me. No?"

"I—oh, what's the use!"

"What was that?" she asked with a chuckle.

"Uh, I'm just about through!" he yanked the sleeve aggressively before running his hand through his hair.

Liyzia smiled knowingly as Markus and Xara appeared simultaneously from opposite ends.

Liyzia adjusted his collar with that same gentle authority that both irritated and oddly comforted him. He wanted to step back, to make some cutting remark about not needing a caretaker. Instead, he found himself standing still, caught between the instinct to pull away and an unfamiliar urge to let someone else take charge—if only for a moment. The fact that she might be something more than she appeared—that her kindness might hide ulterior motives—only made the conflict more complex.

From across the room, he caught Xara's amused smirk, her eyebrows raised in that knowing way that said she'd file this moment away for future teasing. He shot her a warning glare, which only made her grin wider.

The two fell in step behind Liyzia as she led them toward the manor, its silhouette bathed in the glow of sibling moons hanging low and luminous in the night sky.

"Do you see that?" Xara whispered, craning her neck upward.

Markus nodded. The dual moons glimmered with a clarity that made their district's smog-choked skies seem like a distant nightmare. Pinprick stars sprawled endlessly above, forming constellations neither of them recognized. Somewhere in the distance, the soft hum of insects mingled with the rustle of leaves as a gentle night breeze cooled their skin.

"Well," Markus whispered, breaking the moment, "you clean up nicely."

"Likewise."

He hesitated, glancing at her crutch. "Don't you find this odd?"

"What's odd about changing into new clothes?"

"They're perfectly tailored," Markus muttered. "Coincidence?"

"Could belong to her husband," Xara replied with a shrug.

"Xara, seriously—she just happened to have a crutch lying around when she found us? What about the way she approached us? Like she knew exactly where we'd be. Or how she knew our names!"

Xara smirked. "Or the way she keeps looking at you?"

"That's not funny."

"She's peculiar, I'll admit, but harmless," Xara said, brushing him off. "Let's just roll with it. Be grateful for now."

Markus huffed, studying her carefully.

"Why do you keep staring at me? Do I have something in my teeth?"

"No. I just don't recognize you in that getup."

"Silly—you've seen me in a skirt before."

"Well maybe it's time you kept up the act."

As they approached the manor, its grand double doors swung open, and warmth spilled out in a welcoming embrace. The main room was a marriage of refinement and practicality—aged wood polished to a soft sheen, hand-carved furniture, and a hearth that dominated one wall, its light casting long shadows across the space. Trinkets and tapestries adorned the walls, each piece intricate and heavy with history. It was a room that spoke of a household grounded in tradition but lived in with care.

A tall figure rose from a chair near the hearth, his movements deliberate, his presence commanding without arrogance. Nikel, older than Markus expected, carried the weathered dignity of someone who had seen much but held his own. His piercing gaze shifted between the pair as Liyzia helped him to his feet, the two exchanging quiet words in their native tongue.

Nikel's eyes lingered on the shawl draped around Xara's shoulders.

"*Aviero*," he greeted finally in a measured tone. "Markus and Xara. My wife has spoken of you."

His gaze softened as it rested on Xara. "Only the brightest of jewels bear the name *X'araiel*. And a shawl like my wife's on an Earthen woman? Remarkable!"

Xara straightened. "It belonged to my foster mother."

Nikel inclined his head slightly, acknowledging her response before his attention shifted to Markus. He studied him with unnerving precision, his eyes tracing the jagged black scar slashing across his temple. Markus fought the instinctive urge to turn his head, to hide the mark as he'd done countless times before. Instead, he held Nikel's gaze, though his jaw tightened imperceptibly—a habit born from years of having to stand his ground while people stared.

"And you?" Nikel asked. "Her kin?"

"Foster brother," Markus replied, his tone neutral.

Nikel tilted his head, his curiosity sharp. "You were a 'fighter' in Vesper?"

"Not exactly."

"What then?"

"Watchman," Markus replied curtly. "I took out the trash at night."

"It must be some 'tough' trash to handle."

Markus shrugged. "I don't want any trouble here."

"That makes two of us," Nikel responded in an even tone.

"As soon as she's fixed up, we'll be on our way."

"I will make that a priority, then."

Liyzia, standing close to her husband, gently squeezed

his hand. "My Lord," she said with a playful lilt, "would my guest be warmer sleeping in the *icehouse* than under our roof?"

Nikel chuckled, pressing a kiss to her forehead. "No, my dear. Come—be our guests."

* * *

After his warm welcome with her husband, Markus would have just as soon left or crawled under a rock. She led them both to meet more of her folk. He bit his teeth and sucked it up as though he was about to step back into the ring against another opponent. If there was anything he hated more than socializing, it was the uncomfortable glares and glances he'd get. Especially when it came to strangers. And even worse, the stupid questions that followed.

The older you get, the more you get used to it. Just grin and bear it.

Xara, in stark contrast, seemed to bloom in the warm atmosphere. Her eyes darted from face to face, drinking in every detail—the intricate embroidery on Jetza's shawl, the way the children moved with such uninhibited joy, the subtle interactions between the adults. She leaned in, whispering something to Markus that made him roll his eyes.

But to his surprise, it was nothing of the sort. The two other men, Vuchic and Erev, friends of Nikel, were warm and firm in their handshakes. Their wives, Jetza and Niylu, nodded to him with a sparkle in their eyes. And the children? It was more like a classroom—each one with a bounce in their step as they were introduced.

Kneuvah, Teizl, Zeik, Menorah, Evenor, Tavin— he'd lost track after six. At least a dozen faces from six to seventeen, staring wide-eyed at the pair for a brief moment of silence, before reassuming their non-stop chattering and rambling amongst themselves.

Liyzia watched Markus with a knowing smile, her eyes tracking his mounting discomfort like a naturalist observing a rare specimen. She caught his eye just as one particularly loud child careened past, giving him a look that said, "Breathe. Relax."

The children darted between chairs like a pack of playful wolves, their laughter ricocheting off the walls. Markus gritted his teeth, resisting the urge to clamp his hands over his ears.

He watched in disbelief, thinking to himself. How in the world do these people bear so many children? This gathering alone would make a village!

He was about to lose his mind until ...

Right on cue, a loud shrieking whistle from the kitchen pierced his eardrums, calling everyone for supper.

After giving thanks for the bounty, it ramped back up again. And if he thought the children were something, he hadn't seen anything. The three women were even more exuberant. And with the good fortune of having his glowing host seated right beside him, he anticipated the worst. For if it were in her power, she'd probably do everything short of tying him to the chair and propping his mouth open.

The roasted meats had a sheen of honey glaze, their aroma cutting through the earthy undertone of fresh bread. Markus' stomach growled in betrayal, even as he steeled himself against the relentless parade of offerings.

Plate after plate materialized in front of him, each one more colorful and fragrant than the last. It was as if they were trying to drown him in kindness—and food. He'd barely swallowed one bite before another dish appeared, accompanied by Jetza's beaming smile.

The way the women moved, constantly filling plates and urging seconds, reminded Markus of a well-coordinated military drill. He doubted anyone had ever said 'no' to them—and lived to tell the tale.

Markus stared at the swirling amber liquid in his cup. Skylandic beer, they called it. He took the smallest of sips, but his stomach instantly revolted. Smile and nod, he reminded himself. Smile and nod. Only Xara was aware of his sensitivity to alcoholic beverages, and she'd wink at him every time their eyes met.

The first note from the lyre drew cheers from the children, who sprang into motion like wound-up toys. Tambourines and drums followed, the rhythm chaotic and infectious. Markus sank lower in his chair. The clapping was bad enough, but the children's jigs—if you could call them that—made him long for a dark, quiet corner. *Where do they get all this energy?* he wondered. He caught Xara's eye, and silently pleaded for rescue, but she was too busy grinning and clapping along.

Xara, of course, was lapping it all up; even her crutch was tapping out a beat on the floor. Markus shot her a look that said, *Traitor.* She winked back.

As the last notes of the fiddle ebbed, a hush fell over the room, broken only by the crackling fire and the occasional rustle of cloth. Nikel's voice, low and steady, gathered the children like moths to a flame.

Nikel transformed into a storyteller, his body a canvas of narrative. With each gesture, he brought the tale to life—a sword here, a helmet there, his shadow dancing larger than life across the wall. The children hung on to his every word, eyes wide with wonder.

As Markus listened in with heavy eyes, he blinked—and suddenly Liyzia was beside him, so close he could have sworn she wasn't there a moment ago. Her whisper was like silk, translating Nikel's tale. A story of knights, an infant prince, and a rescue that demanded the ultimate sacrifice. As she spoke, Markus could have sworn the words shimmered between them; it was more than mere translation.

Nikel solemnly exchanged his sword for his cane and tapped his knee, while exhaling a long stream of smoke. And as the older man and the three boys turned to observe him, Markus could feel a blanket being laid over him as he drifted away into slumber.

Moments later, Nikel met his wife on the balcony under the clear night of stars.

The cool night breeze brushed against Liyzia's face as she gazed up at the twin moons, their silver light reflected in her eyes. Nikel stood a step behind her with his cane tapping softly against the stone floor.

"I wondered what happened to your shawl. It has been weeks since I have seen it."

"The winds of Canivere snatched it like a thief from my waist."

"You have a way with words, my dear. And did you thank Xara for finding and returning your garment?"

"My Lord, it was Markus who returned it."

He paced and pondered her words. "I am puzzled by

your interactions with this troubled young man. You are drawn to him."

"Yes."

"Is there something about him you wish to share with me?"

Silence.

"I see" he continued, "Right now, I must trust in my judgment. We will get aid for the young lady and send them on their way ... My dear?" he called.

She turned, her eyes reflecting the moonlight. "Your judgment is clear."

Nikel nodded with a thoughtful expression thoughtful, before turning to leave.

Once his footsteps faded into the quiet of their home, Liyzia remained on the balcony. Slowly, she drew an object from within her cloak—a withered flower, delicate and faded, yet still holding a faint glimmer of life—the dying lumidawn.

Its brittle petals trembled, almost imperceptibly, as though responding to her presence. Liyzia ran her fingers lightly over the stem, her touch tender yet curious. The flower's faint stirring mirrored the thoughts swirling in her mind—visions, fragments, and truths she could not yet share.

She gazed back at the moons, the flower cradled in her palm, and whispered a single word under her breath, too quiet for even the night to catch.

* * *

Nestled between Karenthia, Oryndel, and Cyrinth, the district of Vesper had served as a critical stop on the

Levitated Train Network (LTN), connecting the kingdom's eastern and southern regions. Once envisioned as a thriving hub for commerce and industry, it had fallen short of expectations, and had become a haven for miners, merchants, and laborers from surrounding towns. For most, Vesper was a city of hard toil and broken promises.

For Hans Lumen, it was an opportunity.

As Hans sipped his coffee, his gaze swept over the station's worn architecture and the scattered faces of the morning crowd. The city's decline hadn't dampened his ambitions. The mining companies, law enforcement, and even the local crime syndicate—all were cogs in the machinery he was building for himself. The recent elimination of two rivals had only fueled his hunger for power. Now, his plans hung precariously on a single thief: a woman with a satchel containing secrets he couldn't afford to lose.

A gust of October frost swept through the sliding doors, carrying with it the sharp bite of the season. Hans scowled, adjusting his coat as Wendell, one of his magistrates, hobbled inside.

"Mr. Lumen," Wendell greeted.

"Wendell. Can I get you something?"

"No thank you," Wendell replied. "Wanted to catch you before the train arrives—we found her apartment."

"Her?"

Wendell handed him a slip of paper. "Can't pronounce the names. Wrote them down for you."

Hans chuckled as his eyes skimmed the list of aliases. "Splendid, my friend. Is the place covered?"

"Several deputies are watchin' it in case anyone shows up."

"That ship has sailed. Don't touch anything until I get there." He handed Wendell the half-empty cup of coffee just as the distant horn of the Levi train pierced the quiet.

The two men stepped onto the platform, joining the sparse morning crowd. Fog blanketed the horizon like a thick shroud, only to be sliced apart by the bright orb of the oncoming train. The vibrations of its double-decker frame rumbled through the magnetic tracks, causing a mild tremor beneath their feet. Hans barely caught his coffee in time as it threatened to spill.

Minutes later, the mile-long train came to a halt. As its doors slid open to offload passengers, two older gentlemen stepped onto the platform, their sharp eyes locking onto Hans. He straightened, feeling a pang of anticipation. These were the men he had studied, admired, and emulated throughout his career. Yet their solemn expressions warned him that this long-awaited meeting might not unfold as he'd imagined.

"Senator Schweimer. Councilman Pelham. Welcome to Vesper. How was your trip?"

"Not as pleasant as the departure will be."

"I thought we might discuss things over a hot breakfast and ..."

"What in the hell happened?" Schweimer cut him off.

"Care to be more specific?" Hans asked.

The older senator's eyes roamed the passing crowds for bystanders. "Three accounts designated specifically for this operation—thirty million crowns—have vanished. Whoosh! Disappeared. Gone up in smoke. Not even the banks and unions can trace it."

"Who is this remarkable young lady you told us about? This forger? Some sort of magician?" Pelham asked.

"She has quite a record," Schweimer added, "From everything we gathered concerning that bounty in Arduiine. And you let a young lady get the better of you?"

Hans literally felt the arrows sticking out of his back. He took a moment to sip his coffee.

"She's connected with the Vitelli organization, which I am currently rounding up. Should uncover the trail any moment now. In fact, I have some positive evidence to show you, gentlemen."

Within an hour, the trio arrived at a group of apartments, south of Central Square, towards the warehouses, entering the space where Markus and Xara resided. Though it was a minimalist dwelling with sparse furnishings, the dining table was covered in gadgets, widgets, art supplies, microscopes and other contraptions needed for her craft. But not a single scratch of paper was to be found anywhere.

Hans was at first intrigued. But upon rummaging through every drawer and container, he could not find anything—beyond expired ID cards she had used in the past. He'd hoped to find something—anything to connect her to the thirty-million crowns, or even the stolen satchel—but the place was spotless.

He handed the identification cards over to them.

"This is not looking good, Senator. Tell me, did you get the papers?"

Pelham coughed violently to get his attention, then looked towards the doorway at the local magistrate.

Hans patted him on the shoulder. "Why don't you go down and check on your men?"

Once the three were left alone, he continued. "Do

you at least have the papers? The congressional acts and documents which you tasked the young lady in finalizing."

"The transaction is still in progress," Hans admitted.

"You mean it was in progress," one of them added.

"Do you know what else is in her possession, Mr. Lumen? That satchel which she stole from you, containing the classified information for operation 'Aether.' Years of planning are already set in motion. Last thing we need is someone fucking things up."

"She doesn't have any political ties," Hans explained.

"Except you," Schweimer pointed out, "and God knows who else. A young woman like that would catch my eye!"

"And what about him? What's his story?" They pointed to Markus' black-and-white image.

"Bottom of the barrel. Her only family. Get to him? She's not far behind."

"Giving you till Thursday to come up with something."

"I understand."

"Do you? Let's be frank. We are disappointed. Corregan said you were shrewd, but not this sloppy and naïve. He was just as naïve to trust you with this intel. Damn fool."

"And where is Corregan?" Hans asked, "There's no trace of him in Arduiine or the neighboring boroughs. Where did he go?"

If he didn't know any better, from their puzzled reactions, he thought he'd asked a stupid question.

"Disappeared. An expendable piece of shit—like you."

Those words hit Hans like a hammer. Years of effort, of clawing his way up the political ladder, and here he was, reduced to nothing. The warm admiration he once held for these men soured into bitterness. They were not mentors—they were the very thing he had spent his life trying to overcome. Their once paternal smiles were now twisted with malice, revealing their true nature.

"That reminds me, Charles—nomination for the vacant seat in the 'High Council' is coming up." He spoke to his comrade for a moment, briefly ignoring Hans in the most condescending manner. In fact, he even emphasized the word 'High Council' as though dangling a carrot in Hans' ear. Then he added, "I know one name who won't make that list."

Hans could barely save face and keep a lid on his anger. He even placed the Styrofoam cup on the table to steady his trembling hand. It was a personal 'tic' of his whenever he was overcome with such emotion, whether it was nervousness or outright rage.

Hans' eyes were fixated on the lonely dart board hanging on the plastered wall, with his fists clenched. His hands were tempted to grab the darts any second now. No departing words necessary. He only felt them pass by from behind him with each footstep, harsher than the next, like hammers pounding iron nails into his coffin, before fading away.

Wendal, his loyal deputy, showed up moments later. "I need to level with you, Mr. Lumens. It's looking bleak—trying to find this girl, that is. They don't call her a magician for nothing."

"Then look for him instead. You can't miss a face like that!"

"You don't know him like we do, sir. Many of the men don't wanna tangle with him."

"Then fire them! Get some men with some balls to go after him!"

He rushed off with his tail between his legs. Hans paced restlessly, tempted to flip the circular table over. But he gave up. Instead, he pounded his fist against the same plastered wall that had been drilled with thousands of darts over the years.

* * *

The journey from Orwein to Fort Broneth felt like crossing over into another world. Markus had spent days consumed by Xara's worsening condition, desperate to get her medical attention while staying under Han Lumen's radar. The man's reach was vast, his cunning even greater. Markus knew Lumen wouldn't overlook a crash site or stop searching the nearby villages. The specter of pursuit haunted every rattling turn of the carriage wheels.

Leaving Orwein had been bittersweet. Nestled where the Canivere Forest met the winding Donaskan River, the village had a quiet charm—a place of safety and familiarity for Nikel and Liyzia. But even in the shelter of their home, Markus couldn't shake the feeling of a noose tightening around them. They had no choice but to seek help at Fort Broneth, where Xara's injuries could no longer be ignored.

By the time they reached the fort, the air felt heavier, charged with the energy of commerce and authority. Fort Broneth loomed ahead, a naval outpost and stronghold that guarded the kingdom's northern borders. It wasn't just a fortress; it was a beacon of order in a riotous world. Beneath its shadow sprawled the grand marketplace—more than just a collection of stalls. The locals called it the Exchange Grounds, a potpourri of trade and culture where merchants from across the region gathered to peddle their wares.

The Grounds bustled with life. Its sprawling lanes were flanked by awnings of bright fabric and wooden stalls arranged in tidy rows. Unlike Orwein's modest village square, this was a spectacle of organized chaos. Dried fish from the Northern shores hung beside shining brass trinkets imported from the west, stalls selling everything from cured meats and fine textiles to intricate gadgets powered by new technologies—solar-charged lanterns, mechanized tools, and rudimentary communication devices.

Markus felt out of place in the crowd. His nerves were frayed and his focus was entirely on Xara. They hadn't entered the fort yet; Nikel had gone ahead to make arrangements, relying on his status and connections to grant them passage. Markus hovered near the edge of the Galleria, reluctant to stray far from the carriage where Xara rested under Liyzia's watchful eye.

When Nikel returned, the transition into the fort was seamless. With a few well-placed words and the flash of his military insignia, Nikel secured access to the medical facilities inside. Soldiers ushered them in with brisk efficiency; their polished badges and clipped orders contrasted starkly with the lively disarray of the Galleria outside.

Inside the fort, the differences became even more pronounced. The medical facility was pristine, its stark white walls and orderly rows of cots evoking an almost mechanical precision. Markus lingered near the door as medics whisked Xara away. His hand brushed hers one last time and his chest tightened as they wheeled her out of sight. He felt a pang of envy in his gut, watching her receive care. Markus couldn't help but wonder what it might feel like to be the recipient of such attention, to be treated without questions, without having to hide his condition, without the fear of what his blood might do. But there was no time for self-pity. Han Lumen wouldn't be far behind.

"Come," Nikel said, gesturing toward the marketplace outside the fort's gates. "Knuevah's already gone ahead to scout. We'll wait there."

Reluctantly, Markus followed Nikel back into the Grounds. The transition from the fort's ordered calm to the market's controlled disorder hit him like a physical wave. His urban instincts sparked at every unfamiliar sound—vendors' cries atop the hiss of steam vents, the clatter of traditional scales competing with the soft hum of Guild-certified measuring devices. Even the air felt different, heavy with a strange blend of spices, livestock, and the ozone tang of modern preservation units.

Markus' eyes darted over the crowd, scanning for threats while trying to process the strange contrasts around him. A merchant wearing traditional robes adjusted a holographic price display above his wooden stall. Nearby, a group of farmers haggled over hushner feed prices, weathered hands moving in traditional bargaining gestures, while credit markers blinked on their wrists.

The fort's influence was undeniable. Soldiers strolled through in small groups, their modern weapons a stark contrast to the traditional charms and tokens the merchants eagerly pressed upon them. Some vendors called out in multiple languages—modern trade-speak mixed with ancient dialects Markus had never heard before.

A particular stall caught his eye—a flamboyant merchant demonstrating what he claimed was 'authentic Ilyrian crystal technology.' Markus couldn't help but smirk, reminded of Xara's more sophisticated cons. The man's patter was good though, drawing a crowd as he switched between Guild-certified scanning equipment and theatrical flourishes with surprising ease.

The diversity of people fascinated him—western traders with their sleek data tablets, rough-edged Nevrans still using traditional counting stones, and weather-beaten Skylanders whose salt-stained clothes reflected old seafaring traditions. Each group seemed to navigate the market's blend of old and new differently—some embracing both, others stubbornly clinging to the past.

Markus leaned over Nikel's shoulder at a wooden stall lined with starfruit and pulse-wine as the elder acknowledged two men he knew—Varek, an Earthen trader and Solim, a Nevran merchant. The retired knight waited in calm amusement as they haggled over repayment.

Varek tapped the screen of the worn data-slate, glowing faintly with numbers. "I'm not paying by your Nevran cycles! The Sol Standard runs on exact planetary orbits—your system drags centuries behind."

Solim narrowed his eyes.

"Your Sol Standard is meaningless here. This world existed before your ancestors set foot on it. We measure from the beginning of the Second Age, as it should be."

Varek folded his arms. "Fine. Then when exactly does my payment 'cycle' end? Because 100 days in *your* system isn't the same as 100 days in mine."

Solim sighed, rubbing his temple. "You want my goods? You play by Nevran rules"

A nearby Dromelan chuckled, butting in. "That's why we use lunar cycles. Simpler."

Both men shot him a glare. Solim exhaled. "Alright. We compromise. Two cycles in Nevran time, or roughly seven Earthen months. Agreed?"

Varek grumbled, then extended his hand. "Agreed."

Nikel raised an eyebrow at Markus. "Bureacracy's a pain no matter what culture you're in" the elder muttered before he proceeded with the men.

Kneuvah pulled Markus away drifting ahead of him further down the row of merchants. They stopped near a fishmonger's stall, where the sharp tang of salt and brine mingling with the dusty heat of the afternoon. That's when the Skylanders appeared.

Five men, their movements deliberate, emerged from the crowd. Everything about them radiated danger—their swagger, the crude axes strapped to their backs, and the tattoos that spiraled like storm waves down their necks.

"Lost, outsider?" the leader jeered, his voice rough and guttural. A hulking brute with greasy blond hair and a sneer that made Markus' blood simmer, he stepped into Markus' path with a predatory gleam in his eye.

Markus stiffened. He knew better than to

engage—knew he should keep his head down and walk away. But exhaustion and frustration bubbled over, tipping the balance. "Funny," he shot back, his voice low. "I was just about to ask you the same thing."

The blow came faster than he expected, a meaty fist slamming into his jaw and sending him reeling into a stack of crates. Pain flared through his face as he scrambled to his feet, adrenaline overriding caution.

"You've got a sharp tongue for a stray," the Skylander growled, grabbing Markus by the collar. Markus twisted free, shoving the man into a stall draped with tangled nets. But before he could follow through, another thug barreled into him, knocking him to the ground.

The fight spiraled out of control. Markus clawed for anything—a loose plank, a crate—but the Skylanders overwhelmed him, their blows relentless.

Then Nikel arrived.

The older man moved with mastery, his cane a blur of strikes. A jab to the ribs sent one thug stumbling, and a sharp swing of the cane dropped another. "Markus," Nikel barked through the chaos, "Stop flailing and think."

Markus gritted his teeth, grabbed a nearby fishing net and hurled it over the leader, entangling him long enough to land a solid knee to his gut. But it wasn't enough. The man surged forward, pinning Markus with a chokehold that left him gasping for air.

The pressure vanished as abruptly as it had come. Markus blinked, disoriented, as he realized the Skylander had frozen. Nikel's saber glinted against the man's throat, steady despite the slight tremor in Nikel's hand.

"That's enough," Nikel said, his voice calm but unyielding. "Take your bruises and leave."

The Skylanders hesitated, then stepped back, muttering curses under their breath. Their leader glared at Markus, rubbing his throat, before following the others into the crowd.

As the market slowly returned to its usual rhythm, Nikel sheathed his blade and turned to Markus, who was slumped against a stall, catching his breath.

"Impressive," Nikel said dryly. "You managed to turn a simple insult into a public brawl. That's a rare talent."

Markus glared up at him, wiping blood from his lip. "I didn't ask for your help."

"No, but you needed it," Nikel replied, lighting his pipe with a flick of his thumb. "You fight like a man with something to prove. That'll get you killed."

After a long silence, Nikel spoke again, his tone softer. "Next time, think. Your fists aren't your only weapon."

Markus didn't respond. He didn't need to. The lesson was already seared into his mind, along with the burning shame of losing control—the very thing he'd spent years mastering. Each throb of his split lip reminded him how quickly discipline could crack, how easily the careful walls he'd built could crumble. His blood condition had taught him the price of recklessness years ago. Today had just reinforced that lesson, whether he wanted it or not.

* * *

Hours later, Markus lay on the makeshift straw bench in the corner of the barn. His eyes were shut, but his mind was far from rested, wandering back to the fight at the marketplace and the countless other brawls he'd stumbled into over the years. It seemed like trouble had a way of finding him—whether it was bullies, sore losers, or just miserable people looking to pick a fight. He couldn't quite figure out why he always ended up in the middle of it.

The cool afternoon breeze seeped through the cracks in the barn's walls, and his quilt barely offered any warmth. Just as he was about to drift off, he felt something cold and wet against his forehead. Tiny droplets of water, then the cool, soothing touch of a damp cloth on the cut below his eye.

He nearly fell off the bench. "Dammit, woman! When did you come in?" He squinted at Liyzia, who sat calmly beside him, wringing out a wet towel over a bucket. "You did the same thing in the forest! Don't you ever make a sound?"

"The wind is my ally," she replied softly, not looking up from her task. "I'll make more noise next time if you'd like."

"Yeah, tie a bell around your neck while you're at it." He grimaced, half-annoyed, half-impressed by her stealth. "And what do you think you're doing?"

"You're hurt."

"So?" He scowled, trying to sit up but wincing as the pain on his side reminded him of the blows he'd taken.

"It's called helping."

"I didn't ask."

"It's called kindness, then," she said, wringing the cloth again. "Costs nothing."

"I can do it myself," he muttered, ripping the cloth from her hand, but with less force than intended.

"You needn't snatch it." She didn't flinch, her calm presence unnerving him more than the actual pain.

He sighed, feeling the tension ease just slightly. "Look ... I'm sorry. I just don't get why you're bothering me."

"Because my aid and shelter did not include 'fighting' in the marketplace," she said, her tone still soft but now laced with gentle reproach.

He chuckled bitterly. "Seems like trouble follows me everywhere I go."

"Perhaps," she said, sitting back, her eyes on him. "You could leave 'trouble' at the front door next time."

"If it were that easy," he muttered.

Liyzia's lips twitched in the faintest hint of a smile. "Nikel told me how you kept hitting their fists with your face. Quite a unique style."

He couldn't help but smirk at that. "Oh, so you've got jokes now?" He applied the antiseptic she had handed him to the cuts on his face and neck, wincing slightly. "Those foul-smelling Skylanders must be part of the welcoming committee."

Liyzia didn't respond immediately, but her eyes rested on him, making him uncomfortable. She didn't look away, not even when he fell back onto the bench and shut his eyes. He could still feel her there, silently watching.

A broken piece of mirror hung on the barn wall across from him, and in it he caught his own reflection—the black scar stark against his skin in the dim light. He watched Liyzia studying it in the reflection, her gaze neither pitying nor repulsed, just quietly observant. It was almost harder to bear than the usual reactions.

He was used to it by now—the stares, the sideways

glances, the whispered comments behind his back. The scar had been a part of him for so long that he barely gave it a second thought anymore. But the silence between them felt heavy, pressing down on him.

"Don't waste your time asking," he grumbled.

"About what?" she asked calmly, unaffected.

"My face," he replied, his tone sharper than intended. "It's a long story."

"We all have stories to tell," she said, but there was something in her voice that felt like an invitation, not a question.

Before he could respond, the barn door creaked open, and Nikel stepped inside, standing beside his wife. His presence shifted the air in the room—more tension, more immediacy.

"Clean yourself up," Nikel said, his tone curt but without malice. "I need to speak with you and Xara. In the house."

Markus glanced between them, feeling the weight of their unspoken understanding. Whatever was coming next, he wasn't sure he was ready for it—but then again, he rarely ever was.

* * *

The afternoon sunlight slanted through the tall, lattice-framed windows, gilding the room in a soft amber glow. Shadows danced lazily across the polished wood floor, where the faint scuff marks of years past spoke of count-less visitors. The hearth, now subdued, held the faintest trace of ash and warmth from the morning's fire, while the scent of sun-warmed herbs wafted faintly from a bundle of dried lavender hanging near the mantel. The tapestries, vivid in the daylight, revealed intricate details—scenes of distant battles, serene landscapes, and symbols of bygone lore. The room felt less like the stern elegance Markus had first encountered and more like a living, breathing space—welcoming, but still heavy with the weight of unspoken histories.

Nikel faced Markus and Xara near the hearth, where the late afternoon sunlight cast long, angled shadows across the room.

"I'm not one to be—what's the word?—'nosy,'" Nikel began, in a tone laced with mild amusement. "But two couriers returned from the fort. They were accompanied by an officer, an officer who noticed some 'oddities' among your possessions."

He tapped his pipe against the edge of the table for emphasis, gesturing toward the satchel resting on the coffee table before reinserting the pipe between his teeth. Markus and Xara exchanged a furtive glance, both striving to look calm.

"He was about to search it," Nikel continued, his voice calm but deliberate. "Until a soldier mentioned that you were here under my 'supervision,' and I wouldn't take kindly to such prying. I assured him the satchel was mine."

"My Lord," Liyzia interjected smoothly, "you lied."

"Well ..." Nikel paused, exhaling a faint plume of smoke. "Lying sounds harsh. I merely withheld information that wasn't necessary."

"Ah, I see. I think," Liyzia replied, arching her brow.

"And I'm certain our young 'innocent' tulip here can relate to such practices."

The word 'innocent' hung in the air, and Markus and Xara exchanged wary looks. Markus broke the silence first. "The satchel is mine," he blurted out.

"Really?" Nikel asked, leaning forward slightly, his gaze unflinching.

"Yeah."

"Care to explain?"

"This should be interesting," Liyzia murmured, her eyes alight with curiosity.

Markus faltered. He could feel Liyzia's knowing gaze, so subtle yet sharp, and found himself wondering if she already knew the truth.

Before he could dig himself deeper, Xara stepped in, her hand gripping his arm. "Perhaps, Lord Nikel," she began, in a polite but firm tone, "you could simply return the satchel, and we'll be on our way."

Nikel tilted his head, a faint smile tugging at the corner of his lips. "I'm afraid I cannot do that, dear," he said to Xara, his tone cordial but unyielding.

She sighed dramatically, folding her arms. "Very well. Perhaps you'd like to enlighten us about the 'accommodations' in your local jail then."

Markus groaned, dragging a hand down his face. "Nice going, idiot," he muttered through gritted teeth.

"A lot better than your pathetic attempt," Xara shot back under her breath, her eyes flashing.

"I was trying to save your neck."

"You call this saving? It's like watching a bird fly into a window—twice."

"Then why'd you bring the damn satchel in the first place?" Markus snapped. "I told you—one day I'd be visiting you in prison."

Xara jabbed a finger at his chest. "You've got a lotta nerve!"

"Ahem."

The sound of Nikel clearing his throat cut through their bickering. Both Markus and Xara froze and then turned sheepishly toward their hosts.

Liyzia had her teacup poised delicately in one hand, her eyes sparkling with barely concealed mirth. "Please," she said, in a voice smooth as silk, "do continue. It's quite entertaining."

Markus stepped forward, "Look ...," he began, in a firm tone, though his nerves betrayed him in the stiffness of his shoulders, "Lord Nikel, I'll take the fall for her. There's no point dragging this out. Go ahead—call the sheriff."

Nikel blinked, then tilted his head, genuinely puzzled. "The sheriff?"

"Well, yeah," Markus said, confused by the lack of reaction. "Isn't that what you're planning?"

"And why would I call him?"

Markus hesitated, glancing at Xara, who looked equally perplexed. "Because of the contents in that satchel. They're ..." He stopped himself abruptly, remembering Nikel's earlier lesson about withholding unnecessary information.

"Counterfeits?" Nikel offered, his voice light but his expression sharp.

"Dammit," Markus muttered, running a hand through his hair.

Xara threw up her hands. "I knew it!" she hissed, glaring at Markus. "I knew he could read minds, too."

"Yeah, no kidding," Markus retorted. "But not like

her. He's sneakier about it—covert. Not all mystical and ... weird."

Xara turned on him, her jaw dropping at his audacity to speak so openly in front of their hosts.

Liyzia, clearly amused, pressed her lips together, her cheeks flushed as though suppressing laughter. Nikel simply raised an eyebrow, holding his pipe loosely between his fingers.

"Well," Nikel said after a pause, "rest assured, I have no intention of involving the sheriff. Or anyone else, for that matter."

Markus and Xara exchanged a wary glance.

"Why not?" Markus asked, plainly suspicious.

"Because, young man," Nikel said, "there's far more to this situation than you realize. And I suspect you're not yet ready to share the full truth, either."

Markus stiffened, while Xara's grip on his arm tightened slightly.

"Tea, anyone?" Liyzia interjected with a lightness that belied the tension in the room. She rose gracefully, brushing past Markus and Xara as though the entire confrontation were nothing more than a passing conversation.

Moments later, tea and a plate of delicate cakes sat on the low table between them. The warm, soothing aroma filled the room, but it did little to ease the weight of what came next.

As the tension ebbed into a more subdued quiet, Xara finally leaned forward, looking conflicted.

"Lord Nikel, Lady Liyzia," she began, her voice soft but steady, "I think it's time I came clean. You've shown us more trust and kindness than we probably deserve, and it's not fair to repay that with silence."

"Xara, don't—" Markus started, but she cut him off with a glance.

"No, Markus. They need to know."

What followed was a carefully measured confession—one that surprised even Markus with its details. The hearth crackled softly as the weight of Xara's words hung in the air. She had just finished laying the foundations of her story, but it was clear she wasn't done. Markus shifted uneasily in his seat, his expression a tangle of wariness and frustration. Xara drew a deep breath, her gaze turning to Nikel and Liyzia, then lingering briefly on Markus.

"The satchel," she began, in a quieter voice now but no less steady, "contains documents ... forged ones. Very convincing forgeries, I'll admit. Treaties, contracts, decrees—all bearing the monarch's seal. Except," she added, her eyes darting to Nikel, "King Ronan's been gone for ten years. And the real seal is hidden away with his daughter."

Nikel leaned back slightly in his chair, his pipe held loosely between his fingers. His sharp eyes caught a detail on one of the papers. "The dating system is flawless," he observed. "Both Nevran Chronos and Sol Standard."

"Yes—the year 9642 N.C." Xara confirmed. "Or 5510 S.S., depending on who's reading it. Every detail has to be perfect."

"Let me guess," he said, his tone measured. "Notarized as well? Passing the national system?"

Xara hesitated but nodded. "Yes. Every piece bears their mark of authentication. I've made sure of it."

Markus' head snapped toward her. "Wait—*you* made them?"

Her jaw tightened, but she met his incredulous stare with a level one of her own. "Yes, Markus. I made them. Or did you think this whole thing was a misunderstanding?"

Markus groaned, dragging a hand through his hair. "Fantastic. So we're not just on the run from lawmen, we're fleeing from a *kingdom-wide* scandal."

"And now they're in my home," Nikel said dryly, though his tone carried no judgment. "How delightful!"

Xara ignored them both, focusing on Nikel. "I don't know who's using my work or for what purpose, but I've traced one name to it—Hans Lumen, a senator in Arduiine. He's hunting me, not just for what I've done but because I'm ... inconvenient. If he catches me ..."

"You're dead," Nikel finished for her. His calm delivery sent a shiver down Markus' spine.

"Yes," Xara said softly.

Markus scoffed, breaking the tension with a low mutter. "All of this over rejecting a second date?"

Xara shot him a sharp look, but Nikel tilted his head curiously. "Second date?"

"More like a first-and-only," Markus said, his tone dry but edged with unease. "Guess he doesn't take 'no' for an answer."

"Markus ..." Xara began, as a warning, but he pressed on, the sarcasm giving way to genuine frustration.

"Seriously, Xara. I get that you're inconvenient, but this feels a lot like 'you broke my heart, so I'm going to watch your world burn.'"

A glimmer of something crossed Xara's face—guilt, maybe, or regret—but it was gone in an instant. She exhaled sharply and turned back to Nikel.

"This isn't about that. Not really. Whatever infatuation he has, it's just fuel for his ambition. And now he's using my work to fan the flames."

Nikel studied her for a moment, then nodded. "A dangerous man with dangerous tools. One who isn't easily ignored."

"Exactly," Xara said, her voice tightening.

The room fell silent save for the occasional snap of the fire. Finally, Nikel nodded toward the satchel. "Your work is extraordinary," he admitted, "but it's also dangerous. Even I was nearly fooled by the seal. The king's own engineers would marvel at this—though perhaps not as kindly." He gave her a pointed look, but his tone was more impressed than admonishing.

Liyzia, seated elegantly beside him, spoke for the first time since the confession began. "And the fine print?" she asked, in a light but precise voice.

Xara hesitated, her hands clasped tightly together. "Encrypted," she admitted. "The real content is obscured."

"Of course it is," Liyzia said with a wry smile, but her eyes reflected something more profound—respect, perhaps, or a quiet understanding.

Markus leaned forward, his frustration bubbling over. "So what's the plan here? We just sit around while this Lumen guy closes in? Maybe wait for another raid of men to crash through the door?"

"Markus ..." Xara began, but he cut her off.

"No, Xara, this is insane! We can't just ..."

"Enough," Nikel said firmly, cutting through the rising tension. Markus was chastised but still bristling. Nikel's gaze softened slightly as it shifted back to Xara.

"You're right to trust us. This isn't something you can handle alone. I'll take the satchel east to my contacts—craftsmen who can decipher your work. If there's any trace of Lumen's endgame hidden in the fine print, they'll find it."

Xara frowned. "But ..."

"You and Markus will stay here," Nikel continued, brooking no argument. "You'll be safe on the homestead. My web of allies runs deep, and none of Lumen's bounty hunters or bribe-seekers will get close."

Markus groaned audibly, flopping back against the chair. "Great. So we're prisoners now."

"Guests," Liyzia corrected with a smile. "Though if you prefer the term 'prisoner,' I'm sure we could arrange for stricter accommodations."

Her lips curved in a teasing smile, and Xara stifled a snort despite herself.

"Markus," Xara said, placing a hand on his arm. Her voice was softer now, almost pleading. "Please. We need this. I need this. If there's even a chance we can get ahead of Lumen and get out of this, we have to take it."

Markus sighed, his resistance waning under her earnest gaze. "Fine," he muttered. "But if I go stir-crazy, it's on you."

Liyzia leaned forward, her eyes twinkling. "Oh, don't worry. I'll make sure to keep you occupied."

Markus groaned again, while Xara shook her head, a reluctant smile tugging at her lips.

* * *

Liyzia found Nikel in his study, staring at the empty space beside his portrait—the spot where his heir's image should hang. She watched him trace the dusty outline with weathered fingers, his shoulders heavy with unspoken grief.

"They're settling in well," she said softly. "The servants speak highly of them."

"They're not staying." His voice carried an edge she rarely heard. "Once the girl's business with these 'Separatists' is resolved ..."

"You've seen how he watches you in the training yard."

"Like a stray watching scraps fall from a table." Nikel turned, his expression hardening. "Do not mistake hunger for destiny, my dear."

"And do not mistake pride for wisdom." The words slipped out before she could stop them.

Silence stretched between them, heavy with years of empty nurseries and unanswered prayers. Nikel's hand tightened on his cane.

"You see something in him." His words felt more like an accusation than a question.

"I see many things." She moved to the window, where dawn painted the outer yard in soft gold. "But what I see matters less than what you refuse to see."

"And what am I refusing to see?" His voice carried a dangerous quiet.

"Your own reflection." She faced him then, her eyes carrying that otherworldly certainty that had both drawn him to her and unsettled him. "In his determination. His pride. His loneliness."

Nikel turned back to the empty space on the wall. "We are done discussing this."

"For now," she agreed softly, but they had both heard what she left unsaid. Destiny rarely consulted mortal wishes.

She left him there, knowing some seeds needed darkness before they could grow. Whatever path lay ahead, it would be shaped by more than just their desires—though that truth might prove harder for Nikel to accept than any vision she could share.

*** *** ***

In the days following Nikel's departure, Xara mingled effortlessly with Nikel's servants, helping with chores and weaving herself into the warp and woof of the homestead. Markus, on the other hand, found himself far more restless. Liyzia and Kneuvah tried coaxing him out of his shell, but it was like trying to draw water from a stone. Finally, one afternoon, they found him—after scouring the manor, the stables, and even the surrounding woods.

There, under the dim, swinging light of the stable's ground floor, Markus was shadowboxing in a flurry of sharp jabs and weaving footwork. The animals in their stalls watched with wide, curious eyes, as if silently judging the strange human's antics.

"Thought I told you to tie a bell around your neck," Markus called without breaking his rhythm, his voice slightly breathless.

"You wish to strangle me?" Liyzia asked, stepping forward, the corners of her lips twitching.

"No, but I *wish* to hear you coming—before you scare the living daylights out of me."

Liyzia tilted her head, observing his movements with an amused curiosity. "I've seen knights train their sons, but not like this. What do you call it?"

"Sparring," he replied, ducking an invisible blow, "or shadowboxing."

She furrowed her brow. "But shadows don't fight back."

Markus paused in the midst of a swing and looked at her incredulously. "*Duh.*"

"Duh?" She repeated the word like it was a foreign artifact. "Please translate."

Markus sighed, resuming his movements. "The shadow lets me see what I'm doing right—or wrong. Get it?"

"So ... you're anxious to fight?"

"Look," Markus said, his movements growing sharper, "Lord Nikel told us to lay low, and I'm bored out of my mind. Figured you'd know that by now."

"And how would I know that?" she asked innocently.

Markus stopped, turning to her. "Same way you know *everything* else. Don't play games."

"Not playing games," she replied smoothly, stepping closer, her expression thoughtful. "But wait—don't give up on me yet. Let's try something."

Before he could object, she placed her hands over his ears, closing her eyes.

"What are you ..."

"Shhh!" she silenced him with a dramatic gesture her face contorting as though channeling a great force.

Markus exchanged a confused glance with Kneuvah, who had just appeared in the doorway, looking equally perplexed.

Then, Liyzia began groaning—a low, exaggerated sound that had Markus pull back slightly in alarm.

"Uh, are you ..."

"Quiet!" she commanded, her voice taking on a theatrical intensity. "I can hear your thoughts now. Yes, they're clear as the cock crowing at dawn."

She paused, her tone reverting to teasing. "You think this Nevran woman is weird? Mystical. Mad? A lunatic?"

"Now wait just a ..."

"Shhh!" she interrupted again, opening her eyes with mock-seriousness. "There's more. *She is a peculiar nut in this town of fruitcakes, and she will drive me craaaaaazy.*"

Markus stared at her, his face a mixture of annoyance and disbelief.

"There," she said, tapping his nose triumphantly. "Your mind's been read today."

"Very funny," he grumbled.

Liyzia shifted to a more commanding tone. "Restless, are we? Full of energy? Let put that to use!"

Markus perked up, sensing an opportunity. "Now we're talking! What've you got in mind?"

"Work," she said flatly, handing him a broom.

Liyzia crossed her arms, watching him fumble with the broom. "What's the problem?"

"No problem!" Markus said quickly, gripping the broom like a sword. "I've just, uh, never actually *used* one before."

Kneuvah blinked. "You're telling me you've never swept a floor?"

"Not with one of these!" Markus twirled the broom dramatically. "But hey, how hard can it be?"

He raised it like a champion ready for battle, slamming

the bristles against the floor with an exaggerated flourish. Dust exploded upward in a cloud, filling the barn. A nearby Chatterling scurried from beneath a feed basket, making agitated clicking sounds as it disappeared into its burrow.

Coughing, Kneuvah waved a hand in front of his face, grinning. "Oh, this is going to be fun."

* * *

Markus Kane versus rural life: Round One.

Day after day, the disasters piled up like autumn leaves. First came the broom—which Markus wielded like a war hammer, creating dust storms that sent Crownfeathers into a panic, their elaborate plumage fanning out in alarm as they scattered. Kneuvah was left crying with laughter. "Are you sweeping the barn or challenging it to combat?"

Then the woodpile. THUNK went Kneuvah's ax, splitting logs clean in two. BOUNCE went Markus', nearly taking his foot with it. "The wood's supposed to split," Kneuvah called, "not your boots!"

The fishing pole proved an even worthier opponent. While Kneuvah's basket filled steadily with silver-scaled victories, Markus waged war with his fishing line—and lost. Spectacularly. When he finally got a bite, it was less catching dinner and more being dragged into the river like a flailing scarecrow.

"Got one!" he sputtered triumphantly from the water, holding up a massive herring.

"Got soaked, you mean," Xara corrected from the bank, not even trying to hide her amusement. Even the nearby Burrowdiggers paused in their work to observe him, whiskers twitching with curiosity.

But the hushners and hornstriders—those giant beasts—they were his ultimate nemesis. Up, down, crash. Up, down, crash. The pattern repeated so often the stable hands started keeping score.

"The dirt's getting quite fond of your face," Liyzia observed one afternoon, helping him up for the dozenth time.

Flat on his back, spitting out grass, Markus groaned. "This is worse than every street fight I've ever lost. Combined."

Then came the turning point.

"Ready to actually learn?" Liyzia asked, offering both a hand up and that knowing smile of hers.

"Fine," Markus sighed. "Show me."

Slowly, surely, the tide turned.

The broom became an ally instead of an enemy. The woodpile surrendered log by log. Even the fishing line untangled itself more often than not. And the hushners? Well, they at least stopped actively trying to throw him.

The day Markus successfully rode across the pasture, Kneuvah's grudging nod spoke volumes. Even the Specklegrazers paused in their munching to watch his progress. And when his first hunting expedition brought home dinner, the entire household celebrated—though Liyzia couldn't resist one final jab. "Now don't let it go to your head," she called over the congratulatory dinner table. "Or we'll have to start all over with the humility lessons!"

"Just had to ruin the moment, didn't you?" laughed Markus, surprising himself. Somehow, between the bruises and triumphs, he'd found something he never expected: a place where belonging felt as natural as breathing.

Even if that belonging came with a few more mud stains than he'd planned on.

CHAPTER SIX

Hans Lumen watched his two lawmen approach through the precinct's grimy windows. Their slouched shoulders said everything before they even opened their mouths. Another week of failure. Another week of Markus and Xara slipping through his fingers.

The familiar stench of the police station—sweat, stale coffee, and desperation—brought back memories he usually kept buried. That first taste of power: a teenage boy in handcuffs, terrified of disappointing his socialite parents, until he realized how easily money could make problems disappear. Just a slap on the wrist. A seed planted.

It had been like swimming, that first misdemeanor merely a toe in the water. Then came the academic scandals, the bribes, each transgression pulling him deeper until he found himself swimming with sharks— bureaucrats and criminals who recognized one of their own. These days, he didn't just swim with them; he fed them.

The precinct buzzed with his kind of corruption now—beat reporters trading favors for stories, suspects buying their freedom, magistrates he carried in his back pocket like loose change. He'd learned long ago not to play the white knight. Better to be the tragic hero, caught in an endless web of legal depravity he claimed to fight, while secretly spinning it larger.

And now two street rats threatened to unravel it all.

Two of his trusted lawmen approached.

"We're trying, Mr. Lumen. Really. We have every deputy looking. If you give us another week ..."

"I'm afraid you don't *have* another week, Mr. Wendal. A man and a woman don't simply *vanish* into thin air."

"Yessir—aside from the rural villages to the north, the interdistrict is a dangerous void on foot. Hitchhikers, loners, no telling what may have become of them."

"No excuses! If you want to keep this job!"

Within moments, a pair of headlights poured over the trio from the street, as another vehicle hovered nearby and closed in on them. A longer luxury model, geometric and streamlined with glossier finish, and a chauffeur at the steering wheel.

Through the back windows, he recognized his superiors—no doubt demanding an update.

Senator Schweimer greeted him with a mischievous grin in the presence of onlookers. Council leader Pelham, on the other hand, was as sour and stoic as ever. Hans swore, if this crusty old man ever smiled, all the plaster in the world wouldn't not seal the cracks in his face.

"*Mister* Lumens. Why don't you take a ride with us?"

* * *

They knew he didn't have any updates for them. But where in the world would they take him at this ungodly hour of the night?

He slipped on his overcoat, obscuring their view while snatching a sidearm from the magistrate before departing with them.

He sat across from them in the stretched interior, watching their solemn and brooding gaze at him. While one puffed his cigar, the other sipped his scotch. He noticed that neither man offered him a drink.

"Your part in this operation is over," the older man said.

"Please understand, Mr. Lumen, this is in the best interest of the party. Don't take it too personally. You have served your purpose long enough."

"It's best that we move forward with someone more 'capable' in this operation," Schweimer explained.

Hans' finger relaxed on the blaster's trigger beneath his sleeve, believing they might let him walk away into obscurity.

"As far as the senate is concerned, your career is finished," Pelham warned.

"There is just too much at stake here, Mr. Lumen. The donor class will be funding a new candidate from Arduiine to fill the vacated seat."

Hans put on a brave face. His career over in a matter of seconds? Not the news anyone wanted to hear. Yet, when he glanced through the back windows, he noticed the remote dimly lit back roads beyond the factory yards near the edge of the woods.

Why bring him all the way out here to tell him such 'grim' news?

His heart felt like a drum beating from beneath his suit. His necktie seemed to choke against his throat like a pair of hands, and he fought the urge to loosen it.

His index finger tightened the trigger once more.

As Schweimer observed their surroundings through the back window, Pelham casually snuffed out his cigar. The sensations of the rear turbines suddenly felt more alive against Hans' back, while the underside propellers lowered the vehicle to a standstill.

Every little nuance, sound, click, flick of a switch and lever from the chauffeur up front amplified in his head right now.

Then he heard it—the faintest of shrieks—the high-pitched sound when your finger releases the safety switch on a Zarenthian pistol. One of the few stealth guns he was familiar with. Muffled, yet distinct. At least a pair of them.

Hans slowed his breathing and carefully adjusted his forearm across his knee, in their direction; his weapon hidden. No sudden movements.

"Quaint little spot here," Pelham observed once more through the window. "Not a soul around at this hour."

"My sentiments, exactly," Hans uttered, swallowing, then smiling.

"No one will hear you scream."

Hans couldn't pull the trigger fast enough. A crackling display of light and noise filled the vehicle's interior for a few seconds, rattling the windows.

It was over in a matter of seconds.

The young senator covered his mouth at the carnage.

As the smoke cleared, all that remained were the scorched flesh and blast wounds of Senator Schweimer,

Council Speaker Pelham and their driver up front—his body leaning forward against the dash with a blast hole scorched through the back of his head.

He poked their bodies with his smoking weapon for any sign of life, then knocked their pistols from their lifeless hands.

Finally, loosening up his collar and tie, he dropped the weapon and reached for the champagne beneath the portable bar. He guzzled straight from the bottle, spilling it over his shirt, before collapsing on the back seat.

Perspiring, he frantically gathered everything from their wallets, satchels, papers, weapons—even cleaning out the liquor bar. Stuffing all he could in his overcoat, his eyes darted back and forth, from the distant warehouses beyond the fencing, to the dark woods. Every critter, every drop of water, rolling soda can or leaves blowing in the wind caught his eye. In a cold sweat, he fled down the road and into the darkness, getting as far away as possible.

But he wasn't finished yet. In the days that followed, driven by mounting fear and desperation, he moved swiftly—like a man possessed—covering his tracks with ruthless efficiency. First, he paid off local district workers to have the vehicle discreetly towed to an undisclosed location, right under the noses of the authorities. Then, to secure his position, he struck a deal with the devil himself—Vicente Vitelli. In exchange for making the three bodies disappear and tracking down the fugitives, he released Vitelli's men and made a few shady deals. All sins would be forgiven.

With the local crime boss, corrupt law enforcement, and various unsavory individuals in his pocket, his influence was on a level even greater than his own district on the other side of the kingdom. By the time the High Council realized two of their most important leaders were missing, it was too late. He had crossed the Rubicon, elevating himself in just a matter of days to heights he could never have dreamed of in his entire career. Emboldened by his newfound power, he thought, *If I could eliminate two powerful men standing in my way, how could a pair of local fugitives possibly stop me?*

But, as it turned out, the fugitives were more elusive than he expected.

The manhunt had spread across the Canivere Forest and surrounding farmlands, with rumors swirling but nothing officially broadcasted through law enforcement channels. A covert network indeed of corrupt deputies, bounty hunters, and informants connected the kingdom's underworld, all eager to claim the bounty for the Earthen couple!

But in this quiet, rural mix of Nevrans, Earthens and Skylandic folk, outsiders were easy to spot. The locals, well-established in their way of life and fiercely protective of their culture, had a sixth sense for anyone with ill intentions. Even the local magistrates, operating under an unshakable code of honor, stood firm against the corruption creeping in from outside. This was not a place that would easily bend to the will of crooked lawmen, mercenaries, or crime bosses.

The fugitives might have been hiding, but they were hiding in the right place.

* * *

Every attempt to locate Markus and Xara had come up empty. Beyond the crash site in the forests between Orwein and Ninivay, their trail had gone as cold as the approaching winter. Among the Earthen men and couples passing through the region, none fit the description: too old, too young, the wrong accents, or attire that didn't match. Gradually, the rumors and sightings of armed men began to fade, as the roads and passes returned to normal. With the harvest season in full swing and preparations for winter underway, the search quieted.

For two months now, Markus had not only earned his keep on Nikel's farm but also managed to win over Knuevah. He and Xara had been quietly plotting, waiting for the right opportunity to sneak into town behind Liyzia's back. Xara, eager to access the town's communication hubs, longed for any news from Vesper. Markus opposed it fiercely, afraid that any attempt to contact her old allies might alert their pursuers. He finally relented when she sweetened the deal with the promise of a local physician who could examine him— no more costly than a simple barter. Though Markus kept his ailment a secret from her, he was grateful for her concern.

One crisp November morning, with Liyzia away at the market, they made their move. Enlisting Knuevah's help, they slipped through a secluded route leading to the quarters of Prynthor at the town's east end, where the legislature and town hall were located. The plan was simple: split up. Xara, with her sharp command of the native tongue and ability to blend in, would navigate the technological complex on her own. Markus, on the other hand, didn't know enough Nevrish to venture out alone, and rumors about the fugitives still haunted him. To avoid suspicion, he wrapped his head in surgical bandages, covering his scar and most of his face, and stuck close to Knuevah, head down to avoid eye contact. Their first stop would be the healer's shop—a detour Markus had insisted on despite the risks.

The healer's shop seemed to grow organically from the earth itself—half cottage, half living tree, with gnarled roots forming its foundation, while herb bundles and crystals hung from rafters. Markus hesitated at the threshold, the transition from crisp morning air to the shop's heavy warmth making his head swim. Incense smoke curled through shafts of dusty sunlight, while from somewhere, water dripped with steady rhythm into clay bowls.

"Wait here," Knuevah whispered, squeezing his arm before disappearing behind a beaded curtain.

Markus studied the room, street instincts cataloging exits and shadows out of habit. Shelves lined the walls, holding jars of unnamed substances. Bundles of dried plants hung from the ceiling, their pungent scents mixing with something sweeter—like honey but ancient, preserved in clay pots sealed with wax.

He had come hoping to find answers about his blood, but standing here, surrounded by Nevran healing traditions that stretched back centuries, his courage wavered. Before he could reconsider, a voice spoke from deeper within the shop.

"The physician is away."

An elderly Nevran woman emerged, her lavender skin faded with age to a softer shade, almost pearl-like in the filtered light. Her blue eyes held impossible depths beneath silver-brown hair woven in traditional braids. She moved with the measured grace of someone who had spent decades tending to others' hurts.

"I fell," Markus said quickly, gesturing to his bandaged face, the lie coming easily after years of concealing his true condition. "Just need it checked."

Something flickered in those ancient eyes—not quite disbelief, but deeper understanding. "Sit," she instructed in an accented common tongue, indicating a worn wooden chair that seemed to grow right out of the floor.

Her fingers were cool as she began unwinding his bandages, each movement precise yet somehow tender. Markus held himself carefully still. Years of hiding his condition had made him hyperaware of every touch.

Then her hands paused—a long, weighted moment that seemed to stretch like honey dripping from a comb. Through the gaps in the unraveling gauze, her eyes caught something that made her hand fly to her mouth, stifling a sound between a gasp and what might have been a sob. Her other hand trembled slightly as it hovered above his temple, not quite touching his scar.

Their eyes met, and in that endless moment, Markus saw something in her gaze that made his throat tight—recognition, wonder, and beneath it all, an ancient sorrow that made him want to look away. But he couldn't.

"*Ka'aine*," she whispered, the word carrying significance he didn't understand. Then, so softly he nearly missed it: "You survived."

Before he could question her meaning, shouts erupted from the street—voices calling about suspicious travelers seen in the area. The woman's expression shifted, as something like fierce protectiveness replaced her earlier wonder. She rewound his bandages with swift efficiency.

Knuevah was already pulling him toward the back door, but Markus caught one last glimpse of the woman's face. There was something in her expression—not quite grief, not quite hope—that would haunt his dreams for months to come.

The elderly healer stood motionless in her shop. The scents of herbs and incense swirled around her as she touched a worn stone pendant at her throat, so old its original markings had been smoothed by generations of anxious fingers.

Her shoulders seemed to bear a new weight as she moved to her workbench, her movements suddenly those of someone much older. With trembling hands, she reached for a small box carved with ancient Nevrish symbols, its wood darkened by age. She opened it just long enough to place something inside—perhaps a single thread from Markus' bandages—before closing it with the careful reverence of one who keeps dangerous secrets.

"May the stars watch over you," she whispered in her native tongue, "until the time comes!"

As Markus and Knuevah melted into the back alleys, across town, Xara crossed the threshold from the town's rustic surroundings into the remnants of the industrial expansion.

* * *

Xara crossed the threshold from the town's rustic surroundings into what was left of the industrial expansion—a functional relic providing the occasional necessity of modern convenience. Surrounded by the cold steel, the powered generators, and arrays of wires and switchboards, she felt a pang of nostalgia for the life she'd left behind. She had longed for this—the familiar rumble of machines, the sterile efficiency of technology—but now it somehow felt alien. She had grown used to the slow rhythm of rural life, the crackle of firewood, the scent of earth after rain. Yet here she was again, caught between worlds.

After two months in this rural setting, she had grown to appreciate the simplicity and stillness of farm life. There was a peace here—a clarity—that was absent in the fast-paced disarray of Vesper, where blasters, aerglides, and non-stop noise filled every waking moment. For the first time, she understood the value of hearing herself think, of living without constant distraction.

But today, standing in line to pay for a transmit card, the familiar cacophony of technology hit her with the sudden throb of a migraine. After bribing the operator, she was granted privacy at the switchboard. She had only moments to search her encrypted channel in Vesper for any messages—shared only with Markus and a trusted mediator. Reading messages was safe. Responding, however, could trace her location to Orwein, a risk she couldn't afford. As she began to input her memorized key, suddenly, a shadow fell over her.

Her heart skipped a beat as she turned to see Liyzia standing behind her.

"Reaching out to old friends?" Liyzia's voice was calm but knowing.

"My god ... how did you know?" Xara stammered, "Did you listen through the walls?"

"The walls don't need ears," Liyzia said, her voice low. "You think I wouldn't know the moment you set foot here? This is my town."

"I was only checking for messages," Xara muttered, trying to regain her composure.

"Messages? From whatever it is you left behind?"

"Well, not exactly ..."

"Planning to return?" Liyzia's gaze was unyielding.

"No, I ..."

"Or maybe you want to run right into whoever's chasing you?"

Cornered, Xara sighed and shut down the switchboard.

"Now," Liyzia said, eyes narrowing, "where are the other two conspirators?"

* * *

Markus and Knuevah left the town's cobblestone streets behind, emerging onto the open training grounds at Orwein's eastern edge. Before them stretched a vast grass field, well-trampled from countless games and practice sessions. The autumn air carried the sharp scent of damp earth and crushed grass, while wooden posts at the field's boundaries cast long shadows in the afternoon sun. At the field's edge, a row of weathered stables housed the players' mounts, their doors thrown open to release the eager hushners into the practice area.

Across the field, a group of teenagers guided their

hushners through warm-up exercises as the huge wolf-like creatures snorted and pawed at the ground. Numbered cards hung from the riders' chests, fluttering in the breeze as they maneuvered their mounts in practiced formations. The field itself was marked with worn goal lines at either end, testament to countless matches played on this ancient practice ground.

Markus watched with interest, his gaze lingering on the strange, lumbering creatures beneath the riders. He had never seen anything like this back home. Just then, a few of the boys spotted Knuevah and called out in both recognition and challenge. Knuevah was familiar to them; but Markus? They eyed him suspiciously, smirking at his bandaged head.

He felt that familiar dissonance of being an outsider—the sidelong glances, the unspoken challenge. Another new place, another set of rules he didn't understand.

"What do they want?" Markus asked, watching the boys circle closer on their mounts.

Knuevah sighed. "Pay them no mind. Just local troublemakers. They're trying to bait us into playing with them."

Markus raised an eyebrow. "What's the game?"

"The Earthens call it 'Khanz ball.' We know it as *Vélura'khanz*, a traditional game from the high plains of the far east. It's played on wild terradogs by the tribal nations. This is the 'tamer' version for kids."

"So, in your games," Markus asked, leaning closer, "the animals are as much players as the riders?"

Knuevah's lips quirked. "Not just players. Partners. The hushner isn't a tool—it's an extension of the rider's will."

Markus squinted, watching the riders. "So how many times did these kids fall before they got good?"

Knuevah snorted. "Not as many times as you, certainly."

"Hey," Markus grinned, "I'm learning. Eventually."

Knuevah's glance was pure sardonic fondness—of exasperation, and grudging admiration.

Before they could walk away, one of the larger boys—broad-shouldered and smug, wearing the number 66—guided his hushner toward them. Circling like a predator, he eyed Markus, then spat out a string of taunts in Nevrish. Knuevah responded sharply; the melodic language suddenly became harsh in tone.

"They think we're cowards," Knuevah translated, "They bet they could beat us in 'one down.'"

Markus tilted his head. "One down?"

Markus eyed the large boy again, his jaw tightening. "How much you want to bet we could take them?"

"We?" Knuevah's eyes widened in alarm. "No. Absolutely not."

But Markus was already stepping forward, calling out in broken Nevrish. The words were clumsy, but the challenge in his voice was clear. Number 66's smirk widened.

"Markus, don't ..." Knuevah groaned, but it was too late. Within moments, they were being led to the stables to Knuevah's mutterings under his breath about "stubborn Earthens" and "death wishes."

* * *

Before he knew it, Knuevah had mounted a hushner, and wore the number '4' on a card over his chest.

Markus climbed onto his own hushner, awkwardly adjusting the safety harness as a stable hand slapped the unlucky '13' on his chest.

The hushners—with their thick, muscular limbs and bristling fur—towered like war machines. Each one easily dwarfed a horse, with paws that could crush stone, though they moved with a predatory grace that belied their bulk.

Markus handed a sack of one hundred crowns to the bookie, who scribbled their numbers on a blackboard.

Knuevah's eyes widened. "Where did you get all that money?"

"Xara."

"And where'd she get it?"

"Don't ask."

"You bet one hundred crowns? On a game you don't know how to play? On an animal you barely know how to ride?"

Markus grinned. "Relax. Three-to-one odds. We can take them."

"What's this 'we' business?" Knuevah groaned.

But before he could protest further, the whistle shrieked.

Riders surged forward. Mud sprayed. Paws thundered.

Markus struggled. The gait wild and unfamiliar. He lasted seconds before hitting the ground. Hard.

Laughter erupted. Jeers cut through the air.

He rolled. Dodged the stampede. His face burning. Embarrassed. But determined.

He took a deep breath and remounted.

"You're going to get yourself killed!" Knuevah shouted. "Let's end this madness!"

Markus grinned through the mud streaking his face. "I'm just getting started!"

The sky darkened. Thunderclouds rolled. Shadows stretched. Spectators pressed closer. Hushners stomped. Steam billowed. Tension thick as fog. The air alive with snickers and jeers. This crazy outsider was now the main event.

The sky transformed above them, steel-gray clouds swallowing the autumn light. Shadows crept across the practice field as thunder muttered in the distance. The hushners grew restless, their massive forms silhouetted against the darkening sky, steam rising from their fur in the cooling air.

Markus gripped tight, knuckles white.

Another whistle.

The ground turned treacherous. Slick. Chaotic.

Riders crashed.

Beasts bucked.

A muddy battlefield.

Thunder cracked. Rain poured. A quagmire erupted.

Markus saw through the deluge and spotted Xara in the crowd fifty yards away. Frantic. Furious.

He adjusted his technique, removing one foot from the stirrup and loosened the safety belt around his waist.

"You crazy fool!" Knuevah yelled. "Put that back on!"

"I've got a plan," Markus called back, barely audible through the rain.

They lined up once more.

The whistle shrieked. Riders surged forward.

In the storm's twilight gloom, Markus leaned low over his mount, as rain streamed past his face. The mud-slick field flew beneath them, each lightning flash illuminating their desperate charge, like scenes from a vintage battle painting. Through the deluge, the goal posts loomed like ghostly sentinels.

Number 66 charged. His beast snarled. His massive arm stretched and reached for the ball.

Markus stretched out. His fingers extended. The gap narrowed between them.

Number 66 was massive—his weight unbalancing his mount.

But Markus was lighter—quicker.

One desperate lunge.

His fingers yanked the pigskin.

Silence swept the crowd. A collective gasp. Markus clutched the muddy ball to his chest. Knuevah cheered, cracking his reins.

But danger loomed. Markus was slipping from his animal.

One leg dangled free. The hushner's wild sprint continued.

Markus fought to stay upright. Reins loosening. His body was sliding.

Number 66 was furious. Eyes locked. He pursued.

Other riders closed in.

Markus prayed.

Out of options, he bit into the pigskin. Safety belt released. One hand on the muddy reins. The other wrapped around the hushner's torso. His face pressed into its furry, soaked skin.

He held on. Thundering toward the goal.

His adrenaline surged.

And in a flash, he was through.

The hushner skidded to a halt. Markus tumbled into the mud. Dazed. Breathless.

A heavy silence hung over the field, broken only by the sound of rain hammering the ground. The stunned crowd waited.

Markus sat up and raised the pigskin high above his head.

As if marking his victory, the storm began to lift. Rays of late afternoon sun pierced the breaking clouds, turning the rain-swept field into a gleaming mirror. Steam rose from the trampled earth, creating a mystical haze through which the celebrating crowd moved like spirits. The crowd erupted. A tempest of human emotions swept across the field, thundering louder than the sky above. Jeers transmuted to cheers—"13! 13! 13!"—a primal roar of sudden reverence. Players and spectators surged forward, a living wave lifting Markus high above their shoulders. He surrendered to their triumph, baptized by the cold November rain.

This outsider, this clown, had become a hero.

* * *

The celebration of their victory was still in full swing when Markus and Knuevah found themselves cornered in the barn. The triumphant noise of the crowd faded as player 66 loomed out of the shadows, flanked by two leaner and meaner-looking accomplices.

Markus barely had time to react before he was shoved to the ground. He rolled to his feet, wiping mud from his face as his eyes met the brute's furious glare. Knuevah stumbled beside him, clutching the pouch of winnings.

"You've got to be kidding me," Markus muttered under his breath, bracing himself.

Knuevah tugged at Markus' arm. "Let's just go. We've won. No need to ..."

The brute interrupted with a sharp shove. "Cowards," he snarled in his broken Common language. His two accomplices echoed the taunt with laughter, voices dripping with menace.

Markus inhaled sharply, his blood rushing. Every muscle in his body screamed for him to walk away, to avoid the fight. Even his instincts signaled more trouble. The gang wasn't going to let them leave without a confrontation. And Markus knew better than to escalate unnecessarily—especially with Knuevah and his hidden ailment he didn't want anyone to be exposed to.

"Take the money and go, Knuevah," Markus said lowly, handing off the pouch.

"What? No, we're ..."

"Go!" Markus barked, brooking no argument.

Knuevah hesitated, then backed toward the barn door, watching nervously.

Markus turned to face the trio, his hands raised in a placating gesture. He took a step back, subtly positioning himself near a stack of loose hay and an abandoned pitchfork.

66 sneered, stepping closer. "Think you can 'embarrass' me? On my turf?"

Markus continued stepping back, letting the brute advance, and guiding him toward an uneven patch of ground which dipped slightly.

But 66's patience snapped. With a growl, he lunged, fists flying. Markus ducked swiftly, pivoting to the side so the brute stumbled on the uneven ground. Using the momentum, Markus grabbed a nearby bucket and tossed its contents—a mix of water and straw—into the aggressor's face. The brute reeled, spluttering.

His accomplices rushed in, forcing Markus into evasive action. He sidestepped one, guiding the boy into a stack of barrels, which toppled with a resounding crash. The second swung a wild punch, but Markus intercepted it, twisting the boy's arm and shoving him into a wooden post.

Markus tried to stay light on his feet. His heart pounded, but he kept his breathing steady. No cuts. No blood. He couldn't let this turn ugly.

But the brute wasn't done. Roaring, 66 charged again. Markus feinted left, then used the pitchfork handle to trip the larger boy, sending him sprawling into the hay.

The tide turned when one of the accomplices grabbed a broken two-by-four, raising it high. Markus braced himself for the strike but found himself staring as the board froze mid-swing. A hand—strong and weathered—gripped the other end.

The barn fell silent.

Nikel stood there, water dripping from his soaked cloak, his gaze hard and unyielding. The teenager faltered, his bravado melting into fear. Without a word, Nikel twisted the board free, sending the boy stumbling backward.

"Go home," Nikel said, his voice calm yet razor-sharp.

The accomplices didn't hesitate. They fled into the stormy night, leaving 66 alone.

The brute glared at Nikel, then foolishly swung his fist. With startling speed, Nikel stepped aside, letting the boy's momentum carry him off balance. A quick flick of Nikel's cane sent the brute to the ground, writhing and gasping for air.

"Enough," Nikel growled. The brute scrambled to his feet and limped out, clutching his ribs. He steered clear of Knuevah and the women who arrived, soaked in the rain. They too were surprised by the lord's sudden return from his trip. The disappointed look on his face spoke volumes.

* * *

Markus stood frozen, his chest heaving, mud streaked across his face. Knuevah, still clutching the pouch of winnings, emerged wide-eyed from the shadows.

"You're such a fool," Nikel said, in a tone heavy with disappointment as he turned to Markus. "A reckless, stubborn fool. What were you thinking?"

Markus opened his mouth to explain, but Nikel cut him off with a sharp gesture.

"You sneaked into town behind our backs. You endangered yourself—and Knuevah—for what? A game?"

Knuevah tried to interject. "It wasn't his ..."

Nikel silenced him with a look. "Do you think this is a joke? You're under my protection, and this is how you repay it? With reckless fights and gambling?"

Markus' temper flared. "They didn't give me a choice!"

"There is always a choice," Nikel snapped, his tone ice-cold. "You could have walked away."

Markus clenched his fists as the brunt of the criticism settled on his shoulders. He wanted to shout, to defend himself—but deep down, he knew Nikel was right.

The retired knight took the pouch from Knuevah and tossed it to Markus, pelting him in the chest.

"The price for your recklessness—more than enough to send you packing and on your way."

Liyzia stepped forward and met her husband's stone-cold gaze for a moment, before he turned back to Markus.

"I believe we're finished here. My dear, kindly bid farewell to your *honored* guest."

He gestured for Knuevah, who reluctantly gave Markus a remorseful glance before following Nikel into the midday downpour.

Liyzia had Xara wait outside the stable, to be alone with Markus.

"Guess I really fucked things up." he mumbled.

She silently examined his head, with her eyes fixated on his facial blemish. She finally reached forth and touched his dark scar—which stretched as long as her hand.

"You have not told me the story behind this."

"Why the hell do you care about my face?"

"Because there's a greater tale behind it."

"Yeah? Is it a good one?"

"Yes— one that is just beginning to unfold."

Markus combed his fingers through his hair, slinging away the scattered, mud-stained straws and dirt in disgust.

"You're not half-bad, lady—if you weren't so *weird*. You heard the old man. I better hit the road. Oh! I better keep my promise."

He held out the pouch to give to her, remembering to pay her for room and board. But she paused. Her lips trembled, as though she were struggling to say something, but couldn't. And for an instant, he saw that same glimmer in her eyes that first gripped him in the Canivere forest.

"I have something for you," she smiled.

She removed and rung out her rain-soaked shawl, then laid it over his shoulder as she persuaded him to close his eyes and trust her. Though he shrugged at first, he found her touch and presence too calming and soothing to resist, and gave in.

He shifted his weight, suddenly aware of every mud stain and bruise. This maternal concern of hers made him feel like a child again—vulnerable in a way that set his teeth on edge. Yet something in her touch reminded him of a hunger he'd buried so deep he'd forgotten it was there.

Then she started humming a tune soft and low that started to grow, and soon the melody turned into the lyrics of an ancient tongue that rolled off her lips:

Amina sérielian,
Vélith zunar taelis
Ithramiel, ithramiel,
Lunara ve'isia.

The beating of the rain, the soreness of his body, and the frosty chill in the air seem to fade into the back of his mind the longer she sang. Whether it was an enchanting spell that arose through her voice, or whether her voice was as enchanting as a spell, he could not tell. Her native tongue was still very much foreign to him, yet the beautiful words spun and woven from her melodious voice took on various visions and forms in his imagination.

For a moment, Markus forgot the ache in his ribs, the weight of the world pressing down on him. The stars seemed to reach for him, whispering stories he couldn't grasp but somehow felt were meant for him—his vision filled with mythical beings that faded in and out, singing from far above in clouds of colorful mists, arrays of lights, and layers of fog that swallowed him, further away into a realm he did not recognize.

In such dreamlike surroundings, the stars above seemed to fall around him, streaks of gold and silver swirling like a cosmic dance. He felt weightless, carried by an unseen force across endless hills and valleys. The rain faded into a soft hum, replaced by Liyzia's voice— pure, otherworldly, weaving a melody that wrapped around him like a cocoon.

The streaks of light washed over him in a hallucinogenic downpour that blinded him and plunged him into an abyss of unconsciousness.

Slowly, he opened his eyes, blinking away the fog, as though awakening from a long night's dream. He'd lost all sense of time and space around him.

The stable slowly reformed around him, but somehow changed—the ordinary wooden beams now seemed to hold images of the starlight he'd seen, the rain's pattern on the roof was a faint echo of Liyzia's song.

The cold, damp air greeted him, and through the haze, he saw Liyzia kneeling beside him, her arm outstretched.

She did not say a word, just looked at him with a quiet intensity. Her eyes, gentle but powerful, told him something he couldn't quite grasp. Markus reached for her hand, letting her help him to his feet. He stood, speechless, trying to process what had just happened. For a moment, he couldn't tell whether he was awake or still dreaming.

Nikel stood at the stable entrance, his hand tightening around the pipe at his side. For a long moment, he said nothing, his gaze flicking between Markus and Liyzia. The lines of his face hardened, as though he were holding back a thousand unsaid words.

"Was this part of your 'vision' all along?" he asked her finally, his voice like gravel. For a moment, Nikel's face twisted, the mask of anger slipping just enough to reveal something deeper—something raw.

"You could have given your blessing to anyone," he muttered. In the silence that followed, something unspoken passed between them, before he shifted his eyes back to Markus, who stiffened under his glare.

His intensity softened momentarily as he fixed his eyes back on his wife.

"Do you even understand that I have loved you regardless?"

He took a sharp breath, his shoulders rising and falling like a soldier bracing for a blow. "Every tradition. Every custom. Every rule and ritual we live by. You ..." His voice broke off, cracking.

"You've handed it all to *him*?"

Yet, Liyzia's gaze didn't waver as Nikel's anger filled the stable. She stood beside Markus, her posture straight, hands clasped before her—a picture of quiet defiance. Though her heart ached at her husband's words, she remained resolute.

"My love," she said softly, her voice calm yet unyielding. "What's done ... is done."

Nikel's hands trembled as he turned the pipe over and over between his fingers, the slight motion bearing witness to the storm raging in his chest. His voice, when he spoke, was low and tight, as though holding back an onslaught.

"You think you can stumble into my wife's good graces and take something that doesn't belong to you?"

Markus stood frozen, his mind still spinning from whatever magic Liyzia had worked on him. The stable's damp air seemed to shimmer faintly, as though the echoes of her song hadn't yet faded. He barely registered Nikel's words at first—something about dishonor and tradition. Markus blinked slowly, his vision swimming.

Nikel took a long draw from his pipe, as though the smoke might fill the hollow ache in his chest. "You don't belong here. You never did."

Markus could feel the sting of his words after the man turned away and stormed out back into the cold, drizzling wind.

He looked at Liyzia. "I don't understand. I didn't ask for any of this. I didn't ..."

He yanked at the shawl in frustration. But one touch from her hand froze him in place—as if some unseen 'force' was compelling him to yield. She gently laid the damp fabric back over his shoulders.

"Will you reject my blessing?"

Markus blinked at her, his mind spinning, unable to argue.

She met his eyes, unwavering. "You are the one I saw

in my vision. There is a reason for you to be here. And one day, it will fully reveal itself. To both of us."

She finished adjusting her shawl over his shoulders, the damp woven fabric settling like a weight he wasn't sure he could bear. Then, with a quiet grace, she kissed both his cheeks, wrapped her headscarf tighter around her and walked out into the downpour.

Xara arrived, rain-soaked and grinning like she'd just caught the end of a great show. "Well, now you've done it, mister."

Markus frowned, still holding the shawl like it was a foreign object. "I've no idea what I've done."

Xara laughed, sweeping her wet hair from her face. "The matriarch's *blessing*, Markus. Reserved for ... for her kin."

His brow furrowed. "Blessing? Her kin? What does that mean?"

"She's adopted you," Xara teased, a twinkle in her eyes. "Through that shawl are the hands of her ancestry."

Markus, overwhelmed, yanked the shawl from his shoulders. "No way! No *way!*"

Xara laughed harder and threw the garment back over his head. "Oh, yes way. You've got no choice."

He stared at her, incredulous. "You can't be serious."

"I am. And listen," Xara said, lowering her voice dramatically. "You know what's worse than her blessing? Her curse."

Markus' eyes widened. "Wait, what? There's no curse!"

"Oh, there will be if you try to give it back," she said with a mischievous smile. "But you know, what's even worse than that? The curse of *Xara*."

He rolled his eyes, half-laughing. "The curse of Xara? You made that up."

"No, it's real," she said, stepping closer and narrowing her eyes. "The curse where I wrap my tentacles around your neck and strangle the last breath out of you if you ever leave me behind! You're stuck with me now," she said, poking him in the ribs. "Try to leave me behind, and I'll make your life hell."

Markus smirked. "Reckon you'd be safer here than with me."

"Safer, maybe. Happier? Not a chance." She flashed a wicked grin. "So don't push your luck, mister."

Her teasing was familiar territory—something he could grab onto while the ground shifted beneath his feet. Her threats of strangling were almost comforting compared to the intensity of whatever just happened.

He slid the shawl off her shoulders, his fingers brushing against her skin as he looked down at the relic. The profundity of its meaning was starting to sink in.

They both pondered the rain-soaked relic in silence. A piece of hand-knitted fabric that felt heavy in his hands—both foreign and familiar, like a language he couldn't speak but somehow understood. Through the barn's open door, the storm had abated to a soft rain, as if nature itself was acknowledging this moment of transformation.

And for the first time in a long while, he felt like he was meant for something more.

* * *

The morning light bathed the countryside in a soft golden hue and the cool autumn air carried a crispness that signaled change. Markus, already awake, gathered his meager belongings from the barn, his thoughts a tangle of guilt and relief. He didn't want to face Nikel. Not after everything. Confrontations didn't usually bother him, but this one felt different, heavier. Leaving was the best option, for everyone.

The familiar weight of his packed bag brought back echoes of other escapes—slipping out of orphanage windows before dawn, abandoning foster homes when the questions about his condition got too close, choosing the streets over the pitying stares. Running had become as natural as breathing. But this time it felt different.

Xara stood beside him; her expression tight with reluctance. This place, despite its tensions, had been a refuge—a temporary break from the streets that had chased them for so long. They both knew they had overstayed their welcome. Quietly, they collected what the servants had offered them and began walking east, toward the farmlands, the open road beyond the borders of this land. The morning light fractured through the branches, casting long, uncertain shadows that seemed to hesitate across the path—much like Markus' and Xara's own uncertain departure.

But before they could leave the past behind, a familiar sight stopped them in their tracks—a carriage, its wheels rumbling along the dirt road toward them. Nikel held the reins, his face as unreadable as stone, while Liyzia sat beside him, her presence calm and resolute.

The carriage came to a halt before them. Without a word, Liyzia stepped down, her eyes on Markus.

She moved with purpose, reaching for his bag. Markus'

fingers instinctively tightened on the strap—a reflex born from years of protecting what little he could call his own. But Liyzia's eyes caught his, and something in her gaze seemed to reach past his defenses, gentle but inexorable as the tide. Her fingers brushed his as she took the bag, and he felt his grip loosen despite himself, that same unsettling warmth that always seemed to accompany her touch, rendering his usual barriers useless. It was moments like these that made him wonder what she really was—this woman who could disarm him with a look when he'd spent years making sure no one could get close enough to try.

She passed the bag to Xara. "Return to the manor," she said gently, but the subtle wink she gave Xara carried more than just an order.

Then, she turned to Markus. "Get in."

Markus hesitated. "Look, we're leaving. It's better this way."

Liyzia said nothing in response. She simply patted the seat of the carriage, and waited with the kind of patience that was both maddening and reassuring. Nikel sat still, holding the reins tightly, his eyes fixed on the travel distance as though already weary of this exchange.

Markus opened his mouth to argue again, but the words caught in his throat. There was something about Liyzia's silent insistence and calm confidence that rendered his usual defiance useless. Her gaze was steady, warm, but with a power that was hard to ignore. She wasn't forcing him—not really. She was giving him a choice, though one that felt inevitable.

With a quiet sigh, Markus relented and climbed into

the carriage. Nikel and Liyzia exchanged a look, a wordless conversation before Nikel cracked the reins and set the hushners moving again.

As the carriage rolled forward, Markus glanced back. He caught a final wave from Xara, alongside Liyzia, who gave him that same hypnotic gaze that he felt pierce him the day they met, a gaze that seemed to stretch towards him, even as the road swallowed her up behind them.

The road ahead wound through misty fields, tendrils of morning fog clinging to the ground like unspoken words, heavy with meaning but not yet fully revealed.

The silence between him and Nikel grew heavy, and Markus could feel it pressing down on him. He shifted in his seat, uncomfortable with the weight of it all.

"Look," he finally said, breaking the quiet. "Just drop me off somewhere. You don't need to take me along. Xara and I—we were leaving. We have caused enough trouble here."

Nikel's only response was a glance at the shawl Markus tied around his waist. He said nothing, but only tightened his grip on the reins as the carriage rumbled along the uneven path. His spirit right now matched the frost glinting on the carriage's edges—sharp, precise, with a restrained brilliance about it.

Markus rubbed the back of his neck, trying to shake off the awkwardness. "Are you at least going to tell me where we're headed?"

Nikel's voice was low, but clear. "To stay with two old friends. I need time to meditate. To think."

Markus frowned. "Then why bring me?"

Nikel finally looked at him, his blue eyes deep with unspoken thoughts. "You're not the sharpest, are you?"

Markus blinked, unsure how to respond to that. He opened his mouth, but then stopped, hesitating before he spoke again. "It's ... Liyzia," he said, awkwardly. "She creeps me out sometimes. I mean, she is kind, but it's like she can see right through me. Is she ... even human?"

Nikel's expression did not change. "She was born with this ... *gift*," he said, as though that explained everything.

Markus' brow furrowed. "Gift?"

"Yes. She carries traces of those eternal beings who once walked Aerias' soil, whether they be the Celestar, or even the Ilyrians."

Nikel paused to study the young man and his reaction to such tales before continuing. "I've been told that she had a miraculous birth; that she was possibly *touched* by one of these mythical beings and blessed. Can you believe that? She's been called many ... strange things."

Markus frowned, trying to understand. "She can see the future?"

The landscape around Nikel seemed to hold its breath, vast and patient, while he pondered before answering. Distant hills rolled like waves of unspoken thoughts, steady and immovable as his own carefully maintained composure.

"She sees what others cannot," Nikel finally said, his voice taking on a softer note as he spoke of his wife. "Not the future, but deeper truths—hidden things. She can find light where there is only darkness. Flowers in the frost. Fire in the ash. Treasure where others see only ruin."

Nikel snapped the reins, urging the hushners to

hasten toward their destination before Markus could ask any more questions.

Markus fell silent, feeling the weight of the older man's words. The shawl in his possession felt different now, heavier with meaning. She had seen something in him, something he wasn't sure he understood yet. He even wondered if she knew about his hidden blood condition and if it might have something to do with her interest in him.

The road ahead disappeared into morning mist, like the boundary between legend and reality blurring before his eyes. Markus' thoughts were scattered like the leaves in the wind, and though he didn't know where they were going, a part of him felt like he was being led somewhere he was meant to be all along.

CHAPTER SEVEN

The hour-long ride to the harbor town of Altair was not as comfortable as Hans would have liked. Wedged between two bodyguards in the back seat of a vehicle was unsettling enough, but the memories of his recent dealings with his superiors persisted like a stain in his mind. The acrid scent of singed flesh remained. Charred fabric. Lightning-flashes of gunfire. The images haunted him still. How he managed to emerge unscathed still puzzled him, though he reminded himself of it daily. No one suspected a thing.

He kept a cool exterior, a mask he had worn for years in politics. Yet deep down, the paranoia churned, reminding him of the countless ways things could go wrong. There were no witnesses left. No records. Just whispers, and a few too many loose ends now tied too tightly. But even with that certainty, the feeling of knives waiting to slip between his ribs gnawed at him.

The vehicle pulled up to Altair, a town that was more grit than charm. Hans took in the surroundings with quiet distaste. The streets were alive with merchants, hustlers, seamen, and vagabonds—all manner of riff-raff that made him pull his overcoat tighter over his tailored suit. He only heard mention of this place once in a passing rumor that this is 'where the bodies were buried'—leaving the rest of it up to one's imagination. And though it was a far cry from the polished halls of the Capitol, it was still a necessary stop. He entered the busiest inn in town, flanked by his two guards, whose presence was an unspoken signal to anyone watching: he wasn't to be trifled with.

The inn smelled of sweat, stale alcohol, and something burning that might have once been food. He grimaced but kept his composure. In this line of work, showing discomfort was a luxury he could ill afford.

He spotted them easily enough. Two figures at a corner table, barely noticeable to the other patrons; yet they signaled for him. His heart skipped a beat, though outwardly he remained the perfect picture of calm. *Who are they?* How could they have recognized him so quickly in this place?

The first man stood as Hans approached—a human dressed down to blend in with the locals. "Mr. Lumen? Stan Nettles from South Griffin. Third year in the Council."

Hans shook his hand, flashing a polished smile. "Yes, of course. I remember your first speech on the house floor two years ago—quite impressive."

"Thank you," Nettles replied, "but nowhere near as impressive as your own career, sir. May I introduce our guest of honor today? Rathmar."

Hans turned to face the second man, and his breath almost caught in his throat. Rathmar, a Dromelan from the frozen southern kingdom, towered over him. His grip was firm, almost pulling Hans off balance. Yet, the palm of his hand was strikingly warm—a stark contrast to their reputation for being hardened masters of their Arctic domain. The Dromelan's purplish eyes, gleaming like rubies beneath the dim light, took him in with unsettling calm. His greenish-blue skin, adorned with cryptic gold tattoos, shimmered under the glow, and Hans found himself momentarily mesmerized by their intricate patterns.

They sat, and Nettles wasted no time. "Let's not beat around the bush, Senator."

"Just Mr. Lumen," Hans corrected, holding up a hand. "I prefer to keep it informal."

Nettles smirked. "Out here, titles from the Capitol mean little. This town doesn't much care about a government takeover."

Hans leaned in slightly. "I trust the situation is under control—or would I be mistaken?"

Nettles gave a half-shrug. "It's everything you've been briefed on. Your part is clear enough."

Hans nodded but pressed further. "The forged papers ... they didn't go as planned. The forger disappeared. It's becoming a problem."

"That can be dealt with," Nettles waved a hand dismissively. "We have people who can track her down. In any case, condolences to Senator Schweimer and the Council Speaker. Tragic business—with what happened to them."

"Yes," Hans murmured, maintaining a somber tone. "We will arrange a memorial soon. But for now, the second phase of the plan—how is it progressing?"

Nettles' eyes turned toward Rathmar, who had been silently observing the conversation. "Everything is moving forward. The only remaining question is leadership for the next step."

Hans raised an eyebrow. "Leadership?"

"The expedition to Oravon," Nettles clarified, "across the North Sea. We need someone politically savvy to lead the delegation."

Hans blinked, carefully processing the information. "Of course ... though I admit I've been a bit preoccupied with the forger issue."

"Unfortunately, a small issue can become a *bigger* issue if it's not dealt with," Nettles hinted lightly. "You're still the best candidate. The charter is ready to sail. Your task is to meet the governor, attend the festivities, and—using your charm—persuade him to help retrieve the 'asset.'"

"That's it?" Hans asked, sipping his drink to mask his growing unease.

"That's it," Nettles confirmed, with a slight grin. "Though it will depend on your ... persuasive skills."

Hans' eyes narrowed slightly. "If the governor proves ... difficult, I assume you've prepared contingencies?"

Rathmar, speaking for the first time, answered coldly, "We will ensure cooperation. My team is well-prepared for resistance." The Dromelan's voice carried a strange, unnatural quality that Hans found as unsettling as the predatory way the man observed him.

The senator leaned back in his chair, swirling his drink. The pieces were all falling into place, yet something about the way Nettles and Rathmar exchanged glances unsettled him. He couldn't quite put his finger on it, but his instinct told him something was off.

Hans began slowly and steadily, "Before we move forward, I insist on meeting your team. A man in my position doesn't leave himself vulnerable to ... uncertainties."

Rathmar nodded, though his expression was unreadable. "Wise choice. One should always know who they're working with."

Hans nodded, his poker face flawless. "Lead the way. I'm eager to see how far your loyalty extends."

* * *

Hans followed Rathmar and Nettles across the harbor with habitual poise, keeping his nerves locked behind the mask of an experienced politician. The hydro cruiser, sleek and dangerous, stood out among the rugged harbor vessels—a symbol of the power surrounding him on all sides. Hans could only imagine the influence and lengths Rathmar went through in acquiring a state-of-the-art nautical vessel to navigate the high seas.

But as they boarded the ship and descended into its bowels, Hans couldn't shake the uneasy foreboding settling on him.

The cargo hold was vast and cold, and the air was tinged with salt and metal. As they entered the third level, Hans noticed the crew—Dromelans, twelve of them, their eyes tired but alert, their hands resting on blades and strange weapons strapped to their bodies. Their heavy winter attire gave them an almost animalistic bulk. An intimidating sight indeed, as they stood in silent formation.

They approached a hefty steel door, bound with iron latches and thick chains. The room suddenly felt tighter, more oppressive. Even the hardened Dromelans avoided looking directly at the door, their silence adding to the tension. There was something unsettling. Something ominous.

At the top of the steel doors, Hans spotted a small square opening. It was blocked by iron bars and too high for anyone to casually glance through. Whatever was on the other side, it was being contained, and the precautions taken were far more than just for show. Hans felt a shiver crawl up his spine ... a prelude?

Rathmar walked right up to the door and began to speak. Not in Dromelish, nor in any language Hans recognized. The guttural, harsh sounds echoed around the cold steel of the room, something primal and dark in every syllable. The Dromelan crew tensed as they watched their leader. Hans could feel their unease, but it was nothing compared to the icy fear beginning to coil in his chest.

As Rathmar spoke, the temperature in the hold plummeted. Frost formed along the steel edges of the door, spiderwebbing outwards like veins. The air felt heavy as it pressed against Hans' chest, and his breathing became shallow. A low, resonant rumble filled the room—not quite a growl, but layered, vibrating through the metal floor. It was a sound that bypassed the ears and went straight to the bones.

Then came the smell. Faint, acrid, like iron and rot, seeping through the bars of the door. Hans suppressed the urge to gag. He wasn't alone—one of the crew members wiped his nose with a grimace, while another shifted uneasily, glancing at the exits.

When the red eyes appeared, the room seemed to darken, as though the thing behind the door consumed light itself. The eyes moved slowly, scanning the room with unnerving calm, their glow illuminating faint tendrils of frost along the steel bars. Hans felt a wave of heat roll over him, cloying and oppressive, like standing too close to a raging furnace. His instincts screamed for him to move, to flee, but his limbs refused to obey.

A faint clicking sound broke the silence—sharp and irregular, like claws against steel. It wasn't constant, just enough to make Hans' skin prickle. He stared at the red eyes transfixed, but when they landed on him, he quickly looked away. A chill ran down his spine.

Rathmar spoke again in a low rumble in that cryptic tongue. The eyes receded into the darkness, disappearing without a sound. The tension in the room eased, but only slightly.

"Senator?" Rathmar's voice broke the silence.

Hans forced a smile, though his face was pale. "Yes, I'm quite alright."

"What do you think?"

"Charming. Quite charming. Does he come with instructions? Or just warnings?"

Rathmar grinned, showing sharp teeth. "Arrakos is an essential part of my team. I believe the word in your language is 'hunter.'"

"Hunter?" Hans echoed, still unsettled. "And what prey demands such ... extraordinary measures?"

Rathmar let out a deep, throaty laugh. "It's certainly

not you, Senator. Or you, Mister Nettles." He glanced at the councilman, who had been silently cowering behind Hans the entire time.

"Of course," Hans replied smoothly, "And I trust he will perform as expected. After all, our shared objectives are ... ambitious."

Rathmar tilted his head, his predatory gaze lingering on Hans for a beat too long. Then, with a dismissive wave, he turned away. "Ambition, Senator, is a blade. Wield it wisely, or it will cut deeper than you intend."

Hans smiled faintly, though his palms were damp. "Sound advice."

Later, Hans and Nettles found themselves back in the dingy bar in Altair, trying to drown their anxiety in alcohol. The scene from the cargo hold replayed in Hans' mind. The heavy door, the numerous locks, the red eyes staring out from the darkness. He couldn't shake the cold feeling that something far more dangerous than any political maneuver was at play here.

He wiped a bead of sweat from his brow as he downed another glass of whiskey. The burning liquid did little to calm him. Beside him, Nettles leaned against the bar, finishing his own drink in silence.

"What do you know about Rathmar?" Hans whispered, eyes alert to ensure no one was listening.

"He's the leader of their delegation," Nettles replied, equally cautious. "Their kingdom has a personal stake in securing our ... asset. According to the agreement, they are allowed to use their own resources to achieve the objective."

Hans leaned in closer. "And what asset, exactly, are we talking about?"

Nettles hesitated, then whispered, "Her Highness."

Hans stiffened. "The throne's been vacant for years—it's under a regency. Are you telling me there's an heir?"

"She was taken into seclusion following the king's passing, to remain safely until the hour of her coronation. Both her and the coveted seal around her neck."

"The aether stone," Hans uttered softly from behind his raised glass. His eyes shifted, scanning the room for unwelcome eavesdroppers—as if anyone in this town understood the context of their conversation. "The very 'seal' which our talented forger managed to replicate. The one needed to bring down a kingdom."

"Indeed," Nettles confirmed in a barely audible tone. "We've found her! After a decade-long search—hidden remotely in the Heavenly Isles, one of the three islands. She's as secluded as the mist and legend that surround that distant land."

Hans' eyes narrowed. "And the Dromelans think they can get to her? She's surrounded by assassins and Immortals. It's suicide."

Nettles took a long sip of his whiskey. "That's not our concern. The Dromelans have their methods. And that 'hunter' ... well, they say he's killed hundreds, alone."

Hans felt the chill return. "Hundreds?"

"Yes. He's a notorious killer in their kingdom. That's why they keep him bound. For control."

Hans swallowed hard. The pieces of the puzzle were falling into place, and none of them was good. Whatever this operation was, it went far beyond politics. It was dangerous. Deadly. And yet, the allure of power was too great. A seat on the High Council. Control over Pelham and Schwiemer's resources. Unbridled influence.

"I want more than a seat," Hans said, his voice hard. "I want their accounts. Their networks. Their entire empire folded into mine."

"May I remind you, Senator, there is still a party leadership with their eyes on you."

"Is that some sort of ... threat?"

"More of a precaution to keep an eye over your shoulder. Personally, I'm under enough stress myself. Rather it be you leading this mission and not me! The world is yours to claim."

"The world—and a particularly talented young lady."

Nettles stared at him, shocked. "The forger?"

"Precisely. Someone as dangerously cunning as that would make a perfect partner beside me. Don't you think?"

"And how do you plan on achieving that?" Nettles asked. "A custom diamond ring perhaps?"

"My dear councilman. There's more than one way to change a woman's heart." Hans leaned in, his eyes cold. "Think bigger, Nettles. Once we've removed this precious princess, who will stand in our way?"

The silence between them was heavy, but Hans no longer cared. He had crossed the line long ago. Now, it was about survival—and domination.

"Winter is upon us," he said, rising from the bar. "And I intend to claim my prize."

* * *

Onboard the Hydro cruiser's second-level guest quarters, the door to Rathmar's suite stood ajar— unusual for a sect leader who valued his privacy. Gurigor hesitated at the threshold, protocol battling curiosity. The room appeared empty, moonlight spilling through the circular window to illuminate scattered scrolls across the desk.

One particular scroll drew his attention. Its parchment was darker than the others with edges blackened as though burned. Mystical symbols crawled across its surface, their shapes seeming to writhe in the dim light. Gurigor's fingers moved toward it unconsciously, hovering over text that had been forbidden in their kingdom for millennia.

The language itself felt wrong—each character carrying an otherworldly nuance that made his skin crawl. As his fingertip brushed the surface, a jolt of something primal and dark shot through him. He jerked back, heart pounding.

"Beautiful, isn't it?"

Rathmar's voice came from directly behind him—Gurigor hadn't heard him approach. The sect leader's arm appeared beside his own, long fingers tracing the forbidden symbols with intimate familiarity. His voice dropped lower, taking on the guttural tones of that dark speech as he began to read.

Gurigor turned slowly. Rathmar stood impossibly close, his yellow eyes reflecting the moonlight like a hunter. But then his lips curved into an almost playful smile, his hand settling on Gurigor's shoulder with paternal weight.

"Do not fear what calls to us, brother," Rathmar said softly. "Fear only those who would deny our destiny."

The gentle tone somehow made Rathmar more terrifying than any display of anger could have. Here was a man who could read words that could awaken ancient horrors, yet speak of them with a father's tenderness. A zealot whose absolute faith made him more dangerous than any fanatic.

"The text ..." Gurigor managed, his mouth dry. "It's forbidden."

Rathmar's smile widened. "Forbidden by those who fear what they cannot control. But we know better, don't we?" His grip tightened slightly. "We remember what they chose to forget."

Rathmar proceeded towards a decanter of deep amber liquid.

"Gurigor, Brother of Ticuri," Rathmar began in low and measured tones, "your mind has been troubled lately. What weighs on you?"

Gurigor accepted the drink but left it untouched, his brow furrowed. "I've had doubts since before we set out from Krachmeia. I tried reasoning with you then, but you refused to listen. Now that we've arrived and met with our counterparts, I ask you to hear me out."

Rathmar's expression remained unchanged. "Do not dance around the point. Speak plainly."

"It's the kaegar," Gurigor said, his voice tight. "I don't trust him. Just because you've learned his dark tongue doesn't mean you can control him."

"Dark tongue?" Rathmar repeated with a raised brow. "I find it beautiful."

"Beautiful? It's an evil language, Rathmar," Gurigor insisted. "Would you serenade your wife with it?"

Rathmar chuckled, but there was no warmth in it. "Fair point. But control is not my aim with Arrakos. I merely convey the oath, our purpose, our objectives. In the end, we are all brothers—Dromelan, kaegar, even the Earthens. You see dissonance. I see threads of a single tapestry."

"How could I forget?" Gurigor's voice tightened. "It's why we've been forced into hiding, living in the shadows, banished within our own kingdom."

Rathmar turned to the window, looking out over the dark harbor, the lights reflecting faintly on the water's surface. "What else would you expect, surrounded by a society of unbelievers? I have no time for politics. Is it your faith you question?"

"I question this oath," Gurigor said sharply.

Rathmar faced him again, his eyes sharp. "The oath we've upheld for nearly ten millennia?"

Gurigor's tone grew heavier. "An oath that failed us before. History has a way of repeating itself for those who forget."

Rathmar smiled, though it did not reach his eyes. "Perhaps your faith needs renewal, Gurigor."

"Faith?" Gurigor snapped. "Do you even understand the cost of this oath? You've aligned with this senator and his party to help them gain control over their kingdom, but what happens when that kingdom falls? One domino tips the rest. This alliance will swallow them whole. And when the dust clears, who will they blame for their ruin?"

Rathmar waved off the concern in a casual voice yet edged with something darker. "And what would you have me do? These Earthens—these men—have their history books, much like we do. Not that it matters. I seem to know more about their world than they know of ours. If Hans Lumen were a more astute diplomat, he'd have taken the time to study the people he's aligning with. You must always know your enemies as well as your allies ...

"And these men?" He paused, letting the weight of his words sink in. "These Earthens? Blinded by their ambition, gorging on power as if it's inexhaustible. They march to their own downfall, and we need only let them."

Gurigor was silent, processing the brutal logic being laid out before him. Rathmar was always a man of reason, willing to entertain dissenting voices, which had helped him rise within the Sect. Yet Gurigor's doubts had grown heavier, especially after realizing the true nature of their 'cargo' hidden in the ship's hold below.

"So, they're just pawns," Gurigor finally said in a low voice.

Rathmar sighed. "Sadly, yes. Pawns to be sacrificed when the time comes. It's the price, Gurigor. Don't let your sympathies for them cloud your judgment—or your loyalty to the brotherhood."

Gurigor exhaled slowly, resigned. "You've allowed me to speak my mind. For that, I thank you."

Rathmar smiled, a fleeting warmth returning to his voice. "And I thank you, brother. We may not always agree. However, as long as we remain faithful to the oath, we will be fine. Is there anything else?"

"No. It's been a long journey. I need rest."

"Good night, brother. Oh—on your way out, send in one of the guards."

Gurigor nodded and left without another word. The door closed softly behind him, and within moments, one of the guards entered. His face was hidden beneath a mask, his posture rigid and awaiting orders.

Rathmar's voice dropped to a near whisper. "Set a shadow on Gurigor. If his whispers find the senator's ear, I want every word brought to me. Quietly."

The guard bowed slightly. "As you wish."

Alone once more, Rathmar lingered at the window, his reflection ghostly against the harbor lights. Gurigor's doubts were no surprise—there was always one like him, questioning the cost of the oath. But the cost was never theirs to decide. It was carved into their bones, their bloodline. Gurigor would see reason, or he would see consequences.

* * *

Vuchic and Erev approached Nikel across the sprawling fields, the midday sun casting long shadows behind them. Their traditional tunics rippled in the light breeze, but what caught Markus' eye was the belts they wore, each adorned with intricate inscriptions. He couldn't make out the words, but he knew enough to recognize their importance: they carried the story of their lineage, a mark of their status as former knights, now retired like Nikel, but still bound by their shared history.

Though the years had brought them to the autumn of their lives, their posture was still proud, and Markus could sense that even now, they remained formidable. He'd seen them move once—quick, instinctive countermoves with swords or bows, still capable despite age slowing them. But today, there was no such display.

Today, they greeted Nikel with silent nods, acknowledging the man they had served beside. Markus, standing awkwardly at the edge of their gathering, felt their eyes on him. The cold, unspoken scrutiny.

They assessed him from head to toe, not bothering to hide their judgment. His appearance—too old, too foreign—didn't fit the mold of a pupil. He wasn't Nevran, didn't carry their blood, and each scar on his body seemed to them more like a mark of failure than experience. His past was written all over him, and none of it aligned with their ideals.

Without a word, they brushed him aside as though he barely existed, as if he were little more than an afterthought. Vuchic, leading the way, walked him toward the barn without even a glance back, as Erev and Nikel exchanged quiet words. When they reached the structure, Vuchic gestured to the small guest quarters where Markus would be staying. He gave no explanation, no welcome, only a brief glance that conveyed everything: you are not one of us.

Then, without another word, the three retired knights left him there, disappearing to meditate, leaving him alone to bear the chill of their indifference.

With a mix of frustration and boredom, Markus wandered inside. The guest quarters were simple, almost sparse, offering little in the way of comfort. But as he explored deeper into the barn, he stumbled upon something unexpected.

His hand brushed against a piece of equipment, and without warning, he accidentally triggered the electric lighting. The barn lit up, revealing a world beyond imagination. On the far side, away from the livestock pens, an enormous training area came into view, bathed in the soft glow of the lights.

It was a three-story structure, a testament to the knights' former lives. Pulley systems and weights hung from beams and high rafters, along with towering pillars that seemed designed for climbing. There were standing targets with deep cuts and marks, their fabric bodies stitched and restitched from countless strikes. Heavy punching bags scarred from endless blows, swung lazily from chains. The air was thick with the scents of the animals—hushners, crownfeathers, specklegrazers, chickens, all with their younglings, domesticated dogs padding around the corners—mixed with hay, scattered cornmeal, and the faint, earthy odor of manure.

The contrast between the training area and the guest quarters was striking. This was not just a barn—it was a battlefield in disguise, a place where the knights had clearly trained and honed their skills, even now, years after their official service had ended.

Markus stared at the apparatus with a strange mixture of awe and unease. He couldn't help but imagine the three knights here, working through drills, training their bodies long after their duties had passed, keeping alive the warrior tradition. And now, here he was—an outsider, who didn't belong, standing in the midst of it.

The silence returned, settling heavily over him, but now it wasn't just the absence of words from the knights. It was the challenge of this place, the quiet challenge of what lay ahead.

* * *

That evening, Markus entered the dining hall late, hesitant as he approached the long wooden table.

The room felt colder than before. The three retired knights—Nikel, Erev, and Vuchic—sat in stony silence, their expressions unreadable. When he first arrived months ago, they had been cordial. But now, he felt like an outsider in their world. And not wanting to intrude further, he began to turn away.

"Markus! Come sit by me," Jetza's voice rang out, warm and inviting. Her smile broke through the tension like a ray of sunlight. She motioned to the seat beside her, making it clear there was no escape.

Reluctantly, Markus walked over and sat down. Jetza, always full of life, introduced him with enthusiasm. "Do you remember me? Jetza. And my little ones, Evenor and Tavin. Children, you remember Markus."

Her nine-year-old son, Tavin, leaned forward, his face lit up with excitement. "*Vani con gi!* Will you be a knight? Like me someday?"

Markus blinked, caught off guard. A knight? A son? He wasn't sure he belonged at the table, let alone the lineage. The boy's innocent question brought the underlying tension into sharp focus. The looks on Nikel, Erev, and Vuchic's faces said it all. Markus wasn't just here because Liyzia had adopted him—he was here because they expected him to train, to become something more. It was all beginning to make sense now: the cold stares, the silence from the men who had no desire to train someone they didn't see as one of their own. Nikel's spoon clinked once against the bowl. He hadn't looked up since Markus entered.

"Of course!" Jetza's voice burst through his thoughts, her energy relentless. Her eyes lit up like the candlelight above. "Why else is he here? See, children? He carries Liyzia's shawl. That means she's adopted him. And that means he must be ..."

Nikel's jaw tightened as he turned away, clearly displeased. Jetza's sharp eyes missed nothing.

"*Trained* to pass on the lineage," she finished, her voice steady as she glanced at Nikel, daring him to argue. "You think this is a joke?"

Vuchic shifted in his seat, cutting in with his deep voice. "My dear ..." He spoke cautiously, sensing Jetza's tone.

She met her husband's gaze with a respectful but firm nod. "My beloved," she replied, softening her tone only for him. "Liyzia is my sister in all but blood. I will not stand for anyone doubting her choices."

Her eyes swept across the table, landing on each of the men in turn. "Am I the only one here who believes in her?"

The men exchanged quiet glances, unable to argue with her. The tension eased just a little, though it still hung in the air.

"I am sitting between two future knights!" Jetza declared proudly, her hand gently lifting Markus' chin. He almost felt embarrassed. "Sure, you are older, but still young enough for your journey."

She then glanced fondly at her son, Tavin. "You may even fight alongside each other someday, as brothers-in-arms! And I will pray for your safety, Markus, as if you were my own son."

Markus swallowed hard, unsure how to respond. He felt more out of place than ever. Her expectations pressed down on him. Could he really live up to this? Could he ever be more than an outsider in this strange, rigid world?

Jetza was not finished. "You won't find three greater teachers than these three," she said, looking at Vuchic. "Don't you agree, my beloved?"

Vuchic glanced at Markus, and for the first time, a small smile touched his lips. "Yes, my dear. Two future knights indeed!"

Erev rose suddenly, his wine glass held high. "She's right! A toast is in order!" His enthusiasm filled the room, but Markus felt a shudder of discomfort. It wasn't just the sudden attention—it was the sight of the wine itself. How could he tell them he had an unfortunate reaction to alcohol, especially Nevrish liquor?

As everyone stood, Markus tried to quietly reach for his water glass, hoping to avoid the inevitable. But Jetza was too quick. With a smile, she placed a full wine glass in his hand, the golden liquid bubbling over the rim.

"What's that old Earthen saying?" Jetza asked playfully. "'When among strangers, follow their customs'? Something like that?"

"Yes!" Erev grinned, raising his glass higher. "Something like that! Everyone? Glasses up! To Markus! May he carry Nikel's sword!"

He stopped, his words hanging in the air. Every eye turned toward Nikel, waiting for his reaction. The veteran knight, after a brief pause, gave a tight smile, offering the bare minimum of approval.

Erev nodded, satisfied. "With honor!" he finished, and the room echoed with the clinking of glasses.

Markus, however, barely had time to process the moment before the wine hit his throat. He coughed violently, nearly choking as the burn hit harder than expected—not just unpleasant, but almost searing, as if his body rejected it on some deeper level. His face turned red, his eyes watering, and for a moment, the room was filled with the sound of his hacking coughs. The knights looked amused, and even Jetza tried to stifle a laugh.

"Perhaps we should add 'drinking' to his training as well," Erev joked, eyes twinkling with amusement.

Markus managed a weak smile. But even as the laughter faded, a flicker of unease lingered beneath his ribs. He'd tasted drinks before—but nothing had ever scorched like that.

He glanced around the table. Everyone here had a place, a purpose. But he? He wasn't sure where he fit. Yet, Jetza's warmth and steadfast belief in him were the only things keeping him anchored.

For better or worse, this was his life now. He just hoped he could live up to the expectations thrust upon him.

* * *

The dawn had not yet broken when Markus found himself standing on the mat in the center of the barn, face to face with the three knights. They had dragged him out of bed before the first crow, eyes sharp, movements deliberate. There was no warm-up, no gentle introduction. This was his first test—raw, brutal, and immediate.

The training evolved into a series of increasingly impossible challenges. At first, Markus moved like a wounded animal—all raw instinct and desperate survival. The knights didn't coddle him. Each day began before dawn, with exercises that seemed designed to break him. Tightrope walking became a dance with gravity. His first attempts ended in spectacular falls, mud caking his body, bruises blooming like dark flowers. But by the tenth day, he learned to feel the rope's tension, and to move with a precision that surprised even himself.

The sword training started with a heavy two-by-four. His movements were clumsy and predictable. Vuchic would tap his wrist, his elbow, his shoulder—each touch a correction, a silent lesson. "Your body lies," he'd say. "Listen to your bones, not your muscles."

Gradually ... impossibly, Markus began to change.

From the training yard's edge, Nikel often watched in silence—arms folded, face unreadable. He offered no praise, no correction, just a stillness that felt heavier than judgment. Whether he was measuring progress or wrestling ghosts, no one could say.

His punches, once wild street brawler strikes, became controlled bursts of energy. The knights would demonstrate a move once—just once—and he'd spend hours recreating it, muscles screaming, determination etched into every trembling repetition. Meditation transformed from torture to revelation. The silence he once feared became a canvas where he could map his own limitations, then systematically dismantle them.

By the fourth week, something shifted. He wasn't just surviving the training—he was beginning to understand it.

One morning, Erev threw a series of rapid strikes that weeks earlier would have hospitalized him. This time, Markus didn't just block. He anticipated. He moved.

The look of surprise on Erev's face was brief—but it was there.

At the end of another day, Markus' body betrayed every ounce of fatigue. Xara was by his side, half-dragging, half-supporting him as they crossed the yard. She shook her head in disbelief as he managed a faint, crooked smile and a raised thumb towards the men—a silent declaration that he wasn't ready to quit.

As twilight painted the training yard in muted grays, the three knights stood in contemplative silence. They lit their pipes in unison, as the glow from the embers flickered in the dim light. The tension between them hung heavy, as if waiting for someone to break the silence.

Vuchic, whose own son was not yet of training age, spoke first. "Liyzia chose well," he said softly, almost to himself.

Erev glanced at Nikel, reading the tension in his friend's shoulders. "A son," he said, the word hanging between them with weight.

Nikel didn't respond immediately. The word "son" seemed to sit uncomfortably, like an ill-fitting garment. "Not blood," he finally said roughly. "But Liyzia ... she sees things we cannot."

Vuchic understood the unspoken. The pain of child-lessness was a wound they all knew Nikel carried. It was one Liyzia had borne with quiet grace. "The lineage matters," he said carefully. "But perhaps lineage is more than just blood."

Erev nodded. "Your line continues. That's what matters."

The subtext was clear—they were offering Nikel a

path to acceptance, understanding the deeply personal struggle behind adopting Markus.

"He's nothing like the sons we imagined," Nikel said, his voice raw with something unspoken. But was there a hint of something else? Hope, perhaps?

"No," Vuchic pronounced. "He's exactly who he needs to be."

CHAPTER EIGHT

The first light of morning streaked the eastern sky in bands of amber and crimson, casting its long shadows across the training yard as the sun prepared to break the horizon. For a moment, the warmth soothed the constant throb of Markus' scar. These quiet seconds before the day's brutality were precious. They allowed a space to breathe, to remember why he'd chosen this path.

His fingers found Liyzia's shawl, tucked carefully beneath his pillow. The fabric seemed to hold traces of home, of belonging. Of purpose.

Then Nikel's shadow fell across him, and the peace was shattered by the training's familiar violence.

"Up!" the old knight commanded, tossing him the practice sword. "The Guild Engineers think their crystalline blades and energy weapons make them invincible. Today you learn why they're wrong."

The morning air was bitter and cold as Markus followed Nikel to the training yard. The old knight circled him as he took his stance, the practice sword heavy in his hands. Different from the street weapons he was used to, but after weeks of training, its feel had become almost familiar.

"The Guild's technology follows rules—predictable, reliable," Nikel said, demonstrating a move that seemed to ignore physics itself, the blade flowing like water around an invisible energy shield. "But true mastery? That comes from understanding what lies beneath their rules, the power they've forgotten how to use."

Markus attempted to replicate the movement. Once. Twice. On the third try, something clicked. His body found the rhythm Nikel had been trying to teach him—the blade extension perfect, the footwork precise. For a moment, the sword felt like an extension of his arm rather than a tool.

Nikel watched him execute the move again, his expression unreadable. But something glinted in his eyes—pride, briefly surfacing beneath layers of discipline. He caught himself, hardening his voice to mask the slip. "Again."

When Markus mirrored the next sequence, adapting the technique with an instinct that seemed bred in his bones, Nikel's hand tightened imperceptibly on his cane. For a moment, he wasn't seeing a street watchman from Vesper, but something else—something that stirred memories of his own training, of legacy, of succession.

The moment passed. His correction of Markus' stance was gentler than usual, a gesture of unspoken recognition. "The Guild thinks power comes from ownership," he said, demonstrating how to maintain the sword's edge. His fingers traced patterns in the metal that seemed to glint in the light. "But these markings? They speak of belonging. Of tradition. Of power earned rather than bought."

As evening approached, Markus felt the strain of the day's lessons in his muscles, in his bones. But something else lingered too—an understanding of power that went deeper than Guild certifications or street survival. Perhaps that's why, when twilight painted the sky in deep purples and blues, he noticed the way the two figures moved—fluid, precise, and strangely unreal—as if the dusk itself parted to let them pass.

They moved with the grace of myth made real, and Markus' breath caught in his throat. The taller one wore armor that seemed to absorb what little light remained—sleek, functional, entirely black. The other's emerald leather gleamed with gold trim, a crimson cape billowing behind him like a wound in the evening air.

Markus had heard the tales—of Immortals and Zylvan knights, of warriors who blurred the line between myth and man. But stories were wind. This was real. This was power made flesh.

The first figure stepped forward. His armor was obsidian nanotech, smooth as glass and sculpted for war—no seams, no weaknesses. The faint red glow of the Throne's sigil reverberated at his chest like a warning. When he removed his helm, light caught the lines of a face carved by years and loss. This was Draven. A limp betrayed a past injury, but his presence was undiminished. He was built like a fortress—unshakable, unbroken.

Then the second. The contrast struck like thunder. Azlo—elegant, youthful, wrapped in robes of soulsteel that shimmered with motion. His mask resembled a wind-spirit, lenses glowing faintly, and when he removed it, warmth followed—a quiet strength in his eyes, like sunlight breaching storm clouds. Where Draven was gravity, Azlo was grace.

Nikel greeted them both with the easy familiarity of old warriors. But Markus caught something else in his mentor's stance: tension, coiled and ready. Whatever was about to happen, it was bigger than all of them.

From her corner near the hearth, Liyzia's eyes met Markus' for just a moment. In that glance, he read both warning and reassurance. The night ahead would change everything.

* * *

Their footsteps echoed against the timeless floorboards as Nikel led them into the warmth of the sitting room. The hearth's glow caught the metallic accents of their armor, casting dancing shadows across walls where faded tapestries hung like silent witnesses. Vuchic and Erev were already seated, their weathered faces grave in the firelight.

"Your message was urgent," Draven said, his voice low and gravelly. He remained standing, one hand resting casually on his sword hilt. Even at rest, he looked ready to move, to strike.

"The situation requires ... discretion," Nikel replied, reaching for the satchel that lay on the table between them. The leather was worn, unremarkable—the kind of thing that wouldn't draw a second glance, perfect for hiding secrets that could tear a kingdom apart.

Azlo edged closer to the fire in fluid and precise

movements. "We've heard whispers," he said, in a gentle but focused tone—"documents circulating in the Capitol. Treaties bearing impossible seals."

"Impossible indeed!" Nikel agreed. He drew out several papers from the satchel, laying them carefully on the table. The royal seal caught the firelight, gleaming with an authenticity that made Markus' stomach turn. He'd seen Xara work before; but this was different. This was treason given form.

From her corner, Liyzia watched silently. Her presence was a steady anchor in the rising tension. Her eyes never left Nikel, as if lending him strength for what was to come.

"These treaties," Nikel continued, his voice hardening, "speak of abdication. Contingencies should anything happen to Princess Aylin." His fingers traced the seal. "They bear the mark of the aether stone—the very stone that hangs around the princess' neck, the same princess who hasn't been seen in a decade."

Draven's eyes narrowed. "Impossible!" he muttered, moving closer to examine the documents. "The Prefect's guard is impenetrable. No one gets close enough to ..."

"Unless they don't need to," Azlo interrupted softly. He lifted one of the papers, studying it expertly. "Unless someone could replicate the seal so perfectly that even the royal engineers would be fooled."

A heavy silence fell over the room. Nikel straightened, his authority settling around him like a cloak. "Markus," he called, "bring your sister in."

Markus hesitated only a for moment before slipping out to return with Xara. She held herself with a careful dignity that made his chest ache. She'd always been the clever one, the survivor. Now her greatest skill might get them all killed.

Xara met Draven's suspicious glare without flinching. "I forged them," she said simply. "Every document, every seal. Hans Lumen paid well for perfection."

Markus held his breath for a moment, catching Draven's skeptical glance.

Brom, Draven's recruit, who had been lurking near the door, snorted. "A common forger? This is what we're ..."

"Silence!" Nikel's voice cracked like a whip. He turned to Draven, eyes fierce in the firelight. "This isn't about some petty criminal scheme. These documents? They're preparation. Insurance. The kind you only need if you're planning something bigger."

"An attempt on the princess," Azlo said quietly. "Timed for her approaching coronation."

"The Separatists would need these to legitimize their power grab," Vuchic added, speaking for the first time. "But they're worthless without ..."

"Without my decryption," Xara finished. Her voice was steady, but Markus saw her hands trembling slightly. "I encrypted details in the fine print. A fail-safe. It's why I'm still alive."

"These treaties need both," Nikel said, lowering his pipe as the realization struck. "Your presence, and the princess' aether stone—both must come together to reveal whatever the Separatists have planned."

Draven's scarred hand tightened on his holster. "So we don't just need to warn the Prefect. We need to somehow get both your forger and these documents before the princess herself."

The impossibility of the task hung heavy in the air.

215

A glimmer of respect crossed Draven's face. "Clever girl," he murmured. "But it also makes you a target."

"She's protected here," Nikel said firmly. His hand rested on his cane, but his stance was that of a warrior ready to defend his own. "The question is, what do we do with this information?"

The silence was deafening. Liyzia moved then, just slightly, the rustle of her dress drawing all eyes. She didn't speak, but her presence seemed to fill the room with unspoken purpose.

Draven paced with a limp more pronounced in his agitation. "Even if we believe all this, we can't reach the princess. The Prefect trusts no one. Approaching him with forged documents would be suicide."

"Unless," Azlo began thoughtfully, "we had a reason to be where she'll be. A legitimate reason that wouldn't raise suspicion."

Draven stopped pacing, his expression shifting. "There might be a way." He glanced at Azlo, who gave him a slight nod. "The princess ... she attends the Feast of Solstice in Oravan. December 21st."

"Impossible," Erev breathed. "The Prefect would never allow her out of his sight. Not even for ..."

"Among thousands wearing masks and disguises, who would know?" Draven's voice countered. "The festival provides cover, even for the princess. I know because Mercury guards her. He's one of the Inner Court—the Prefect's most trusted Immortals—and he's always in attendance."

The fire crackled in the silence that followed. Markus watched as understanding dawned on the faces around him, as the import of this secret settled in the room.

"This information cannot leave these walls," Azlo added softly. "Mercury's duty is to protect her. If word got out ..."

"Her last festival in seclusion," Nikel mused, stroking his chin. His eyes took on a calculating gleam that Markus had learned to recognize. "But how to get close enough? The Prefect ..."

"Even if we could find him in Oravan before the festival," Vuchic said, "why would he trust us?"

The room fell silent save for the pop and crack of burning logs. Nikel's gaze swept the room, settling first on Brom in his cadet uniform, then on Markus. Something sparked in his eyes.

"Unless we had a reason to be there. A legitimate reason."

Xara caught the tone in his voice, shooting Markus a quick, knowing glance. Whatever was coming, it would be either brilliant or terrible.

"Markus will train in the Trial by Fire," Nikel announced, referring to the legendary endurance training held in Oravan. "And Xara will attend."

"I will?" Markus' voice cracked slightly. Doubt crept over him at first, along with every fall, bump, bruise and past failure. But then again—why not? When you've been down for so long, sometimes the only way to go is up.

Vuchic and Erev exchanged wide-eyed looks. Even Draven seemed taken aback.

"Yes," Nikel continued, warming to his plan. "And Xara will accompany him as ... his nurse."

Xara opened her mouth, then closed it again. In the corner, Liyzia's quiet laugh was barely more than a breath.

Brom's face split into a smug grin. "Now this is going to be as funny as …"

"Funny as what, you pompous oaf?" Nikel's voice cut through the room like steel. He turned on the cadet, eyes flashing. "So you've passed the Academy's military requirements? Shall I fetch you a medal?"

He turned to Draven, jabbing his cane toward Markus with the authority of a man who would suffer no more doubt.

He glanced at his wife. She raised her eyes, parted her lips—but said nothing. That was enough.

"My son," he said—voice steady, like a blade drawn from a sheath—"is training for something far greater. To be a Zylvan knight."." His voice hardened. "Unless you deem your military academy to carry more weight than the ancient order of the High Kingdom of Niri?"

Liyzia's breath caught at the word "son." The word echoed in Markus' chest, pressing against wounds he hadn't realized still ached. He wanted to speak, to say something—anything—but years of learned silence held his tongue. In the hearth's warm glow, he saw Nikel not as the warrior who'd trained him, but as something he'd stopped hoping for long ago.

Nikel stood beside Azlo now—past and present warriors united—speaking of a future neither of them could fully see.

"Lord Nikel," Draven said carefully, "no man has ever dared to carry such a burden. To cross both lines, endure both journeys, knight and Immortal—both—the training alone could break even the strongest spirit."

The fire crackled in the silence.

"He is no ordinary man," Vuchic rose slowly, his voice

firm with the weight of years spent judging the worth of warriors.

"Aye, that he's not!" Erev joined him, both men looking at Markus with something akin to pride.

Draven's eyes narrowed. "Are you only suggesting this to reach the Prefect?"

"No," Nikel's response was immediate. "Finding the Prefect will be *your* task, Immortal. This is another door opening for Markus. And should he pass?" A slight smile touched his lips. "That seal about his chest ensures not only his future but Xara's as well."

He met Draven's eyes meaningfully. "A Zylvan knight's word carries weight even with the Prefect's court."

Hope lit Xara's face as the implications sank in. Azlo nodded slowly, his silence of greater consequence than words.

Nikel reached into his vest, pulling out something that gleamed gold in the firelight. A pendulum on a ribbon. "One last thing," he said, his voice softening with memory. "King Ronan gave me this, years ago, for my service. The princess will recognize it."

When Draven reached for it, Nikel shook his head. Instead, he stepped forward and placed it around Markus' neck. The weight of it—both physical and symbolic—made Markus' protest die in his throat. His fingers found the ancient metal, still warm from Nikel's hands.

Before he could find his voice again, Liyzia was there, unwinding her shawl. As she laid it in Markus' lap, their eyes met, and in that moment, all his doubts and fears quieted under her gentle telepathic touch.

The room, the mission, the impossible odds—all of it seemed to fade into a singular purpose.

Draven looked to Azlo, seeking something in his friend's face. The younger knight studied Markus for a long moment before nodding—not with confidence, but with faith. Sometimes, Markus realized, that was worth more.

Draven's gaze flicked between the pendant, the shawl, and Markus' still-lowered head. *The young man hadn't asked for this—yet he stood anyway.* That mattered.

The Immortal turned to Markus and extended his hand. Even the fire seemed to still.

Markus looked around the circle—at Nikel who had called him son, at Liyzia whose quiet strength filled the room, at Xara who gave him a subtle wink that spoke of a thousand battles already fought together. Then he stood and clasped Draven's hand.

The die had been cast. There would be no turning back.

MILES

0   10   20

DUNIDUIIR

VELUCIA

VELUCIAN RIVER

MOORWOOD FOREST

DRESSEN

BRESSELORN

NENEVUIIM

NUBENSOYRA

DURENVEL

NANISUIIR

LESSADOR

TRELUSYA

CENOVIRA

ORAVON

NORTH SEA

Map of Oravon – Northern Kingdoms and Forest Realms

PART II:

ALLIES AND ENEMIES

CHAPTER NINE

Morning's first breath stirred over Orwein's marketplace, washing the sky in soft ribbons of coral and gold. Early risers shook off the last vestiges of slumber, moving through the streets like shadows—farmers arranged their carts, bakers stoked ovens, merchants unfurled awnings in preparation for the day ahead. The morning air carried the sharp bite of autumn, heavy with dew and woodsmoke.

Finnor wove through the awakening marketplace with the peculiar ease of one who walked in two worlds at once. He tossed a coin to a fruit vendor without looking, yet somehow caught the apple that arced toward him as if it had called his name. Children giggled as he passed, delighting in the funny faces he pulled and the nonsense songs he hummed. Even the marketplace's many animals seemed drawn to him—cats wound between his legs, and the massive hushners lowered their heads for a friendly pat.

He paused at the market's edge, where the view opened to the distant Donaskan mountain range. The peaks rose like ancient guardians, their snow-capped summits ghostly in the morning light. Two young women, sorting through harvest fabrics nearby, caught him staring at them, and exchanged knowing looks.

"The great Donaskan peaks have a question," Finnor announced suddenly, turning to them with twinkling eyes. "They're quite curious as to why you chose tangerine orange for your harvest colors instead of sapphire pink. They find it a bold choice."

The women's laughter rang out like bells, but something in their eyes suggested they weren't entirely sure whether to take him seriously.

When Nikel appeared through the thinning mist, Finnor's demeanor shifted subtly. The seer's ever-present smile remained, but his eyes took on a sharper focus. Without a word exchanged, they fell into step together, leaving the marketplace behind for a winding path that led up the wooded hillside.

The path twisted through Shadowvein trees whose pale striations seemed to quiver in the strengthening morning light. Nikel's cane tapped a steady rhythm against the packed earth, marking their progress toward Finnor's dwelling. But halfway up the path, both men stopped short.

Liyzia stood before them as unexpected as a star at midday.

"I thought you decided to stay in your garden," Nikel said, his voice carrying equal measures of surprise and concern.

"Can a woman not change her mind?" Liyzia's lips curved in that mysterious smile that never failed to both charm and unsettle. "Besides, I need fresh air."

The two men exchanged glances. The distance between

Nikel's homestead and the market was not insignif-
icant—several miles at least. With Nikel's knee, he'd
taken their carriage. Yet here stood his wife, as if she'd
simply stepped out of the morning mist.

Liyzia moved past them up the path, humming a
melody that made the leaves shiver on their branches.
The question of how she'd arrived hung in the air
between the men, unasked and unanswered. It was
another mystery to add to the growing collection that
surrounded her— another whispered suggestion that
perhaps those who called her 'touched by the Ilyrians'
weren't simply repeating old wives' tales.

Finnor's garden appeared around the next bend.
This was a spiral of controlled chaos where medicinal
plants grew in patterns that followed some logic known
only to him. Crystal wind chimes hung from gnarled
branches, carrying messages in a language only he
seemed to understand. At the garden's heart stood an
enormous Mistweep tree with branches weeping morning dew.

The warmth of the morning sun had begun to assert
itself, so they gathered in the garden rather than entering the cottage. Finnor moved between his plants with
familiar ease, occasionally touching a leaf or flower as
if in greeting. But now his usual whimsy had faded; it
was replaced by something more solemn.

"I feel there's a coming darkness on the horizon,"
Nikel said, breaking the morning quiet.

Finnor acknowledged Nikel's words with a grave nod.
"The 'Whispering winds' have spoken these things to
me from afar."

"It is nearer than you think," Liyzia said quietly. Her

fingers traced the edge of a leaf with absent affection, but her eyes held a distance that suggested she saw far beyond Finnor's garden.

"I speak of a ... kaegar." Finnor uttered the word with careful precision. The very air seemed to shudder—leaves trembled without wind and the crystal chimes fell eerily silent. Even the morning birdsong ceased, as if nature itself recoiled from the word.

"Even the ancient spirits of the forests and animals detect their presence and react, in the same way they react to all of the magical beings in this world." His eyes fixed meaningfully on Liyzia.

"Don't you agree, Lady Liyzia?"

She met his gaze steadily, neither confirming nor denying the implication in his words.

"Kae..." Nikel started, then thought better of it. Even he, with his practical warrior's mindset, knew better than to speak such words in a Nevran seer's sanctuary.

"But only *one* of these beings' presence has been felt," Finnor pressed. "Lady Liyzia, does your heart confirm these things?"

"Deeper things than this occupy my mind." Her eyes found Nikel's, remembering his earlier words about darkness. "Darker things ..."

"Is the presence of a ..." Finnor caught himself from repeating it, "what I spoke ... roaming these lands, millennia after the great war? Is that not dark enough?"

"Finnor ..." she began.

"It is 'Elithor,' Lady Liyzia. Please." He bowed slightly, but there was an edge to his correction.

"I speak of another. I speak of those who walk between two worlds. Between two planes." Her voice remained soft, but it carried an authority that made even the Mistweep's branches still their weeping.

Nikel's expression darkened. "I only know of certain beings still lurking in darkness, capable of that."

"Yes, my Lord," she responded, "your thoughts are accurate."

"Shadow walkers," he spoke carefully, noting how the words seemed to have less impact than the forbidden term Finnor had used earlier.

The seer himself leaned forward, intrigued. "Very few can glimpse into the 'other' side and see them," he remarked.

Liyzia swallowed, dropping her hand from the plant she'd been tending. "I ... have seen one."

The silence that followed was absolute. Even the rustling leaves seemed to pause.

"Days ago—before everyone else departed."

"Are you ... sure?" Nikel's voice carried more concern than doubt.

"I am certain one was near. I felt a presence. For a fleeting moment. As swift as a breath from my nostrils. Swirling between shadow and light. It shuddered and fled the second I saw it."

"Were you frightened?"

"I do not frighten so easily." A faint smile touched her lips. "But I was ... disturbed."

"As I've spoken earlier," Finnor began, "it takes a special individual to see such things."

As Nikel took her hand, they watched Finnor move through his garden with renewed purpose. The seer bent to examine each plant in turn, catching every detail. But it was the way he kept glancing back at Liyzia that finally wore through her patience.

When he lifted a withered lumidawn flower in his palms, studying her reaction, she strode over and blew a sharp puff of air at it, rattling its dried petals. "There!" she said, acid sweetness in her tone. "I made it move. Shall I make it rise up and dance too for your entertainment?"

"Such modesty from a being who's walked with starlight!" Finnor murmured. "All it takes is a slither of a petal here ..."

Liyzia's hand flashed out, swatting the dead plant from his palm. It fell apart on the ground. Her eyes, usually warm and maternal, blazed with something primordial and ferocious.

"There! Now I made it disappear!" Her voice had a saccharine edge. "Shall I turn you into a cloud of smoke next?"

"My dear!" Nikel stepped forward, more concerned about offending a powerful seer than his wife's threats.

Finnor merely hummed, tilting his head as he studied her with that infuriating mystical gaze. "It is okay, Lord Nikel. The last thing you want to do in the presence of an Ilyrian is to ignite their ire ..."

Nikel moved swiftly between them as Finnor, suddenly finding great interest in gathering the scattered lumidawn remnants, crouched down while still humming his ethereal tune.

Liyzia's eyes rolled skyward, but the look she gave the seer could have withered his entire garden. "If you call me that one more time, Finnor ..."

"My dear!" Nikel's hand found hers, squeezing gently. Rising with the dead plant cradled in his hands, Finnor glanced between it and Liyzia. "I was going to ask you to use your powers to heal it ..." A slight smile played at his lips, "but I won't push my luck."

"Finnor!" Nikel's patience had worn thin. "What is the purpose of our visit? For you to rattle my wife's nerves?"

"Oh, I am not rattled, my Lord." Liyzia touched his hand, then fixed Finnor with a steady gaze. "I know why we're here. Finnor has something to share—a rare word in the old language that he's hesitant to speak out."

Nikel looked to the seer. "And what word is that?"

"*Ka'ene*," Finnor uttered, and Nikel's eyes narrowed. "You mean ... *Kane*. Don't you?"

"The one she's given her blessing to, Lord Nikel."

"His name is Markus."

"His *identity* is Ka'ene."

Silently, Nikel met his wife's eyes as all traces of whimsy fell away from the seer.

"That name came through the 'whispering winds' to me that day when .... when *he* drew near to you, Lady Liyzia. In the marketplace. It was as though Nature recognized him as he approached. He carries a thread—a rare, long-lost thread connected to the old world."

Liyzia's expression remained carefully neutral, neither confirming nor denying the seer's words.

Finnor's gaze was intentional and sincere. "Surely, you recognize this? Surely, you see these signs in him?"

Though her lips parted, she hesitated. "I see greater things in him, Finnor."

"Greater? Such as?"

"A purpose."

He smiled. "Your charity is both a noble and powerful virtue. But ..."

"Finnor," she cut him off, though her voice remained calm. "Do the whispering winds tell you anything else concerning my dear Markus?"

The seer glanced at Nikel respectfully. "They are silent ... for the moment."

Her gaze lingered on the seer as though searching inside of him. She then turned to her husband. "The air has grown thick and rather suffocating here. I will wait till you two are finished."

She moved away, drawing her cloak tight as she gazed toward the distant mountains.

Nikel turned to face the seer, once his wife was out of earshot, yards up the forest trail. "Anyone could have crossed through these woods that day."

"True. But these things of old do not stir for just *anyone*," Finnor whispered, and stepped closer. "You've even asked yourself, why him? I believe we will soon find out."

"We?" Nikel raised an eyebrow.

The weather-beaten seer smiled. "I am just a lore keeper, like you. If the legends are true, he will need every watchful eye covering him with protection— should that storm ever rise again."

Nikel pondered on the seer's words before exchanging a farewell.

Finnor moved to sweep away the crushed petals. But he stopped short. Where moments ago, lay only dust, the lumidawn stood whole again, its petals carrying an impossible sheen that caught the morning light. More than that, it seemed to radiate a faint inner radiance, as if touched by something older than the kingdom itself. The seer's laugh was soft but knowing. Some questions, he knew, answered themselves.

Moments later, Nikel caught up to his wife and they began their walk back toward the marketplace.

"Good old Elithor," Nikel joked, using the seer's true name.

"'Finnor,'" Liyzia corrected firmly, "until he regains my respect."

"My dear, we cannot take the whispering winds lightly, nor can you use it to hold a grudge when you disagree."

"It is not a grudge I hold. But what's hidden in my heart, that I protect."

"And what is that?"

"That young man will need our guidance, and your training: that we're to play an important part in his road ahead. And from that I will not waver."

"Another side of you is coming out. Like one of the great woolly bears of the Frigid Mountains, who protect their young against the courageous hunters! You must remember—he is not a child. There are battles he will face on his own."

"Of course! But it does not hurt to come to his aid every now and then. To look in on him."

Nikel chuckled. "Come to his aid?"

"Yes. Do I amuse you?"

"They are bound for Oravan. A thousand miles away! Will you swim across the swells of the great North Sea to reach him?"

Liyzia laughed, the sound bright as morning bells.

"My *Levuiilia*! Don't be ridiculous! Why swim? When I can simply ... walk!"

Nikel's laughter died in his throat as her words sank in. He stared at her, suddenly uncertain whether his wife had made a joke or casually revealed something impossible. The question of who—or what—she truly was pressed against his mind like hoarfrost.

But Liyzia had already begun humming her own melody, continuing down the path as if she hadn't made such a wild suggestion. Behind them, the crystal chimes in Finnor's garden rang out in harmony with her tune, though whether by wind or something else, who could say?

* * *

Markus stood at the edge of the ship's railing, staring out at the vast expanse of the Great North Sea. The world before him was a breathtaking merger of myth and reality, a realm both wondrous and ominous. Far in the distance, shrouded in mist and legend, lay the Heavenly Isles—their very name a whisper of something beyond human comprehension, perched on the edge of the known world.

"Quite the view, isn't it?" said Xara with a hint of awe as she joined him at the railing. Her usual sharp wit had softened in the face of such majesty. "Makes Vesper look like a child's playground."

The sea, usually a tempest of fury, was calm this morning. Unnervingly so. The smooth, glassy surface rippled in the first light of dawn, a golden path stretching out before the ship as if beckoning them forward. The hydro-cruisers cut through the water with ease, their streamlined forms gliding like sea creatures through the arctic blue.

He could still feel the weight of their parting gifts— Nikel's dagger at his hip, Liyzia's shawl around his waist. Xara absently touched the half-pendant around her neck, its twin resting against Markus' chest, the alq'arus, split between them as a reminder that neither walked this path alone.

"You're brooding again," said Xara, nudging him with her elbow. When he didn't respond, she sighed. "I know that look. You're wondering if I should have stayed behind."

"Can you blame me?" He turned to face her, lowering his voice. "Hans is dangerous enough when he's playing politician. Now he's desperate. If he recognizes you ...?"

"Then I'll handle it." She cut him off in that familiar steely voice. "I survived his attention before, didn't I?"

"That was different. You were just a forger then. Now you're ..."

"Now I'm what? A liability?" Her eyes flashed. "Need I remind you who got us out of Vesper? Who navigated us through that crash? Who ..."

"Who's arguing this early?" Draven's gravelly voice interrupted as he approached with Azlo close behind. The Immortal's dark armor seemed to absorb what little morning light reached it, while the knight's emerald leather caught the dawn like captured fire.

"Just a friendly disagreement about roles and capabilities," said Xara, her diplomatic mask sliding into place. "My brother seems to think I need constant protection."

Azlo's lips quirked in a slight smile. "And you disagree?"

"Vehemently."

"Then perhaps," the knight suggested, "we should test those capabilities. The journey is long, and the training need not be limited to one student."

Draven shot his companion a sharp look, but Azlo continued. "Unless you object to learning some of our ... particular skills?"

A sly grin spread across Xara's face. "Object? I thought you'd never ask."

Markus groaned. "You're encouraging her."

"No," Draven corrected, "we're acknowledging her. There's a difference." He fixed Markus with a steady gaze. "Your sister's talents kept you both alive this long. Rather than stifle them, why not help her refine them?"

"Besides," Azlo added, in a lighter tone, "would you rather have her unprepared when trouble finds us? Because it will find us, my friend. It always does."

Markus looked between them—his sister's determined face, Azlo's quiet wisdom, Draven's pragmatic acceptance—and felt his resistance crumbling. "Fine. But we do this carefully. Methodically."

"Of course," Xara agreed all too quickly.

"I mean it, Xara. No showing off, no unnecessary risks."

"You worry too much, brother dear." She was already following Azlo toward the training area, stepping light with anticipation. "Besides, isn't unnecessary risk my specialty?"

Draven clapped a heavy hand on Markus' shoulder. "She'll be fine. After all," he added with the ghost of a smile, "she survived you all these years, didn't she?"

Markus watched them go, with a mixture of pride and concern. The rising sun caught Xara's hair as she walked away, turning it to flame, and for a moment she looked like something more than his scrappy foster sister—a co-warrior in the making.

The sea stretched endlessly before them, breaking into gentle crests that caught the morning light like scattered gems. They were crossing more than just water, Markus realized. They were crossing into a new chapter of their lives—one where his role as protector would have to evolve into something else. Something equal.

He just prayed they were all ready for what waited on the other side.

Markus stood on the deck, ignoring the throng of passengers that swarmed around him as they disembarked. The approaching port of Cenovira, the southern gateway to Oravon, embodied the clash of old and new that defined these northern territories. Dozens of vessels plied the busy harbor; sleek hydro cruisers with Guild-certified propulsion systems glided past traditional sailing ships, timeworn wooden hulls reinforced by modern alloys. Between them, hybrid vessels showed how necessity bred innovation: steam-powered frigates retrofitted with salvaged hover technology, their crews adapting to survive outside Guild control.

"Look at that," Xara whispered, appearing at his elbow. She'd traded her usual attire for something more subdued—rough-spun wool and leather that helped her blend with the local merchants. "No crystalline towers. No hover lanes. Just raw survival against the elements."

Between the sturdy harbor buildings and long-houses, Markus caught glimpses of skiffs, speeders, and driftcycles zipping by in droves, but few carriages. Most people here appeared to prefer getting around on foot, braving the damp, frost-covered brick roads that wound inland toward the heart of the region—a center of governance and commerce where Guild influence waned against older powers.

The people of Oravon came into clearer view—a melting pot of races and species that stretched across the known world. He saw Nevrans from the eastern lands, some from distant colonies draped in Guild-certified heating cloaks, while others from tribal nations were wrapped in traditional furs. There were Dromelans, towering figures from the arctic empire, whose technology the Guild Engineers still struggled to understand, a rare, formidable sight. Northmen from the Skylands, bulky and brutish, mingled among the frail-looking Earthens, who already seemed overwhelmed by the bitter wind.

"Be cautious," Draven warned, in a low and firm voice. "This isn't a place for pleasantries. We're a long way from home. You'll find more warmth from an iceberg than from the folks on this boardwalk. At least till you get inland."

Before they reached the customs zone, Draven pulled them into the shadow of a harborside warehouse. Behind them, the loading cranes creaked over empty cargo bays, while ahead, the customs buildings marked the official entry into Oravon's port.

The Immortal's black armor seemed to drink in what little light reached them as he unslung a weapon case from his shoulder. "Oravon isn't kind to the unprepared."

He kept his voice low as he unlocked the case. Inside, nestled in foam padding, lay a NS-7 "Phantom" Resonance Pistol. "Markus, this is a step up from your Stinger."

He lifted the weapon, its dark chrome finish reflecting an iridescent sheen. "Guild-engineered resonance core. Creates a sonic disruption wave on impact that can incapacitate targets through most armor. Integrated thermal optics." He demonstrated the modular grip system. "And if things get ugly, the secondary plasma mode can cut through shield barriers."

Azlo stepped forward, presenting Xara with a VX-9 'Specter' Tactical Sidearm. "More subtle than your Whispershot," he explained, his voice gentler than Draven's but no less serious. "Quantum-stabilized rounds that phase through cover before re-materializing. Perfect for when stealth is paramount." He showed her the crystalline power cell. "The targeting assist links to your neural patterns—it'll feel like an extension of your arm after a few practice shots."

Xara ran her fingers over the weapon's sleek contours. "Adaptive harmonics in the barrel?"

"Good eye," Azlo nodded. "It learns from each shot, adjusting the quantum frequency for maximum effectiveness. The Guild's latest achievement in miniaturized format."

"These aren't standard issue," Draven added, handing them both specialized power cores. "They're prototype weapons from the royal armory. Use them wisely—and keep them hidden. The wrong people see these, and they'll know exactly who sent you."

Markus weighed the Phantom in his hand, feeling the

subtle vibe of its resonance core. This was far beyond the street weapons he was used to—this was the kind of technology that could change the course of a fight, or a mission.

Draven's warning rang true as Markus took in the sight of the locals. Beneath their thick furs, leather hides, and winter pelts, weapons of all kinds were barely concealed—holsters, grips, and blades. Even with the local militia patrolling the docks to keep the peace, it was clear that violence could erupt at any moment. Here, strength was as common as breath, and peace was something earned, not given.

Xara's hand brushed his arm—a signal they'd developed in their street days. Her eyes motioned toward a group of men moving through the crowd with too much purpose—"We're being watched."

Markus nodded imperceptibly. He'd noticed them too—the way they cut through the crowd with practiced ease, too coordinated to be random dock workers.

"Wait here," Draven instructed Markus and the others, gesturing toward the harbor's food court. "We'll secure transport."

The recruits made their way to a table by a large window, seeking temporary refuge from the chaos outside. Inside, the air was no less overbearing—the scent of strong ale and spiced meats, competing with the pungent perfumes of passersby. The din of the harbor seeped through the walls—the low drum of cranes, the blare of ship horns, the chatter of voices speaking in a dozen different languages.

The tavern was abuzz with chatter and clinking glasses. Markus sat at his table, eyes focused on the grime-streaked window, through which the harbor was faintly visible. Xara sat with her back to the wall, her posture relaxed but her eyes constantly moving. She'd positioned herself perfectly—able to watch both the door and the window while appearing to simply be enjoying her drink.

Her fingers tapped an idle pattern on the table, but Markus recognized it as their old code: *Danger. Three men. Coming in.*

He didn't need to turn around to know who it was. A familiar voice cut through the noise.

"You gentlemen thirsty? Drinks are on me."

Hans Lumen's refined tones were as out of place here as a silk scarf in a gutter. Markus felt Xara tense beside him, though nothing in her posture betrayed it. She'd drawn her shawl closer, letting its hood shadow her features—as if just another weary traveler seeking warmth.

Luc and Cypran, two other recruits, practically fled toward the bar, eager to escape the sudden shift in atmosphere. Coins clinked on the table as Hans stepped into view, taking a seat across Markus. His back was to the window, facing the harbor beyond.

The noise around faded as Hans settled into his chair.

"What a small world this is, Mr. Kane!" Hans said, his aristocratic voice carrying that same unsettling warmth it had in Vesper.

"Not small enough," Markus replied, the words clipped, his gaze steady.

Hans smiled, gesturing to a waiter with two fingers. The man brought over their drinks—coffee for Markus, something more refined for Hans. The two men, though separated by their differences, shared a cautious stillness. They were both far from home, in unfamiliar territory, each knowing that the other wasn't alone in this foreign city.

Markus took a sip of his coffee, eyes never leaving Hans. Every nerve in his body was telling him to get up—strike, do something. But it would be foolish. Whatever protection this restless city gave him, it wouldn't last if he made a move here. And Hans, with all his connections, knew that.

"Life's gotta suck," Hans began, breaking the silence, "with the type of work you do."

Markus shrugged, the bitterness hidden beneath his casual tone. "It's a livin'."

"Is it?" Hans pressed in. "I've read about you—your suspension from boxing after nearly killing two men. Fired from the mines and docks. Now scraping by on whatever you can find. No credentials, no future."

Markus' jaw clenched. "You're a senator. You looking to fix that?"

"The two of you turning yourselves in would be a start."

From the corner of his eye, Markus caught the slightest of pauses in Xara's movements—a breath held too long—before she resumed her careful anonymity.

"You're one to talk," Markus said. "Your hands are all over the mines in the Bronze Hills. Bankrolling those dirty lawmen and deputies. How much of the pie is Vitelli giving you?"

Hans leaned forward slightly, his voice dropping just enough to seem personal. "Corruption is profitable. So is counterfeiting and forgery. You should know."

"There's a difference," Markus said, "between sitting at the table and clawing for scraps underneath it."

Hans chuckled softly, shaking his head. "The cards you're dealt don't matter, kid. You can have every-thing—the right people in your corner, all the power in the world—and still feel empty."

"Yeah? In that case, I guess we're both feeling pretty at home here."

Hans' smile faltered for a second, as his eyes scanned the room as if making sure no one was listening too closely. "Did you and your friends come here alone? Looking to get away?"

"That depends," Markus said coolly, "on your defini-tion of 'friends.'"

"And the young woman who keeps patching you up? She's not with you, is she?"

Markus' grip tightened around the cup. Behind Hans, through the grimy window, he could see Draven and Azlo returning across the dock. "She's smart enough to stay away from criminals like you."

Hans reached inside his coat, slowly, carefully, and slid something across the table. Markus' eyes fell on the pamphlet—a bounty poster with Xara's face staring back at him. Five million crowns! The artist had cap-tured her perfectly: the determined set of her jaw, the intelligence in her eyes. Everything that made her both remarkable and dangerous.

Xara's fingers had stopped their tapping entirely. She sat perfectly still, like a prey to a predator's approach. But Markus knew better—she wasn't afraid. She was calculating.

Hans rose from his chair, his movements deliberate.

"In case you get tired of running," he said, dropping a card onto the table with his contact information. "I'd keep an eye out if I were you. No telling who you'll run into in a place like this."

As Hans walked away, Markus caught Xara's reflection in the window. For just a moment, their eyes met in the glass. In that brief glance, he saw everything— her fury, her determination, and beneath it all, a fierce joy at having outwitted Hans yet again. She might be in hiding, but she was far from helpless. If anything, being this close to Hans, while remaining undetected, was its own kind of victory.

The tavern seemed to exhale as Hans disappeared into the crowd, just as Draven and Azlo arrived with Luc and Cypran in tow. Markus scanned the room one last time. No sign of Hans. He took another sip of coffee, but it tasted bitter now. His mind replayed every moment, every word, while beside him, Xara resumed her quiet observation of the room, anonymous as ever.

But there was something different in her posture now—like a coiled spring waiting to be released. Hans hadn't just threatened them. He'd challenged them. And if Markus knew his sister at all, she was already planning her response.

* * *

Three days in Lessador had taught them the rhythm of the old quarter, where aging brick and weathered stone pressed against modern metal façades like reluctant neighbors. Steam from the underground vents mingled with the December chill, creating an ever-present haze over streets where hover vehicles steered cautiously past horse-drawn carts.

Draven's silence had grown more pronounced with each passing day. No word from Mercury meant no way to reach the Prefect through official channels, which left them with far riskier options.

"The communications facility," he'd finally said that morning, conveying the gravity of a decision long-considered. "If there's any contact between the Prefect and the Governor, it will pass through there."

Xara had smiled then, the kind of smile that reminded Markus of countless schemes back in Vesper. "Well then," she'd said, "it's a good thing you have someone who speaks their language."

They huddled in the shadow of an abandoned merchant's stall, whose weather-beaten awning provided cover from both the winter wind and prying eyes. Markus kept his hood pulled low, while Xara had traded her usual attire for the garb of a local servant.

Draven's voice was low as he studied the facility's entrance from behind stacked crates of apples. "The main hub is on the third floor. Security will be minimal—they rely more on authorization protocols than guards."

"Good thing I brought my own protocols," Xara said, patting the hidden pocket where she'd already stashed a stolen ID card. Three days of watching the facility's routines had taught her the operators' schedules, their habits, their vulnerabilities.

Markus shifted beneath his hood, clearly unhappy with the plan. "If Hans' people should spot you ..."

"Then I'll give them something else to look at," Azlo

interrupted smoothly, adjusting his formal attire. He looked every inch the visiting dignitary, the perfect distraction, if need be.

The communications facility rose before them with its crystalline spires contrasting starkly with the brick and stone buildings around. Modern security sensors swept the entrance, but Xara had marked the blind spots days ago. More importantly, she'd noticed how the veteran operator always took his lunch break precisely at two bells, leaving only his young apprentice to watch the monitors.

Draven melted into the crowd, a shadow among shadows. Markus followed, though his stillness carried more tension than stealth. Time to move.

Xara nodded to Azlo and began their approach, with measured steps. She'd done this dance countless times in Vesper. The key was to belong—to move with such natural confidence that your presence was never in question by anyone watching.

The apprentice barely glanced up as they entered the lobby, Azlo's noble bearing drawing what little attention there was. Xara kept her movements fluid and unhurried, as she drifted toward the restricted access door. Three floors up, encrypted transmissions held the information they needed. But first ...

She spotted their target—the senior operator, right on schedule, heading for his afternoon meal. His security badge gleamed at his hip, practically begging to be stolen. Xara brushed past him, her fingers dancing through the motion she'd perfected in Vesper's crowded markets. The badge vanished into her sleeve.

One piece down. Now for the hard part.

The service lift carried them upward. Azlo positioned himself casually by the door, his enhanced senses alert for any approach. The stolen badge felt warm in Xara's palm. Too many things could go wrong. But then, that had never stopped her before.

The doors opened to sterile white corridors lined with vibrating technology—a sharp contrast to the aged stonework below. Glass-walled offices branched off the main hall, most of them empty at this hour. The few technicians they passed barely glanced up from their data screens

"Third door on the right," Xara murmured, from memory. "The main hub. Restricted access."

Azlo gave an almost imperceptible nod, taking up position near a window with clear sightlines in both directions. To anyone passing, he appeared absorbed in reading transmissions on his personal tablet.

The security panel chimed softly as Xara swiped the stolen badge. Inside, rows of crystal terminals cast a pale blue glow across the empty workspace. The operator's station still displayed active transmissions—he hadn't even logged out before leaving. Sloppy, fortunately.

Her fingers moved swiftly across the interface, muscle memory from years of forging documents that guided her through encryption patterns. Cargo manifests, routine communications, security protocols ... there! A heavily encrypted channel, recently active.

A soft whistle from the corridor—Azlo's warning. Someone approaching.

Xara's hands flew across the keys, trying to access the encrypted data. The screen flared to life. Vessel documentation. The Nightshade. Arrival manifest sealed under highest security clearance. Just a glimpse of the cargo hold specs before ...

Heavy boots in the hallway. Not the operator's familiar tread.

Xara slid beneath the desk, heart racing. Through the gap beneath the door, she saw black boots pause. A moment of absolute stillness.

The door opened with deliberate slowness.

A tall figure entered like liquid shadow, a predatorial grace about his movements. Her fingers curled around the small blade hidden in her sleeve.

But his attention was fixed on the screen, still displaying the Hydra's manifest. One gloved hand reached out, hovering over the interface.

Now. While he was distracted ... Xara slipped from her hiding spot, every movement calculated to avoid detection. Three steps to the door. Two. One ...

His head snapped around, eyes locking onto the space she'd vacated a heartbeat before. But she was already through the door, moving with the silent precision that had kept her alive in Vesper's deadliest alleys.

The tall figure emerged from the room with the casualness of a carnivore ready to pounce on its prey. His yellow eyes scanned up and down the hall with a hint of a sparkle in them, as he laid eyes on her from behind.

Rathmar.

* * *

The corridor stretched before her, suddenly endless. Behind her, Rathmar emerged from the office with unnatural quiet. No running footsteps, no shouts of pursuit. Just that steady, inexorable presence drawing closer.

Xara wove between startled technicians, her movements fluid as water. A dropped datapad here, a stumbling worker there, small obstacles in her wake. But Rathmar moved through the clutter like smoke, undeterred.

The lift was too obvious. The stairs too enclosed. Which left ...

She caught Azlo's eye as she passed. The knight's expression didn't change, but his hand moved slightly, gesturing toward the western exit. The maintenance access.

Rathmar's reflection ghosted across a glass partition. Closer now. Still moving with that terrible patience.

Xara slipped through the maintenance door, into a maze of service corridors lit by stuttering crystal lamps. The air grew colder, carrying the scent of metal and old stone. Above, pipes and cables twisted along the ceiling like mechanical vines.

A shadow fell across the wall ahead—but from the wrong direction. Rathmar was herding her, she realized, using her own escape route against her.

Without notice, she changed direction, relying on muscle memory from years of evading Vesper's guards. Down became up. She grabbed a pipe, swinging herself into a maintenance shaft as Rathmar's form entered the corridor below.

The shaft opened onto the facility roof. Bitter wind cut through her clothes as she emerged into fading daylight. Below, Lessador's mix of historic and modern architecture presented a deadly puzzle of ledges and drops.

Behind her, the access hatch opened silently.

"Impressive," Rathmar's voice carried across the roof, cold as the wind. "But ultimately futile."

Xara didn't waste breath responding. The gap to the next building was wide—too wide for most to attempt. But she wasn't most people.

She ran, building momentum. The edge rushed toward her. No time to second-guess.

She leapt.

For a moment, only wind and sky and the sickening drop below. Then her feet found the opposite ledge, decades of rooftop escapes guiding her into a roll that absorbed the impact.

Rising, she risked a glance back. Rathmar stood at the edge, making no move to follow. But his stillness carried a certainty that chilled her more than any pursuit.

He knew something she didn't.

Movement caught her eye—dark figures emerging onto neighboring rooftops. Not guards. Something worse. More Dromelans ... positioned to cut off her escape routes.

The hunt was just beginning.

* * *

Xara spared a precious second to scan her surroundings. Three of Rathmar's hunters on adjacent rooftops. Two more scaling the building to her left. Their movements held that same unnatural grace as their leader— too fluid, too precise to be fully human.

Below, afternoon crowds thronged the streets, unaware of the deadly game playing out above. Market stalls and vendor carts created a maze of color and motion. Somewhere in that maze, Draven and Markus waited. But getting to them meant getting down. And getting down meant ...

A crossbow bolt whistled past her ear.

Right. No more planning.

She sprinted across the rooftop, boots gripping the rain-slicked tiles. The first hunter reached for her as she passed. Xara dropped, sliding beneath his grasp, her momentum carrying her toward a slanted section of roof. No time to slow down. She let herself fall.

The world tilted. Wind rushed past. Her hands caught a decorative ledge, redirecting her descent toward a stone gargoyle. She swung, muscles straining, launching herself toward a merchant's awning two stories below. The fabric caught her, tearing but slowing her fall. She rolled off onto a balcony, startling a woman hanging laundry. "Sorry!" Xara called, already moving. Through the apartment, past a shocked family at dinner, out their front door into the building's stairwell.

Boots thundered above. They were following her down, trying to cut off her exits. But they didn't know these kinds of buildings like she did. In Vesper, every runner learned that old buildings held secrets.

There it was—beneath the stairs. A maintenance tunnel, probably centuries old, back when the building relied on steam power. She pried the rusted grate loose and slipped inside.

The tunnel was a tight fit, thick with dust and cobwebs. But it led downwards, angling toward the street.

Behind her, voices argued in some unrecognizable language. They'd lost her trail.

Light filtered through another grate below. The street was close, but ...

She stopped breathing. In that shaft of light, she saw it. A thread of a shadow that moved wrong, curling like smoke against natural laws.

They weren't just following her trail. They were scenting her somehow.

New plan.

Xara backed up three feet and kicked the grate with everything she had. It burst outward in a shower of rust, taking a chunk of wall with it. The noise would draw them instantly.

Perfect.

She swung out of the tunnel into a storage room, her exit masked by the falling debris. Not stopping to see if her diversion worked, she shouldered through a door into what had to be the building's old boiler room. Antiquated pipes created a lattice of shadows and steam.

A figure dropped from above, landing between her and the exit. Another hunter followed, this one wearing some kind of fitted mask that covered its entire face.

Behind her, more shapes moved in the steam.

Surrounded.

* * *

Steam hissed through the old pipes as Xara studied her surroundings. The Dromelan's measured steps echoed behind her—unhurried, confident. No wasted movement. Even without knowing his identity, she recognized the calculated precision of someone who enjoyed the hunt.

The boiler room's architecture offered a tangle of pipes and valves. But he was herding her, she realized. Each step had been orchestrated, driving her exactly where he wanted.

His voice carried through the steam.

"Fascinating," he said, the word marked with an accent she couldn't place. "Such skill. Such grace. I begin to understand the senator's ... fixation."

Xara's breath caught. He knew who she was.

Her blade found the pressure valve without looking. Ancient metal shrieked as steam erupted between them. She was already moving, years of evading Vesper's guards guiding her through the jumble.

But his reaction wasn't what she expected. No shouts. No pursuit. Just that same measured pace, as though her escape attempt amused him.

The maintenance tunnel beckoned ahead—her final gambit. But as she reached it, his shadow fell across the wall.

"A shame," his voice came ... impossibly close by. "That such talent serves such limited purpose."

Xara didn't waste breath responding. The gap to the next section of tunnel was narrow—too narrow for his larger frame. But she wasn't running blindly anymore. That calculating tone, the way he'd mentioned Hans ... he wasn't just trying to catch her. He was assessing her.

She had become quarry in a larger game.

* * *

She moved like liquid shadow, every motion calculated. Not running—that's what prey did. Instead, she flowed through the narrow gap, her movements as precise as any forgery she'd crafted.

Light filtered through gaps ahead. Street sounds. Freedom. But it felt too easy now.

"The senator sends his regards," Rathmar called after her, still making no move to pursue. "Though I suspect we'll have our own conversation soon enough."

The exit was just ahead. Xara could taste cold air, hear the marketplace beyond. But his words followed her like ice down her spine. This hadn't been a chase—it had been an introduction.

She burst into afternoon sunlight, immediately merging with the crowd's flow. Azlo materialized beside her, his casual stride masking combat-ready tension.

"Company?" he asked quietly.

Xara risked a glance back at the building. No sign of pursuit. Just the memory of that calculating voice, those knowing words.

"Worse," she managed, her voice steadier than she felt. "Politics."

They found Markus and Draven in the predetermined location—a dimly lit corner of The Broken Barrel, a tavern frequented by dock workers where strangers drew less attention than usual. The smell of spiced ale and woodsmoke provided comfortable anonymity as Xara slid into the booth, her heart still racing from the chase.

Her brother's eyes searched her face, reading the tension there. She forced a smile, and made her shoulders relax.

Some truths were better left unspoken. Hans knowing she was here would change everything— force them to abandon their plans, maybe even leave the island. No. Better to carry this danger alone, at least until she figured out the game these hunters were playing.

"No word on the Prefect, or any vessels from Celavon," she reported instead, focusing on the mission. "Just private vessels arriving from the mainland. Custom containment systems in the cargo hold. Transporting spice and other 'non-mentionables.'"

But even as they discussed next steps, she let Rathmar's words sink in. She hadn't just been discovered—she'd been measured, evaluated. And, somehow, that felt far more dangerous than mere pursuit.

CHAPTER TEN

The unexpected news in the intelligence reports brought Governor Tarnsford to his study before dawn. The room offered a commanding view of the harbor, where morning fog rolled in from the North Sea.

The governor was forced to confront two valuable documents in his possession whose implications kept him from sleeping. They laid before him upon his executive desk—carrying secrets heavier than the gathering storm clouds.

The first bore two signatures: his own, and the late King Ronan's, its ink long since devolved to the color of dried blood. The second, hastily concealed beneath trade reports entered by his aide, detailed tonight's shipments along the Velucian river—the kind of manifest that never saw official ledgers.

Duty and profit. Honor and necessity. The balance had seemed simpler once.

A discrete knock on the door broke the silence—three soft taps, identifying one of his most trusted advisors.

"Enter."

His aide, Callum, closed the door behind him before

approaching the desk. The man's face was drawn, his usual composure missing. Callum leaned in close, "My Lord, they've been spotted. Making port in Cenovira." No names needed—they both knew who 'they' meant. The governor's fingers briefly stroked the wax seal of the late King's signet impression on one of the documents.

"Far ahead of schedule."

Tarnsford's hands moved swiftly, sliding the spice manifest beneath a faux panel in his desk drawer. The action wasn't lost on Callum, whose careful blank expression suggested years of practice at not seeing such things.

"The weather service reports ..." Callum began at normal volume, smoothly shifting to their public conversation.

"How long?" Tarnsford interrupted softly.

"Given the terrain between here and ..." Callum's eyes pointed meaningfully upward—the north, where the Velucian river wound through Moorwood's forest. "They could reach the location by nightfall."

The governor's jaw tightened. A day's ride, perhaps less, with the resources at the Prefect's disposal. But moving an entire security detail through his territory without drawing attention was no small matter.

"Send word to Captain Doren," he ordered. "The Sentinels are to mobilize quickly. No uniforms, no insignia. They're to secure the perimeter without being seen. And, Callum ..." He paused, choosing his next words carefully. "There have also been reports of increased activity along the river. Unauthorized vessels."

"The usual traders, my Lord?"

"Perhaps. But spice runners usually don't operate so

boldly. Unless it's someone else testing my defenses, sniffing around that area."

"I'll send some of our scouts ..."

"No," Tarnsford interrupted softly, "That's what the sentinels are for."

The governor's eye caught a glimpse of the ominous clouds lurking on the distant horizon beyond the sunrise. "Have our Nevran advisors reported anything ... unusual?"

"They've been unsettled, my Lord. Speaking of strange things like 'whispers on the wind.' Of darkness stirring. These people have a peculiar way with their words."

"Don't you believe in such things, Callum?"

"My beliefs in the Nevran's cryptic forecasts have little import, my Lord. Though I would advise you to be bit more *pragmatic* and inquire from modern meteorologists whose ..."

"Whose blind reliance on modern equipment dismiss subtle omens."

Thunder rolled in the distance, as if emphasizing his words. Tarnsford moved to the window, studying the clouds gathering over the North Sea. They were darker than any he'd seen this season, and moving against the prevailing winds.

"Double the patrols along the Velucian river," he said finally. "Discreetly. Whatever game these strangers are playing, Zone 33 remains sacrosanct." He turned back to Callum. "And send word through our ... unofficial channels. I want to know who's asking questions about restricted areas."

The aide bowed and withdrew, leaving Tarnsford alone with his thoughts and the growing darkness beyond his window. The oath he'd sworn to the late King Ronan went beyond mere politics. Zone 33 wasn't just a sanctuary—it was a trust, paid for in royal blood.

But as he watched the storm approach, a deeper unease settled in his chest. Some prices, once paid, kept collecting interest. And he couldn't shake the feeling that accounts were about to come due.

* * *

The back room of The Wandering Huntsman was all shadows and secrets, where even the lamplight seemed reluctant to reach the corners. Maps of Oravon lay scattered across a heavy oak table, their edges curling in the damp air from the harbor.

Hans preferred it this way—let the more prominent establishments draw attention, while real business happened in places people tried not to notice. The tavern's name, meant to draw in simple wilderness guides and trackers, held no hint of the ancient predator they planned to unleash.

The mariner's hands shook as he placed the glass back on the table, spilling drops of amber liquid across the carefully arranged maps. Sweat beaded on his forehead despite the room's chill.

"You're certain?" Hans asked, his voice carrying that dangerous calm his associates had learned to fear. His own hands were smooth and steady as he poured his guest another drink.

"The Prefect arrived ahead of schedule?"

"Y-yes, sir." The mariner's eyes darted to the corners where shadows seemed to move of their own accord.

"Is it reliable?"

"My ... contact in the Governor's mansion is well established. The Governor's Sentinels are mobilizing—quietly. No uniforms. They're heading toward the upper Velucian."

Hans exchanged glances with Rathmar, who stood like living darkness in the corner. The Dromelan's presence seemed to absorb what little light reached him, as if the shadows themselves were drawn to him. "Zone 33," Hans mused. "Tell me, what makes a governor deploy his elite forces to protect an empty stretch of forest?"

The mariner swallowed hard. "There's more. One of the Governor's Nevran advisors ... I heard him warning about dark omens. About forgotten evil walking again."

Hans' eyes met Rathmar's with a casual nod and a manipulative gaze, balancing their mutual understanding with a subtle hint of contention.

"Mr. Rathmar, I believe he's speaking your language."

"Indeed, Senator. Arrakos' hour has come."

The words hung in the air like icicles. Hans studied Rathmar's expression, noting how the Dromelan's usual calculated calm had shifted to something hungrier. They both knew what waited in the hold of The Nightshade—a power older than the islands themselves, straining against bonds that even Rathmar's elder tongue could barely control.

* * *

Dawn crept through the barracks window, painting golden stripes across Markus' face. For a moment, the warmth soothed his scar's constant throb. These quiet seconds before the day's brutality were precious. They allowed a space to breathe, to remember why he'd chosen this path.

His fingers found Liyzia's shawl, tucked carefully beneath his pillow. The fabric seemed to hold traces of home, of belonging. Of purpose.

Then the batons struck iron.

All fifteen recruits jolted awake to the sharp clatter of the iron batons striking their bed frames. Some sprang up instantly, others fumbled in panic. The instructors moved silently through the barracks; their presence was more threatening than any shout could be.

Markus pulled on his fatigues, fingers catching on the nameplate stitched above the pocket. KANE. The letters seemed to burn under his touch, and for a moment, the world tilted. Voices from his past crowded his mind— the taunts, the jeers, the cruel laughter that followed that name through every orphanage and street fight.

"Check the freak's face," a nearby voice cut through his memories. "What kind of scar is that?"

Ryder and Ellis. Of course. Their sneers were familiar; he'd seen that same look in every alley and fighting pit in Vesper.

The words died as Draven's hand landed on Ryder's shoulder. The Immortal's grip must have been brutal, but his voice remained eerily calm.

"See this?" Draven traced a deep scar of his own along his forearm. "Each mark tells a story of survival. Mock another man's battles again, and I'll give you some stories of your own to tell."

The tension crackled. Markus continued his preparation, movements precise, controlled. But something was different. His temples throbbed with a familiar heat, and his vision swam at the edges. Whether these symptoms were from the arctic air, or just the forebodings of something that awaited him, he couldn't ignore them for long. They were getting worse.

* * *

The first few days were a blur of brutal conditioning beneath Oravon's steely skies. Their breath frosted in bursts during the pre-dawn exercises, the push-ups continuing until arms gave out against the frozen ground. Runs seemed endless through terrain that alternated between frost-hardened earth and treacherous mud, where the weak arctic sun never fully warmed the soil. Combat drills left them bruised and gasping in the biting wind that swept down from the northern peaks, carrying the promise of deeper winter.

Through it all, Markus felt the changes in his body—a slow burn that grew hotter with each passing day, in sharp contrast to the numbing cold that claimed more recruits every morning. Some dropped, their bodies unable to adapt to both the brutality of training and the merciless climate. Others learned to move with the cold, to use its bite as fuel rather than let it break them.

Markus endured, but each night the nightmares grew worse. Dreams of endless mirrors where his reflection moved independently, observing himself with eyes that weren't quite his own. He saw corridors that twisted into Moorwood's bowels, where shadows reached for him with hungry hands. Sometimes he had glimpses of his younger self—scenes of his blood turning black as it dripped from his temple. Other times, something antediluvian and predatory stared back from his reflection, as if his cursed blood recognized a darkness older than time.

He would wake gasping, as his scar throbbed in the darkness, never sure if the shadows in the corners were real or imaginary. The symptoms were changing too—his blood didn't just burn now; it seemed to quicken with an awareness of something drawing closer. Even awake, he couldn't shake the feeling that his reflection might show something else if he dared look too long—something that had always been there, waiting to be discovered.

His scar drummed like a second heartbeat, and sometimes, in the pre-dawn darkness, he could swear the shadows moved against the light.

* * *

Dawn came again, different this time. Markus woke before the batons, his scar burning hotter than ever. The golden light that had once soothed him now felt like fire against his skin. Four days of brutal training had changed him; but something else was changing too.

He pressed his forehead against the cool window, watching distant storm clouds gather against the wind. Below, the training ground waited like an arena. His muscles ached from countless pushups, endless runs, but it was the deep burn in his blood that concerned him.

He felt a familiar presence move to his side. It was Xara, posing as an attendant to the camp's physician.

"Can't sleep either?" Xara's whisper came from the

shadows. She moved to his side, in her nurse's attire. Her presence was a reminder of why he endured this. Her fingers brushed his scar, recoiling at its heat. "That thing on your face—it's getting darker."

Markus touched his scar reflexively. The tissue felt hot, almost alive.

Before he could answer, the batons struck iron. Another day. Another test.

* * *

"Again!" Viktor barked, but Markus caught the concern in the Immortal's eyes. All the instructors had been watching him closer lately, their usual stoic demeanor cracking just enough to show unease.

The day progressed in waves of exertion and pain beneath a sun that hung low and heavy on the horizon. Other recruits dropped from exhaustion, but Markus was engaged with something deeper. Each hour brought new symptoms—heightened senses that made every sound too sharp, every shadow too deep. His body felt like a weapon being forged—though for what battle, he couldn't say. Through the bitter cold, the setting sun painted the winter sky in fierce oranges and crimsons. But even as the natural fire faded from the sky, the burn in his blood grew hotter.

* * *

The mess hall buzzed with tired voices; its warmth contrasted sharply to the darkness pressing against frost-rimmed windows. Modern heating elements drummed beneath stone walls, but it was the massive hearth that drew everyone closer. Xara slid the intelligence report across the wooden table to Draven. Her movements were casual despite the tension in her shoulders. Her attention kept drifting to where Markus sat alone in the shadows beyond the hearth's glow, absently pushing food around his plate.

"There's something ... odd about him," Draven said quietly.

Her fingers stilled on her cup, a subtle warning.

"Well?" Draven continued, "You're his guardian angel, aren't you? What's his story?"

Her eyes glanced toward Markus, then back to her plate. "Some stories aren't mine to tell." She paused, then continued softly. "Even I don't know that one. Never asked. Never needed to."

The protectiveness in her voice made further questions die in Draven's throat.

* * *

That night, Markus barely slept. His scar throbbed with each passing hour, as if counting down to something inevitable. When the batons struck iron in the pre-dawn darkness, he was already awake, his blood singing with strange anticipation.

The march to the cliffs took them through terrain that grew steadily more treacherous. Rocks slippery with frost threatened every step as they approached the coast. The North Sea's fury grew from distant thunder to deafening rage and the wind cut sharper here as salt spray and bitter cold penetrated the bone.

Then the Walls of Dressen appeared through the morning mist.

At first, Markus could only stare in wonder. Three hundred feet of rock stretched toward the gray sky, its face carved by millennia of wind and waves into something that looked more like a sleeping giant than mere stone. The sight stirred something in his blood—a recognition of age and power that both awed and unsettled him.

"The Walls," one of the recruits whispered with native dread, "legends say they hunger for climbers."

Markus might have dismissed such talk as local superstition, if not for the way his scar trembled in response to the rock face. Below, massive swells crashed against the cliff base, sending spray high enough to drench the first thirty feet of stone. Those who chose the sea route would face not just the frigid water, but the risk of being smashed against the rocks by waves that seemed to reach like hungry hands.

"Last test before sunset," Viktor announced, his voice barely carrying over the howling wind. "Choose your path. The sea. Or the wall."

Even the safety lines seemed a meager comfort as Markus studied the wall. The sea was certain death—he had barely survived the harbor swim. But something about the cliff face made his scar throb with warning. The ancient rock seemed to watch them, patient and hungry.

The first recruits had already begun their ascent when he heard it—a sound that shouldn't have been possible. A low groan emanated from within the rock itself, like some giant stirring from sleep. One of the handholds suddenly shifted, melting back into the wall as if it had never existed. A recruit's scream cut through the wind as he lost his grip, the safety line snapping taut with a crack that made everyone flinch.

"The wall is living!" someone shouted. "It's moving!"

"It's moving!" The words echoed off the cliff face, answered by another chilling groan from the rock. Markus watched in horrified fascination as sections of stone twisted and extended like living clay, forcing climbers to leap or fall. The wall wasn't just alive—it was awakening, stretching itself after ages of slumber.

His vision blurred at the edges, the familiar heat rising in his temples. But beneath the initial terror, something clicked. The wall's movements weren't random—they had a pattern, like a deadly dance. Each shift and groan came with subtle warnings—if you knew how to read them.

Drawing a deep breath of salt air, he began his climb. Each handhold was a gamble.

Again, the wall groaned beneath Markus' fingers, ancient stone protesting like a living thing. He froze, but pressed against the cold surface, as a tremor rippled through the cliff face. Above him, someone cursed as their handhold crumbled to dust.

"Left!" Viktor's voice cut through the wind. "The whole section's about to ..."

Before he could finish, the wall shifted as massive blocks of stone ground against each other like teeth. Markus lunged sideways, his fingers latching on just as his previous position collapsed into air. Heart hammering, he watched chunks of rock disappear into the mist below.

A cry from above made him look up. There was Cypran hanging by one hand as his feet scraped desperately for a foothold as the wall continued its terrible dance. Their eyes met for a fraction of a second before the younger recruit's grip began to slip.

Without thinking, Markus moved, scaling the shifting surface with desperate speed. His muscles screamed as he reached up to catch Cypran's wrist just as the last of his strength gave out. For one terrible moment, they both hung suspended between sky and stone, while the wall rumbled with predacious hunger.

His fellow recruit recovered, grabbing hold of a ledge, with a nod of gratitude, as Markus took a second to focus.

The rock groaned and shifted beneath his fingers, slick with sea spray and treacherous with frost. Yet, instead of fighting it, he moved with the wall's rhythm. His street fighter's instinct—the ability to read an opponent's moves before they struck—translated to this vertical battlefield. When a section collapsed, he was already reaching for the next grip. When spurs of rock shot outward, he used their momentum to propel himself higher.

A massive wave crashed below, its spray reaching high enough to drench him. The bitter cold threatened to numb his fingers, but the heat in his blood burned hotter, keeping him moving. Halfway up, the symptoms hit hard. His scar felt branded with each pulse of blood like fire in his veins. The wall's movements began to blur with his nightmares—twisted shapes, grasping hands, the sensation of being hunted. But he couldn't stop. Not here. Not now.

"Focus, Kane!" Draven's voice cut through the wind and haze. The Immortal watched from a nearby outcrop, his expression unreadable through the swirling mist.

Markus gritted his teeth. The name didn't sting this time—it fueled him. Every taunt, every scar, every nightmare had prepared him for this moment. His body moved on instinct now, finding impossible paths between the undulating stone. Below him, recruits who'd fallen back faced their choice—brave the murderous sea or admit defeat. One by one, they chose to retreat, leaving him alone on the wall's face, in a dance with the menacing stone that seemed determined to claim him.

When his hands finally gripped the summit, the sun was setting over the North Sea, turning the waves to molten copper. Markus collapsed, his legs giving out beneath him. For a moment, his careful control cracked—a sound escaped him, somewhere between a laugh and a sob. His heart was still pounding but his blood was cooling for the first time in hours. Below, the wall settled back into deceptive stillness, as if it had never moved at all.

"Well done," Draven said quietly. He offered Markus a hand up, his eyes lingering on the black scar. "Though something tells me you're fighting more than just the wall."

Markus couldn't answer. The symptoms were fading, but they left questions in their wake. Why had the wall affected him so differently? Why did his blood burn hotter with each passing day? And why did he feel like this was only the beginning of his trials?"

* * *

Three days after the Wall, the symptoms were getting worse. Markus' victories felt hollow against the growing burn in his blood, and the way shadows seemed to move at the corner of his vision. Even Draven noticed, though the Immortal kept his concerns to whispers with the other instructors.

The cross-country run would be their final test before the final trial, twenty miles through Nenevuiim's fields toward the darkness of Moorwood. As Markus took his place at the starting line, his scar quivered with a new kind of warning—not of failure, but of something waiting. Something that could sense him as surely as he could sense it.

* * *

Markus continued lumbering up the dirt road though the grassy fields of Nenevuiim—passing multiple property lines through distant farmlands where the harvest was already gathered. Five remaining recruits struggled to keep up with the seasoned instructors who by now were tiny specks in the distance, leading them into the lower elevations of the High Plains and then eastward, through Moorwood forest.

A break in the clouds brought the first star of the evening, luring his thoughts away for a moment. Murith—a sailor called it, onboard the futuristic hydro cruiser that carried him here. It was the heart of the archer, Aldra, a constellation that climbed high above the world out of the west horizon.

With each step, the path gradually faded into dusk as a pale greenish and violet shade crept upon the land just moments before twilight.

He'd hoped to make it out of Moorwood long before nightfall. The thought of running through this dark ancient forest in a land permeated by both myth and magic only forced him to quicken his pace—especially after nearly being consumed by those otherworldly cliffs.

By now the woods had become denser, closing in on both sides of him. The trees towered over him like a group of dark watchers with enormous sprawling branches reaching out to him. Knotted, twisted long-fingered hands from all angles seem to stretch forth. Every silhouette leaned, bent, peaked or hovered all around like disfigured figments of his imagination.

Then the symptoms started—first, a strange metallic taste in his mouth, followed by a tingling sensation that started in his extremities and spread inward. Next, a cold chill began spreading over his body with sensations that began like a fever, but deeper—a heat that coursed through is veins with each heartbeat. His scar burned, almost like a migraine along the side of his face. It was like a sharp awareness that seemed to be pulling on him like a compass needle straining towards a magnetic north.

The only sounds he could hear were his boots scraping against the slippery soil, along with the gravel and crunching leaves beneath his feet. Each step felt heavier, as if the very air was thickening around him.

The forest had fallen unnaturally silent—no birds, no insects, not even the whisper of wind through leaves. The Nightcallers' songs cut off abruptly. And the Starfawns, usually visible at twilight, had vanished entirely. Nature itself seemed to be holding its breath—as though recoiling at his very presence. And in that unnatural silence, Markus felt something stirring inside of him. An unshakable sensation. A symbiotic recognition of something atavistic tugging on him.

In that moment, movement flittered at the edge of his vision, as something dark passed across the light between two trees.

Then he saw it.

A dark massive form emerged like a nightmare taking shape—taller and larger than any man or predator. Between the rustling of grass and snapping of twigs, the tremors of each footstep shook the ground, causing Markus to backpedal and stagger, nearly tripping over the foliage behind him.

He couldn't take his eyes off it as the scattered remnants of moonlight brought it into view. Its purple-black skin seemed to absorb what little light remained. But it was draped in something that shifted like wet fabric—part cloak, part shadow—blurring the edges of its form. He couldn't tell where the creature ended and its hooded shape began, as though even its silhouette defied the laws of light. It moved, yet the shroud around it didn't stir. Red eyes blazed beneath the hood—fiery like amber, eternal and searching. Every instinct screamed at him to run, but terror had locked his muscles.

Then the thing's head tilted, studying him with a terrible intelligence. Its mouth opened, revealing rows of teeth that gleamed like black glass. But it was the recognition in those burning eyes that truly terrified him—as if it had been waiting for him. Hunting him specifically.

A low sound rumbled from its chest, more felt than heard, and the very air seemed to vibrate with ancient malice. This kaegar had found what it sought.

Then the spell broke. Markus ran.

He could hear this being behind him, charging straight for him. Up ahead, the path along the trail turned a corner into the deeper woods. Scrambling for his life, Markus skidded and made the cut. Instinctively, he looked to his left and dived off the trail, falling headlong into a dark ditch at a sharp drop.

Within seconds, heavy footsteps had turned that same corner and skidded to a halt, scattering dirt and leaves. But because of the foliage and angle in which Markus was lying, he wasn't detected. It couldn't see him. Yet, he had the feeling that it could still sense him because it hadn't moved. In fact, all it had to do was step forward a few steps off the trail, lean over and look down, to snag him.

He remained face-down in the damp grass and weeds, fighting to muffle his heavy breathing. The stench nearly gagged him—like a rotting carcass scorched by fire. Charred flesh. Ash. As if it had crawled from a furnace and never cooled.

He heard it sniffing the air, slow and deliberate. The low rumble in its chest rose and fell with each breath—a wet, animal hiss layered beneath growls and guttural clicks, like some monstrous exhale from a cracked throat.

Then it leaned closer.

Not quite to strike.

As if it were *listening*.

Markus' scar flared—hot and sharp—just as the creature exhaled across the back of his neck.

He didn't understand it. He didn't want to. But something inside him stirred—deep and ancestral, like a compass needle twitching toward a terrible truth. Something in his bones answered back.

An overwhelming sensation of dread—of something so carnivorous and wrong it defied comprehension—began crawling over every inch of his body.

Thankfully, he heard it moving away in the opposite direction ... but not very far. It was still on the trail, somewhere, pacing back and forth, still searching. Markus held even the tiniest breaths, praying this thing couldn't hear him exhaling.

Suddenly—everything fell quiet.

Where had it gone?

Was it still there?

Was it silently waiting him out?

It was either fight or flight. But fight with what? All he had was a dagger tucked in his sock. He could feel the ice-cold cross guard and pommel against his calf. But just pulling up his trousers may cause a stir.

Dammit!

The seconds turned to minutes—at least twenty minutes of brooding silence, before he finally summoned enough courage.

Slowly.

Fearfully.

He lifted his head.

* * *

The mist curled low over the trail, thick and soupy. Markus blinked into the half-light, squinting at a hunched shape ahead. A stump, maybe. Or a boulder. The shadows played tricks in this forest.

Then it shifted.

Not a trick. Not a stump.

Until it rose to its feet.

It was the same towering form he'd fled from—the same breath, the same red eyes, the same impossible presence.

A hood shrouded its head, and something—cloak or skin or shadow—flowed behind it, not caught by the wind, but held by something deeper. It made the figure look both regal and wrong.

Markus' breath hitched; his heart pounded in his chest. He wished he'd never set foot in this cursed forest. If only he could go back, back to the safety of the barracks, back to a world that made sense.

The creature's head tilted, slightly. Watching. Not charging—not yet.

And still, those red eyes locked onto him like twin brands.

Something in him twisted. He didn't know if it was terror... or recognition.

Then the figure stepped forward. That was enough for Markus.

He tumbled down the steep hillside, fumbling and crashing through branches, his descent chaotic and uncontrollable. Behind him, the thunderous sound of pursuit grew louder, raining dirt and debris down upon him.

Suddenly, the ground gave way beneath him. He

plunged into the open air, free-falling through the trees. Desperately, he reached for anything to stop his fall, smashing into branches and limbs with brutal force. His chest slammed into a thick branch, knocking the wind from his lungs as he tumbled into the dense underbrush below.

The kaegar followed—not crashing, but flowing through the branches with terrifying ease. It moved like a shadow with weight, tearing through limbs only when they dared to be in its way. When it hit the ground, the forest didn't shake. It held its breath.

Markus lay motionless, his battered and broken body half-buried in overgrown grass and twisted roots. He could hear the creature approaching, its heavy footsteps crushing twigs and leaves as it closed in. Every fiber of his being screamed to flee, but he couldn't move. He barely had the strength to breathe.

It loomed over him again. Not striking. Not feeding. Just... watching.

A slow inhale—almost thoughtful.

Markus' scar flared again.

He didn't know if it was pain or recognition. But it was *shared*.

Then, a blaster shot ripped through the night, startling him. Another blast followed, then another, lighting up the darkness with searing bursts of energy. The kaegar roared so loudly, it sent a jolt of shock through Markus' spine. He cringed and shivered fearfully beneath the towering bipedal before it darted off into the forest, vanishing into the shadows. Distant blaster fire erupted overhead, voices shouting as they chased the fleeing predator.

Markus finally exhaled, relief flooding his body. Whatever had been hunting him was gone—for now. But the feeling didn't last. Footsteps approached from behind, cautious but deliberate.

He held his breath, slowing his breathing to remain unnoticed.

Was it another mysterious being?

A soft scent drifted toward him—powdered jasmine and warm clove. Not at all like the ash and char that still clung to the trees.

A shadow knelt beside him, cloaked in violet.

Through the haze of pain and fading light, Markus caught a glint of silver—a mask, ornate and still. But it was the eyes that held him. Calm. Watchful. Not unkind.

Not Liyzia's warmth. Not the kaegar's dread.

Something else entirely. Something *unknown.*

She didn't speak. She simply laid a hand against his brow.

And then everything went black.

CHAPTER ELEVEN

The warmth of the presidential suite did nothing to thaw the atmosphere as Hans studied the three men before him. Rathmar stood like a shadow against the twelve-foot window revealing the dark ribbon of the Velucian river, while Nettles and Gurigor waited with poorly concealed tension.

"Gentlemen," Hans said, his cultured voice precise as a blade. "Would anyone care to explain how a supposedly controlled operation degenerated into blaster fire and chaos?"

When no one immediately responded, he gestured to the bar with exaggerated courtesy. "Perhaps a drink would loosen tongues?"

"The kaegar," Rathmar said, ignoring the hospitality offered, "was drawn to something. Someone."

"Drawn?" Hans' smile didn't reach his eyes. "Like a common beast catching a scent? I was under the impression your ... pet ... was more sophisticated than that."

"Arrakos and I would appreciate a little more respect, Senator."

"*Arrakos*—is that the *name* of that ungodly apparition?"

"Yes—and I am quite impressed. I understand you are not the most eloquent speaker in any language beyond your political rhetoric."

"Go on," Hans answered calmly ignoring the remark.

"He's never disobeyed before," Rathmar said with a tone of genuine concern. "Something about that man ... drew him. Like a predator sensing its ... *own* kind."

"Man?" Hans asked.

"Whether the intent was to hunt or kill, I couldn't tell! But it drew him in, either out of aggression or curiosity. He chased him straight through towards the ravine. Only the sounds of blaster fire drew it away, and back towards my call. Unscathed."

"Perhaps the man was a sentry, patrolling the path," Nettles suggested.

"No weapons," Rathmar answered, "He was completely alone. Except for an injury."

"Injury?"

"Yes—a peculiar black scar along his face, an injury that should have killed him. Perhaps the lighting and shadows played tricks on my eyes."

The two politicians traded subtle glances, as though waiting for the other's cue. Hans didn't skip a beat. "I wouldn't be concerned. May have been some lost soul in the woods—triggering some hereditary hunting instincts in him. I'm sure it will ... subside."

"And what about the blaster fire? Someone spotted him."

"Indeed."

Hans laid out the table-sized map of the land before

them, giving careful attention to the Southeastern region, within distance of Zone 33. "64° 10' 0" N, 51° 44' 0" W. This was well within the two-hundred-yard radius designated as a buffer zone.

"What do you think?" asked Rathmar. There's little wildlife beyond the Velucian river to the west. Hunters maybe?"

"Hunters don't foolishly light up the woods like that over mere 'wildlife.' Only the threat of an intruder would trigger warning shots from sentinels."

"Are you apprehensive?" Rathmar asked.

"After tonight's debacle? I'm not entirely convinced of this current plan on action."

"We don't have any other leeway here" Nettles added, "Every resource, spy, even the 'plant' I have working in the interior administration can't get that close to the governor."

"And that's the problem! We rolled the dice once this evening. We'll roll it again. We'd better be damn sure about it."

"What do you suggest?" the sect leader asked him.

Hans studied the three men in the room carefully while refilling his wine. He was already apprehensive about the Dromelan delegation, and this mishap only added to it. Was that man really Markus? The same Markus Kane he fortunately walked up on at that pub in Cenovira? His mind juggled between the young watch-man, a frightening hunter, a room full of conspirators and a master plan that was now hanging by a thread.

"Senator?" quizzed Rathmar.

"Give it forty-eight hours."

"Why the wait?"

"My own discretion, Mr. Rathmar. I need time to re-evaluate."

"I believe we should act sooner."

"Really? I sat there with you in the brush and observed that kaeger with my own two eyes! I have no doubt, by its sheer presence alone, he'd tear up a man limb from limb. But there's a militia protecting that sector, and the finest fighters in the land protecting that asset. It wouldn't take much for the slightest alarm to alert them a second time. Assuming this is the location."

"And I assure you, Senator—you have no idea what he is capable of. You can inquire about his abilities as they are documented in the accounts of the Great war and ..."

"Legends and monsters," Hans said, swirling his glass with deliberate panache. "While you speak of ancient powers, I deal in modern realities. Money. Politics. People's predictable little weaknesses. These are Immortals you're dealing with, Mr. Rathmar. Capitol assassins armed with modern tech aren't anything for your hunter to sniff at!"

"Well!" Rathmar remarked calmly. "Allow me to 'rattle' your modernity, Senator, with our 'Old World' ways. A demonstration?"

Though Hans didn't feel it was any sort of threat aimed at him personally, a moment of caution passed between them at the mention of the word 'demonstrate.' It caused him to discreetly rub his hand down his left side, as he casually felt for the ion pistol in his waist.

"What do you mean by ... demonstration?"

"Find me an Immortal," Rathmar said quietly, his ageless eyes fixed on Hans. "Watch what the kaegar does to one of your kingdom's finest warriors. Then we can discuss ... sophistication."

Hans' laugh was pure silk over steel. "Shall I arrange that over drinks? Perhaps a nice café in Lessador?" His voice dripped sarcasm. "I'm certain the women and children would provide an appreciative audience for your demonstration."

"You mock what you don't understand, Senator." Rathmar turned to the window, but his reflection showed the faintest of smiles. "Tell me, amid all your political schemes, have you ever seen an Immortal die?"

Nettles grew nervous, finding it odd that he would make light of the situation and the mysterious hunter whose very presence struck fear in him. Gurigor was just as perplexed, carefully bracing himself between the two. Surprisingly, Rathmar was not a man who was so easily triggered. He brushed the senator away and turned his back to him, staring out the overhead circular window. But through the glass's reflection, Hans caught a solemn expression on his face.

"Do you know what it takes to kill one?" Rathmar uttered.

Again, Hans' hand drifted to his concealed weapon, a gesture not lost on anyone in the room.

"Precisely," Rathmar continued. "Stick to what you know, Senator. Leave the killing to those who remember how."

Hans shook the ice in the bottom of his glass, while peddling his index finger to his head as though thinking. "By all means," he said, his cultured tones carrying just a hint of steel, "demonstrate your creature's abilities. But remember who finances this little venture."

The Dromelan's smile carried a millennia of secrets. "Money," he said softly, "is such a young form of power, Senator."

The door sealed behind Rathmar and Gurigor with a pneumatic hiss. Hans waited three heartbeats before throwing back his drink.

"You think it's wise to antagonize him?" Nettles asked softly.

"What I think," Hans said, moving to the map table, "is that we have a more immediate problem." His finger traced the location of the night's debacle. "A man with a black scar. Here, of all places."

"Kane?" Nettles barely breathed the name.

"Twice now," Hans muttered, swirling his drink. "First the harbor, now here. Either Kane is the luckiest street rat alive, or there's something we're missing. And I don't believe in luck." Hans' carefully maintained composure cracked slightly. "What is he doing here? And more importantly, who's helping him?"

"The Immortal we saw him with ..."

"Which is precisely why we need to move carefully." Hans pulled out a freshly printed document—Markus' face staring up from the page alongside Xara's.

"We have forty-eight hours. Find him. I don't care how."

"And the girl?"

Hans' smile was cold as winter. "Oh, I have special plans for Xara. Assuming she's nearby—and she always is, isn't she?"

Neither man noticed the shadow that paused momentarily outside the door, or the way Rathmar's lips curved in a knowing smile as he walked away with secrets of his own.

* * *

Markus felt the cold dew of the grass soaking into his hands and face, as the slimy grit of dead leaves pressed against his chest. The earthy dampness clung to him, grounding him in the woods, though where exactly, he didn't know. He hadn't opened his eyes yet. His nose was clogged from the chill, but no strange scents reached him. Familiar sounds drifted to his ears: the chirping of distant birds, the rustling of creatures in the underbrush, the creaking sway of tree branches in the breeze. All normal.

When he finally opened his eyes, beams of morning light streamed through the dark canopy above, blinding him for a moment. Slowly, cautiously, he pushed himself upright, sweeping his gaze across the tranquil surroundings. The chaos of the night before felt like a distant memory. He was alone, lying between the massive roots of two Mistweep trees, not another soul in sight.

But then, something caught his eye.

A mirror.

It stood upright on the forest floor, framed in an ornate brass design, an elegance entirely out of place among the wild thickets and trees. The mirror faced the shadows, away from the sunlight filtering through the leaves. Markus froze, unease curling in his stomach.

He glanced around, scanning the trees for any sign of someone—anyone—who might have left it here. But the woods remained silent. With cautious steps he approached the strange object. Circling it, he examined its back: plain wood, sturdy and unremarkable. His fingers brushed the smooth brass frame as he moved to face it directly.

The mirror reflected the forest behind him with perfect clarity—the twisted roots, the mossy undergrowth, the endless sprawl of trees. But as Markus stepped into view, his reflection vanished.

The glass turned black, an inky void that seemed to swallow light itself.

He stepped back instinctively, and the reflection returned, nature's serenity once again filled the surface. Frowning, he leaned forward, watching as the image faded and dissolved into darkness again. No matter how long he stared, the void remained, impenetrable and unnerving.

A chill ran down his spine. He tapped the glass. Solid. Real. He tapped his knuckles against it, but the sound was muted. Markus' breath quickened; his unease grew. There was something deeply wrong with this.

Suddenly the forest around him darkened.

The sun, which had been streaming through the trees moments ago, vanished in an instant. Shadows raced across the ground as dusk fell unnaturally fast. Markus blinked, disoriented, as a cold wind whipped through the woods, stirring the leaves into a frenzied dance.

The creaking of branches grew louder, almost menacingly, as if the trees themselves were restless.

A low, shivering howl echoed through the air.

Markus' fingers, still pressed to the mirror, jerked as a force grabbed him. Something unseen yanked his arm with terrifying strength, pulling him forward. He stumbled, his shoulder slamming into the glass. To his horror, the surface rippled like water and began to swallow him whole. His arm disappeared into the void, followed by his shoulder.

Thrashing, panic clawing at his mind, he struggled to pull free. The mirror's grip was unrelenting, dragging him inch by inch into its abyss. His muscles burned, his nails scraped against the brass frame; but it was useless. The void devoured him as his head plunged into the suffocating darkness.

Then, two fiery red eyes flared to life within the blackness, staring directly at him.

A thunderous crack split the air ...

Markus tumbled backward, landing hard on a bright marble floor. Heart pounding in his chest, he gasped for breath. The oppressive darkness was gone; it was replaced by sunlight streaming through slatted blinds. The green walls of a room surrounded him, and the faint bustle of morning filled the air. He found himself tangled in bed sheets, his body trembling as he struggled to make sense of what had just happened.

He ran a hand over the cool marble beneath him, trying to ground himself. A dream. It had to be a dream. But the vividness lingered, gnawing at the edges of his reality. His chest felt tight, the fear refusing to let go. These nightmares were getting intense with each passing night. They weren't just dreams anymore—they felt like something more, something that blurred the line between his waking and sleeping worlds.

And then he heard it.

A shuffle nearby.

Markus' head snapped toward the sound, eyes sharp, muscles tense.

An Immortal stood leaning casually against the wall, as

still and silent as a statue. The warrior wasn't one of the others he'd met before. Not Draven. Nor any other familiar faces. This one's armor bore intricate carvings and gold regalia, whose plated shin guards and armlets glinted in the light. His face was rugged, lined with age, and streaked with early strands of gray in both his hair and goatee. He seemed completely uninterested in Markus, casting only a dispassionate glance toward the window.

Markus forced himself to move, slowly crawling back onto the bed, every muscle aching from the strain of the nightmare. He could feel the warrior's eyes on him as he climbed under the blankets, cold sweat still clinging to his skin.

Their gazes met briefly, and Markus saw a hint of curiosity in the Immortal's eyes as if he expected Markus to tremble or react with awe. But all Markus could feel was exhaustion.

The warrior squinted at him through the sunlight, studying him carefully, as though searching for something hidden beneath the surface.

"Who are you?" Markus asked.

"I'll ask the questions around here," he answered with a bassy voice. "What were you doing in this neck of the woods?"

Markus returned the silent favor, ignoring him to glance out that same window towards the rising sun above the distant treeline.

"Would you like to do this the hard way?"

An odd question, Markus thought. With everything running through his mind right now, why was this man even threatening him? He hadn't the slightest clue where he was or how he'd got here.

It all started with the Immortal recognizing the faded gray fatigues Markus was wearing—the signature attire of recruits. Not for the National Army, but for a special few—young men 'selected' and 'sponsored' to serve the throne of the kingdom. First, they had to prove their worth by surviving their rigorous series of evolutions.

Markus felt compelled to describe the stress and ordeal from the past couple of weeks. At this, the Immortal's hardened façade softened—though not completely. With a scattered smirk here and a chuckle here, he recalled his younger days when he too faced such challenges as the Walls of Dressen and the ice-cold swells of the North Sea harbor.

It was when the man introduced himself as Cael Veridian that the lightbulb went on in Markus' head. This was him—the Prefect, the person that Draven had been trying to locate through another Immortal named 'Mercury.' He was certain of it. And though he was usually cautious with strangers, having learned from Xara to always keep his cards close to his chest, he ventured to share more of his escapade.

Whether it was the stress from the training or the aftermath of what he'd just escaped from by the skin of his teeth—he was compelled to go all in right now. Play with house money, so to speak. He told Cael of what chased him in the forest at night—this ungodly entity that echoed the beings of Old in these ancient and mystical woodlands.

He described the Camp at Nenevuiim. Draven. Azlo. Xara and her rare and sought after 'gift' of forgery— with an eye sharp enough to counterfeit the seal of the monarchy with such precision and accuracy as to pass authenticity.

But by the time he was finished, Markus failed to realize that the door to his room was ajar. and two more warriors were silently observing him, taking in every word. He knew these men were elite, cunning and efficient. The mastery of stealth just added another layer to their reputation.

Markus shifted his attention back toward Cael, who was deep in thought as he paced the window then back again.

"You expect me to believe," Cael's voice dripped with aristocratic disdain, "that a street watchman and his forger sister have uncovered a separatist plot that my entire intelligence network missed?"

Markus met the Prefect's gaze steadily, though his scar burned under the man's scrutiny. "The evidence is in those documents."

"Documents that your sister forged." Cael's laugh was sharp as broken glass. He turned to Mercury. "Is this what the Immortals have come to? Recruiting gutter rats to protect the throne?"

"Those 'gutter rats' exposed a breach in your security," Mercury said quietly, "one that cost two Council leaders their lives."

Something glimmered in Cael's eyes—doubt, perhaps, or fear quickly masked. "The Council's affairs are not my concern. My duty is to the princess, and to traditions that have kept this kingdom stable for centuries." His gaze returned to Markus' scar. "Though some traditions, it seems, are being ... diluted."

The implication hung heavy in the air. Markus felt

his blood heat, but kept his voice steady. "Traditions won't stop Hans Lumen. Or what he's brought to your shores."

"Ah yes, your mysterious 'monster.'" Cael's smile was cruel. "Tell me, did this creature leave that mark on your face? Or is there another story you're not sharing?"

Mercury stepped forward, but Markus raised a hand. "My scars are earned, Prefect. Can you say the same about your position?"

The temperature in the room seemed to drop. Cael's mask of civility cracked just enough to show the rage beneath. "Watch yourself, boy. Greater men than you have disappeared in Moorwood's depths."

"Well, I see I've arrived at a 'touching' moment," said a surprisingly pleasant female voice. The two warriors, who'd been leaning with folded arms, eased up and parted a way for the petite young Earthen woman to gracefully slip in through the doorway between them, followed by another masked warrior. His voice was muffled from behind the visor, yet audible enough to understand. "Sir, you're needed at the perimeter."

Cael acknowledged the young lady, then turned the others. "Watch him *closely*."

He gave Markus one last glance, before making his exit.

The girl looked as young as Xara—twenty, petite, fair, and proper in her attire and stature. She glided as gracefully as Liyzia, though not as silently, and when she sat, crossed her legs with ease, the morning light casting highlights in her blonde ponytail. She reached into her leather sack and pulled out a pulse pistol, X-27 Whispershot. Markus chuckled on the inside, recognizing the familiar weapon that Xara carried for the longest time. Light enough for delicate fingers.

She laid it across her lap, then smiled. "Good morning—'Kane,' is it?"

For the first time in forever, that name didn't pierce, poke or bring a shriek to his ears. Then again, he couldn't remember it ever rolling off anyone's lips in such a friendly manner.

"Who was your friend?" he asks, "Remind me to stay clear of him."

"Oh. That was Cael—the head of my security. Charming fella."

"*Your* security?"

"I am Danae, the lady of the house. Somehow, you have stumbled upon my private estate. You must have slipped or tumbled over into the ravine somewhere off the trail."

Markus thought for a second and wondered if he were actually in the presence of *the* princess, the object of everyone's obsession. Though tempted to probe further, he resigned himself to just observing. These armed warriors still present in the doorway studying him from behind their faceless helmets gave him as much concern as the weapon that laid across her lap.

"I didn't 'stumble' off anything. Something—chased me."

"Chased? By what? An animal? We are too far south for quadrupeds. Wait. Don't tell me—the little forest critters ganged up on you for trespassing their trees and holes in the ground!"

She managed to get a half smile out of him, even for a second. "I wish it were."

"Then what then?"

"I pray you never run into it. You'll never know a good night's sleep again."

Her glowing demeanor began to sour. "Is that what you've been dreaming about? For the past two days? Your sleep has been restless."

"Two *days*?"

He thought to himself—*It felt like I've been out for only a frightening minute!*

"Are you alright?" she broke his thoughts.

"I don't know what's come over me, but it's started ever since I've stepped foot on this soil. My dreams were much different when I had ..." He felt his waist, front and back frantically. "No. Where is it? Did I lose it?"

"Lose what?"

"I must have lost it somewhere out there." He started rambling, between checking himself, then beneath the covers and looking all around the room. "It's gone!"

"Lost something?"

"A scarf, I mean—a shawl. I was wearing it. Have you seen it?

"Shawl?"

"Yes. I had it on me! It was given to me. Tied and tucked behind my belt. It was given to me—have you seen it?"

"A hardened young man like you carrying such a thing about his waist? Don't be ridiculous!"

"Yeah, I know it sounds weird. I won't argue with that! But that's where she tied it."

"Who tied it?"

"The Nevran woman who adopted me, so I wouldn't lose it."

"What does it matter? It's just a rag around your waist."

"Just a rag around my waist? Don't you know anything about their customs? Traditions? That is their lineage, as old as forty generations, sewn in that fabric! You think this is a joke?"

"Yeah? Who's lineage? Can you even pronounce it?"

"The house of Q'irrev," he answered as accurately as he could remember. "From the line of Nikel. Given to me by his wife—Liyzia, daughter of Ruvira. Is that good enough for you? Don't know why I'm wasting my time talking to *you* about it!"

As he threw his hands up in disgust, she reached into her leather sack by her chair; she carefully lifted the neatly folded and cleaned garment, and presented it to him.

"I assure you. I am well-versed in our brethren's culture and traditions from the east. I just needed to make sure ..."

"Make sure this hideous looking freak isn't some random thief?"

"I was not going to say that!" she snapped.

"Yeah, sure! All Hallow's Eve's all year round with a face like mine! Trust me, I've heard it all."

"No such thought has crossed my mind, mister. You have no right to judge someone you just met! And neither do I. We held the garment for safe keeping while the nurse looked you over. Also took the liberty of washing it."

"Thank you," he answered softly as he received it with a sigh of relief

She then held up the necklace from Xara. "The wings on your golden alq'arus have been clipped."

"No" he answered, holding the ornament up before her, as it glowed in the morning sunlight. "Not clipped. My foster sister wears the other half, until we are reunited."

He tied it around his neck, beneath his fatigues.

"And this?" Danae handed over Nikel's custom crafted dagger, decorated in the cryptic symbolism and markings of the High kingdom from the east.

"My mentor. For his 'unlikely' pupil."

"So ... you have family back in the mainland."

"Family?" he thought. It had not dawned on him until now. Although neither Nikel nor Liyzia had verbally spoken such words to him, her ritual blessing was evident to everyone. He was not sure such a word as 'family' ever existed in his own vocabulary till now.

"Why are you here thousands of miles away?" she continued.

"To train."

"Seriously." She answered, "Tell the truth."

"That is the truth."

"Only the boldest are foolish enough to come here. And only the craziest who think they can cut it." She gestured to the door and winked at the Immortal well within earshot of their conversation.

"With all due respect," he answered, "I believe I have what it takes."

"Yeah? Who sponsored you?"

"Draven Handley and Azlo, son of Izikiur. Three thousand crowns at three-to-one, backed by Nikel, and two other knights, Vuchic and Erev."

Markus paused. His voice faded off into a subtle tremor. Their conversation had drawn in an unexpected audience, of not one, but now *three* Immortals gazing upon him in the doorway. He couldn't see their faces but could distinguish them by the different shades of color on their belts and the color guards decorating their breastplates. He remembered how intimidating the recruits found Viktor, Kratz, and Dalton at first sight that day down at the harbor. And he'd seen Draven fully armored upon meeting him in Erev's home. But these three men peering through the door with their heavy gear and arms were much too close for comfort, leaving him with no means of escape except for the closed window.

This was neither some bulky type of steel or iron, nor even the thinner-patched, puzzle-fitting, armor worn by the infantry of any coalition force. This was a sleekly crafted, advanced fusion of nanotech and poly-alloy, layered to a vibrant and luminous shine almost as luminous as steel. He imagined an endless process and meticulous detail of forging this coveted substance into the form-fitting pieces, including the signature seal seared into the pectoral of their breastplates.

One of them entered and stood before Markus. The young watchmen glanced up at the titan-like warrior, seeing his tired face reflected in the warrior's brilliantly polished view plate.

"Interesting," one uttered.

"Very few people are familiar with those names," another said.

"Didn't know Nikel had an 'heir'—till now." The third one said, "Why did he adopt an Earthen?"

"Earthen. Dromelan. Nevran. Or any other species— what does that matter?" Danae asked.

"Cause we're reckless," one of them joked, "We lack the patience, virtue and upbringing to follow the Zylan Order."

Danae touched the warrior's metal gauntlet. "Perhaps that's exactly why he was chosen."

She took a hold of a corner of the shawl hanging from beneath Markus' belt, which he had tied back into place.

"An Earthen, adopted by a Nevran, who will train for knighthood—all while undergoing 'The Path' of the Immortals. What do you think? Were the stars aligned upon his birth?"

"A diamond in the rough maybe?" one of the Immortals added.

"Or Draven's rotten luck," the third Immortal piped in with a chuckle, "Hopefully you won't share the same fate as his last three trainees."

"And what fate was that?" Markus asked.

"Why do you think it's called the Trial by *Fire*?"

He could only see his reflection in the man's faceless steel mask. With a cold and stoic undertone, the words came across as either a sadistic joke or a dire warning to the young recruit.

"What are you talking about? What happened to them?"

"Pay them no mind," said Danae, waving her hand.

"But they just said ..."

"They wish to intimidate you—it's all they have! Now come!"

* * *

Danae guided him by the arm through the grand outer halls of the Manor. The sound of their footsteps and those of the silent Immortals echoed over the gleaming marble floors. Portraits of unknown figures adorned the walls—faces of power and import, though there were none he recognized. They walked past towering columns that reached towards twelve-foot ceilings, past parlors filled with furnishings so extravagant they seemed out of place in this isolated, hidden corner of Moorwood. There were no outsiders here. Just the Immortals and their silent servants.

As they stepped out through the patio doors, the sprawling courtyard and sloping lawn spread out before him to rolling hills bathed in the soft early morning light. The architecture of the manor struck him as something ethereal, an intricate web of ornate designs and impossible detail, as though it had been crafted by other-worldly hands. Yet here it stood, alone in the woods, unseen by any but the select few who dwelled within its walls.

His thoughts drifted. Five Immortals guarded her. Five. Perhaps this Danae was more than she appeared to be. The sternness of their gaze rested on him, reminding him that he was constantly being watched and guarded from all sides.

Ahead, beneath the limbs of a sprawling Ghost Oak, a table was being set for lunch. Markus caught sight of a figure sitting there already—a spindly young man with spectacles buried in a book. He grinned at their approach. His name was Thelonius or, as he called himself, 'The Scholar.' Danae murmured something to Markus, but her words dissolved into the background, lost to a whisper, as everything around him began to blur.

It was then that his eyes lifted beyond the lawn toward the pond at the far edge of the estate.

Time seemed to slow.

At the pond's edge, a majestic swan drifted closer to shore, its white feathers catching the sunlight in a halo of gold. Rays of light danced across the water's surface where gentle ripples broke the glassy stillness, creating a shimmering path to the bird, like a bridge between worlds.

Through this veil of light a pale hand appeared, fingers extended with such gentle patience that the great bird showed no fear. The swan's head tilted ... considering ... before finally accepting the offering. As the scene widened, the hand became an arm draped in dark velvet, illuminated by scattered beams through the overhanging branches. Then it resolved into a cloaked figure kneeling at the water's edge. The swan leaned in, pecking curiously at the woman's fingers before resting its beak in her palm—a quiet gesture of trust.

Though her features were mostly concealed by an ornate silver mask beneath her hood, her movements carried an innate grace that left Markus breathless. Her emerald eyes gleamed like jewels, catching the same ethereal light enveloping her, and around her throat, a pendant cast a mystical glow. The sunlight seemed to seek her out, creating a soft aureole that separated her from the mundane world around her, while catching the shimmer of a ring on her hand, a soft glint of gold, as she gently stroked one of the ducklings before returning it to the flock.

The scene felt like a pastoral painting come to life. Time itself seemed to pause as he watched her, his heart quickening in his chest. Those eyes were familiar, though he couldn't place them. How could eyes, so striking, so full of silent emotion, belong to this stranger?

Danae and the woman exchanged gestures in fluid, silent language that Markus barely noticed. His gaze remained fixed on the cloaked figure, whose face was concealed by the mask except for her eyes, as his mind raced with questions. Who was she? And why did it feel as if, at this singular moment, something unspoken yet profound had passed between them?

Her name, as Danae told him, was Lily. She was her sister. Lily was mute, yet her presence spoke louder than words. Or so he was told. Whether it was a true affliction or part of the guarded persona surrounding her, Markus couldn't tell—and didn't dare ask. Even her silence felt deliberate. Measured. Part of the mystery they were all protecting.

Yet, despite the invisible barrier that seemed to exist between them, Markus couldn't tear his gaze away from her. The grace in her movements, the sadness in her eyes, the soft glow of her pendant—all of it drew him in, tugging at something within him. It was as if the world had faded, and for that fleeting moment, nothing else existed but the two of them.

Even as lunch was served beneath the oak, and Thelonius began to chatter endlessly across the table, Markus found it difficult to find his bearings. His mind was still with Lily, standing by the pond. He could feel her presence across from him, her gaze meeting his in brief, stolen glances through the slits of her mask. He'd learned long ago not to stare at people too long, but with her, it was impossible not to. Every time he looked away, he felt her eyes on him, as if she, too, was searching for something in him.

The lunch passed in a blur of words as they dipped into the food. Thelonius' ramblings were little more than background noise. All the while, Markus couldn't shake the feeling that there was something more to Lily. The necklace she wore, now tucked out of sight, haunted his memory. Where had he seen it? He knew it from somewhere, but the connection hovered just beyond his consciousness.

And then there were those eyes—sad, searching green eyes that left him with an inexplicable ache. Was it just curiosity? Or something deeper?

With his attention tugged from all sides between his three hosts at the table, the guards lurking nearby, and servants tending to their every need, a hidden hand slipped a sedative into his cup while he was not looking. Before he realized it, a foggy heaviness had overtaken him, drawing him into gradual slumber with all eyes on him.

CHAPTER TWELVE

A slight squeeze to his shoulder was all it took for Markus to open his eyes. The second hand was placed on his chest to keep him from getting startled. Through the haze of waking, he made out two figures—the towering Immortal's armor gleaming in the late afternoon shade of the barracks, and beside him, Xara's familiar silhouette. Right on cue when he awoke, the sight of the warrior leaning over him was enough to frighten him. But the Immortal caught and braced him, while Xara's steady hand on his chest anchored him. Within seconds, Markus returned to his senses.

It was late afternoon as he sat up on one of the empty beds in the barracks at the camp in the region of Nenevuiim. He recognized the Immortal, remembering him from the distinct signature marking on his helmet—that 'M' engraved behind the visor. Xara hovered nearby, her face tight with the kind of worry she usually tried to hide behind sarcasm.

The engraved emblem in the Immortal's chest plate finally clicked with Markus. He remembered now. It was the seal of the monarchy. Many nights he'd catch Xara carefully redrawing and sketching the symbol, then forging it on her counterfeited pamphlets with great precision using her magnifying tools. However, it was not necessarily the Seal, but the unique jewel that served as the centerpiece in the design, the 'Aether stone' as Nikel called it—the unique necklace worn around the monarch's neck.

The gem around Lily's neck looked so convincing that he'd bet his life on it. He was certain that was the coveted stone, though he was unable to get a closer look beneath its sparkling features. Why else would this young lady be covered up and so closely guarded in the presence of a stranger who stumbled upon her secluded location? It was starting to add up from everything Nikel disclosed to him and Xara.

For a moment, their eyes met and Markus wondered if this man could read his mind. Xara shifted uncomfortably beside him, no doubt wondering how much they should reveal.

"I've only seen glimpses of Draven's armor from beneath his trench coat," Markus admitted as an excuse for staring at the breastplate's emblem.

"His is a bit scruffy compared to yours."

"You sure it's not the emblem? You seem to recognize it," the warrior uttered.

Xara's hand tightened on his arm—a warning or encouragement, he was not sure which.

"Maybe I've seen it on some transcripts from time to time," Markus deflected, though Xara's slight head shake told him he was not being convincing.

"Yeah? And how many government transcripts pass underneath the nose of a mere ... watchman? You recognized it so keenly"

Markus froze at his startling revelation. To his surprise, the warrior tapped the side of his helmet, near the engraved, scripted letter 'M.' The other Immortals' helmets carried similar signature markings that had caught his attention earlier.

"My name is Mercury," the warrior revealed, tapping the side of his helmet near the engraved, scripted letter 'M.'

Xara exchanged a quick glance with Markus as her mind visibly worked through possibilities. She reached for her satchel with deliberate movements. "Then perhaps you'll be interested in why Hans Lumen wants the princess," she spoke in a steady voice despite the risk she was taking. From the satchel, she withdrew several documents, whose royal seals caught the afternoon light.

Mercury's posture shifted subtly. "And you are?"

"The forger he's been hunting." She held out one of the documents. "These bear the mark of the Aether stone—a mark I learned to replicate perfectly. That's why Hans needs me. That's why he's here."

Markus tensed beside her, but she continued, her voice gaining strength. "The Prefect didn't believe my brother. But maybe he'll believe these. Hans plans to use my forgeries to legitimize whatever he does to her Highness."

She laid out more documents, each bearing the impossible perfection of her work. "The question isn't whether I can forge these seals. It's why Hans needs them in the first place."

Mercury studied the documents with growing intensity. "The Prefect needs to see these."

"No." Xara began gathering the papers in swift but careful movements. "These stay with me."

"You doubt the Prefect's protection?"

"I doubt his willingness to listen," she countered. "He dismissed my brother once. And without these ..." she tapped the satchel meaningfully, "I have no leverage with Hans."

Mercury's silence suggests understanding, even respect. "Then what do you propose?"

"Keep them close," Xara said, meeting his gaze steadily. "When Hans makes his move—and he will—the Prefect will need proof of his true intentions. We'll be ready."

Markus watched this exchange, recognizing his sister's careful maneuvering. She had shown enough to plant doubt in Mercury's, mind while maintaining their only leverage. It had been the kind of strategy that had kept them alive in Vesper's shadows.

Mercury adjusted his posture from interrogator to messenger. His gaze swept the empty barracks, taking in all the made-up beds. Out of twenty, only four had been disturbed recently.

"I don't know you," Mercury uttered, the words pregnant with what was to come, "But I do know this evolution. By now the last few have already begun the deadly 'Trial by Fire' some twenty miles north—for which you'll never make up in time."

The words hit Markus like a physical blow. He tried to prize off the nameplate on his fatigues—KANE—but the damn thing wouldn't budge. Just like everything else in his life, it clung to him, mocking his attempts to become something more.

"Any last remaining survivors must reach the peak of

the Crater at Duniduir by sunrise on the seventh day, come hell or high water, ice, snow, blizzard, frostbite, starvation, injury—or predator."

He yanked at the nameplate one more time until he gave up. With a snarl of frustration, Markus seized the nearest bed, flipping it with a crash that echoed through the empty barracks. The sound wasn't nearly loud enough to match the roaring in his chest. His boot connected with a footlocker, sending it skidding across the floor—but even that felt hollow.

Xara watched him, her earlier confidence fading as her brother's rage spent itself against innocent furniture. She knew this wasn't just another setback. This was different. This time, he'd allowed himself to hope.

Markus strode to the window, his breath coming in sharp bursts. The dawn was breaking over the eastern hills, painting the sky in glorious shades of gold and crimson. Somewhere out there, the others were continuing their journey while he stood here, trapped once again by what he was— or wasn't.

His scar throbbed with familiar heat as he pressed his forehead against the cool glass. The rage was fading now, leaving that hollow space he knew all too well. But, beneath his exhaustion, something else stirred—a restlessness in his blood that felt different from his usual anger. Like his body knew something his mind didn't, pulling him toward a destiny he couldn't see.

"We should go," Xara said quietly from behind him. She didn't offer empty comfort or try to tell him it would be alright. She knew him better than that.

Markus nodded, his reflection fractured in the window's glass. Just another failure. Just another dead end.

But even as he turned away from the dawn, some part of him knew that this wasn't the end of his story. It was barely the beginning.

* * *

The next morning at sunrise, Markus and Xara set out from the camp, their packs loaded with what dry rations they could gather. Their steps fell into the familiar rhythm they'd developed over years of watching each other's backs in Vesper's streets.

"Heading south to Lessador?" Xara asked, adjusting the satchel at her hip.

"You don't have to come."

"Right. Because you've done so well on your own lately." The familiar edge of sarcasm in her voice almost made things feel normal. Almost.

"Xara ..."

She cut him off. "The festival's in two weeks. Hans will be there. The Prefect too, probably, if he's smart enough to hide the princess in plain sight."

Markus paused in his stride. "It's suicide."

"So is letting Hans win." She squared her shoulders. "Draven's given up. The Prefect won't listen. We're all that's left."

"And what exactly are we supposed to do?"

"What we've always done." She patted the satchel. "Survive. Adapt. And maybe ..." a dangerous smile touched her lips, "make Hans regret ever crossing us."

Markus studied his sister—the steel in her spine, the fire in her eyes. This wasn't just about warning the Prefect anymore. This was personal.

They followed route 54, the island's main highway connecting the local municipalities that ran south towards Lessador. According to their map, it was a good twenty miles on foot. With barely two hours before sunset and the temperature dropping for the evening, they hadn't made it as far as they'd hoped. Being strangers in a foreign land, neither wanted to risk traveling after dark.

They passed several inns along the way—the kind mentioned to recruits who might need rest between here and the southern harbor. But money was tight, and they'd learned long ago to be careful with what little they had.

"The stables," Xara suggested, nodding toward the buildings between two adjacent inns. They were only half full this time of the year, leaving plenty of space to bed down for the night. From here they could see the distant lights in the nearby taverns, hear the raucous laughter, and smell the nauseating stench of strong brew.

"Of all the places on earth. Why here?" Markus muttered, his nose wrinkling at the scent of Nevrish ale. "Hopefully, I'm so tired that I'll fall asleep quicker than I can bear that stench!"

"At least it's warmer than the streets of Vesper," Xara remarked, already scanning the area for the best defensive position. Old habits die hard!

Shortly after, three Nevrans arrived to join the small group of weary travelers making do with the stables instead of the inn. Markus could tell they were from the far east, further, in fact, as they were not dressed in the similar colonial fashion of Nikel's household, or that of the Nevrans of Orwein. No, they were more like the traditional nomads and eastern tribes, wrapped in their massive animal skins to keep warm. Shortly after, a few drunken merchants showed up and flopped down nearby, much to Markus' disdain."

* * *

He had fallen asleep for just a short spell, when he rolled over on the ground. When he opened his eyes, he noticed that his leather carrying pouch was missing. Looking around, the campfire was barely lit with a few embers underneath, yet there was still plenty of light from one of the twin full moons overhead. Half the men were fast asleep, while others were sitting around. But he couldn't find his pouch. Did he drop it? He was certain he just had it. He jumped to his feet, searching desperately, back, and forth, at everyone, and every spot in the ground, every quilt, every spot, even everyone's head.

Finally, he spotted it.

Three large drunk men were holding it, laughing and joking around, as they sat off to the side on a log. Infuriated that they would just steal something that didn't belong to them from right under his nose, he stormed over there and snatched it out of his hands.

Without a word, one of the older, heavier men snatched it back. But Markus would not let go, and instantly started a tug of war. Back and forth they went before he used his weight to shove the recruit to the ground. The three middle-aged drunkards mocked him in amusement.

"Look at that face," one of them jeered, pointing at Markus' scar. "What kind of freak show did you escape from?" they mocked, making exaggerated gestures at the black mark that ran down his temple.

"Bet he's cursed," another one called out loud enough for the other travelers to hear. "Probably bring bad luck to anyone who sleeps near him."

A few of the bystanders chuckled nervously, others averted their eyes, pretending not to notice as they always did when confronted with his disfigurement. Some even shifted their bedrolls away.

Xara saw it happening before Markus moved—that dangerous stillness she recognized from their street days. But this was different. His scar had darkened, and there was something in his eyes she hadn't seen in years. "Markus," she said quietly, but he was already rising, his blood brimming with rage.

He attacked again. This time the other two pounced on him from behind with their large elbows, not looking to hurt him but swat him away like a gnat—their heavy forearms pounding him to the ground like a hammer.

To them, it was all a joke, as more bystanders sneaked up on him. Markus, on the other hand, was tired and worn out, not to mention dealing with three hefty men. Once more he struggled, grunted, and wrestled with all three of them, and again they pounded him repeatedly, finally tossing him off like a twig into the shadows of the grass with one of them giving him a final stomp on the face with his boot.

The rage was different this time—not just anger, but something deeper stirring in his blood. The humiliation of Mercury's dismissal, and now these thugs ... his scar throbbed darkly as memories flooded back. Those two boys who'd crossed him years ago and their screams as his cursed blood turned their victory to horror ... he'd sworn never to lose control like that again.

But right now, he didn't care about promises.

His muscles coiled, ready to unleash everything he'd been holding back. Then Xara's hand locked onto his arm—not gentle, but fierce with street-forged preservation.

"Not here," she hissed, her voice sharp with urgency rather than concern. "You start this, every guard in Oravon will know where we are. Hans will know."

Her grip tightened as the thugs laughed again. "They're dead anyway if they stick around. But we survive first. Always have."

Her words hit like ice water, but the rage still churned beneath his skin. Markus yanked his arm free from her grip, shooting her a look that would have made anyone else back down. But Xara just stared back, unflinching.

"Fine," he spat, snatching up what gear he had left.

He stormed toward the far end of the stables, needing distance before he did something they'd all regret. The thugs' laughter followed him, but Xara's warning rang louder in his head. She was right—and that only made it worse.

He didn't see the Nevran chieftain watching from the shadows, didn't notice how the old man's eyes lingered on the darkness pulsing beneath his scar. But the elder had seen everything—the rage, the restraint ... and something else.

Xara's fingers twitched toward her concealed blade.

Her jaw was clenched so tight her teeth might crack. The familiar calculation ran through her mind—how quickly she could incapacitate the first man, use his bulk as a shield, then take down the second before the third could react. She'd handled worse odds in Vesper. But that would mean exposure they couldn't afford. Her eyes locked with the leader's for one dangerous moment with one of her looks that made his laughter falter.

"Aww, does the pretty nurse need to hold the baby's hand?" one of them sneered, recovering his bravado. "Maybe she should kiss his wounds better."

"Come over here, sweetheart. We'll show you what real men look like."

The Nevran chieftain seemed to materialize from the shadows, his sudden appearance making the Skylanders stumble back. Their drunken bravado withered under his steady gaze. In the darkness beyond, his two sons sat alert, hands resting with calculated casualness on their weapons.

The trio retreated, mockery dying in their throats.

"The shawl you wear," the chieftain's voice cut through the bitter night air, deep and steady as an oak. "It bears the mark of the house of Q'iirev."

Markus stood apart, still quivering from barely contained rage. But something in the old man's presence commanded attention. The chieftain studied him with careful consideration, catching the pulsing beneath the scar. "Interesting," he mused without judgment. "A knight claims an outsider as his own, marking him with our most sacred traditions."

Xara watched the exchange with sharp eyes, reading

the subtle shift in her brother's posture. The old man reminded her of Nikel—that same quiet authority that somehow reached past Markus' defenses.

"I am Yewwa. These are my sons. Ditta, Nix." He gestured to the fire—not a request but a gentle command that carried its own gravity. "Come. Share our fire. Let us speak of home."

Xara moved first, accepting the invitation with the formal Nevran greeting Liyzia had taught her. But her hand stayed near her blade; respect didn't mean trust. She glanced back at Markus, letting him choose his own time to approach.

He stood alone for several long moments, the rage gradually giving way to exhaustion. The fire's warmth beckoned, and something about Yewwa's calm presence reminded him of long evenings in Nikel's study. Finally, his feet carried him forward of their own accord.

As they settled around the flames, the night's ugliness began to fade into something different— not peace exactly, but a kind of weathered understanding. Yewwa didn't press them with questions, seeming to know that some wounds needed silence to heal.

"The threads that bind us," Yewwa said finally, studying them both, "are not always the ones we expect." His sons exchanged glances but said nothing. They'd clearly learned to wait for their father's wisdom to unfold in its own time.

The elder's eyes rested on the shawl, its curious patterns catching the firelight. "Sometimes the strongest weaves come from threads that seem not to match. The High Kingdom knows this— their knights have always seen what others miss." A slight smile touched his weathered face. "Nikel was ever one to recognize strength in unexpected places."

Markus stared into the flames, letting the words wash over him. Tomorrow's uncertainties could wait. For now, there was just this: the fire's warmth, his sister's soothing presence, and the quiet acceptance of strangers who asked nothing of him but to be.

The fire crackled, sending sparks toward stars that suddenly seemed closer than before. For the first time since leaving Nikel's home, they felt the promise of something familiar. Not safety—they knew better than that. But perhaps ... understanding.

As Markus and Xara finally dozed off, feeling secure in the presence of Yewwa and his sons, the elder took out the cloth that had caught Markus' blood earlier. His bluish eyes lit up brighter than the dying embers on the campfire in front of him. The two sons came over on each side of him as he held up the cloth to discover a hole that had been burned through, surrounded by crusty, dried, blackened edges as though something toxic and acidic had made it. The elder swiftly shielded Nix's fingers from touching it, then in his native tongue, told them to get some rest. He would examine it later.

Once his sons had settled into sleep, Yewwa sat alone by the rekindled firelight, slipping on his spectacles. His weathered fingers traced the cloth's scorched edges before reaching into his collection. Among the bronze, metal, and quartz arrowheads, he searched for one particular bundle wrapped in aged leather, handling it with the reverence of one who carries history itself.

The leather was stiff with age, its surface covered in faded script—the kind of high Nevrish that few could still read. As he carefully unwrapped it, black arrow-heads caught the firelight like captured shadows. He lifted one with a gloved hand, studying how it seemed to drink in the flame's glow. Holding it beside the scorched cloth, he drew in a sharp breath. The similarities were impossible to ignore.

Almost without thought, his fingers found the ancient text, tracing words that hadn't seen firelight in generations: "*Ka'ene ...*" he whispered, the old tongue feeling strange on his lips. The rest of the inscription was too worn to read clearly—something about darkness, and sacred weapons, and a warning that made his blood run cold.

Yewwa's eyes found Markus' sleeping form, seeing him differently now. The young man's scar seemed to tremble faintly in the dying light, while the shadows around him moved strangely, as if responding to his presence. The elder carefully rewrapped the arrowheads, murmuring a protective charm passed down before his grandfather's time.

Some truths, he knew, revealed themselves only when the moment was right. For now, he would watch, and wait, and remember stories that spoke of powers older than kingdoms.

The fire crackled once more, sending sparks toward stars that suddenly seemed much more distant.

* * *

Morning came with shouting. Markus blinked awake, his muscles aching from sleeping on hard ground, to find the inn's yard in chaos. The magistrate's men had the Skylanders in irons, their protests drowned out by the innkeeper's accusations about stolen livestock and pilfered stores. The same men who'd seemed so imposing last night now looked quite pathetic, tripping over their own feet as they tried to explain why stolen chickens had mysteriously appeared in their rented room.

Something soft bumped against Markus' leg. His knapsack—mysteriously returned, with two chicken feathers laid across it like a signature. An apple struck his chest, and he caught it reflexively.

Xara lounged against a fence post, the picture of innocence as she bit into her own apple. The wink she gave him said everything—no words needed. Of all the skills his sister possessed, justice was her specialty: delivered quietly, precisely, and with just enough bitter aftertaste to remember. The fact that the stolen chickens had somehow managed to roost in the Skylanders' beds was, to be sure, purely coincidental!

They joined Yewwa's group on the south road, where autumn had transformed the landscape into a tapestry that would have made Nikel proud. Amber and gold leaves danced on the morning breeze, while the distant mountains wore crowns of early frost that sparkled in the sunlight. Even the Mistweep trees seemed less mournful, their drooping branches adorned with crystals of ice that caught the light like countless tiny prisms.

The Nevran chieftain's secure presence seemed to calm the very air around them, while his sons' quiet competence made the journey easier than expected. The morning sun cast long shadows across the frost-dusted path ahead, promising a clear day's journey even as the crisp air hinted at winter's approach.

CHAPTER THIRTEEN

The port of Cenovira emerged through the morning fog like a city under siege, though its invaders came bearing festival banners instead of weapons. Markus and Xara stood at the harbor's edge, watching the endless stream of vessels dock and unload their human cargo. The sight made both of them tense up, for street instincts died hard and crowds meant danger as much as cover.

"This can't be normal," Xara muttered, counting the ships with the same attention she'd once used to track guard patrols in Vesper. "Even for a festival."

The harbor churned with activity as far as the eye could see, in an overwhelming sea of humanity that made Markus' chest tighten. Wide-eyed travelers poured out from the vessels, carrying everything from traditional blessing-rings to freshly cut pine trees. Their faces shone with an excitement that felt alien to both former street runners.

"Perfect cover for Hans," Markus said quietly, scanning the crowd with practiced wariness.

"Or perfect cover for us," Xara countered, though her

hand never strayed far from her hidden blade. "No one looks twice at festival guests."

They worked their way through the crowd, years of partnership making their movements fluid and coordinated. Xara took point, her smaller frame slipping between groups while Markus followed in her wake, his broader shoulders creating space they could both use. It was a dance they'd perfected in Vesper's markets, though the stakes here were infinitely higher.

A commotion near the harbor master's office drew their attention. A cluster of officials huddled around weather reports, their faces grave. Xara drifted closer, in a casual posture but with ears pricked up.

"Storm front moving in from the south," she reported back in a low voice. "Early winter storm. They're talking about moving the festival grounds inland."

"Where to?"

"Nubensoyra." She nodded toward the distant hills. "About a day's journey up the trade road. They're announcing it now."

The news rippled through the crowd like wind through grass. Excitement shifted to confusion, then determination as people began reorganizing their plans. Street vendors hurriedly packed up stalls they'd barely finished setting up, while officials tried maintaining order among the press of bodies.

"Chaos," Markus observed grimly. "Perfect time for someone to make a move."

"Or perfect time for us to disappear." Xara's eyes tracked the movement of the harbor guards. "Question is—do we follow the festival, or use this as cover to slip away?"

Before Markus could answer, a cold wind cut through the crowd, carrying the first bite of the approaching storm. Something about it made his scar throb, a warning that had nothing to do with the weather. Beside him, Xara stiffened—she'd learned to read his reactions better than he could himself.

"That wasn't just wind, was it?" she asked quietly.

Markus touched his scar, the tissue burning beneath his fingers. "Something's coming. Something worse than storms."

Xara nodded, her decision made. "Then we follow the crowd. Better to face whatever's coming with people around than alone in the wilderness." A ghost of her usual smile touched her lips. "Besides, I've always wanted to see how the other half celebrates."

As they navigated the crowd, an elderly Nevran woman appeared before them, her arms full of elaborately woven holly corsages. Silver bells and crimson ribbons caught the weak sunlight as she moved through the crowd with surprising bounce, bestowing her creations on locals and travelers alike. Her weathered face bore the serene joy of someone who'd performed this ritual for decades.

"*Tarnüra*, young ones!" she called, pressing a corsage into Xara's hands before Markus could steer them away. "None pass through Cenovira's gates without winter's blessing!"

Xara accepted it with the perfect mix of grace and gratitude that had fooled so many in Vesper. But Markus saw the genuine warmth in her eyes as she admired the delicate weaving. Street life hadn't completely hardened her heart to simple kindnesses.

"For the gentleman," the woman insisted, holding out another corsage. Markus stared at it blankly, as something foreign to him as the concept of celebration itself.

Xara's lips twitched with suppressed amusement. "Here," she said, taking the corsage and reaching up to fasten it to his collar. Her fingers were quick and sure, the same hands that could pick any lock in Vesper now handling festival flowers with surprising tenderness. "Try not to look so terrified. It's holly, not handcuffs."

The old woman beamed, already moving to her next target. Around them, more festival-goers were emerging from ships bearing similar decorations—bright splashes of color against winter clothes that transformed the commotion into something almost magical. Children darted through the crowd trailing ribbons laughing in sharp contrast to the guards positioned at strategic points around the harbor.

"Feels wrong," Markus muttered, resisting the urge to tug at the corsage. "Playing at festivals while Hans is out there."

"Maybe that's exactly why we need it," Xara replied softly. Her hand brushed his arm, a gesture that had calmed him countless times in Vesper's darkest alleys. "Sometimes the best disguise is simply allowing yourself to be part of something."

They continued through the crowd, now marking more than just escape routes and guard positions. Xara's sharp eyes noted which vendors were legitimately preparing for celebration and which might be using festival goods to hide less innocent wares. Markus cataloged faces, searching for any that might belong to Hans' people, while trying to ignore how the holly at his collar seemed to pulse in time with his scar.

Beneath their winter clothes, weapons lay ready. Behind their festival masks, street instincts stayed keen. But for just a moment—watching children hang blessing-rings from lamp posts while their parents sang traditional winter songs—they caught a glimpse of the peace they'd never known. A peace that, if Hans had his way, might not be theirs by midwinter.

* * *

The crowd's movement pushed them toward the eastern docks, where the press of bodies thinned enough to breathe. Markus' scar had been throbbing steadily since they'd arrived, but something about this section of harbor made the pain more acute. Beside him, Xara noticed his slight flinch—she'd learned to read the signs of his 'condition' over the years, though he'd never let her understand its true nature.

"You should rest," she said quietly. "Find a medic in town ..."

"I'm fine." The response was automatic—years of deflection.

"Right. Like you were 'fine' all those nights in Vesper when you'd disappear to that clinic." Frustration tinged her voice—the same frustration she'd felt every time he'd shut her out of this one part of his life.

Before he could respond, a movement caught his eye—a figure among the fishermen's stalls, too still to be a merchant. The old Nevran's eyes found Markus through the crowd, and something in that gaze stopped him in his tracks. Beside him, Xara tensed, her hand drifting toward her hidden blade.

"The whispering winds speak of darkness," the seer said, his accent thick with the islands' cadence. He reached out, not quite touching Markus' face, his hand hovering near the black scar. "But you ... you carry a different song. Like two tides pulling against each other."

Xara stepped slightly forward, placing herself between Markus and the stranger—a protective gesture, honed by years on the streets. But Markus caught her arm. There was something about the seer's words that was holding him in place.

"I'm nobody," Markus said, though the words felt hollow even to him.

"No." The seer's eyes seemed to look through him. "The winds whisper of a primordial hunter, awakened after ages of sleep. Its presence taints the very air." His hand moved to his chest, as if feeling some invisible weight. "But you ... your blood sings with both shadow and starlight. A contradiction, a ..."

He stopped abruptly with widening eyes. Markus felt it too—a sudden chill that had nothing to do with the morning air or the approaching storm. The mist seemed to thicken, moving against the wind.

Xara's grip tightened on Markus' arm. She'd seen enough strange things since leaving Vesper to know when something was truly wrong. The seer's words about Markus' blood stirred memories—nights she'd found him burning with fever, moments when his wounds seemed to heal differently than they should. But she'd never pushed, never demanded answers.

Now, watching his scar throb with an almost visible darkness, she wondered if that had been a mistake.

"Go," the seer whispered, making a sign neither of them recognized. "It hunts. And somehow ... it hunts for you."

The words hit Markus like a physical blow, and suddenly he was back in Moorwood forest. Red eyes blazed through darkness as that massive shadow moved against nature itself, the stench of charring and decay. His scar burned with the memory, an echo of that primal terror that had nearly stopped his heart. The flash lasted barely a heartbeat, but it left him cold despite the press of bodies around them.

Xara's hand pulled him back to the present. "We need to move," she motioned quietly in a steady voice despite the fear she couldn't quite hide. Whatever had just passed through her brother's mind had left him pale beneath his tan.

Still reeling from the memory, Markus let her guide him into the crowd. But through his haze, he had picked up the way she glanced back at the seer, and the slight tremor in her usually steady hands. She'd spent more time with Liyzia than he had, and learned more about Nevran ways. He recalled how she'd fallen silent during Finnor's cryptic warnings that first day in Orwein, and how she'd started taking the old stories more seriously after witnessing Liyzia's powers firsthand.

Now that same wariness crossed her face as she kept close to him, scanning the crowd with new vigilance. If Xara—who'd always found a way to laugh in the face of danger—was this unsettled by a seer's words, perhaps the threat was graver than even his memories suggested.

The festival preparations were underway, but to him each laugh seemed hollow, each celebration masking something darker at work beneath the surface. His scar throbbed with renewed intensity, as if agreeing with the seer's warning. Whatever hunted him had followed them across the sea. This time, he couldn't protect Xara by keeping from her what he truly was.

The festival crowds swallowed them once more, but not before the winter wind carried one final whisper from the direction of the seer's stall—words that seemed to chase them like shadows through the busy harbor.

* * *

The morning mist clung to Orwein's streets as Finnor approached Nikel's home. His usual whimsy was replaced by something darker. Around him, the village prepared for its own modest winter celebrations—garlands of holly appearing on doorways, blessing-rings woven with fresh pine. But the seer's attention was fixed on the horizon, where storm clouds gathered against an otherwise clear sky.

"The winds speak of shadow," he said without preamble, finding Nikel and Liyzia in their sitting room. "Something is stirring in the north."

Liyzia stilled at her place by the window with a festival wreath half-formed in her hands. Silver ribbons caught the light as they slipped through her fingers. "Not shadow," she corrected softly. "Hunger. Long buried and now awakened."

The air in the room seemed to thicken with her

words. Nikel drew his pipe from his lips, watching his wife carefully. In all their years together, he'd learned to read the subtle shifts in her presence—the way the light seemed to bend around her when she sensed something beyond mortal ken.

"The seer in Cenovira has seen him," Finnor continued. "Your ... son."

The word caught her like sunlight through crystal. *Son.* She had called him "My Markus" since that day in the woods had woven protection into his shawl with all the fierce tenderness of her heart. But *son?* The word rang with an authenticity that nearly took her breath away.

"He carries ancient blood marked by the old world," Finnor pressed. "The winds whisper of shadow and light dwelling in one vessel. Of power stirring from long sleep."

The wreath in Liyzia's hands stilled. Nikel drew his pipe from his lips, and for a moment, husband and wife exchanged a look charged with unspoken understanding. That first night, when she'd brought the stranger home, Nikel had sensed something in him—an echo of something older than their known histories. His years of training had taught him to trust such instincts.

But Liyzia merely returned to her work, her fingers weaving ribbons through evergreens as though Finnor's words carried no weight.

"The winds whisper of shadow and light dwelling in one form," the seer continued, frustration in his voice. "Of power awakening."

"And what would you have me do?" Liyzia's voice carried that same gentle certainty that had named him in the forest. Her fingers traced patterns in the air, as if touching a thread that stretched across the sea. Through the shawl's ancient weave, she could almost feel him—not the scarred warrior others saw, but the soul beneath, bright as any star.

"You speak as if he were in the next room," Finnor observed carefully, "not leagues away in dangerous lands."

Liyzia smiled in an expression holding secrets older than the forest itself. "He may walk far from my reach, but never beyond my knowing."

Nikel and Finnor exchanged troubled glances, but Liyzia had already returned to her wreaths, humming a forgotten melody. The air around her seemed to shimmer, just slightly, like heat rising from summer stones.

"Do not fear for him," she said softly, though whether she spoke to them or to someone much further away, neither man could say. "I will watch. I will know when he needs me."

The morning light caught her form, and for a moment—just a moment—she seemed to fade at the edges, like a watercolor. Then she was solid again, merely a woman preparing for a festival, though the power in her gentle certainty lingered in the air like the chime of distant bells.

"The kaegar is hunting him," Finnor said abruptly, the forbidden word hanging heavy in the air. "You know what this means."

Liyzia's hands never paused in their weaving, but something in the air grew sharp, like the moment before lightning strikes. "I know what hunts my son," she said, her voice carrying a knowing that made both men step back. "I know what darkness stirs. But you forget, Finnor, he carries my blessing now. My protection."

"And what protection can you offer against such hallowed depths of evil?" Finnor challenged, though his voice wavered.

Liyzia finally looked up, and both men caught their breath. Her eyes held something older than the forest, deeper than the sea. "You see only the darkness in his blood," she said softly. "I see the light that will transform it."

Nikel pressed his pipe between his lips, watching his wife with a mixture of wonder and concern. After all these years, her mysteries still unfurled like endless ribbons, each answer leading to deeper questions. He caught Finnor's eye, but the seer merely shrugged, as if to say some riddles were better left unsolved.

The pipe had gone cold in his hands, yet Nikel continued to hold it, lost in thought as Liyzia's soft humming filled the room—a mysterious melody that seemed to reach across seas and shadows toward their adopted son.

Liyzia's melody faded into silence as shadows lengthened across Orwein's streets. The storm clouds that had caught Finnor's attention now stretched toward Cenovira, as if nature itself conspired to darken the paths ahead.

* * *

Beneath the belly of the docked cruiser NightShade, the telecommunications chamber droned with artificial life. Hans watched his operators work as their fingers moved nimbly across crystal-powered boards that painted their faces in cold, unnatural light. Modern marvels that had helped build his empire of influence—predictable, controllable, everything that power should be.

The lights dimmed on command, but when Rathmar moved through the shadows behind him, they lit up of their own accord. Even the ship's systems seemed to recognize something older than circuitry and crystal, something that made Hans' carefully constructed world suddenly feel fragile.

Three ghostly figures materialized in holographic gold, a technological seance that had cost millions of crowns in Guild engineering. These were 'the three wise men,' as Nettles called them, Franz Schwartz, Karl Williams, and Herman Klaus. Their projected forms towered over the chamber—to reveal masters of industry and manipulation present in light and shadow.

Hans might have smiled at the irony. Here they all were, using the pinnacle of modern achievement to dismantle a throne older than their bloodlines. But Rathmar's presence behind him kept the smile from his lips. The Dromelan moved like someone who had walked with older powers, who understood forces that couldn't be bought or controlled with modern ingenuity.

"The three wise men," Nettles acknowledged quietly, while the operators made their final adjustments. Something in the transmission made the holograms waver, like spirits struggling to maintain form.

"Wise?" Rathmar's voice carried a hint of amusement. "They grasp at power through machines and money, yet know nothing of true strength." He moved closer to the projections, and the distorted images around him that seemed repelled by his very nature. "Your masters play at being gods, Senator. But they have forgotten what real power feels like."

Hans straightened his tie, an increasingly hollow gesture. "Power is power," he said, though the words tasted like ash. "Whether it comes through technology or ..." he hesitated, unwilling to name the forces Rathmar commandeered.

"Does it?" Rathmar's yellow eyes reflected the holographic light like a predator's. "Then why do your machines tremble when I draw near? Why does your artificial clarity blur at the edge of deeper truths—those carved before memory?"

As if to confirm his point, the transmission wavered again. The three wise men's faces faltered like masks about to fall, while somewhere far below in the ship's hold, something primal and hungry stirred in its chains.

The three holograms stabilized, though their shadows seemed to writhe at the edges. Schwartz spoke first, his artificial form looming larger than the others.

"Let's make this cordial and brief, Senator Lumen. We need you to expedite this operation as swiftly as possible." His voice carried the seasoned authority of someone unused to being questioned. "Our sources confirm the local authorities are already coordinating with nearby regiments to increase security. The coronation has been confirmed for New Year's Day."

Williams' ghostly fingers tapped an unseen surface as he leaned forward. "You are to deliver the seal and expedite it, no matter the cost. We have more than enough to compensate the Dromelan delegation for their part in the mission."

Hans felt Rathmar shift behind him at the casual mention of compensation. The Dromelan made no sound, but the temperature in the room seemed to drop.

"The forged documents must be transferred immediately," Klaus added, swirling what appeared to be brandy in his projected hand. "Our proposal for the new government must be ready following a respectful 'bereavement' at her Highness' demise."

The casual way they discussed assassination made even Hans' stomach turn, though he was careful to keep his face neutral. These were men who ordered death over breakfast, who reshaped kingdoms from the comfort of their distant offices.

"Of course, this will include securing the number of votes needed to elevate you to the High Council," Williams continued, "along with appropriate financial compensation."

Rathmar's quiet laugh made the holograms shudder. "They offer you scraps from their table, Senator, while speaking of powers they barely understand." His voice carried the weight of centuries. "The aether stone they covet so carelessly has outlasted a thousand such 'wise men.'"

The three figures shifted, their expressions hardening. "Is there a problem with our Dromelan allies?" Schwartz asked, his tone suggesting that the word 'allies' was generous.

"No problem," Hans said quickly, shooting Rathmar a warning look that the Dromelan ignored. "Everything proceeds as planned. Though the timing ..."

"The timing is not negotiable," Klaus cut in. "You have our instructions. We expect confirmation of success, nothing less. Good day, Senator. And Happy Holidays!"

Their forms dissolved into static, leaving the chamber feeling darker and emptier. Hans turned to find Rathmar studying him with those unsettling yellow eyes.

"Your masters play their games well," the Dromelan said softly. "But they forget—some powers cannot be bought. Some hungers cannot be controlled by men who think gold is strength."

In the shadows beyond the chamber's door, Gurigor watched silently as his leader baited the senator. Like Hans, none of these 'wise men' understood that Rathmar served purposes far older than their petty politics. The kaegar was just the beginning.

"Time grows short," Rathmar continued. "Shall we show your masters what real power looks like?"

Hans straightened his jacket, a man clinging to familiar gestures in an increasingly unfamiliar game. "Power is power," he repeated, but the words sounded hollow even to him. Somewhere above them, the approaching storm clouds gathered like an omen, while below, ancient forces crouched in the inky darkness of the ship's hold.

The telecommunications chamber powered down, modern marvels fading to darkness. Hans turned to find Nettles at the door with a scout—one of the men who'd been watching the ravine. The man's report came quickly: five black vehicles spotted, advanced XL17 models with blacked-out windows. The Governor's sentries were moving like clockwork through the perimeter.

"The festival grounds have been moved inland," Nettles added, "to Nubensoyra."

Hans studied the map, tracing the route with his finger. "They'll have to pass through Moorwood's outskirts. The road narrows there, cutting between the forest and the ravine." He glanced at Rathmar. "A perfect place for your hunter."

"The aether stone will reveal her location," Rathmar said quietly. "One echo calls to another—old power recognizes its twin." His yellow eyes gleamed. "When the kaegar draws near, the stone will betray her presence—a beacon in the darkness."

"And the Immortals?" Hans asked. "Even with your ... creature, they won't be easy to overcome."

Rathmar's smile showed teeth that seemed sharper than they should be. "In open ground, away from crowds and witnesses, the kaegar will show you what true power looks like. Your men need only prevent their escape. The hunter will do the rest."

Hans tried to hide his unease at Rathmar's certainty. "My scouts will track the vehicles, confirm when they leave the festival grounds. We strike on their return journey—clean, controlled, away from prying eyes."

"Yes," Rathmar said, though something in his tone suggested he found Hans' need for control amusing. "Let them enjoy their festivals and masks. Let them dance and celebrate." He moved toward the door, shadows clinging to his form. "The old powers are patient. We will wait in the dark places, in the deep woods where their modern weapons mean nothing."

As the storm clouds gathered over Oravon like a shroud, ancient powers stirred beneath modern ambitions. In the ship's hold, something remembered the age before the kingdoms dreamed of its coming freedom.

And somewhere between festival lights and gathering shadows, a man with cursed blood felt the weight of powers he didn't understand pulling him toward a destiny he couldn't escape.

The winter festival approached, putting on a bright face against the gathering darkness. But this year, more than just the old year would die when the celebrations ended.

CHAPTER FOURTEEN

The sun dipped low, painting the sky in hues of red and orange, signaling the eve of the Winter Solstice. The town of Nubensoyra and its fields transformed into a tapestry of old-world magic and modern revelry—a celebration five millennia old, yet somehow new each year. Thousands of lanterns twinkled to life from every rooftop and porch, their light catching the crystalline frost that dusted the pine branches. Holly and mistletoe were entwined with ribbons of scintillating colors—deep crimson, midnight blue, and shimmering gold. The scent of mableberries filled the air mixed with woodsmoke and spices from a hundred different lands.

For those who had traveled from across the kingdom, this was more than mere celebration. Merchants from the harbor towns traded stories with highlanders from the frost-covered peaks. Nevran tribal elders walked alongside Earthen craftsmen, while Skylander children darted between stalls with faces painted in starlight patterns. Tonight, all boundaries were blurred—between peoples, between traditions, between the world that was and the one that might be.

For Markus, it was suffocating. The crowd, the laughter, the overwhelming crush of people—they felt like a tide threatening to pull him under. His recent failures weighed on him, dragging his steps. Even the warm glow of the lanterns couldn't chase away the cold certainty that he didn't belong in this tapestry of joy and belonging.

"Stop brooding and help me choose." Xara held up two masks, her eyes bright with an enthusiasm he hadn't seen since their childhood. The first was a delicate swan, graceful lines and pale feathers. The second emblazoned with crimson and gold was a phoenix rising from flames. "Which suits a master forger better?"

"The swan's more subtle," Markus offered, but Xara was already fastening the phoenix mask in place.

"Since when have I been subtle?" Her smile flashed beneath the beaked visage. "Besides, I've already picked yours."

She produced another mask from her satchel—a saber-wolf, fierce features fashioned with unsettling detail. Something about it made Markus' scar throb. The craftsmanship was extraordinary, the kind only found in the highest markets of the kingdom. Yet here it was, in a street rat's hands.

"A wolf?" He touched the mask's snout cautiously. "Why?"

Xara's expression softened behind her phoenix mask. "Trust me," she said, reaching up to fasten it around his head. Her fingers brushed his scar with familiar gentleness. "Some things choose us before we choose them."

From the shadows between stalls, a cloaked figure

watched their exchange. Mercury's hand rested lightly on his concealed weapon, but his attention was fixed on the dark scar visible beneath the wolf mask. Beside him, another masked observer in a flowing dress nodded almost imperceptibly. Danae had spotted him too.

Around them, the festival swelled with life. Yewwa and his sons donned their own masks—birds of prey whose feathers caught the lantern light. The air was filled with the scent of roast meats and spiced wine, pulling at memories of Liyzia's kitchen. But even that comfort felt distant now, lost in the press of masked revelers and the weight of all they'd left behind.

* * *

The drums began as distant thunder rumbled far and wide on the winter wind. Deeper than mere music, the sound seemed to rise from the earth itself—an age-old heartbeat that awakened something primal in the blood. One by one, the festival's other musicians joined in: pipes that wailed like wind through mountain passes, strings that sang of stories older than history.

"Now this," Xara said, as her phoenix mask caught the lantern light, "is more like it." Her fingers tapped against her leg in time with the drums, muscle memory from countless nights of timing guard patrols in Vesper's alleys.

Markus watched the dancers gather, grateful for the wolf mask that hid his unease. Couples moved together like leaves in a whirlwind, their own masks transforming them into mythical creatures—deer and dragons, owls and mighty giants of yore.

"Don't even think about it," he muttered as Xara's hand closed around his arm.

A familiar laugh cut through the music. "Too late for that."

Through the crowd came a figure in a sheep mask that couldn't quite conceal the grace of noble bearing. Markus recognized her immediately—Danae, the lady of the manor who had shown him kindness when he'd stumbled into her estate. Her eyes sparkled with mischief through the mask's openings. "The lost recruit returns," she said warmly. "Though perhaps not so lost now."

Xara's posture shifted subtly. Markus felt her assessment of Danae—quick, thorough, born of years of reading marks and threats alike. But something in Danae's genuine warmth seemed to settle her street-honed instincts.

Behind Danae, a cloaked figure that Markus recognized as Mercury moved with studied casualness. The Immortal's nod was barely perceptible, but Markus caught it. So did Xara, whose fingers brushed his arm in silent recognition of an ally.

"A dance?" Danae asked, extending her hand. The simple gesture carried echoes of that morning in her manor—the same offer of normalcy in a world that had gone sideways.

Markus started to refuse, but Xara surprised him. Instead of the protective warning he expected, she gave him a gentle push forward. "Go on," she said softly. "Not everyone who offers kindness has an angle."

"I was going to say no," he protested weakly.

"You always say no." There was something in Xara's

voice—protectiveness and hope that made his chest tight. "Maybe it's time to say yes."

As Danae pulled him into the whirl of dancers, Markus caught one last glimpse of his sister. There she stood with her phoenix mask gleaming, watching him with the same fierce pride she'd shown when he'd survived his first street fight. But now that pride carried something new—a wish for him to find moments of joy in between the shadows they lived in.

The music blared, and Markus found himself caught in the whirl of the dance. Danae moved with measured grace, but there was laughter in her voice as she guided his clumsy steps. "Relax," she whispered. "You faced the Walls of Dressen. Surely a dance can't be worse?"

"The walls didn't laugh at my footwork," he muttered, but found himself nonetheless smiling.

Behind her sheep mask, Danae's eyes softened. "No, but they didn't offer friendship either."

The dance swept them through patterns of light and shadow, each turn of the crowd revealing new facets of the festival's spontaneity. Markus struggled to match Danae's steps, aware of his own awkwardness against her natural grace. But she moved with the music as though it were a game, making every stumble feel intentional.

"You're thinking too much," she said, guiding him through another turn. "Feel the rhythm instead."

"Easy for you to say," he muttered, narrowly avoiding collision with another couple. "You probably learned these steps before walking."

Her laugh carried a hint of sadness. "Actually, I learned them in secret. Father thought dancing was ...

unnecessary." Through the slits of her mask, her eyes sparked with remembered defiance. "So naturally, I practiced twice as hard."

Around them, the celebration swirled in ever-widening circles. Yewwa and his sons had joined the dance, their bird masks bobbing like exotic fowl through the sea of revelers. Even Mercury's cloaked form moved with surprising agility at the edges of the crowd, though his vigilance never wavered for an instant.

The music picked up tempo. Danae's grip tightened on his hand as she pulled him into a faster step. "Trust me," she said, and before he could protest, she was leading him through a spin that somehow didn't end in disaster. "Not bad for someone who claims to be done with surprises!" she teased, her breath quick with exertion and laughter.

The crowd pressed closer, forcing them to move together. Despite his initial resistance, Markus found himself caught up in the moment—the warmth of her hand in his, the way she made each misstep feel like part of the dance rather than a failure. For a brief moment, the burden of his recent defeats felt lighter.

Through a gap in the dancers, he caught sight of Xara. His sister had found her own partner—a young Skylander whose enthusiasm made up for his lack of rhythm. But even as she moved fluidly through the steps, her eyes never stopped their careful sweep of the crowd. Always watching, always protecting, even in the midst of celebration.

"Your sister," Danae said softly, following his gaze, "she carries the weight of both your worlds, doesn't she?"

The observation caught him off guard. "We carry each other," he corrected.

Danae's eyes met his through their masks—the sheep and the wolf, prey and predator, moving together in defiance of nature's rules. "Sometimes," she said, "the heaviest burdens are the ones we choose."

The music reached a crescendo, drums and pipes weaving together in a final flourish. Couples around them spun faster, their masks creating a blur of mythical faces in the lantern light. Markus felt Danae's hand steadying him through one last turn before the song ended, leaving them both breathless.

"See?" She squeezed his hand. "Not everything has to be a battle."

But even as she spoke, a chill wind cut through the warmth of the crowd. Above them, clouds were gathering against the festival's lights, while in the distance, thunder rolled like mythical drums coming to life. The storm that had been threatening all evening was finally approaching, carrying with it omens that neither mask nor music could keep at bay.

* * *

The festival's energy gradually shifted as evening deepened into night. The frantic rhythms of the dance gave way to softer notes, while overhead, twin moons emerged from behind scattered clouds—one casting purple light, the other emerald, painting the world in ethereal hues.

Markus had retreated to the quieter fringes of the celebration, seeking refuge from the press of bodies and memories of the dance. His wolf mask hung loose around his neck, the cool night air welcome against his flushed skin. From this higher vantage point, the festival below looked almost dreamlike as thousands of lanterns swayed like earthbound stars, and masked figures moving through pools of moonlight.

A soft sound of footsteps drew his attention. Even before he turned, something in him recognized the presence—that same otherworldly energy he'd felt at the manor. Lily stood a few paces away, her form ethereal in the dual moonlight. She wore two masks now—an ornate hawk over her usual silver faceplate, yet her green eyes were unmistakable through the layered openings.

For a moment, neither spoke. The festival's sounds seemed distant here, muted like underwater music. Lily moved with that same grace he admired, and took a seat on a weathered stone wall that overlooked the celebration. After a heartbeat's hesitation, she patted the space beside her—an invitation as silent as she was.

Markus found himself accepting, though he kept a careful distance. Up close, he could see the aether stone's glow beneath her cloak, pulsing faintly like a captured star. Its light seemed to resonate with something in his blood, though he pushed that thought away.

He sat stiffly at first, unsure where to look. Her beauty wasn't loud—it was quiet and unguarded, like a song you only heard if you were still enough. But his eyes kept finding hers through the mask. And he hated how clumsy he felt next to her grace.

<<The moons are beautiful tonight,>> her hands signed in a graceful and practiced movement.

Markus nodded, his own hands replying with the simple signs he'd learned. <<Yes.>>

Her eyes lingered on him as she continued. <<Only seven times a year do both appear as full as they are tonight. They're closest to us now. Almost close enough to touch.>> She reached up, as if to grasp the celestial lights. <<Do you watch them often?>>

The gesture held such innocent wonder that Markus felt something in his chest tighten. He looked away, his hands moving slower, uncertain. <<Some things ... they're just not meant for us. Too far out of reach.>>

The words carried more bitterness than he'd intended, but Lily's eyes softened behind her masks. There was understanding there—not pity, but recognition of a kindred spirit. Both of them were isolated, though for very different reasons.

Her hands moved again, playful despite her hidden expression. <<I've reached them before,>> she signed, pointing toward the moons.

<<Back then, it was easier to believe in impossible things.>>

Her hands paused, uncertain. <<Before the masks. Before the silence.>>

Markus raised an eyebrow.

<<When I was a child,>> she began, her movements carrying a wistful note, <<my father would lift me in his arms during nights like this. He'd tell me I could touch the stars, and for a while, I believed I could. He'd lift me higher, and I'd reach out as if I could grab them.>>

The memory seemed to catch her off guard, her hands stilling. She drew closer, the subtle shift bringing with it a scent of flowers ... and something older ... like the pages of ancient books. The aether stone at her throat gleamed brighter, catching the crystalline frost that had begun to form on the grass around them.

<<I remember it like it was yesterday,>> she signed, as her eyes shone with an impossible mix of loneliness and light. <<All I have are my memories with him. But memories ... they can't overcome the loneliness of tonight.>>

She reached up, undoing the clasp that held the stone.

Markus tensed. It felt too intimate, too exposed.

In her palm, it glimmered with inner radiance, brighter than any star...

Markus forgot to breathe—not just from the stone's beauty, but from the trust in exposing it. She didn't do this for strangers. He was certain of that now.

His hand moved of its own accord, drawn to the timeless jewel. When his fingers met hers, warmth spread through him like sunlight breaking through storm clouds. Above them, the twin moons cast their ethereal light, while below, the festival continued its dance of shadows and joy.

<<Memories are good,>> he signed, surprising himself at the gentleness of his motions. <<They give you something to hold onto. The nights your father spent with you, reaching for the stars ... hold onto those memories like you would this stone. Not everyone has them.>>

He immediately regretted the words, feeling foolish. What had possessed him to say something so sentimental? <<I know that probably sounds stu ...>>

Lily gently placed a hand on his fingers, silencing him. <<Don't ruin the moment,>> she signed with eyes twinkling with warmth.

<<Moments like this are rare for me,>> she signed. <<I don't share them easily.>> Beneath her mask, Markus sensed a hidden smile, one she only half revealed.

<<There's much more to you than you realize,>> she continued softly. <<Your mentor, Nikel ... his name is spoken with reverence in my father's journals. He wouldn't take in just anybody.>>

Markus looked away, shaking his head slightly. <<He took in a 'nobody,'>> he murmured. <<Crazy, huh?>>

Her hand found his wrist, a light yet firm touch. <<This 'nobody' warned us through Mercury. Even if others wouldn't listen ... I am grateful.>>

The words carried layers of meaning—gratitude not just for the warning, but for trying when most would have walked away. Some part of him wanted to argue that the warning had fallen on deaf ears, that the Prefect's dismissal had made his efforts worthless. But something in her eyes stopped him. They carried a wisdom beyond her years that suggested she understood more than she could say.

The warmth of her gratitude felt too palpable, too pure for someone like him. He started to rise, to retreat back into familiar shadows, but her grip tightened ever so slightly. <<We will meet again when you receive the seal of the monarchy. You *did* complete the training—right?>>

The question struck like winter frost. Markus' eyes lowered, defeat washing over him anew. He began to pull away, but Lily's hand remained steady on his wrist, neither demanding nor releasing.

In that moment of shared silence, something passed between them—an understanding deeper than words or signs could convey. Above, the dual moons painted the world in impossible colors, while on the horizon, storm clouds gathered like deep-seated powers arising from sleep. The festival's warmth felt distant now, as if this moment existed in some space between celebration and shadow, between what was and what might have been.

Lily's eyes held his again, green as spring leaves. In their depths, Markus saw not just the lonely girl reaching for stars, but something older, something that resonated in his own blood like a song half-remembered. The aether stone danced once more between them, its light a promise or a warning—he couldn't tell which.

The wind picked up, carrying with it the first wisp of the coming storm. But for now, they sat together in comfortable silence, watching the last remnants of twilight fade into a night that would change everything.

CHAPTER FIFTEEN

The winter air bit through layers of wool and leather as Xara moved through the festive crowd, her travel coat doing little against the arctic chill. Her phoenix mask caught firelight from the hanging lanterns, while her hand unconsciously touched the half-pendant at her throat. Around her, revelers in elaborate costumes twirled beneath strings of crystalline lights, their breath frosting in the December night.

At first, she thought exhaustion was playing tricks on her eyes. A serpent mask emerged from the crowd near the wine pavilion, its silver scales catching moonlight. Before she could process the sight, another identical mask appeared by the musicians' stage. Her heart quickened as she spotted a third by the merchant stalls—each figure wearing the same tailored black overcoat, each moving with calculated purpose through the revelry.

Years of reading marks in Vesper's shadows had taught her to notice the subtle tells—the way wealth carried itself, the difference between practiced grace and natural movement. Two of the serpent-masked figures moved like actors in borrowed clothes. But the third ... he stalked the crowd with the easy confidence of a predator.

Xara kept her movements casual, drifting between groups of dancers, while tracking all three figures in her peripheral vision. The real Hans was searching for something. Or someone. She touched her mask, grateful for its concealment as she plotted her next move.

The decision was taken from her when a gloved hand touched her elbow. She hadn't heard him approach—a rare feat that sent ice through her veins.

"A dance?" Hans' cultured voice carried none of the warmth she remembered from The Hive. His fingers brushed the half-pendant at her throat, and she could hear the mockery in his words. "I remember this piece. Though it seems ... incomplete now."

Xara could flee. Create a scene. Disappear into the crowd as she'd done countless times before. But something in his tone—that mix of threat and curiosity—made her turn to face him instead. The serpent mask's silver scales seemed to move in the lantern light, its empty eyes studying her through the slits.

"Quite bold of you," she said, letting him guide her into the dance. "Approaching a woman you barely know."

"Oh, but I do know you ... 'Persia,' I believe." His hand settled at her waist as they moved to the music. "Or do you prefer 'Xara' now?"

She matched his steps with rehearsed grace, thankful that Liyzia had insisted on teaching her proper form. "And I know you, Senator. Tell me—does the Nightshade's cargo hold feel crowded these days?"

His grip tightened slightly—the only sign her words had struck home. Around them, other couples danced and laughed, unaware of the dangerous game being played in their midst. The festival music rang through the wintry air, covering their low voices.

"Impressive!" Hans said, guiding her through a turn. "Though I wonder what else you know."

"Enough to make the National Army very interested." She kept her tone light, playful even. "Spice running is one thing, Senator. But your other cargo? That would end more than just your political career."

The serpent mask tilted, studying her. "You've grown bolder since our last encounter. I admired that fire in you then. Still do, if I'm honest."

"Flattery?" Xara laughed softly. "I expected better of you."

"Not flattery." His voice dropped lower, meant for her ears alone. "An offer. Think about it— your skills, my resources. Together we could ..."

"Build an empire?" She cut him off with a smile that didn't reach her eyes. "I've seen what happens to your partners, Mr. Lumen. Two Council leaders learned that lesson recently, didn't they?"

The music shifted to a slower beat. Hans pulled her closer, his next words carrying an edge beneath their silken surface. "Careful, my dear. Some dances end more abruptly than others."

"Is that why you're here?" She kept her movements light, despite the tension coiling in her chest. "To end something? Or someone?"

His laugh was genuine, which somehow made it more frightening. "I'm here to celebrate the festival, like everyone else. Though I admit, finding you was an unexpected pleasure."

His thumb brushed the half-pendant again. "Tell me, how is your brother enjoying Oravon? You're certainly not here alone."

The mention of Markus made her pulse quicken, but years of running cons kept her expression impenetrable behind the phoenix mask. She let Hans lead her into another turn, using the moment to scan the crowd. His other masked accomplices had drawn closer, creating a loose perimeter around their dance.

"My brother can take care of himself," she said guardedly.

"Can he?" Hans' voice carried a dangerous undertone. "The failed watchman, the street fighter with a temper ... yet somehow he caught the attention of Zylvan knights and Immortals. One might wonder what they see in him."

Xara forced her voice to remain steady. "You seem fascinated by my family, Senator. Should I be flattered? Or concerned?"

"Both, perhaps." His hand at her waist guided her deftly past other dancers. "You're both remarkable in your own ways. The forger who could replicate the impossible. The watchman who survived what should have killed him." He leaned closer, his mask's silver scales glinting. "Tell me—what else runs in those shared veins?"

"We're not sharing anything tonight," Xara said, her light tone evading the warning in his words. "Especially not blood."

"No?" Hans' chuckle was soft. "Five million crowns

says otherwise. Arduiine's bounty hunters are very motivated these days."

"And yet here I am, dancing with you instead of rotting in their cells." She smiled beneath her mask. "Perhaps you should question their motivation."

The music's tempo increased. Hans matched it, his movements precise but with an underlying tension she hadn't noticed before. "You're playing a dangerous game, my dear. The pieces are already in play. Wouldn't you rather be on the winning side?"

"Winning?" She let skepticism color her voice. "Is that what you call unleashing something you can't control?"

His steps faltered—just slightly—but enough to confirm her suspicion. The cargo in the Nightshade's hold wasn't just illegal. It was dangerous. "You know nothing of control," he said, his cultured tones hardening. "But you will. Soon enough, everyone will."

A flash of crimson caught her eye—Markus' wolf mask moving through the crowd with Lily. They were heading toward the hill overlooking the festival. Away from Hans' line of sight, but also away from her protection. The dance had served its purpose, revealing more than Hans intended. But now she needed to end it.

"A shame," she said, beginning to pull away. "But all dances must end."

His grip remained steady, not forceful enough to raise the alarm but present enough to remind her of the danger he represented. "Indeed, they must. Though I wonder which of us will lead the final step." His voice dropped lower. "The festival's not over, my dear. And tonight promises ... unexpected entertainment."

Something in his tone made her pause. That casual threat was expected, but there was something else—an undercurrent of uncertainty that seemed out of character for a man who orchestrated every move.

"Careful, Senator," she matched his quiet tone. "Draw too much attention, and you might not like what answers."

Hans released her with studied grace, his serpent mask catching the lantern light. "An interesting choice of words. I look forward to discussing them further—after tonight's events unfold." He stepped back with a slight bow. "Do give my regards to your brother. While you can."

Xara watched him disappear into the crowd, her mind racing. His masked accomplices had vanished as well, but she didn't trust this apparent retreat. Hans was many things, but never careless. If he was letting her go this easily ...

She touched the half-pendant at her throat, scanning the festival grounds for Markus. Whatever Hans had planned, she needed to warn her brother. But first, she had to understand what game the senator was really playing.

* * *

Hans moved through the festival with polished calm, though his thoughts churned like a winter storm. Two of his masked accomplices fell in step behind him, while the third maintained position near the main pavilion. Their synchronized movements had worked perfectly in identifying Xara—too perfectly. She'd known exactly who he was, and had played him as skillfully as he'd played others.

He found a secluded spot beneath the merchant quarter's awnings, where the festival's glow barely reached. "Leave me," he ordered the faux serpents. Once alone, he yanked off his mask, letting the bitter air cool his face. His hand shook slightly as he pulled out his transmitter.

The Nightshade. How had she known about the ship? More importantly, what else did she know?

The transmitter crackled. Nothing. He tried another channel, stilling the urge to crush the device. Rathmar had insisted on radio silence until the signal, but too many pieces were sliding out of his control. Xara's apparent knowledge of their ship—and possibly their operation—had him on edge.

A sound made him turn—just wind through the awnings—but his nerves were raw. He was a senator, not some common criminal jumping at shadows. Yet here he stood, hiding from a street forger who should have been nothing more than a tool in his plans.

The festival music seemed to mock him now, its mirth grating on his darkening thoughts. Somewhere in that celebrating throng, the princess danced beneath her own mask, the aether stone pulsing at her throat. Everything he'd worked for, every calculated move, rested on tonight's success.

But Xara's words had shaken him more than he cared to admit.

"You know nothing of control."

His own words thrown back at him felt prophetic now. He had bedded with ancient powers he barely understood, trusting Rathmar's promises of victory without questioning the price. The sect leader spoke of revenge, of powers older than the kingdom itself, but what did that matter to a man who dealt in modern currencies of influence and fear?

The transmitter crackled again—this time with purpose. He pressed it to his ear, listening to the encoded message with growing unease. Movement in the woods. Something stirring ahead of schedule.

"Hold position," he ordered, his voice steadier than his hands. "No one moves without my signal. Is that clear?"

The response was lost in sudden static. Hans looked toward the forest's edge, where festival lights failed to penetrate the darkness. For a moment, he thought he saw something—a shadow moving against the shadows, too large to be human?

Control. He almost laughed. Perhaps Xara had been right after all.

He replaced his mask with methodical precision, checking that his weapon sat ready beneath his coat. The night's plans might be fraying, but he was still Hans Lumen. He hadn't climbed from district clerk to senator by letting fear rule his actions.

The festival crowd parted as he emerged from the shadows, his serpent mask once again a symbol of authority rather than deception. Let Xara play her games. Let Rathmar keep his secrets. In the end, power belonged to those who seized it, not those who merely dreamed it.

* * *

The aether stone at Lily's throat glimmered with unusual brightness, its glow visible even through her layered garments. She touched it uncertainly, feeling its warmth against her palm.

Beside her, Markus suddenly stiffened.

The symptoms hit without warning. First came the metallic taste in his mouth, followed by that familiar cold sweat. His temples throbbed as nausea rolled through him in waves. These episodes had become more frequent since arriving in Oravon; but this felt different. Stronger. More immediate.

<<Are you alright?>> Lily's hand touched his arm, steadying him.

<<Something's wrong,>> he managed to sign, fighting to keep his fingers steady. His scar burned as if he were newly branded, sending bursts of heat through his veins. The festival lights blurred at the edges of his vision, while distant music seemed to fade beneath the sound of his own blood rushing in his ears.

* * *

The festival's lights barely touched the forest's fringe, where age-old trees stood like sentinels against modern revelry. Three young boys darted between the shadows. Their game of hide-and-seek was carrying them deeper than they intended. Here, where celebration met wilderness, their laughter wafted strangely.

The first sign was silence. Birds stilled their evening songs. The wind itself seemed to pause. Then came the sound—a steady hissing, like steam escaping antiquated pipes, rising and falling with rhythmic precision. A deep, bassy rumbling followed, more felt than heard.

The kaegar watched the children from the darkness, almost invisible despite its size. Red eyes studied their movements with predatorial intent, but something else stirred in its primordial consciousness. Recognition, perhaps? Memory? How long since it had seen such innocent play? How many centuries trapped in darkness, waiting?

Two boys caught sight of it first, their young faces draining of color as their minds struggled to process what stood before them. The third child, still unknowing, watched his friends scramble backward through the undergrowth.

The kaegar lowered itself to one knee, its massive frame dwarfing the remaining child. Its hooded face drew close, nostrils flaring as it drank in the scent of mortal fear. The boy stayed frozen, trapped between terror and fascination as those burning eyes studied him.

Behind its bestial exterior, thoughts moved like glaciers—ancient, inexorable. This was not its prey. Not what called to it through the darkness. Something else pulled at its senses, a beacon that made its very blood surge with recognition.

The aether stone's vibrations were clear now, singing to it across the festival grounds. But there was something else ... something that made its primal instincts scream with hunger. A scent. A presence. Something that should not exist in this age of men.

The kaegar rose to its full height, its black cape spreading like wings in the winter wind. The boy fled, finally finding his legs, but the hunter paid him no mind. Its burning gaze was fixed on the festival lights, where two signals called to it with maddening intensity.

Rathmar emerged from the shadows, his words forming in that forbidden tongue. *{The stone is here. Somewhere. But we must wait in retrieving the woman who wears it as I have instructed you. The hour will soon be at hand.}*

But the kaegar's focus had shifted. Its massive head lifted, testing the air. Something was wrong. The scent it caught was impossible—an echo of its own kind, though diluted, but all the same unmistakable.

{A familiar scent. Here somewhere!} Its response came in snarls and snaps, defying Rathmar's control.

{Listen to me!} Rathmar's command carried desperation now. *{You are the only one here. There is no other!}*

But the kaegar was already making its move, drawn by a hunger older than its captivity. Each massive step cracked roots and branches beneath it. Festival lights beckoned through the trees, and with them, the promise of something it had thought had been lost to time.

The hunt had begun, but not for the prey Rathmar intended.

* * *

The festival's sounds struck the kaegar like physical blows—too strident, too strange after millennia of silence. Lights pierced the darkness in ways its rudimentary mind struggled to process. The scents of thousands of humans mingled with unfamiliar smoke and artificial smells, was an assault on senses honed in a simpler age.

But through this tangle of modernity, that impossible scent called to it. Familiar yet wrong. Pure yet corrupted. Blood that echoed its own, but diluted through countless generations.

The first humans to spot it reacted with confusion rather than fear. Caught in the revelry, they mistook its massive form for an elaborate costume, a planned spectacle. Even its movement through the crowd drew more wonder than terror at first.

Its cloak—neither cloth nor skin—shifted not with wind, but memory. Each movement smeared the air, as though even light recoiled from touching it.

Even its presence confused the senses—too large, too silent, too fluid. People clapped, others gasped.

"Look how big it is!"

"What incredible craftsmanship ...!"

"Is it part of the ceremony?"

One reveler—staggering and slurring, his breath reeking of cheap spirits—lurched too close. He laughed and reached for the cloak, thinking it some illusion.

The kaegar recoiled. Not from the man, but from the *stench*. It turned away in disgust—nose flaring, lip curling—not in fear, but distaste.

Their ignorance stirred something akin to pity in its ancient thoughts. *These frail creatures have forgotten what real power looked like. Forgotten why their ancestors had learned to fear the dark.*

Then someone screamed. The sound cut through the music like a blade, triggering more cries as understanding dawned on the spectators. The kaegar's bulk moved with surprising agility, each step precise despite its growing agitation. Humans scattered before it like leaves.

A brave fool approached with some kind of weapon—all bright lights and artificial thunder. The kaegar swatted him aside with casual force. More came, their weapons just as useless, their deaths just as quick. The creature felt no pleasure in the killing, no more than a storm feels pleasure in flooding a valley. Self-preservation was its only motive as it stalked its real prey.

But that scent ... that impossible bloodline ... it kept growing stronger. The kaegar's head lifted, nostrils flaring as it tracked the source. Through the panicked crowd, up toward the hill where ...

There.

* * *

The festival erupted into pandemonium. Masks that had transformed revelers into creatures of myth now became grotesque mockeries as terror stripped away civilization's veneer. People tripped over elaborate costumes, their festival finery becoming death traps in their panic. Children's screams pierced through the clamor while parents frantically searched through the sea of masks, unable to distinguish their loved ones from strangers.

Lanterns swayed violently as people crashed into their supports, casting wild shadows that only heightened the chaos. Festival stalls collapsed, sending goods and debris flying. The music stuttered and died, replaced by a cacophony of screams, breaking glass, and the thunderous sound of thousands trying to flee all at once. The revelry that had celebrated humanity's resilience to winter's darkness became a stark reminder of how quickly that same humanity could shatter.

The kaegar moved through the panicked crowd, its consciousness fixated on that impossible scent. But something else stirred in its awareness—a recognition that went both ways. Its prey was not just marked by old blood; it was *responding* to its proximity. The diluted bloodline might be weak, but it remembered. It knew.

Above, on the hill, Markus collapsed to one knee. His body felt like it was trying to tear itself apart, every cell screaming in recognition of something it should never have known. The scar on his temple had darkened to an impossible black, pulsing in time with his frantic heart.

Lily's aether stone flared brighter, its light seeming to resonate with both Markus' pain and the approaching hunter. Ancient powers clashed, calling to each other across centuries of silence.

* * *

On the east end of the field, as others fled for their lives, Yewwa led his two sons from behind the scattered and frightened militia. He pulled the boys down in the grass, ordering them to change their spearheads. The elder revealed special arrowheads—black, larger, shinier headpieces, polished to razor-sharp points. As the pair changed them out, they watched their father prepare two arrows for his longbow before proceeding, trying to flank the creature from the south.

* * *

Before Cael and his men could reach the couple, the kaegar lunged forward like a raging demon. The three Immortals opened fire, their twin-barrel heavy blasters raining blasts of lightning, hammering the giant backward in a fiery blaze.

But to their horror, when the smoke cleared, the kaegar rose again. Though its stony, gargantuan body was charred and steamy from the laser blasts, it still breathed. Unscathed, with eyes glowering red, it lunged once more. In disbelief, the assassins aimed their fire again, this time taking turns to reload between rounds. But even their long-range blaster rifles and carbine guns were reduced to only a beating—but not penetrate its steely hide to kill it. Its speed, strength and dexterity overwhelmed the brave assassins, pounding and punishing the trio in a violent, three-on-one struggle.

* * *

Xara spotted the child frozen in terror as the crowd surged around her. Without hesitation, she dived through the mass. Her shoulder slammed into a falling beam as she pushed the girl to safety, the impact sending white-hot pain through her arm. Mercury appeared through the chaos, pulling them both back as the structure collapsed where they'd stood moments before.

"Get her to safety," Xara gasped, her arm hanging useless at her side. She could spot Markus on the hill, but the distance between them now felt like miles. "I can't ... I can't reach him."

"Stay with the girl," Mercury ordered, already moving toward the hill. "We'll find him."

* * *

The symptoms hit like a tidal wave—familiar yet deepened. When the kaegar's roar shook the air, Markus felt it in places he didn't know existed. It resonated not just in his bones but in whatever dark ancestry slept in his cursed bloodline. His body reacted violently with his muscles seizing as two natures warred within him. Human consciousness fought against primal instincts he'd never known he possessed, each breath a battle between what he was and what his blood remembered.

<<Run,>> he signaled to Lily, though every word was a battle. <<Please ... run ...>>

The young princess fled towards the fringe of Moorwood.

His relief in watching her escape was short-lived. Between the pounding in his head, and the chills and nausea in his throat, he could feel the kaegar's approach. The piercing grunts, snaps, gurgling and slashing of its razor teeth brought an overwhelming dread over him as the growing shadow seemed to engulf his entire body.

Lacking any firepower to save himself, he remembered Xara's gauntlet. He scrambled with his remaining strength to roll up his sleeves and snap it on right at the last minute.

An onslaught of heavy, steamy breath beat down upon him, each exhalation sprinkled with droplets of saliva and blood. Rocky fingers balled up into fists, grinding like stone against stone.

Instantly, one of the massive hands clamped down on Markus' throat and lifted him. He could feel the air in his chest being strangled by the massive, jagged fingers, pinching through the skin of his neck! His legs kicked. His arms flailed. His teary eyes flinched beneath the pressure as his face turned crimson, mere seconds away from suffocation.

Then, distracted for a split second by some movement, the kaegar turned its head and spotted the princess seventy yards away.

She stood frozen, her body trembling beneath her cloak as she faced the impending nightmare. The aether stone at her throat vibrated frantically, as if recognizing something it was never meant to encounter. Through the slits of her mask, her green eyes widened with a terror deeper than mere fear—the kind of primal dread that lived in ancestral memory. Her hands moved in aborted attempts to sign, but terror stole even that from her. When the creature's burning gaze fixed on her stone, she clutched it protectively, every fiber of her being screaming to run yet knowing that no distance could truly free her from her assailant.

Time seemed to stand still between the trio. The bestial red eyes glanced between them, like a predator caught deciding which one to prioritize. Its indecision was both curious and intimidating, filled with delayed purpose and hideous delight.

The creature pulled Markus closer. He couldn't move— just gagged and gasped for air as its grip crushed the breath from him.

Those monstrous eyes examined him up close. A steamy breath rushed over his face, laced with a venomous hiss and the slick snap of teeth.

Something in it knew him. And something in him knew it.

It turned back to Markus. Then to the girl.

Its breathing quickened—almost impatient. There was recognition in both. But only one carried the stone.

Then it roared. The sound tore through him like a living thing—a punch to the chest, a scream in his bones. A hundred hounds couldn't match the monster's voice.

Without warning, it flung him aside, as if throwing away a broken branch.

* * *

Hacking, coughing, and scratching for every breath, Markus' throat was on fire, the skin on his neck burning from nearly being crushed beneath the kaegar's enormous hands. As he slowly struggled to his knees, Ditta raced forward with his spear. Markus, fighting for air, pointed towards the woods. But he barely had enough strength to stand right now, much less take off into the treeline to chase after Lily. Jittery and shaken, he collapsed. The last thing he remembered was watching this alien giant tearing off into the dark woodlands right after the princess. Another deafening roar rattled the underbrush, as the bipedal plowed through the darkness.

Then everything fell silent.

The two young men look back into the smoky mist for any signs of help or reinforcement. All they could hear were scattered cries and weeping off in the distance. And as the smoke cleared, the shiny remnants of the Immortals' obsidian armor came into view. To their horror, all three had fallen—but one seemed to be moving. Markus and Ditta approached cautiously.

It was Cael—the stern and aggressive prefect who had

been personally charged with protecting Lily. The three men had met their ghastly fate when they attempted to physically take on the giant. Someway, it managed to rip through their armor to their vital organs, fatally wounding them.

Cael, bleeding from beneath his rib cage just beneath his breastplate, struggled to remove his helmet.

Solemnly, Markus and Ditta took a knee and assisted in removing the view plate, then the outer cavity. It revealed an Immortal, rugged, ravaged, peppered hair and stubble with the face of a care-worn father figure. His eyes lit up momentarily as he smiled at the two young men, knowing he didn't have long. Blood seeped from his mouth, and he turned to the side to spit it out. With his dying strength, he grabbed Markus' wrist, pulling him closer to show him a device he carried on his utility belt.

He powered on the gray box, and the console lit up, displaying a panoramic field of view for a three-mile radius. A light green dot, or a 'blip' was barely visible, moving about, fading in and out.

"That's her," he whispered with a cough, "See? That's her right there."

"Lily?" Markus whispered.

"Yes. Three-mile radius—until you lose her." He coughed out more blood, almost choking on it as the two tried to make him comfortable. "Don't lose her ..."

His voice faded with his final breath, his brown eyes still staring into Markus' as his fingers relaxed, still clutching Markus' wrist.

Ditta bowed his head momentarily, followed by Markus in a moment of silence.

Markus collapsed in the tall grass, fumbling with the tracker, frantically trying to figure out how it worked. The signal grew fainter with each passing second as it registered a distance beyond two miles. Soon it would be completely out of range.

"A bloody massacre," he muttered, gazing over the scattered bodies on the fairground below. "What the hell is that thing?"

"My father says it's a warrior from antiquity," Ditta answered, "But that cannot be possible!"

"That could have been me," said Markus, massaging his throat where the kaegar's grip had nearly throttled him. "Why didn't it finish me?"

His voice caught as another thought hit him. "Xara. I need to find her! Where's Xara?"

"She's alive," Ditta says quickly. "My brother is attending to her now. The injury is not fatal—she's alright."

The tracker's signal blipped again, threatening to fade entirely. Markus stared at it, torn between his sister and the princess. The weight of Cael's final words pressed down on him.

Mercury emerged through the smoke, his armor torn open from shoulder to hip, revealing a wound that gleamed with unnatural darkness. Where the kaegar's claws had struck, the flesh seemed to resist healing, as black veins spread outward with each heartbeat. Even his immortal constitution couldn't fight whatever secret poison now coursed through him.

"The inner court ..." he gasped. "Where is she?"

"Still alive," Markus held up the tracker, its signal growing fainter. "For now."

Mercury tried to rise but collapsed, the darkness spreading visibly through his wound. "How long?"

"Two miles and fading," Markus checked the device again. "Minutes before she's out of range."

"Go," came Xara's voice, sharp with pain but determined. She limped forward, supported by Nix, pale but resolute. Her eyes met Markus' just for a moment, carrying everything they'd never needed to say aloud. "I'll watch him. You find her."

The tracker beamed once more, weaker than ever. No time for goodbyes. No time for doubt.

Ditta pressed his spear into Markus' hands, the black arrowhead gleaming. "My father and brother will find you. Now go!"

As Markus turned toward the dark woods, Xara called after him. "Come back to us."

A distant roar shook the air, and something primal stirred in Markus' blood in response. He looked back once, memorizing their faces, before plunging into Moorwood's inky darkness.

PART III:

TRIAL BY FIRE

CHAPTER SIXTEEN

The once vibrant festival ground had collapsed into a nightmare. Overturned tables and torn banners lay scattered like a battlefield, while the air hung heavy with smoke and the acrid remnants of hundreds of celebratory fireworks turned to weapons. The shrieks of revelry had given way to the moans of the wounded and the shocked silence of survivors.

Governor Tarnsford's response was swift and decisive. His call to arms drew two hundred men to the Legislative Manor—local sheriffs, deputies from as far as Nenevuiim—even foreign merchants bearing whatever arms they possessed. They gathered beneath candlelight, a hastily assembled force against an enemy few could comprehend.

Never had the capital square known such frenzy. What should have been the land's most prosperous week had descended into carnage.

Among the outer grounds of the manor, two other men also descended on the disorder. Hans Lumen, bearing a long rifle, kept his transmitter buzzing, waiting for the signal to pick up. He finally located the man he'd been looking for the past half-hour. In a heated moment of vengeance, he plowed through the multitude and nearly tackled him, along with several others. A chain reaction broke out, with more pushing and shoving among a group of anxious men, before they could finally separate themselves from the crowd.

Hans confronted Rathmar, shoving him into the iron railing.

"Let it out, Senator—if it would help you *feel* better."

"Look around, Mr. Rathmar! Any chance of stealth and successfully pulling this off have now gone up in flames! The whole damn island is about to go on the hunt for this thing! What the hell happened?"

The sect leader took a moment to gather himself. "I witnessed it. Arrakos left the forests, and marched directly through the crowds, across the fields—not to kill. Do you understand? It was only in self-defense! It was as though something or someone was luring him."

Hans' eyes darted about making sure no one was eavesdropping.

"How? This is the second time this has happened!"

"He told me," Rathmar swallowed, "He told me that he sensed '*another*.'"

"Another? Are you telling me—there are *others* like him?"

The sect leader parted his lips, hesitatingly. "His species is all but extinct—except for a remaining few. But I swear to you, Senator—he's the only one here."

"He's headed directly for the princess," Hans whispered.

"You saw her?"

"Her identity was hidden, but the seal of the

monarchy—the aether stone—it's on her necklace. Markus Kane was with her."

"Markus Kane?"

"The man with the scar." Hans leaned over the rails, while watching an overflow of volunteers being turned away and sent home. "This is the second time he has encountered him—and drawn him near."

Rathmar pondered, "I've been chasing this man half-way around the world and once again—he's becoming a thorn in my side. Either he had help delivering those plans to warn them, or something else is going on. Arrakos has eliminated the Immortals just as I foretold, Senator. If this 'Kane' fella's still alive, he's all alone. Certainly, we can handle *one* man—can't we?"

Hans thought long and hard, before pulling out a small tin of brandy to warm himself on the frigid night. "Wait here."

* * *

The two were barely able to squeeze into the crowd of volunteers surrounding the governor's manor. Here local board members and magistrates gave brief statements and took questions during this emergency town hall.

Hans listened in on Governor Tarnsford's assessment of the situation. It was everything he feared. This ancient warrior named Arrakos—the name transliterated by Rathmar in modern Dromelan—had exceeded his own expectations.

This kaegar was not human and was everything that Rathmar projected. A hunter, bred for warfare,

carnivorous, impervious to pain, and of singular purpose—to find its quarry. To that end, it would stop at
absolutely nothing in its path—by force, by blood, by
slaughter.

And though the senator had managed to build up his
own team of mercenaries to join the armed men from
the mainland, he was still greatly outnumbered in this
makeshift militia of two hundred volunteers. But fortunately, the politician had a few contingency plans up
his sleeve.

Rathmar had been waiting outside the Governor's oval
office, next to a couple of armed guards. Hans exited
between the pair and gestured for the Dromelan to keep
up as the two made a hasty retreat from the manor.

"Talk to me, Senator. What is happening?"

"I've managed to buy us a little time" Hans patted him on the back "I've talked our esteemed host,
Governor Tarnsford, into allowing my team to assist in
this manhunt. We'll take the southeast. Everyone else
will take the northwest corner of Moorwood."

The two were now far enough away from Lessador's
legislative branch and the dwindling crowds where they
could speak more freely.

"Are you sure you have the means for tracking your
'hunter'?"

"Of course, Senator. My scouts are quick and accurate.
But what about the governor? And the militia gathering?
Doesn't he suspect our motives?"

"I informed him that I'm representing the lower senate in the high council and that we have a personal
stake in the matter. I also threatened to expose his
illegal spice smuggling out of the port of Duniduiir.

Always carry an ace up your sleeve, Mr. Rathmar. Any further questions?"

"And if we encounter Kane?"

Hans sighed in frustration. "Take him alive if you can. But the seal and girl come first."

"All I want, Senator Lumen, is that stone. At all costs."

* * *

The makeshift infirmary buzzed with urgency as healers moved between the wounded festival-goers. Xara sat on the edge of a cot, ignoring the healer's attempts to check her injuries. Her eyes remained fixed on the doorway, as if willing her brother to appear.

Nearby, Mercury lay propped against the wall. The removal of his damaged armor revealed deep gashes across his chest. The wounds weren't fatal, but they'd keep any normal warrior down for days. Mercury wasn't normal.

"How much longer?" he asked the healer attending to him, his voice tight with impatience.

"These need proper ..." the healer began.

"How. Much. Longer?"

Xara recognized that tone—and felt the same restrained desperation in her own chest. "He's out there alone," she said quietly. "With that thing hunting them."

Mercury's jaw tightened. "The princess ..."

"And my brother," Xara cut in, meeting his gaze. A look of understanding passed between them—both sworn to protect, and both forced to watch their charges slip into danger.

"We don't even know which direction," Mercury said, though his eyes had already moved to his weapons.

Xara stood, shrugging off the healer's protests. "When has that ever stopped either of us?"

A ghost of a smile touched Mercury's lips. "The wounds will slow me down."

"Then it's a good thing you've got a street rat to watch your back," said Xara, gathering supplies despite her own injuries. "Besides, Markus is useless at tracking. They'll need us both."

Mercury watched her for a moment, measuring his options. Then he pushed himself up, ignoring the fresh blood seeping through his bandages. "We move in ten minutes."

The healers exchanged worried glances, but neither Xara nor Mercury paid them any attention. They had failed in their duties once tonight. They wouldn't fail again.

* * *

It had been an hour since Markus entered the dark woodlands, maneuvering through the undergrowth, tangled roots, saplings, and towering timbers. Moonlight filtered in faint patches through the dense canopy forty feet above, casting jagged beams that barely illuminated his path. His watch read a quarter past two in the morning, central time. With a spear in one hand and a blaster in the other, he moved cautiously, on a swivel as he trudged northward over the uneven terrain.

The tracker's signal was weak, fading in and out. He couldn't leave it on continuously as the battery was critically low. But turning it off risked losing both her direction and the signal entirely. The faint clicking beeps and soft hum of the console might draw unwanted attention, but silence was a luxury he could ill afford. Lily's life was at stake, and every second mattered.

His last encounter with the kaegar haunted him. The memory of its jagged fingers tightening around his throat sent an ache down his neck. His body still trembled in an aftershock more chilling than the frigid night air biting through his thin fatigues. Those eyes—sinister and red—were etched in his mind, a burning image of inhuman malice that seemed to taunt him in every shadow.

The forest around him was no less unnerving. Disfigured shadows stretched and twisted in the moonlight, and every creak of a branch or rustle of leaves set his nerves on edge. A pair of bright yellow eyes flashed in the darkness before a great-horned owl took flight, brushing past him with its wings. A sharp knocking sound from behind made him spin around, raising his blaster, only to find a thrush smashing a snail against a rock. When his back brushed against a pair of outstretched branches, he stumbled, nearly losing his footing. He hit the ground, the flashlight trembling in one hand, the pistol shaking in the other as he aimed at nothing but twisted shrubs and thickets.

His breath was fast and shallow. His heart pounded erratically, each beat echoing in his ears. Between the relentless tension and sleep deprivation, he felt as though he might lose his grip on reality. The shadows seemed to move, taunting him toward paranoia.

But every moment spent fighting his mind's tricks was another minute lost. Cael's final words replayed endlessly in his head: "Don't lose her. Don't lose her. Don't lose."

Markus' jaw tightened at the memory of the man. Cael had been brusque, unyielding, and stubborn, but he'd been honorable, a soldier devoted to protecting the monarchy. Even in his last moments, he had handed Markus the tracker, trusting him with Lily's life. And now Markus was failing.

The tracker's power dial wavered below critical levels as the console's screen faded into darkness. Desperately, he shook the device and held it up to the faint moonlight, hoping for any response. The switches refused to react, and the yellow circumference bars blinked weakly before disappearing entirely. He slammed the device against his palm, cursing under his breath, and stumbled backward. His heel caught on a gnarled root, and he fell hard against a clump of rocks. The impact shattered the console screen into a web of useless cracks.

Markus sat there, cradling the broken tracker, and trembling with rage and despair. The frustration choked him, and for a moment, he couldn't even muster the energy to curse aloud. He simply threw his hands up and collapsed backward into the unforgiving dirt. How had it come to this? How had he been drawn into this nightmare? And why couldn't anything go right?

Above him, the light of one of the moons shone through the skeletal branches, illuminating his weary face. His body ached, his eyelids were unbearably heavy, and the horrific memories of the festival replayed in vivid detail in his mind—the screams, the chaos, and the sight of the kaegar tearing through Cael and the other bodyguards. He flinched, his hand instinctively massaging his neck as he remembered those monstrous, clawed fingers choking the life out of him.

Markus' eyes snapped open, his chest heaving as he struggled to ground himself. Cold sweat clung to his skin, and his fingers trembled as they gripped the edges of the shawl hanging from his belt. The familiar fabric brought a sliver of comfort, a reminder of Liyzia's steady presence in his life. He clutched it tightly, willing its mysterious power to anchor him.

But exhaustion was overtaking him. His heavy eyelids fluttered once, then again. The third time, they remained closed for a moment longer. When he opened them, a shadowy figure loomed above him, eclipsing the pale moonlight. Markus' body tensed, but before he could react, sleep claimed him, pulling him into its depths.

* * *

Lumidawns. That was what the Nevrans called them—the distinct flowers with translucent petals that seemed to capture and amplify light. The petals spiraled outward in a double-helix pattern, each one slightly iridescent with an inner luminescence. Markus remembered the faint scent from the withered one Finnor had handed him that day in Orwein.

Out of nowhere, that sweet, spring-like scent tickled his senses and pulled him from unconsciousness. Awake? He couldn't remember falling asleep.

The morning sun, peeking through the treetops

welcomed his sore eyes. When had daylight come to his rescue so swiftly? Was he even safe now?

The forest was alive with the rustling of leaves in the breeze and the chirping of birds. The crisp, cool air made him sniffle and shiver in his underdressed fatigues. The earthy scent of frosted moss mingled with morning dew, while, faint but unmistakable, was the scent of a wildflower—out of place and out of season.

He blinked. Surely he was imagining things, but there it was: a single lumidawn flower lying across the frozen ground. Its spiral petals glowed with a light that seemed to defy winter itself. Shifting from silver to pale blue, its glow cast delicate shadows. The sight evoked something deep within him, a memory tied to someone he couldn't yet name.

Then, just as suddenly as it appeared, the flower faded like morning mist, its light fragmenting and gathering into shapes. A presence touched his consciousness— gentle, ancient, like starlight given form. He should have been afraid, should have reached for his weapon, but something in his blood recognized her before his eyes did.

"You're not dreaming," said Liyzia softly.

She sat on a fallen log as if she had always been there, as natural as the forest itself; yet somehow more real than everything around them. The air shimmered faintly where she appeared, like heat rising off summer stones, carrying that same hint of otherworldly light he had glimpsed in Orwein.

Markus blinked, struggling to form words, but his foggy mind wouldn't cooperate. He parted his lips, but she spoke first.

"No," she said again, answering the question in his head. "You're not dreaming."

Of course, she would read his thoughts. Why was he not surprised?

"You shouldn't be," she said, as if hearing his inner dialogue aloud. "By now, I'm sure you've sensed many strange things about me."

Markus stumbled to his knees, rapidly scanning the forest. The shattered tracking device lay where he'd dropped it the night before, its screen cracked beyond repair. Slowly, the events of the previous evening came crawling back: Moorwood forest, his fall, the suffocating fear. His hand instinctively went to his holster.

"No need for the weapon," she said calmly. "There's no one around for miles."

"How would you know that?" he muttered.

"Must you question everything?" she replied with a faint smile, patting the log beside her.

He rose unsteadily, his eyes fixed on her, still half-convinced she was an illusion. He rubbed his eyes, slapped his cheek, even gave her shoulders a squeeze as if to confirm her tangibility.

"Did you stow away on one of the ships? How'd you find me? How did you get here?" he asked in rapid succession.

"I felt your turmoil in the night and came," she said simply. "Did you sleep well?"

His mouth opened, "What do you mean—you came? How?"

"Come, sit," she said, dismissing his questions with a wave. "Eat. Your mind is racing faster than your appetite."

She pulled him down beside her and unwrapped a

warm loaf of bread. Its nutty, fruity aroma was so fresh it might have just come from the oven. Dumbfounded, Markus stared as she tore off a piece and placed it in his open mouth.

"Are you not happy to see me?" she asked with a comforting smile.

"I am! But—what's the use? I've given up trying to understand this ... this *power* you have!" He paused, shaking his head. "Xara and I thought you were some crackpot when we met you. No offense."

Liyzia chuckled. "I've been called worse."

Her serenity only made his frustration grow. "What are you doing here?"

"I've come to encourage you."

He scoffed. "A little late for that. Things have gotten crazy. I was dropped from the 'evolution.'"

When she didn't react, he frowned. "Did you hear me?"

"Yes," she said.

"Then it doesn't mean anything to you?"

"I haven't given it much thought."

Her calmness was infuriating. "What the hell am I doing here, then? You've got me thinking I can be like Draven and the others. That I'm good enough. Where is this great warrior you've been preaching about?"

She studied him for a moment, then said, "You are years behind and lacking the proper upbringing for this path. Nikel and I both know it. All adolescent males in our culture are sent away for a time of great stress and isolation before their true training begins."

Markus snorted. "Oh, so you sent me here to break me, is that it?"

"I have other reasons," she said. "I know you don't sleep at night."

"I'm a night owl. So what?"

"You don't sleep," she said, pointing to his chest, "because something chases you. Not out here, but in here."

Markus stilled. He thought of the predator hunting the princess but knew she meant something deeper.

"There are monsters buried inside you," she continued. "And they will resurface when you least expect it."

Her words chilled him more than the winter air. For a moment, he stared at her, grappling with the weight of her insight. "Is that why you scare me? Because of things you can see in me?" he asked.

"Perhaps," she said. "But hopefully, they will disturb you long enough for you to face them."

Markus looked away towards the woods. The sounds of morning filled the air—rustling leaves, the distant calls of birds—but the weight of her words stayed. He thought of the nightmares, the fear that gnawed at him, and this kaegar that still hunted the princess. His stomach twisted, and his fingers brushed the crusted stains on his fatigues, a bitter reminder of the prior evening's horrors.

His thoughts spiraled, dragging him back to that suffocating moment—the kaegar's clawed grip at his throat, the monstrous red eyes boring into his soul. The tremor in his hands started again, and he clenched them into fists. He had to shake this, had to keep moving.

"Come back," Liyzia said gently, squeezing his arm.

Her voice grounded him, pulling him out of the storm

in his mind. He turned to her, his breathing uneven. "I don't think I'm gonna make ..."

"Shh!" she interrupted, tightening her grip. "If you believe you won't, then you won't."

Markus took a deep breath and nodded, forcing himself to focus. She was right. He had to keep going—for the sake of the princess, for the others who had fallen. His gaze dropped to the shattered tracker lying in the dirt. Cael's face flashed in his mind, along with the lifeless bodies of the princess' guards. His chest ached at the memory of their sacrifice.

Liyzia's expression suddenly sharpened, her eyes lifting to the treetops with an alertness that sent a jolt through him. "What is it?" he asked, his voice tense.

"You should get moving," she said, pointing northeast. "That way."

"Danger?"

"No," she replied, though her tone carried a subtle urgency. "But you must make haste."

Markus stood, his mind racing. He had so many questions, so many things he wanted to say, but he knew better than to delay. He studied her, searching for some clue, some explanation, as though committing her image to memory. His hands found her shoulders again, squeezing them gently.

"I'm going to watch you this time," he murmured. "Make sure I'm not going crazy."

She smiled, her gaze soft but steady. "*Zyria eth'véliu,*" she whispered.

Before he could respond, she turned him by the shoulders, guiding him toward the northeast. When he glanced back, she was gone.

＊＊＊

Markus stood there, stunned by her sudden absence. The morning breeze stirred the air where she had been, carrying her faint, sweet scent. In his hands, the warm loaf of bread remained, its aroma still fresh. At his feet, two distinct footprints made their mark the soil.

A smile tugged at his lips. Her presence had left him with a renewed sense of purpose, the rest and nourishment he hadn't realized he needed.

Uninterrupted, he thought. I haven't slept that peacefully since ...

His thoughts faltered. Nightmares. The kaegar. The Immortals. Cael. His mind raced back to the present, to the task at hand. He wasn't out of the woods yet. Raising his pistol and gripping his spear, Markus set off, heading northeast with cautious determination.

The sun continued its ascent, filtering through the trees in a golden light. It illuminated the path ahead, guiding him forward. He moved carefully, his senses heightened by the rustling leaves and the sudden stirrings of birds taking flight. Climbing over rocks and weaving through mossy patches, he descended into a clearing surrounded by jagged cliffs and dense thickets.

It was a dead end.

The encircled rocks and twisted branches offered no clear way forward. Markus scanned the area, boots crunching against frosted gravel. Then he noticed them—drag marks in the dirt. They weren't straight but scattered, as though left by trembling fingers clawing through the earth.

Curiosity pulled him to his knees. He pressed his

hand into the soil, tracing the marks with his fingers. They matched. His breath hitched as he leaned closer. The moss-covered ground stirred faintly, a faint shift beneath the tangled debris. Gravel shifted nearby, followed by a muffled cough.

Markus froze, his hand instinctively tightening around his spear. Slowly, he poked the pile of moss with cautious and deliberate movements. Stained leaves, gravel, and debris spilled out, revealing something hidden beneath. Dark, velvety material peeked through the shadows, followed by the tip of a worn suede boot. His heart raced as he recognized the golden emblems sewn into the black cape.

He reached for the gloved hand that appeared, but it retracted swiftly. The figure beneath the moss stirred, trembling, and a pistol emerged, aimed directly at him.

Markus raised his hands, his pulse pounding in his ears. The weapon wavered, the hand holding it trembling uncontrollably. A single misstep could end him, but when he turned his face to the side, revealing himself, the figure lowered the gun lowered, and the masked woman emerged from the growth and collapsed at his feet.

He reached down, pulling her free from the debris, cape and mask muddied and torn. Her frame was weak and trembling as he cradled her.

<<Kane,>> she signed weakly. <<How did you find me?>>

<<Took a miracle,>> he replied, his eyes scanning their surroundings warily.

<<Cael. Lepou. Mercury. My Immortals?>>

Markus hesitated, then shook his head. Her shoulders

tensed, and tears pooled in her eyes beneath the mask. He instantly regretted his honesty, knowing how close her loyal guards had been to her.

She rested her head against his chest, clutching his hand tightly. In their shared moment of relief, Markus felt the enormity of their ordeal settle over them both. This creature was still out there, hunting. Its monstrous visage seared into his memory. His hands trembled at the thought, and he gritted his teeth, ashamed to show fear in front of her.

<<Come back,>> she motioned, her grip on his hand firm.

Markus nodded, returning to the present. He wasn't out of the woods yet.

CHAPTER SEVENTEEN

A state of emergency was declared in the mainland, which stretched its resources between finding safety for several thousand extra occupants and organizing a massive local manhunt, Hans had only a brief window of opportunity to act. In the back seat of his Radeon V28—one of the fastest aerglides on the market—he ripped through the countryside like a bat out of hell.

His team arrived on the outskirts of the district of Nenevuiim, just two miles beyond the hedges of the southeastern woodland country. The three streamlined vehicles came to a screaming halt beneath the six-foot overgrown hedges just before noon, accompanied by half a dozen more men zipping in from the rear. They swarmed in like hornets—loud, fast, precise. From a distance, the locals assumed they were with the authorities. The truth was much worse.

Two dozen men exited the vehicles, arming themselves to the teeth with silent sonic weapons, short-range pulse pistols, long-range energy rifles, among their heavy assortment of gear. After synchronizing with each team leader, the head split the group into three directions.

Hans watched through binoculars, flanked by his councilman, the Dromelan leader, and three others.

"We don't have much time," Hans uttered. "Are you sure this will work?"

"You're talking about thirty square miles of thick, dense, uneven land south of the Velucian river. These are the best we have right now. The speeders are only a last resort."

"Mr. Rathmar. Anything you want to add?"

"All is on schedule, Senator. I've given him direct orders to rendezvous with the asset back at base camp. Before nightfall."

"I still don't like how this turned out," Hans snapped.

"If you're worried about this fellow—Kane—perhaps you should have eliminated him when you had the opportunity."

Nettles looked at Hans, who remained calm under the accusation.

"Perhaps that wouldn't have been necessary, my friend, if this kaegar would directly obey your orders. Does he not understand them? Is it not as simple as giving a command to 'sit' or 'stay'? Or am I missing something here?"

"As I've stated, Senator," Rathmar began, seething and struggling to maintain his composure, "on both occasions, there's been one and only one correlation that has derailed his behavior—and that is Kane. Now, as for what exactly is triggering or luring him in? I don't know! Fortunately, he just happened to lure us toward the 'asset' last night, getting us closer to our objective."

"Yes, I'm incredibly grateful for that, my friend. But what I'm not grateful for is the bloody mess it's made and the attention it's brought! It won't be long before the Central Kingdom gets notified."

"Yes, yes, I understand. If all else fails, we head for the docks beyond Duniduiir. I've relayed that over and over to everyone. Despite the unfortunate turn of events, Senator, we're still on pace to reach our objectives. I hope you're not considering ... aborting."

"Aborting?" Hans questioned. "Where'd you get that idea? We're playing with house money here. Regardless, I'd bet my life that if Niri or the Capitol gets wind of this, they'll sweep in faster than either of us can handle."

"I agree. I only wanted your reassurance," Rathmar acknowledged and turned away momentarily toward the vehicles.

Rathmar exhaled slowly and motioned toward the convoy.

"Before we leave, I need a word with the men," he said, his voice flat.

Hans folded his arms, unmoved. Nettles shifted beside him, sensing something off.

The soldiers stood near the transports—ten of them, including Gurigor.

Rathmar walked slowly. Purposefully. His boots struck frost-hardened soil like metronome beats. He stopped before Gurigor, who straightened.

"I've been reviewing last night's chain of comms," Rathmar said, loud enough for all to hear. "There was a... lapse."

A few soldiers exchanged glances. Gurigor remained still.

"This operation demands unity. Precision. Obedience." His voice sharpened. "I don't tolerate hesitation."

He turned his head. Not toward Gurigor.

But toward the youngest soldier—Niv.

"Step forward," Rathmar said.

"Sir?" Niv blinked. "I—I didn't—"

The gunshot cracked like bone.

Niv collapsed face-first into the snow. A hiss of steam rose from the spreading pool beneath him.

No one moved.

Rathmar holstered his sidearm.

"Let that be a reminder," he said. "You breathe because I allow it. If anyone—and I mean *anyone*—feels the need to question my choices, speak now... or stay silent forever."

The only sound was the wind scraping over the hilltop.

Gurigor's jaw clenched, but his eyes stayed forward.

Hans stepped beside Rathmar, voice casual.

"Bit dramatic, don't you think?"

"Disloyalty spreads if you let it fester," Rathmar said.

"Mm." Hans's tone was dry, unreadable. "Shame about the boy. Thought for sure you had another name in mind."

He gave Gurigor a brief glance—neutral, knowing.

Hans whispered to Nettles, "See, this is what happens when you bring in monsters to chase ghosts. Eventually, the men start wondering who's really giving the orders."

"We may continue now, Senato", Rathmar acknowledged.

Hans watched the Sect leader heading back with the other mercenary while patting down his own winter coat to locate his weapon. It was the behavior of someone who had literally just dodged a bullet. It could also have been both a warning to the Dromelan and a threat to Hans himself.

The other two vehicles revved up their turbines and begin levitating. The councilman spoke as he climbed into the back seat next to the Senator. "Think he's trying to send a message to us?"

"He's clearly lost control of the situation. It won't be long before the Council gets wind of this mess!"

"The Senate can brush it under the rug," Nettles responded.

"Don't be a fool! Under the Council of Regency, the generals will get wind of it."

Hans leaned over, out of earshot of the driver up front. "They'll storm this place like a cyclone, searching for her. Their loyalties lie with the throne—as long as she has breath."

"Then we need to find her and get the hell out of here!"

"Easier said than done!" Hans remarked.

"And what about Kane?"

"What about him?"

"Are you gonna find a better forger than Xara? We've invested too much time and energy to start from scratch!"

"Flip a coin, Councilman."

"What?"

"Heads, he dies. Tails, he finds her."

He didn't even reach for a coin. Just watched the storm rolling in.

* * *

Markus led Lily through the narrow, winding path, checking his compass to keep heading north. The pair continued to use sign language, their footsteps careful and as quiet as possible. Lily animatedly insisted she knew the way and could navigate the woods better than him. She claimed to have memorized the path back north to the secluded manor—one the Immortals had drilled into her since adolescence for times of emergency.

Yet Markus remained the voice of reason, understanding they couldn't strictly adhere to their designated path. There were variables, unknowns and, most importantly, a menacing seven-foot-tall bipedal, who was already responsible for a dozen deaths in the past twelve hours. He had no idea if anyone was coming for her.

The Skylands, Markus had always thought, were an untamed frontier beyond the kingdom's borders, a melting pot of brutality, crudeness, and lawlessness. The thought of crossing into that domain with Xara would have stressed him beyond measure. He could only imagine the types of individuals passing through these infamous harbors—smugglers, scoundrels, and riffraff, who'd seize any opportunity to exploit their situation and plunge the holiday season into further chaos.

Despite their constant back-and-forth, they managed to advance in a northeasterly direction without incident. The trails were obvious, open, and revealing heavy disturbances from both man and beast. Forced to leave the main path, they moved through thickets, rugged terrains, gorges, and fallen trees. Even though the journey had become more strenuous, it was the wisest decision.

Her bickering—or constant gesturing—tested his patience. Fatigued, delirious, and nearing breaking point, she finally pushed him so far that he ticked her off. This only worsened his plight as she pestered him to explain the gesture. Unfortunately, Xara's street-learned vulgarity wasn't part of her academic sign language repertoire.

With tensions running high, they eventually agreed to stop for food and rest. After a meal of wild herring Markus had caught from a nearby stream, they rested beside the trunk of a fallen pine beneath the dense underbrush. Before continuing, Markus returned to the stream to filter and refill their water supply.

Cautious of his surroundings, Markus stepped into the open meadow. The air was crisp, cool, and still, with subdued shades of gray, pale green, and rich brown blending harmoniously in nature. The faint whisper of wind threading through the trees was the only sound.

As he knelt beside the water, the forest's rhythm changed.

The Mistweep above him ceased dripping, its droplets hanging in the air like paused thoughts. Beneath his boots, the roots of a nearby Shadowvein gave a subtle thrum, a low vibration that pulsed once—*in rhythm with his own heartbeat.* Somewhere nearby, the wind caught a Songbark's edge, drawing out a hollow hum that trembled in his chest.

Markus unscrewed the bottle's lid and paused. The air felt dense. Not dangerous. But aware.

Leaning over the stream, he caught his reflection— then stopped cold.

The hand holding the bottle was no longer his.

Scaled. Ridged. Clawed.

Mottled in gray-blue textures like stone worn smooth by time. Fingers that curled with coiled precision.

And behind him—in the mirrored surface—a twisted shape emerged. Tall. Predatory. *Watching.*

Blood-red eyes met his own.

His pulse roared in his ears. The Kaegar's features grinned in the reflection, its jaw widening unnaturally, grating sinew stretching as if in mocking delight. No sound. No movement. Just poised violence.

Then, as if in response to his rising panic, the stream rippled—not outward, but inward—toward the reflection.

A wordless breath passed over the surface.

Not a voice. Not quite.

Just the shape of one:

"Ka'aine."

Markus flinched, stumbled back, and dropped the bottle. The water swallowed it with a soft splash.

Lily was already approaching. Her mask tilted in concern. Markus pointed at the stream, panting, trembling.

But when she looked—there was nothing.

The reflection showed only ripples. Trees. Sky. Him.

The forest sounds slowly returned—the whispering branches, the gurgle of water. The moment passed.

But the name lingered.

Not in his ears—but in his bones.

The forest sounds gradually returned—the gurgling stream, the whispering trees. Embarrassed and shaken, Markus turned away, stumbling as he tried to catch his breath. Shivering in a cold sweat, the predator's image stayed vividly in his mind. He tried to write it off—exhaustion, trauma, maybe a lucid dream from the herring. Once he composed himself, he rose and faced Lily, whose mask-covered eyes showed visible concern. He gestured to her.

<<Don't worry. You'll soon be free of me.>>

A part of him wanted to push her away, while another part yearned to flee. He imagined sprinting to the coast and diving into the North Sea, where he'd either swim away or drown. Yet, when he trudged past her, she caught up and squeezed his arm gently as they disappeared into the underbrush.

* * *

Sunlight filtered through Moorwood's canopy, casting dappled light on the forest floor. Xara, Mercury, and the others moved in formation, their pace steady but watchful.

They'd veered north, taking trails known only to smugglers and seers. Behind them, the trees thickened; ahead, they thinned—colder, quieter.

"The tracks split here," Mercury said, crouching. His wound still burned with black veins beneath the skin. "Two sets, both heading toward the river."

Yewwa knelt beside him, fingers brushing leaves. "They passed through. But something else followed. The forest trembles."

Xara felt it too. The birds had gone silent. Even the trees seemed to lean away.

A sound drifted through the woods—not howl, not scream. It came from nowhere... and everywhere. Ditta and Nix moved closer, spears drawn.

"The Wraithwoods," Ditta whispered, pointing southwest. "Those sounds—"

"We go north," Yewwa cut in. "Even the kaegar won't tread there."

Mercury stayed crouched, hand near his weapon. "Legends won't help if Hans gets to them first."

Yewwa's fingers paused over a dark stain. "Both are true—the old and the new. But what hunts your princess is drawn by more than blood. The forest remembers what your weapons can't fight."

Another cry pierced the air—closer. Grief, hunger, fury, all in one.

Xara gripped her half-pendant. Her instincts said run. But she followed Yewwa.

They crested a ridge. The trees ahead grew darker—not with shadow, but age. Gnarled and scorched, they twisted like cursed things.

"That's the edge," Mercury said.

"Thought those were just stories," Xara muttered.

"So did I," Mercury replied. "Till I camped too close once. Woke up screaming—with my voice on the wrong side of the fire."

Nervous chuckles passed between them. But no one laughed long.

"Let's hope we don't end up there," Xara said.

"Hope won't help us," Mercury muttered. "But maybe a head start will."

They pressed on. But the forest's silence felt full of watchers—and Xara couldn't shake the sense that whatever hunted Markus had stirred up more than just the kaegar.

* * *

Through discreet, calculated maneuvers, Markus and the princess pressed northward—slipping through thickets, skirting rocky ledges, always staying beneath the treeline. The forest sounds wrapped around them: wind brushing the canopy, twigs crackling under careful steps.

Then: a distant hum.

Lily paused.

<<What is that? Sounds like a swarm of bees.>>

Markus tilted his head. <<Mechanical. Gears shifting. Not bees.>>

He pulled her down behind a gnarled hedge as the sound rose, the earth trembling faintly beneath them.

<<Driftcycles,>> he signed.

<<Drift... what?>> she asked, brow raised.

<<Speeders you lean into. Ride low and fast.>> He glanced uphill. <<Two of them. Maybe more.>>

<<Are they following us?>>

<<Not yet. But let's not give them the chance. Stay low.>>

He gripped her hand, leading her deeper into the grass and scrub, sticking to the shadowed bends of the landscape. The rumble swelled as two riders broke across a distant clearing, turbines slicing tall grass and spitting dust. The air shook with their passage—no attempt at stealth, just brute sound and speed.

<<They look fun,>> Lily gestured, smirking. <<I want to ride one.>>

Markus gave her a look. <<Loose cannons zip around my district on those. Real subtle.>>

<<Where?>>

<<Vesper. West coast. Mining zone's dumpster.>>

<<Sounds charming.>>

<<Oh, it is. The seagulls even rob you.>>

She grinned beneath her mask.

<<Old friends?>>

<<Not unless they're trying to kill me.>>

<<They're here for me then?>>

<<More than likely.>>

They crouched lower. Markus tracked the binoculars of one rider panning their direction. His finger hovered near the trigger, breath held.

The gaze passed. The cycles veered and peeled off, engines roaring eastward.

Markus exhaled. Checked his compass.

<<We're farther north than I thought.>>

<<I know a pass near the Velucian River,>> Lily signed. <<It leads back to the manor.>>

<<Anyone there?>>

<<Just sentries. Everyone else is still at the festival. The other Immortals, my companions—no one knows I left.>>

<<That's what worries me.>>

<<What do you mean?>>

Markus hesitated. <<Hans Lumen isn't working alone. Someone wants you gone. And that creature...>>

<<The one hunting us?>>

<<It's not just after you. It's chased me before. Ever since I got here, something's been... tracking me. Or waiting.>>

Lily's fingers paused in mid-sign.

<<You think we're linked somehow?>>

He didn't answer. Just looked down the tree line.

The forest was quiet again—but unnaturally so.

Not peaceful. Poised.

Aylin noticed his stillness. Touched his shoulder.

<<What is it?>>

<<Just thinking about all the Immortals sworn to protect you... and not one of them is here.>>

She squeezed his hand. <<Then I'm glad you are.>>

<<Let's keep moving.>>

He led them on, hugging the forest's spine, weaving off-trail. The sky dimmed. The path narrowed. Once— just once—he glanced up and realized there were no birds. Not even wind. Just *that hum* still pulsing in his chest.

Not engine. Not wind.

Something else.

* * *

Over the next day, somehow, the pair managed to stay low while maintaining a reasonable pace northward. Occasionally, they heard sounds that hinted of nearby animals and their movements. During the night, Markus swore he caught a foul stench, one that coincided with another spell of an upset stomach.

He kept them safe by building a makeshift lean-to—a low shelter covered with grass, leaves, and dirt—to conceal them long enough for some much-needed sleep and protection.

By noon the next day, the two found a brief reprieve beneath the shade of a massive fallen trunk near a cluster of giant oaks on a grassy incline.

Lily, suddenly excited, grabbed Markus' attention and pointed toward a distant sight she hadn't seen before.

Through gaps in the trees, massive shapes emerged from morning mist like living legends— creatures unlike anything Markus had seen. They moved with fluid grace despite their size, each one easily seven feet at the shoulder. They were like hushners but larger, wilder, their muscled forms speaking of untamed power.

Markus recognized them as adult terradogs. He'd heard Knuevah speak of them—ancient breeds that roamed these northern lands before humans claimed them. The nearest one lifted its massive head, nostrils flaring as it caught their scent.

Markus felt the need to remain hidden and avoid drawing attention. But he couldn't help but consider the possibility: could he tame one of these beasts and ride it to hasten their journey?

Markus remembered Liyzia's lessons about the way to approach wild creatures—not with fear or dominance, but with respect. With Lily behind him, he made his cautious approach, raising his hand slowly, palm out in the gesture she'd taught him. The largest terradog's eyes held an intelligence that reminded him of his first days with the hushners, when everything in this world had seemed alien and frightening. One by one, each member of the pack sniffed the air, recognizing friendly humans. Their gigantic tails wagged and they panted loudly.

Their heavy breathing and saliva were as thick and overwhelming as their sheer size, yet their manner was affectionate. One terradog submitted to Markus' hand, allowing him to scratch its large, wet nostrils. The creature sniffed him thoroughly before lathering his face with its enormous pink tongue.

However, the pack growled at Lily, backing away from her, growling. She drew back, uncertain and cautious. <<Did I do something wrong?>>

Markus pointed to his own face as one of the creature's wet nostrils drew near to him, sniffing the back of his head.

She lowered her head, turning away. And Markus turned back to the terradog beside him, feigning nonchalance. He admitted to himself that part of him was curious about Lily's appearance. To outsiders and much of the world, she was an enigma with her face concealed behind her intricately designed mask. Given the threats to her life, the precaution made sense.

After years of secrecy and protocol, she finally relented. With deliberate care, she pulled back her hood and removed her inner veil. Her long dark hair cascaded freely in the late-afternoon breeze. As the mask lowered, Markus found himself holding his breath.

The mask lowered in a fleeting shimmer.

Her olive skin glowed with a natural radiance, smooth and luminous. Her green eyes, no longer shadowed by the mask, carried both wisdom and vulnerability. Her face was deep and expressive, carrying a quiet strength he recognized—not the remote princess of legend, but a young woman as complex as the world she inhabited. As two of the terradogs approached and sniffed her approvingly, her expression brightened with a gentle, enigmatic smile that spoke of countless untold stories.

When their eyes met, Markus didn't shy away. He smirked and gently held her mask in his hand. <<I think they prefer this version of Princess Lily.>>

She stood up to face him. She was no longer mute and spoke in a husky lilting voice.

"Aylin," she said quietly. "Only a few know it. Fewer still hear it."

She gestured to the mask.

"It's easier, sometimes, to let the world think I can't speak. They listen more kindly to silence."

He'd imagined her voice might sound like wind or bells. But it wasn't. It was low. Measured. Real.

And now, hearing her speak, he wasn't sure what stunned him more—her voice, or the fact that she trusted him enough to use it.

Markus nodded, acknowledging her words. "Have you ever ridden one of these?" he asked, patting the terradog's massive shoulder.

"I've been escorted on hushners, but these terradogs are much bigger and taller!"

"Well, there's a first time for everything. This one seems friendly. Let me get it to kneel."

Markus used the calming gestures and techniques he'd learned to coax the terradog into lowering itself. He climbed onto its back, and Aylin followed, wrapping her arms around his waist. The giant beast rose, grazing briefly before joining the pack, trotting, and breaking into a slow, bouncy gallop.

Markus felt a glimmer of pride. Under such duress, he'd managed to build fires, shelters, find food, and now tame a wild terradog on his first try. It was a small but hopeful victory, a second wind in their race for survival. He was certain they could reach the Velucian River before nightfall on the backs of these powerful creatures, sparing them the grueling trek on foot.

The terradogs moved with freedom and excitement, their massive paws silent on the forest floor. Their coats, blending with the earthen tones around them, ranged from sleek to shaggy in hues of black, gray, tan, and gold. Markus marveled at their fluidity—graceful beasts with strides that dwarfed even the fastest hushner.

Though each ran with its own rhythm, the pack remained unified, following Markus' lead. Their joy, wild and contagious, surged through him as Aylin's arms wrapped tighter around his waist. He couldn't tell what lifted his spirit more—the wind against his face, the pulse of the creatures beneath him, or the feel of her there, close and real.

Then it shifted.

A knot tightened in his stomach. The fiery sensation rose in his throat, choking him. Metallic. Wrong.

He pulled the lead terradog to a halt. The others slowed in kind.

Aylin sat up, concern in her eyes. The terradogs began to snarl and huff, sniffing the air. The meadow fell unnaturally silent.

No birds. No breeze. Just pressure.

Markus scanned the tree line ahead—thick trunks of ghost oaks, where sunlight barely broke through.

Then something moved.

At first, it looked like a fallen banner caught on a limb. But it swayed with purpose—too heavy, too fluid.

A limb followed. Then a second.

The cape dragged across the pine needles, a massive shape behind it. The air warped around the figure like it brought its own gravity. From within the cowl, two eyes glowed red, piercing the shadows.

Markus felt the gaze—not a look. But a recognition.

The Kaegar stepped forward, not rushing, but *arriving*.

The cape flowed behind it, more alive than cloth

should be. It shifted with the rhythm of breath, coiling and trailing like smoke off a battlefield. Its sheer size disrupted the grass as it moved. Still only part of it was visible—a chestplate's glint, a thick leg, the edge of something jagged beneath the hood.

Markus didn't breathe.

The creature tilted its head—just slightly. Enough.

Then it hissed.

The terradogs exploded with growls. Their bodies surged with energy, restless, coiled.

From the east, came the hum of driftcycles cresting the hill. Two riders—mercenaries—saw the scene and froze.

Predator. Prey. And them—caught between.

Markus whispered, "Don't let go."

The Kaegar charged—limbs piston-fast, cape flaring behind like a shadow unchained.

The terradogs scattered at Markus' command, leaping in unison. One slammed shoulder-first into the creature's path. The impact staggered the Kaegar, but it twisted, using its own momentum to slide across the grass with impossible grace.

Another terradog lunged, jaws snapping near its neck. The Kaegar's arm shot out—not to strike, but to catch. It flung the beast aside like a sack of bark. The terradog rolled, yelped, then rose again, growling, unbroken.

The driftcycles roared into motion. One rider peeled right, blaster raised. The other weaved wide, trying to flank.

Aylin drew her pistol and fired—quick, precise bursts that forced the riders off course. Their blasts lit the grass in streaks of orange heat. Markus veered his mount hard, shielding her with his back as they crashed through a thicket.

Laser fire cracked around them. A terradog snarled as it took a hit and barreled into the shooter, throwing both man and machine into a tumble.

Markus caught a glimpse of the Kaegar through the smoke—not chasing, but tracking, cape drawn around it like wings. It didn't rush. It stalked.

Then a blast grazed them.

Aylin slipped from the saddle, tumbling hard onto the ground. He reached for her—too late. She was already up, pistol blazing. Her shot clipped the lead rider, forcing him to veer wildly and vanish between the trees.

They ran.

They ran—into tight trunks, hanging mist, and shifting shadow. The hum of driftcycles echoed in impossible directions. Markus yanked Aylin behind a massive Shadowvein, bark cool against their backs, their breathing loud in the stillness.

A cycle passed. Then circled. The rider slowed, scanning.

Aylin lifted her pistol.

Markus pressed her hand down.

Wait.

The hum dropped to a low purr as the mercenary hovered closer.

Then he moved on.

Aylin exhaled, barely a whisper: "They're herding us. Pushing east."

Markus nodded, already moving. They ducked between trees, bursts of fire chasing them, bark splitting in sprays of embers. One shot scorched the earth beside them, the stink of burning root thick in their noses.

A mercenary broke through the smoke ahead—blaster up, teeth bared.

Markus didn't hesitate.

The spear left his hand like an answer to a question.

It struck true—burying deep into the man's chest. His driftcycle careened off-course, metal shrieking as it struck a tree. The explosion that followed was deafening, flames licking up the bark like hungry tongues.

Aylin spun to fire on the second rider. Her shot connected—chest, then shoulder—spinning him from the saddle. The driftcycle tumbled and struck an Emberwood, detonating in a plume of fire and sap.

Silence.

But not peace.

The trees glowed faintly, scorched bark peeling. Smoke twisted in unnatural shapes—lines, runes, marks in forgotten tongues.

Markus turned.

He didn't hear it.

He *felt* it—pressure behind his eyes, heat prickling in his scar.

Aylin's hand tightened on his arm. She leaned in close, not speaking. Her breath warmed his cheek. A stray strand of her hair caught the wind and brushed the side of his face—the scarred side.

In the thinning smoke, the figure stood. Not rising. Not approaching.

Waiting.

It didn't roar now.

It didn't need to.

It saw him.

And it remembered.

* * *

The forest changed around them—trees drew closer, their branches clawing across filtered light. Aylin's steps grew more certain, guided by memory and fear.

"The river's close," she gasped. "I used to play here—before..."

She trailed off, her childhood flickering behind her eyes.

"There's a place where the stones break the surface."

Behind them, a roar shattered the silence. Bone-deep. Closer.

The Kaegar's footfalls pounded the earth in slow, vile rhythm.

They crested a rise—and there it was.

The Velucian River. A silver serpent carving through the forest, its waters churning with forgotten power.

Aylin grabbed Markus's arm. "There," she pointed. "Where the stones form a crossing. The Immortals used it on patrol."

The Kaegar broke from the trees.

It didn't lunge.

It emerged—slow, deliberate, as if daylight required it to shed some part of its myth.

The cape flowed around it like ink in water. Its hood shaded most of its face, but the glow of its eyes pierced the day, locking onto Markus.

Not them. *Him.*

Markus stepped forward, instinct warring with logic. Aylin held him back.

"Wait," she whispered, gaze locked on the creature. "It's... studying the river. Like it remembers."

It stood still. Chest rising. Cape fluttering as if

reacting to an unseen wind. It inhaled, slow and deep, like it was tasting the air.

"Old stories," Aylin whispered, "say some beings feared sacred waters. Couldn't cross without... some ancient right."

Markus looked at her. They had no time.

The Kaegar stepped forward.

They ran—into the river.

The shock of cold hit like stone. The current seized them, pulling with ancient strength. Roots twisted below like fingers, trying to drag them down.

Markus fought to keep them above water, gripping Aylin as they surged toward the far bank. She kicked hard, matching him stroke for stroke.

Behind them, the forest held its breath.

No cry. No charge.

Only the sound of water and the soft rise of the figure's cape as it reached the river's edge.

It did not cross.

It watched.

Water shook from the trees in ripples. The creature paced, but didn't step forward. Its cape curled around its frame like a shield.

On the far bank, Markus and Aylin collapsed onto the stones, breathless and soaked.

"It's not just hunting," Aylin said, staring back. "It's remembering."

She looked at Markus. His scar burned faintly, pulsing with heat.

The creature's head tilted, scenting the air. Then, slowly, it turned—and stepped backward into the forest, vanishing like a shadow into sunlight.

The river rushed between them, ancient and unmoved.

Markus pulled Aylin to her feet. They trembled—cold, shaken, alive.

The river behind them surged like a boundary between what had passed... and what was awakening.

For now, they were safe.

But safety, Markus was learning, was only a pause in the story fate had already begun writing.

CHAPTER EIGHTEEN

The twin moons hung like luminous coins in the darkening sky, their dual light casting strange shadows through Moorwood's canopy. Xara watched frost gather on fallen leaves while Ditta and Nix moved through their evening rituals—checking weapons, testing bowstrings, movements that carried the fluid grace of those born to the forest. Even here, miles from the Wraithwoods, their eyes kept straying westward where distant howls echoed unnaturally between the trees.

The group made camp in a hollow carved by the roots of a great Shadowvein tree, its pale markings barely visible in the gathering dark. The small fire cast dancing light across Mercury's face as he maintained his watch, though the wounds from the kaegar had spread like black veins beneath his skin, defying his immortal properties. Each breath seemed to cost him more than the last, yet his vigil never wavered.

"We should press on," Mercury said in a voice tight with pain and urgency. "Every hour we rest is another hour lost."

Yewwa crushed herbs between his fingers, sprinkling

them over the flames. The smoke took strange shapes, curling like written words before dissolving. "The old stories speak of nights like this," he said, his voice barely above a whisper. "When the veil between worlds grows thin. Look."

"Speak plainly," Mercury uttered, "where our educated ears can understand."

"Very well." Yewwa pointed to where mist had gathered unnaturally, flowing against the wind. "The forest remembers things your modern maps have forgotten. Is that plain enough, Immortal?"

A distant howl cut through the darkness, making them all turn westward. It wasn't the sound of any natural creature—more like grief-filled voice, or ancient rage echoing through time.

"There it is again," Xara whispered, drawing closer to the fire.

"Just the trees," Mercury muttered, though his hand never left his weapon.

"Could be glade ghosts," Ditta offered, his young face serious in the firelight.

"The what?" Mercury asked.

Xara leaned forward, her eyes reflecting the flames. "I heard a local's tale—soldiers doomed to wander after falling to some ancient curse. They say they still fight, never knowing their war ended centuries ago."

Yewwa lit his pipe, watching his sons with quiet pride as they added to the tale.

"Some say they were warriors cursed for their hubris," Ditta said.

"Others claim they're spirits of slaughtered villagers, forever protecting their homeland," Nix finished.

A branch snapped in the darkness, causing all of them to tense. Ditta and Nix moved to defensive positions, their spears ready, while Mercury's hand tightened on his weapon. But it was only a terradog, enormous and wild, drawn perhaps by their fire.

The animal paused at the edge of firelight just long enough for Ditta to catch something on the wind. He inhaled deeply, his eyes meeting his brother's. Nix nodded slightly - he'd caught it too.

"The beast has crossed paths with them," Ditta said softly to Xara, keeping his voice low enough that Mercury couldn't hear. "Your brother's scent lingers in its fur."

Yewwa's lips curved in a subtle smile as he tamped his pipe, having noticed what his sons detected. The terradog melted back into the shadows, but its visit left them with something precious—confirmation that somewhere in the vast darkness of Moorwood, Markus still moved through the night.

Xara's hand found her half-pendant, hope ignited in her chest like the embers spiraling above their fire.

The Nevran elder studied something in his pouch—a cloth with strange black stains, scorched at the edges if by acid. "Some places," he said finally, "hold memories older than stone. These lands remember when darker things ruled here. Before kingdoms. Before the light." He held up the cloth, letting firelight catch its mysterious damage. "Only older things would awaken such memories."

"Does the kaegar awaken them?" Xara asked in barely a whisper. "Disturb them?"

Yewwa's eyes met Mercury's across the fire. "Surely

even your modern eyes can sense it, Immortal? The stirring of ancient powers?"

"And what of her Highness?" Mercury demanded. "While we sit discussing legends, she's out there somewhere."

"And Markus," Xara added, her hand finding her half-pendant.

Yewwa smiled gently. "Do you know anyone smarter than your princess, Immortal? Or anyone more stubborn than your brother?" He squeezed Xara's hand. "I pity the mythical beings who dare engage with such a pair. We will see them again."

He settled back against the Shadowvein's roots, his pipe glowing softly. "There are enough burdens here to last a lifetime. Let us find what rest we can."

Xara took first watch, her eyes scanning the shadows. Somewhere in the shadows of Moorwood, her brother moved through the night. Though miles separated them, her vigilance remained steady—a silent promise to the family they'd forged in Vesper's shadows.

* * *

Moonlight silvered the grounds as Aylin led them through the silent manor, with precise and purposeful movements. She navigated familiar paths between protruding roots and massive trunks where the forest had claimed parts of the grounds. They emerged into a clearing that Markus recognized—the pond where he'd first seen her feeding swans, though it felt like a lifetime ago. The water's surface reflected the twin moons overhead, still and black as obsidian.

The manor loomed before them, beautiful and abandoned. No lights burned in its windows; no movement disturbed its perfect stillness. They moved through empty rooms where furniture waited like patient ghosts, as their footsteps echoed in halls that seemed to hold their breath.

They crept across a large dining hall towards a grand fireplace on the opposite end, where she intentionally pulled on a wall lantern—not a real one, but a cleverly hidden lever. Within seconds, the mahogany wall panels had slid apart, silently, smoothly, and swift enough for her to draw him into the darkness before the panels shut back into place on their own accord.

The switch illuminated a hidden hexagonal chamber. No windows divided these walls, but shelves lined every surface—some filled with leather-bound books, others stocked with provisions. Markus glimpsed bread and cheese, jars of preserved fruits, and carefully packed tarts. A cabinet revealed more of Aylin's elaborate masks and ceremonial attire, while a small hearth occupied one wall. Three rolled sleeping mats waited in a corner, as if the room had long anticipated its purpose.

The space felt both prepared and untouched—a sanctuary waiting for a moment they'd hoped would never come.

* * *

The fire crackled in the small hearth while they shared a simple meal of bread and preserved fruits. Neither spoke much at first as the weight of recent events pressed down on them. Aylin methodically arranged their supplies, carrying the precise dignity she'd been taught, though her hands trembled slightly.

A distant howl pierced the silence of their sanctuary, making them both look up from their meal. It wasn't the sound of any natural creature—more like rage echoing through time.

"The Wraithwoods," Aylin whispered, her hand finding the aether stone at her throat. It quivered faintly in the chamber's warmth as its light caught the elaborate carvings on the shelves around them. "When I was small, my nurse would tell stories of what lived in those dark groves. Olden things that remembered when these lands belonged to darker powers."

The stone's glow strengthened briefly, making shadows dance across their faces. Markus felt something stir in his blood—a recognition he couldn't explain. He focused instead on checking the room's defenses, trying to ignore the way the stone's light seemed to pulse in time with his own heartbeat.

"I've only been in here only once before," Aylin said finally, in soft tones, as if trying to change the subject. "When I was twelve. Mercury showed me the entrance, and made me memorize every detail. 'A last resort,' he said."

"For emergencies," Markus observed, studying the well-stocked shelves.

"Yes." She touched a shelf of books, trailing her fingers over familiar spines. "Though I never truly believed ..." Her voice caught, "Cael and the others ..."

Markus shifted uncomfortably, recognizing her loss while at the same time instinctually wanting to maintain distance. "They died protecting you. Protecting what you represent."

"What I represent," she repeated quietly. "Sometimes I wonder if that's all anyone sees." Her eyes met his. "Except you. You don't look at me like I am a symbol."

Markus found himself fidgeting with the half-pendant at his throat, a habit he'd developed whenever his thoughts turned to family and belonging. Aylin noticed the movement, and was drawn to the broken edge of the golden alq'arus.

"Tell me about your sister," she said softly, recognizing his need to speak of his own connections. "The one who shares your pendant."

His fingers traced the familiar contours of the broken bird. Despite everything, a smile touched his lips. "Xara. She found me when we were kids. Dragged me home like a stray cat." His expression softened at the memory. "Wouldn't take no for an answer."

"She sounds formidable."

"You have no idea. Probably tearing apart the woods looking for me right now." He paused, remembering something. "Your tutor—Theo. You mentioned he studies ancient things?"

Aylin's face lit up. "He's brilliant. Eccentric, but brilliant. He believes the alq'arus still exist, beyond the Frigid Mountains where no one dares venture. Everyone thinks he's mad, but ..." She glanced at the stone's steady glow on her necklace. "Sometimes I wonder if the old stories hold more truth than we know."

The fire popped, sending sparks spiraling upward. Markus watched them fade, thinking of Liyzia's quiet power, of the way the kaegar had looked at him with kindred recognition, and of all the questions he'd never dared ask about his own nature. "Sometimes," he said carefully, "it's safer not knowing."

But the stone's light flashed once, as if in disagreement, and Aylin's eyes held questions she was too wise to voice. Not yet.

The fire crackled between them, its warmth drawing them closer despite themselves. Outside their sanctuary, the night pressed heavy and silent—too silent, as if the forest itself held its breath.

When Aylin spoke again, her voice was so soft that Markus had to lean slightly to hear her. "What good is a fire without a story?"

He looked at her oddly, caught off-guard by the request. "Do I look like some storyteller?"

"Please?" The firelight caught her eyes, turning them to emerald. "Theo's tales are all scholarly text and dusty facts. But you ..." she hesitated, then continued carefully, "you've lived real adventures. The way you speak Nevrish, the way you move—there must be stories there."

Markus shifted uncomfortably, conscious of their proximity, of the way the stone's light seemed to strengthen whenever he moved closer. But her gentle insistence reminded him of quieter evenings in Nikel's home, of tales told by firelight while winter pressed against the windows.

When he began speaking of the tale of 'The Prince of Niri,' his voice found its cadence. The Nevrish words came naturally, as if they'd been waiting to spill out. He told the story simply, without flourish, unaware of how his rough voice softened on the ancient words, and how his scarred face transformed in the telling.

Aylin watched him with growing wonder, seeing past his self-consciousness to something he couldn't yet see in himself. Here was no polished courtier or accomplished storyteller, but something rarer—a man who carried truth in his scars and poetry in his unwitting grace.

"Your Nevrish is remarkable," she said when he finished. "And your voice ..." She caught herself, then added more carefully, "It's odd that you chose that tale in particular."

"It's the first one I heard. The one that moved me most."

"It moved you because you see yourself in this tale," she said softly. Something in her tone made him look up. "Though I wonder if you realize—I've heard this story before. About Lord Nikel and his companions, rescuing the infant prince." Her eyes held his. "And now here you are, his chosen heir, trying to protect another royal charge."

Markus averted her knowing gaze. "Don't kid yourself. I'm no knight. No Immortal. And this is just ..."—he gestured vaguely at their hidden sanctuary—"survival."

"Is it?" she asked. The aether stone throbbed again gently, casting a soft light between them. "The stories we choose tell us more about ourselves than we realize."

"Maybe," he said quietly, "I just understand what it's like to be lost. To need someone to ..."—he trailed off, uncomfortable with how close to truth his words strayed.

The fire had burned lower now, its warmth wrapping around them like a blanket against the gathering dark.

It cast tired shadows across walls that held both safety and imprisonment as night settled heavily around their hidden sanctuary.

When Aylin's head grew heavy against his shoulder, Markus involuntarily tensed—touch wasn't something he welcomed easily. She glanced at him with a gentle smile. Her simple look and acceptance made his defenses waver. When she settled back against him, he found himself relaxing despite old habits, though he still kept his scarred temple turned slightly away.

Her breathing gradually evened out as exhaustion overtook her, while the aether stone's light dimmed to a soft tremor, like a heartbeat in the darkness.

Markus kept his vigil, ears straining for any sound beyond their shelter. Tomorrow would bring impossible choices—to stay hidden until their supplies ran out, or venture into a forest that held both human hunters and ancient horrors.

But for now, in this moment between moments, he allowed himself to feel the strange peace of having someone trust him so completely. His hand found the half-pendant at his throat, thinking of Xara somewhere in the vast darkness, two siblings watching through the night, each protecting their own charge, each carrying their own burdens.

A final howl echoed from the distant Wraithwoods, closer now, carrying emotions no natural sound should hold. The stone at Aylin's throat lit up briefly, and Markus felt that familiar stirring in his blood—a warning, or a recognition, of things better left unnamed. Not yet. Not here.

He settled back against the wall, one hand near his

weapon, the other protectively close to Aylin. Whatever tomorrow brought, for tonight at least, they were safe in this pocket of warmth against the gathering gloom.

* * *

Ancient stone seemed to breathe around Rathmar as he descended into the abandoned facility's depths. Each level he passed felt older than the last, as if the very architecture were drawing him backward through time. The wine cellars had been merely the beginning—now the walls bore markings that predated the kingdom itself, scripts that even scholars had forgotten how to read.

His black robes whispered against weathered stone, the sound echoing strangely in corridors that had not known light in centuries. The air grew thicker with each step with the weight of buried secrets. Even the shadows felt different here, moving like living things at the edge of sight.

Rathmar's fingers brushed the medallion beneath his robes, its cold surface a reminder of power and duty. Yet something had changed in him since the kaegar's hunt began. Questions that had never occurred to him in centuries of service now gnawed at his certainty like rats.

The iron-bound door waited at the passage end, its surface marked with symbols that seemed to shift when viewed directly. Rathmar sealed himself inside, the hollow boom as it closed reverberating like destiny itself. A single torch cast a weak light across the chamber's bare stone, illuminating only the pedestal at its center.

With a deep breath, he began to chant in a voice that was not entirely his own. The words of the ancient Dromelish tongue scraped against the air, harsh and cryptic, each syllable vibrating with power. The lights dimmed as his voice deepened, the shadows in the room seeming to stretch and reach toward him, as if drawn to the presence being summoned.

The medallion responded. Its emerald glow intensified, casting an eerie green light across the chamber, and bathing Rathmar's face in its spectral hue. A low hum filled the room, both mechanical and otherworldly. From the medallion, a holographic orb began to form—green, spinning slowly, fading in and out of solidity as if caught between this world and another. The orb hummed louder, a pulsating rhythm that matched the cadences of Rathmar's chant. It spun faster, casting fractured rays of light across the room, and finally stabilized to hover just above the stone.

The first voice that emerged from the orb carried the weight of mountains—deep, immovable, laced with contempt for anything that dared challenge the old order. The second spoke like winter wind through dead branches, sharp and biting. But it was the third voice that truly chilled the blood—quiet, almost gentle, yet somehow more terrifying in its softness.

{*Rathmar,*} the first voice rumbled, timeless as mountains. {*You disturb our contemplation. This had better warrant such ... boldness.*}

The green orb quivered with each word, casting sickly shadows that crawled across the chamber walls. Rathmar bowed his head as centuries of conditioning warred with his growing unease.

{*My Lords,*} he began, but the winter-wind voice cut through his words.

{*Spare us your formalities, Sect Leader. We taste your doubt like poison in the air.*}

The third voice slipped between them, soft as falling snow. {*Let him speak, brothers. Our dear Rathmar has never wavered in his devotion. Until now.*}

That gentle observation carried more threat than any rage. Rathmar's hands trembled slightly as he withdrew the meditation beads from his robe—black stones that seemed to drink in the torchlight.

{*The kaegar strays from its purpose,*} he said, each word carefully chosen. {*It hunts... for something. Something that calls to its primeval blood.*}

The mountain-voice laughed, a sound like boulders grinding to dust. {*Your beast merely tests its leash. It knows nothing of purpose beyond what we grant it.*}

{*With respect, my Lords ...,*} Rathmar's fingers tightened around the beads. {*I have served the Sect for three centuries. I have never known the kaegar to defy my commands. But now ...*}

{*Now?*} The gentle voice seemed to smile. {*Now you question what cannot be. Tell us, dear Rathmar, what impossible thing haunts your thoughts?*}

The chamber grew colder. Frost crept across the pedestal's surface despite the torch's heat. Rathmar drew himself up, knowing his next words might condemn him.

{*A Furi walks these lands.*}

Silence fell like a blade. The orb's light flickered, its green glow momentarily dimming as if even magic itself recoiled from the word.

{*Impossible!*} the mountain-voice growled, but there was something beneath its certainty—the faintest tremor of unease. {*The bloodline was ended. We saw to that ourselves.*}

The winter-voice hissed. {*Your time in the mortal realm addles your mind, Rathmar. Perhaps we should ...*}

{*Peace, brother,*} the gentle voice interceded, somehow more unsettling in its calm. {*Our faithful servant would not speak such words without cause. Would you, dear Rathmar?*}

Rathmar's throat felt dry like ancient dust. {*The kaegar senses something in one of them. A resonance in the blood. Like recognizing like.*}

{*Them?*} The gentle voice curled around the word like smoke.

{*A pair of Earthen siblings. The brother ...*} Rathmar paused, remembering the black scar that had seemed to vibrate in the kaegar's presence. {*There is something different about him. Something that calls to powers older than our understanding.*}

The mountain-voice rumbled with derision. {*You chase shadows, Sect Leader. The Furi were more than mere blood. They were living bonds between realms, bridges between what was and what could be. Such things do not simply ... appear.*}

{*Yet the kaegar hunts,*} Rathmar pressed. {*It remembers what we would prefer to forget.*}

The orb's light intensified, bathing the chamber in a sickly yellow. When the gentle voice spoke again, its softness carried an edge sharp as broken glass.

{*Your loyalty is not in question, dear Rathmar. Not yet. But do not let curiosity blind you to your purpose. The aether stone*} *must be secured. The girl must not reach the throne. All else is ... irrelevant.*}

The finality in those words sent a chill through Rathmar's ancient bones. Yet as the orb's light began to fade, he couldn't shake the memory of the kaegar's recognition—that moment when predator and prey had seemed to share some deeper understanding.

The orb dimmed to nothing, leaving Rathmar alone in torchlight that suddenly seemed feeble against the darkness. He remained kneeling, his meditation beads clicking softly as age-old memories stirred—fragments of knowledge from times before the kingdom's rise, whispers of powers that had once walked freely between realms.

Three centuries of existence had taught him to recognize patterns, to see the subtle shifts that preceded great change. These were like ripples before a storm, or the first tremors before mountains fell. He had witnessed the slow dance of power many times—the rise and fall of kings, the ebb and flow of ancient forces.

But this ... this was different. The kaegar's reaction had awakened something in him—doubt, yes, but also recognition. Not of the young man himself, but of what his existence might mean. Some bloodlines ran deeper than nobility, older than kingdoms. Some powers refused to die, no matter how thoroughly they were hunted.

Rathmar rose slowly, with movements carrying the weight of centuries. The medallion felt heavier now against his chest, its cold surface a reminder of oaths sworn in darker times. He had been many things in his long existence—servant, hunter, keeper of forbidden knowledge. But never before had duty and instinct pulled him in such opposing directions.

As he made his way back through the corridors, each step echoing with his masters' warnings, a single thought burned in his mind: What if the dark lords, in their arrogance, had overlooked something vital? What if the kaegar's defiance wasn't mere rebellion, but recognition of something that even the Sect had forgotten?

The facility's shadows seemed to reach for him as he ascended, as if trying to pull him back into their secrets. But for the first time in centuries, Rathmar felt something beyond duty stirring in his blood—curiosity, and with it, the first dangerous whispers of doubt.

* * *

The morning sun spilled through ancient branches as Mercury led them through paths known only to the Immortals. Their small group moved with practiced stealth—Xara with her Whispershot ready, Yewwa's sons eagerly gripping their Guild-crafted weapons while their father carried his traditional longbow with quiet dignity.

"Perfect time to try these out, yes?" Ditta adjusted the crystal lattice on his Starpiercer, earning an eye-roll from his father.

"Kids these days," Yewwa muttered, though his lips twitched beneath his beard. Xara caught his glance and smiled, but her eyes never stopped scanning the shadows.

The manor emerged through the morning mist, its stone walls holding secrets older than any of them.

Mercury moved with heightened tension now, each step deliberate. He knew where the princess would go if she had survived—knowledge earned with years of training and trust.

Movement darted in the shadows. Markus materialized like a ghost, his Ghost Strike pulse blaster unwavering—until Yewwa raised his hand, calm as summer rain.

"Markus! Your Highness! You are safe!"

The hidden panel slid open with ageless grace. Aylin emerged first, sunlight catching her mask's silver edges, while Markus followed with the watchful tension of a predator protecting its own.

Mercury started to bow, but Aylin crashed into him instead, her embrace fierce enough to rattle his damaged armor. "Don't you dare," she threatened, and for a moment the immortal warrior's composure cracked.

Then Xara moved with a glare sharp enough to cut steel as she crossed the space between them. Markus lifted his hand, and opened his mouth to speak, but she ignored it completely. Her embrace nearly knocked him back as years of shared survival compressed into a single moment. When she finally pulled back, her fingers found his half of the pendant, pressing it to her lips before letting it fall back against his chest.

"Told you my father would find you," Ditta grinned, but something shifted in Markus' stance—that familiar tension Xara knew too well.

"We need to go," he said, reaching for her hand. But Aylin stepped forward.

"As blunt as you are bold," she chided. "And where exactly do you think you're going?"

"Getting the hell out of here," Markus replied in a rough voice. "Your champion's here now." He gestured to Mercury, something bitter creeping into his tone. "I failed the evolution. I'm nobody, remember? All of this could have been avoided if your Prefect ..." He caught himself, seeing the flash of pain cross Aylin's face, "rest his soul ... but he didn't listen the first time. Why would he?"

The words hung in the morning air. Sunlight streamed through high windows, dust particles dancing in the beams, while outside birds called to each other as if nothing had changed. But everything had.

Mercury stood very still, his discipline battling with something darker. When he spoke, his voice carried the weight of years of service. "He's right."

"No," Aylin started, but Mercury cut her off.

"Yes, he is." The Immortal's carefully maintained control cracked. "Cael was always ... stubborn." The word seemed to catch in his throat as memories crashed over him—years of training, the pride of being chosen by King Ronan himself, the brotherhood of the Immortals now all gone.

The chair crashed against the wall before anyone could move, the sound reverberating through empty halls. Mercury stalked away, his footsteps fading into silence.

Aylin moved then, placing herself between Markus and the door. "You were right," she said quietly. "Cael didn't listen. He was ..." She paused, struggling for composure. "He was like a father to me. In his love, his protection ... even at the end, when he gave you the tracker to find me ... Now they're both gone," she whispered ... the words seemed to echo in the space between them.

Yewwa stepped forward, drawing all eyes. The Nevran chieftain carried wisdom in his bearing, earned through years of watching the cycles of life and death in his beloved forest.

"No, your Highness," he said gently. "They're still here. They live in you." His eyes held hers, ancient understanding meeting fresh grief. "Their time was purposeful, but brief. They would not want you to grieve in vain. One chapter has ended ..."

He glanced around the room—at his sons with their blend of old ways and new, at Xara's street-hardened eyes, at Markus who stood caught between running and staying.

"And now another begins," Yewwa continued. His fingers found Liyzia's shawl at Markus' belt, touching it with reverence. "This one starts right now, with new participants. New guardians." His voice carried the weight of prophecy: "If you'll accept the task."

The morning light seemed to strengthen, casting long shadows behind them all—shadows that stretched like destiny itself.

Markus shifted uncomfortably under Yewwa's knowing gaze as his hand felt for the shawl at his belt. "I'm not ..." he started, but Xara's fingers wrapped around his wrist, silencing him.

"Listen to me," she said, her voice carrying the same fierce protection that had saved him so many times in Vesper's shadows. "You've spent your whole life running from problems. Running from fights. Maybe it's time to stop and face them."

"It's a no-win battle," Markus said, in a voice saturated with street-wise cynicism. "Hans has everything—money, power, an army."

"And we have nothing," Xara's eyes glinted dangerously. "That's what makes us dangerous. You don't survive Vesper's streets by playing fair."

A bitter laugh escaped him. "Tangling with a forger? A small-time thief? And a lowly watchman?"

Aylin moved closer, her presence drawing Markus' attention like gravity. Her hand found the aether stone at her throat with its gently pulsing light. "It's not about who you are on the outside —but on the inside that counts."

"Strong words," Markus muttered, but his resistance was wavering.

"Are they not?" Mercury's voice made them all turn. The Immortal had returned, his earlier anger replaced by something deeper. "My Lady, Cael and the others ... they died upholding an oath sworn generations ago. But perhaps," he glanced at Markus, "right now, it's time for a new team. New guardians."

"The old powers stir," Yewwa added, his eyes distant. "Old and new. This kaegar hunts more than just blood. It hunts destiny itself." He touched the shawl again. "Perhaps Liyzia saw this moment. She chose you, Markus, before anyone understood why."

Markus looked around the room—at Mercury's quiet strength, at Yewwa's age-old wisdom, at Ditta and Nix's eager hope. At Aylin, whose face somehow held more truth than any he'd known. And finally at Xara, who had never stopped believing in him, even when he couldn't believe in himself.

The morning light painted them all in gold, and for a moment, just a moment, Markus felt something shift inside him—like the pieces of a puzzle finally falling into place.

"I don't think we're people you want right now," he said finally, his voice rough with emotion.

Aylin's hand found his, warm and steady. "You're the ones we need right now."

The aether stone's light seemed to strengthen, casting soft shadows that danced like memories of ancient powers. Outside, birds called to the rising sun, while inside, the weight of choice and change hung in the air between them.

"Well?" Xara asked, that familiar street-fighter's grin. "Ready to stop running?"

Markus looked at Aylin, seeing past the princess to the person who'd trusted him when she had every reason not to. "Fine," he said, the word carrying years of choices. "But we do this our way."

Relief softened Aylin's features. "Agreed. Though I suspect we all have secrets yet to share." Her gaze rested on his scar, then to the aether stone at her throat. Both beamed with subtle light, as if acknowledging each other.

Mercury straightened, years of training asserting themselves. "We'll need to move quickly. Hans won't stay blind to this location forever."

"And the kaegar?" Xara asked, her hand never far from her weapon.

"It still hunts," Yewwa said gravely. "But perhaps ..." He studied Markus with those knowing eyes. "Perhaps what it hunts is not what we assume."

Xara's fingers brushed the satchel at her hip, where Hans' stolen documents waited. "Then maybe it's time we understood exactly what we're dealing with." She met her brother's eyes. "All of it."

Markus nodded slowly, recognizing that look. It was the same one she used to wear in Vesper when unraveling particularly dangerous mysteries. "The forgeries," he said. "Everything you took from Hans ..."

"Secrets have nearly gotten us killed more than once," Aylin said with quiet authority. "Let's not repeat past mistakes."

Morning had fully claimed the sky now, as sunlight streamed through the windows. They gathered closer, the revelations yet to come hanging between them like mist before dawn.

* * *

Afternoon light slanted through tall windows as they gathered in the manor's upper study. The massive map of the three islands dominated the oak table, its parchment edges curling slightly in the winter air. Xara emptied the satchel with deliberate care, each document falling like leaves of destiny.

"The aether stone will reveal what's genuine," Aylin explained, lifting the jewel from her throat. "And what's ... not."

The stone's light intensified as she held it over the scattered documents. For a moment, nothing happened. Then metallic seals, each one bearing the stone's carefully forged imprint, began to change. Like frost touched by sunlight, their surfaces liquified, running in silver rivulets across the parchment. The false seals dissolved completely, leaving stains that marked them as counterfeits.

But three documents remained untouched, whose seals remained solid and pristine.

"Those are mine," Xara said with a hint of pride in her voice. She reached for a slender cylindrical device—something between a jeweler's tool and a lockpick. As she slipped it over her fingers, faint crystals along its length began to form.

"Watch," she told Aylin, moving her hand in a precise gesture over the first document. Ultraviolet light emanated from the device, revealing text hidden beneath the surface ink. Words shimmered into view like stars emerging at dusk—a secret message woven into the very fabric of the parchment.

"Guild encryption tech," Mercury observed, studying the device. "Modified, I assume?"

"Among other things." Xara's smile was razor-sharp. "The seals might fool most eyes, but the hidden text ... that's where the real art lies."

"Quite a gift," Aylin breathed with genuine admiration in her voice.

"Now we understand why you're in such high demand," Mercury said, studying the revealed text with an Immortal's expert eye.

"You'd be surprised," Markus muttered, but there was a hint of pride beneath his gruffness. His sister had always been brilliant, even when that brilliance got them into trouble.

They leaned in together, shoulders almost touching as they read. The hidden text revealed layers of conspiracy—new powers rising, old ones falling, all carefully orchestrated like some deadly political dance. And at the center of it all, Hans Lumen's name gleamed like a poisoned blade.

The silence that followed felt heavy like armor. No one needed to speak the obvious—Aylin's intended fate was written between every line.

"We need Governor Tarnsford," Mercury said finally, in a tone that carried the weight of centuries of protocol.

"He's compromised." Xara's voice cut through the formal suggestion like a street blade through silk.

Mercury's eyes narrowed. "How would you know that?"

"Trust me." It was the same tone she'd used countless times in Vesper's shadows, when trust meant the difference between life and death.

"He's sworn an oath to my father," Aylin said. But uncertainty had crept into her voice. "Zone 33 is protected by his own sentries."

"All of whom are conveniently nowhere to be found right now," Markus pointed out, exchanging a knowing look with Xara. They'd survived too long on the streets to believe in convenient coincidences.

"And just why would—he pull them back?"

"To let Hans' team come sniffing around." Xara's fingers traced the documents' edges. "Why else?"

"I find that difficult to believe." But Aylin's protest sounded weaker now. "His oath to protect the throne is invaluable."

"Not as valuable as his illegal spice smuggling out of Duniduiir." Markus' words fell like stones in still water.

Aylin turned to Mercury, and something in her

expression made them all pause. It wasn't just shock or betrayal in those innocent eyes—it was the slow, painful awakening to a world far more complex than the one she'd been trained to rule.

"Illegal smuggling." Aylin tested the words like unfamiliar weapons.

Mercury's expression softened with understanding. "Sadly, your Highness, they're right. Cael knew, even when we kept you in Celavon. A difficult compromise between secluded protection and ..." he hesitated, "unwanted attention."

Aylin turned to Markus, something sharper in her gaze now. "And just how do you know these things?"

His sidelong glance at Xara held volumes of shared history. "A little birdie."

"The executive logs in Lessador," Xara shrugged, but her casual tone didn't quite mask her pride. "I just happened to stumble upon the Governor's dirty laundry."

"Well, aren't you the most gifted artist!" The mix of shock and admiration in Aylin's voice almost made Xara smile.

"Whoa, first of all," Markus cut in, "she's a saint compared to the other characters you're up against right now. And second, this wasn't just hacking. This was authorized ..." He stopped abruptly, memory striking like lightning. "Draven. And Azlo."

The names hung in the air like smoke. Suddenly the room felt colder as they all remembered the two elite warriors who'd started this journey with them, from that first meeting in Orwein, across the North Sea, to those early days of training. Had it really been only a week? Maybe longer. Since then, everything had changed.

"Viktor, Kratz, Dalton," Markus continued softly, counting off the instructors. Four more Immortals plus a Zylvan knight—all of them unaware of what had unfolded here.

Mercury's head snapped up, meeting Markus' gaze with sudden understanding. They moved as one to the map's edge, fingers finding Duniduiir like a lifeline.

"The Trial by Fire," Mercury breathed. "It's nearly finished—if any of the recruits have survived. They give them ten days."

"What's the date?" Markus asked, tension threading through his voice.

"December 20th," Xara answered, and the passage of time pressed down on them all.

"Three days." Markus' finger traced the distance they'd need to cover. "They'll wait, won't they?"

Mercury's laugh held no humor. "Three options. Finish, quit and find civilization ..." He paused. "Or survive the crater."

"And the third?" But Markus' tone suggested he already knew.

"Isn't it obvious?" Mercury's eyes gleamed with something almost feral. "Surviving that forsaken tundra—weather permitting. Not to mention the local wildlife. Lynxes, scraperbacks, spiked-badgers, and the deadliest of all ..."

"Saberwolves," Markus finished, catching Xara's wide-eyed expression. "Either you guys are truly elite or just crazy," he said, shaking his head.

Mercury's chuckle held dark pride. "It takes a special breed to make it." His expression sharpened as he turned to Aylin. "That's it, your Highness. That's our play!"

"What is?"

"Draven. The others—five additional elite assassins."

"Against Hans Lumen's men?" Xara's skepticism cut through the air.

"And this hunter from another world?" Markus added.

"Assuming we can make it that far." Aylin traced the distance on the map. "Duniduiir? The crater? In three days?"

"For what—a last stand?" Xara's voice rose. "There's a storm coming. It's suicide!"

"On foot? Out of the question." Mercury's eyes gleamed with something almost predatory. "But by the best and fastest means available ..." He gestured toward the window. "We have an older aerglide in storage. Bit dated, needs repairs ..."

"That can be fixed," Xara cut in, her mind already racing through possibilities. "But one vehicle can't hold all of us."

"No, you're right." Mercury's smile grew sharper. "That's why we'll need two."

"Where exactly are we getting a second car?" Markus asked. "We're not exactly near a Guild-sponsored dealership."

"Certainly someone in this room is capable of coming up with a second vehicle." Mercury's gaze settled meaningfully on Xara, "Don't you think?"

The look that passed between Markus and Xara carried years of shared survival, close calls, and impossible odds. But this time, neither had a quick response or reassuring smirk. This would either be their finest moment or their greatest failure.

Aylin watched them both, reading the gravity of the

moment in their silence. Then she straightened, her royal will asserting itself like steel. "Well then," she said quietly, "we better get started."

* * *

Aylin found Mercury at the manor's eastern window, his wounds dark against his tarnished armor. Below, the courtyard bustled with preparation, but her eyes were drawn to the siblings working on the aerglide.

Xara lay beneath the diagnostic panel with the tools spread in precise order beside her, while Markus paced the perimeter, checking sightlines. Without a word, he shifted position, placing himself between his sister and the manor's entrance. Even here, they never stopped watching for threats.

"Look at that," Mercury said softly. "He's got better defensive positioning than half my trained guards."

"They move like dancers," Aylin observed. "Always knowing where the other is."

Through the window, they watched Xara emerge from beneath the panel, making a subtle hand gesture. Markus responded instantly, tossing her a tool she hadn't even asked for yet.

"No formal training," Mercury mused, "yet they've developed their own language, their own way of surviving." His voice carried grudging respect. "Though I'd never admit that to their faces."

"They shouldn't be here," Aylin said, but there was wonder rather than dismissal in her tone. "This isn't their fight. Their world. And yet ..."

"And yet they're exactly what we need." Mercury's

hand unconsciously touched his wounded side. "Sometimes the best guardians aren't the ones who follow protocol."

* * *

"Pass me the fusion wrench," Xara called from beneath the craft, her voice muffled by machinery.

Markus scanned the meticulously arranged tools. "The what now?"

"The blue one. No, your other blue. The one that looks like it could crack someone's skull."

"That's how you remember tool names? By their combat potential?"

"Says the guy who organized the medical supplies by 'which wounds need stitches' versus 'which ones we can walk off.'"

He slid the wrench into her waiting hand. "Hey, that system works."

"Until you need actual medicine instead of street triage." A loud clank punctuated her words. "Speaking of which, did you reinforce the rear panel like I showed you?"

"Added extra plating where you marked it." He crouched to check her progress. "Though I still say we should rig the fuel line to detonate if someone tries to disable it."

"No explosives." She emerged long enough to give him a pointed look. "I'd like to actually survive this escape."

"That was one time ..."

"Three times."

"The third one barely counted." He helped her up, both of them automatically shifting to cover each other's blind spots. "Besides, your security bypasses aren't exactly subtle."

"They work, don't they?" She wiped grease from her hands with customary efficiency. "Unlike someone's 'punch first, ask questions later' approach."

"Got us this far."

"Yeah." Her voice trailed off slightly as she ran diagnostics. "Further than we had any right to get."

They worked in comfortable silence for a moment, punctuated by mechanical hums and the soft beep of testing equipment. Neither mentioned the storm gathering on the horizon, or the battles waiting ahead. They didn't need to.

"If that coupling doesn't hold," Xara said finally, "I'm blaming you."

"If that coupling doesn't hold, we'll have bigger problems than blame."

"True." She closed the panel with a decisive click. "But I'll still blame you."

Markus grinned, catching the rag she tossed at his face. Some things never changed, even when everything else had.

CHAPTER NINETEEN

Moonlight painted the manor grounds in shades of silver and shadow, each breath of wind stirring leaves that seemed to whisper ancient warnings. Hans Lumen moved between the trees with practiced stealth, his boots silent on the frost-covered ground. Around him, two dozen mercenaries took their positions, their modern weapons in stark contrast to the manor's timeworn stones.

Through his tactical visor's enhancement, Hans watched heat signatures move within the manor's walls, red and orange blobs drifting like ghosts, unaware of the net slowly closing around them. Or so he thought.

"Teams in position," Nettles's voice crackled through his earpiece. "North and east secured. Waiting on your signal."

Hans adjusted his coat, feeling the reassurance of his sidearm. "Status of the governor's men?"

"Nothing. Zone's clear, just as promised."

A bitter smile touched Hans' lips. Amazing what leverage could accomplish! One whispered threat about spice shipments, and the governor's sentries had vanished like morning mist. Everything was falling into place.

Almost everything.

Inside the manor, where candlelight cast long shadows across the walls, Yewwa's head snapped up from the maps spread across the oak table.

"Father?" Ditta whispered, recognizing that distant look in the elder's eyes.

"They're here," Yewwa said softly. "Moving like shadows, but the trees remember their passing."

Mercury's hand found his weapon, while Xara moved instinctively closer to her brother. Markus felt the familiar burn beginning in his blood as his scar throbbed in rhythm with the aether stone at Aylin's throat.

"How many?" Mercury asked, his voice carrying the weight of centuries of combat.

"Two dozen, maybe more." Yewwa's eyes remained distant, reading signs others couldn't see. "They think they're hidden, but the forest knows their intentions. Violence walks among the roots tonight."

"The vehicles?" Markus asked, his hand finding Xara's arm.

"Ready," she replied. "Though getting to them might be interesting."

Aylin stood by the window, moonlight catching her mask's silver edges. "We knew they would come," she said quietly. "Hans isn't known for his patience."

"Or his subtlety," Xara added, checking her Whispershot's charge. "Two dozen men for one girl? He's either desperate or ..."

"Scared," Markus finished. Something in his blood sang with recognition of approaching danger. "He knows what else hunts these woods."

Outside, Hans raised his hand, ready to give the signal.

His men tensed, weapons ready. The manor waited in deceptive peace, its windows gleaming with patient eyes.

The shot came from nowhere.

One of Hans' men crumpled, clutching his shoulder where a precise blast had found the gap in his armor. Before anyone could react, more shots rang out from the darkness. Not from the manor, but from the trees themselves.

"Contact!" Nettles shouted. "Multiple hostiles in the ... "

Another shot cut him off. Hans dived for cover as more blasts illuminated the night. Through the chaos, he caught glimpses of figures in the trees—sentries who should have been miles away, their loyalty to the crown apparently stronger than the governor's threats.

"Damn them!" Hans snarled, returning fire. But even as his men regrouped, something changed in the air. The night itself seemed to hold its breath.

Then came the sound—a low, rumbling growl that caused even hardened mercenaries to freeze. Hans felt it in his bones, a recognition of something that should not exist in this age of men.

The kaegar had caught their scent.

Inside the manor, Markus' scar burned black as pitch. Aylin's hand found his in the darkness, while Xara's fingers tightened on her weapon. Through the windows, they watched the night erupt into gunfire—blaster fire painting the darkness in desperate colors while shadows moved with terrible purpose between the trees.

"Time to go," Mercury said quietly, but his eyes held the weight of impossible choices yet to come.

The night had only begun.

* * *

The firefight painted the night in strobing flashes, each burst illuminating fragments of the unfolding chaos. Hans' men scattered for better positions, their tactical formation dissolving under the sentries' targeted fire. Through his visor's enhancement, Hans counted at least six positions in the trees—each one occupied by a marksman who had clearly trained under Mercury's exacting standards.

"Meet up on the north side!" Hans ordered, but even as the words left his mouth, something massive moved through the shadows behind his men. The darkness itself seemed to shift, and a familiar dread pulled at his chest.

From her position near the manor's west window, Xara caught movement through the trees—the sleek outline of a vehicle, partially concealed by foliage. Two mercenaries were crouched behind it, using its bulk for cover as they fired toward the manor.

"Mercury." She touched his arm, nodding toward the vehicle. "Think I found our second ride."

His eyes narrowed, catching her meaning instantly. "How many guards?"

"Just two." A smile touched her lips. "Almost unfair."

Aylin stepped up beside them, her ion pistol humming with charged energy. "Need a distraction?"

"Your Highness," Mercury started, but she cut him off with a precise shot through the window. The blast caught a tree near the mercenaries, sending them scrambling.

"Like that?" she asked innocently.

Xara grinned. "Exactly like that. Cover me."

Xara moved like water through shadow, years of Vesper's streets guiding her path between laser bursts. The firefight's disarray worked in her favor—none of Hans' men expecting an attack from behind while they were focused on the manor.

The first mercenary never saw her coming. Her garrote wire found his throat as she emerged from beneath the vehicle, a silent and efficient takedown. Before his partner could turn, she'd already slammed his head against the aerglide's frame. Both men went down without a sound— street fighting refined to an art.

Her fingers danced across the security panel, bypassing codes with accustomed ease. The engine ignited just as a laser blast scorched the ground where she'd been moments before.

"If anyone wants a ride," she called softly into her comm, "better hurry."

Inside the manor, Markus felt it before anyone else. His scar was burning black as pitch as ancient blood recognized its own kind. The kaegar's roar shattered the night, its massive form emerging through fire and smoke like judgment itself.

"Move!" Markus grabbed Aylin's arm, but she was already in motion, royal dignity transformed into combat-ready efficiency. Ditta and Nix sprinted for their prepared vehicle while Mercury, despite his wounds, provided covering fire.

Through smoke and chaos, Markus glimpsed his sister across the grounds—her stolen vehicle roaring to life as Yewwa reached it, bow already drawn. No time for goodbyes. No time for plans. Just survival instinct and desperate choices made in fragments of seconds.

"Split up!" Mercury's voice cut through their comms. "Northwest and east. Rendezvous at the fallback point!"

The kaegar's form stood terribly still among the flames, those burning eyes tracking both vehicles with primal intelligence. Unlike Hans' frantic men, it moved with singular purpose— not wasting energy on those who didn't interfere, but focused entirely on its true quarry.

"Stick close to the trees," Xara's voice crackled through the comm. "We'll draw them east."

"Like hell you will," Markus started, but Aylin's hand found his arm.

"She's right," she nodded. "We're the ones it wants."

The night dissolved into fire and shadow. When the smoke finally cleared, both vehicles had vanished into darkness into separate paths carved by necessity and chance. Only then, in the quiet aftermath, did the impact of separation hit them all.

Miles apart now, brother and sister each realized the same thing Not since Vesper had the silence between them felt so final. They faced the darkness alone— knowing the other might not return.

* * *

The aerglide's turbines screamed as Xara dodged another volley of blaster fire. Hans' vehicles pursued with military precision, trying to flank them on both sides. A shot clipped their rear stabilizer, which sent them lurching toward the tree line.

"We're losing power to the port engine," she called, fighting the controls as their trajectory spiraled. The dawn light caught unfamiliar terrain through breaks in the ancient forest, paths they hadn't meant to take.

Another blast forced them deeper into unknown territory. The trees began to change, their bark growing paler, their branches reaching like grasping hands toward stars that seemed suddenly distant.

Too late! Recognition dawned in Mercury's eyes. "Pull back," he ordered, his immortal's composure cracking. "We've strayed too far east. These are ..."

"The Wraithwoods!" Yewwa's voice carried quiet dread. The very air had changed around them, becoming thick with memories older than the kingdom itself. There was no turning back now.

Ethereal mist clung to the twisted trunks, and in that mist, shapes began to form. Ghostly figures shimmered between the trees, their forms more suggestion than substance. For a moment, Xara thought she saw faces of impossible beauty—until they turned toward the vehicle, revealing something ancient and terrible beneath their serenity.

Through her mirrors, she watched Hans' vehicles enter the Wraithwoods behind them, their headlights cutting through the mist. The mercenaries' faces showed the first hints of uncertainty as they saw shadows move with unnatural purpose between the trees.

Xara could have sworn those ethereal beings were smiling—an expression of such pure joy it made her heart ache. But there was something wrong about those smiles, something that sat uneasily beneath their radiance. She clenched her teeth and drove on, but the laughter—soft and lilting—brushed her ears like cobwebs.

"Keep going," Yewwa commanded, though his voice muted to barely a whisper. "Whatever you hear, whatever you see—don't stop."

The spirits drifted closer to their vehicle, those beautiful faces pressing against the windscreen with terrible curiosity. Yewwa's bloodied hand gripped the dash, his lips still moving in that ancient tongue. The phantoms seemed to pause, tilting their heads as if listening to something only they could hear. Then, like water parting around stone, they flowed away from their craft, turning their attention with hungry purpose to Hans' pursuing vehicles.

"They recognize the old ways," Yewwa said quietly as Xara guided them through the ethereal tide. "Blood freely given carries different power than blood taken by force."

Hans' vehicles entered the Wraithwoods behind them, their headlights cutting through the mist. The ghostly figures turned toward the intrusion, and in that moment, everything changed.

Their ethereal beauty twisted; faces elongated into something ancient and terrible. Jaws distended to impossible lengths, revealing rows of teeth that could never exist in any natural creature. Their light turned from silver to sickly green, while their reaching hands became claws that could rend reality itself.

Through her mirrors, Xara saw those ethereal figures turning their faces toward the headlights, beauty shimmering before it cracked like ice. Smiles split into maws, and screams filled the forest.

Hans' men fired frantically at the spirits, but their blasts passed harmlessly through writhing forms somehow both there and not there. Xara caught glimpses in her mirrors—mercenaries being dragged from their vehicles by things that had no right to exist in any sane world. Even Hans' face, usually so controlled, showed pure terror as the phantoms tore through metal like paper.

"Now!" Yewwa commanded, drawing his knife. Before Mercury could stop him, Yewwa sliced his own palm, blood spilling freely to the Wraithwood's roots below—an offering older than language, older than light. The words he spoke belonged to no language Xara had ever heard, sounds that made her teeth ache and her vision blur.

The spirits responded instantly. Their terrible forms coalesced into a tide of horror that swept over Hans' vehicles like a wave of nightmares given flesh. Through the chaos, Xara kept the aerglide steady, her knuckles white on the controls as otherworldly screams filled the night.

Markus' party emerged from the Wraithwoods' far side into blessed darkness. Behind them, Hans' remaining vehicle limped away in the opposite direction, its frame scratched by claw marks that couldn't possibly exist. The spirits remained at the forest's edge, their forms once again beautiful and terrible as they swayed like dancers in the mist.

"Seven hells," Mercury breathed, his immortal composure finally cracking. "What were those things?"

"The ancient dead," Yewwa replied simply, binding his bleeding hand. "Those who walked these lands before light came. Before kingdoms rose." His eyes met Xara's in the rearview display. "They remember their own kind."

Xara's hands trembled slightly on the controls, but her voice remained steady. "And the blood offering?"

"A reminder." Yewwa's expression was grave. "That some prices are paid in flesh, not coin."

They drove on through the night, leaving the Wraithwoods behind. But in every shadow, in every trace of mist that clung to their vehicle, Xara thought she saw fragments of that ethereal light— beautiful and horrible, ancient and eternal—a reminder that some powers survived beyond death itself.

* * *

The aerglide's turbines whined as they cut through Moorwood's canopy, whipping past branches close enough to scrape paint. Markus kept his eyes fixed on the terrain ahead, trying to ignore how his scar pulsed in time with ancient blood.

"Two vehicles," Nix reported from the back, tracking their pursuers through modified binoculars. "Three hundred meters and closing."

Aylin checked her ion pistol's charge. "They're herding us east."

"Away from the Wraithwoods," Ditta added. "Smart of them."

A massive impact shook the forest behind them— the sound of trees being torn aside by something that moved with terrible purpose. Markus' hands tightened on the controls as that familiar burn spread through his veins. Not fear this time, but recognition. "It's not following them," he said quietly. "It's following us."

Through the rear viewport, they caught glimpses of

the kaegar's menacing form—its movements deliberate and relentless as it carved a path through the forest. Unlike the frantic pursuit of Hans' men, the creature advanced with cold calculation, each stride eating up distance with mechanical efficiency.

"Hold on!" shouted Markus as he yanked the controls hard, sending them into a sharp dive between twisted trunks. The pursuing vehicles split up, trying to flank them. Laser fire cut through branches overhead, filling the air with burning leaves.

Aylin leaned out her window, returning fire with deadly aim. Her shot caught one vehicle's stabilizer, sending it spinning into the underbrush. "That's for Cael," she whispered, but there was no triumph in her voice.

The remaining pursuit vehicle drew closer, its head-lights painting their cabin in harsh glare. Through the light, Markus recognized the driver—one of Hans' personal guards, the kind that gave other killers nightmares.

"We can't outrun them forever," Ditta warned, notching an arrow to his bow. "And we're burning fuel too fast."

As if in response, the aerglide's reserve lights began flashing. Ten minutes of power, maybe less. Markus fought to keep his focus as another wave of burning swept through him. The kaegar was closer now—he could feel it in his blood, like a compass needle strain-ing toward magnetic north.

"There!" Nix pointed toward a gap in the cliffs ahead. "The old mining tunnels!"

"No!" Aylin started, but Markus was already turning

the wheel. The vehicle shot toward the narrow opening, its sides scraping stone as they threaded the needle. Their pursuer tried to follow but miscalculated the angle. The sound of shrieking metal echoed through the night as their vehicle wedged itself in the gap.

The tunnel swallowed them in darkness. Emergency lights cast everything in red as they flew through former excavations, between the walls close enough to touch. Behind them, the kaegar's roar reverberated through stone, frustrated but not deterred.

"It'll find another way through," Markus said, fighting another wave of burning recognition. "It always does."

"The fuel won't last much longer," Ditta reported. "We need to ..."

The tunnel ahead had collapsed. Markus yanked the controls, barely managing to turn down a side passage. The aerglide's wing clipped stone, sending them into a spin that ended with a bone-jarring crash against the tunnel wall.

Silence fell, broken only by the dying whine of their engines and the distant sound of pursuit. The emergency lights beamed once, then died, leaving them in complete darkness.

"Everyone alive?" Markus asked, tasting blood where he'd bit his lip.

"Define 'alive,'" Aylin muttered, but her hand found his in the darkness. Through their shared contact, he felt the aether stone pulse gently—its rhythm somehow steadying the burn in his blood.

Footsteps echoed through the tunnels—Hans' men following on foot now. And beneath those sounds, something else moved in the darkness. Something primordial that made the very stone tremble.

"We need to move," Markus said, helping Aylin out of the wreck. "The tunnels branch ahead. We can ..."

His scar flared with sudden heat. Through the darkness ahead, two points of red light burned like dying stars—primal eyes that carried terrible recognition.

The hunt was far from over.

* * *

The darkness pressed around them like a living thing. Markus' handlight cast wild shadows across rough-hewn walls, illuminating support beams that might have been old trees once, whose surfaces were worn by time. Water dripped somewhere in the darkness, each sound echoing strangely through tunnels that seemed to breathe.

"This way," Ditta whispered, his hunter instincts reading signs the others missed. Old rail tracks ran deeper into the mountain, their metal surfaces dulled by years of disuse. Guild-tech lighting strips still clung to some walls, dead now but hinting at more recent operations.

The tunnel opened into a larger chamber where multiple shafts connected. Disused mining equipment lay scattered like the bones of metal giants—ore carts tipped on their sides, rusted conveyor systems reaching into darkness. But there was something else about this space, something that made Markus' scar burn hotter.

"Look at these marks," Aylin said, as her hand brushed stone walls that seemed almost polished in places. "This isn't just Guild mining. Some of these tunnels are older."

A sound echoed through the darkness—the scrape of claws on stone, still distant but drawing closer. Markus felt it in his blood, that terrible recognition growing stronger in the confined space. The kaegar was hunting them through the mountain's cavernous spaces, as patient as the stone itself.

"Multiple levels," Nix reported, studying a faded map bolted to one wall. "These shafts go deep."

"Too deep," Ditta added. His voice carried the weight of old stories—tales of things that slept beneath mountains, of powers better left undisturbed.

Markus' handlight caught something that made them all freeze—massive claw marks into solid rock, old and weathered but unmistakable. The kaegar wasn't the first of its kind to walk these tunnels.

"Move," he ordered. But another sound froze them in place—voices echoing from a side tunnel, Hans' men, closing in.

"Up there." Aylin pointed to a higher passage, accessed by metal stairs that looked barely stable. "The old ventilation system might lead to the surface."

They climbed as quietly as possible, metal groaning beneath their weight. Markus took rear guard, watching darkness press against the edges of their light. His scar vibrated with each heartbeat, while the aether stone at Aylin's throat cast its own soft response to ancient powers resonating in the depths.

A crash echoed through the tunnels—it was the kaegar forcing its way through another passage. Closer now. Through the darkness below, Markus caught a glimpse of burning red eyes, searching with malice. For a moment, their gazes met, and something passed between them—recognition deeper than blood, older than kingdoms.

"It's not just hunting us," he whispered, the realization hitting him like physical force. "It's searching for something. Something it sees in ..."

The stairs gave way with a shriek of tortured metal. Aylin's hand caught his arm as they tumbled backward, but momentum carried them over the edge. They fell into darkness, as the shouts of the others were lost in the clamor of falling debris.

Markus' world dissolved into impact and shadow. When his vision cleared, he found himself in a lower tunnel, separated from the others by tons of collapsed metal and stone. Aylin lay beside him, dazed but alive; the aether stone's light was their only illumination.

Through the wall of debris came Ditta's muffled voice: "Find another way up! We'll meet at the surface!"

"If we live that long," Aylin muttered, but her hand found Markus' in the darkness. The stone's light strengthened slightly at their contact, pushing back shadows that seemed to move with purpose now.

From somewhere in the darkness came that sound again—ancient claws on stone. But it was the living presence that made Markus' cursed blood reply with recognition.

They were not alone in the deep places.

* * *

Rough stone scraped their shoulders as they pressed through narrowing passages. The aether stone's light caught crystalline formations in the walls—not natural growth, but something that seemed to pulse faintly in response to their presence.

"These tunnels," Aylin pointed out, her hand trailing across the strange patterns. "They're not just mines, are they?"

Before Markus could answer, his scar flared with sudden heat. He pulled her into a side passage just as heavy footsteps echoed through the darkness ahead. Hans' voice carried through the tunnels, closer than expected.

"Find them! The girl must not reach Duniduiir."

They pressed deeper into the passage, but Markus' blood warned. The kaegar's presence was closer too— moving with dreadful intent, driving them toward ... something.

"Look!" Aylin's voice barely carried over the sound of dripping water. Her hand trembled slightly as she pointed ahead.

The tunnel opened into a chamber that no miners' tools could have reached. Perfect archways of stone rose into darkness, their surfaces covered in script that seemed to shift when viewed directly. At the chamber's center, a circular platform bore similar markings—but these were scorched, as if something ancient and powerful had burned them into the rock itself.

"I've seen these marks before," Aylin breathed, the aether stone's light growing stronger as she approached the platform. "In Theo's oldest books. They're ..."

A roar shook dust from the ceiling—closer than ever. At the same moment, Hans' voice echoed from another tunnel: "This way! Fresh tracks!"

They were being herded, Markus realized. Every twist

and turn had led them here, to this chamber that felt older than the kingdom itself. His scar burned black as pitch, responding to something that called from even deeper in the mountain.

"We need to move," he said, but Aylin's hand caught his arm.

"Markus." Her voice carried an edge of realization. "It's not just following us. It's following you."

Before he could respond, heavy footsteps entered the chamber—Hans' men spilling from one tunnel while that other, more terrible presence approached from another. They were trapped between modern hunters and ancient horror, with nowhere left to run.

The aether stone's light caught Hans' face as he emerged from shadow, his weapon trained on them with unwavering precision. But there was something in his expression beyond mere triumph—a hint of desperate fear as that other presence drew closer.

"It ends here," Hans said softly, but his words were drowned by another sound—ancient claws on stone, drawing closer with unstoppable purpose.

They stood at the nexus of modern ambition and ancient power, trapped between forces that would shape everything to come. Above, somewhere in the darkness, their companions searched for another way to reach them. But here in the deep places, surrounded by script that spoke of mysterious powers, Markus and Aylin faced their pursuers.

The hunt was about to end. Or perhaps, something even older was about to unravel.

CHAPTER TWENTY

The aether stone's light caught ancient script like frozen lightning, each symbol burning with impossible clarity. Markus felt power radiating from the circular platform—old magic that made his cursed blood sing with recognition. Hans' men spread through the chamber's shadows, weapons trained on both exits, while that other presence drew closer.

"Last chance," Hans said softly. His voice carried none of its usual polish—just raw desperation masked as control. "Surrender the stone, and this ends cleanly."

The kaegar's roar shook dust from the ceiling. Not hunting now—*herding*—driving them toward something that resonated in the mountain's depths. Markus' scar was black, while the stone at Aylin's throat cast wild shadows across weathered stone.

"You don't understand what you've awoken," said Aylin with quiet authority despite their desperation. "What you've unleashed."

"I understand power." Hans' smile was cruel in the strange light. "The kind that builds empires or breaks them. The kind your father ..."

The stone walls *shuddered*.

Ancient script blazed with sudden light as massive claws tore through the tunnel's mouth. The kaegar emerged, a nightmare in the flesh—its granite skin catching crystal reflections, those burning eyes fixed on Markus with hungry recognition. But there was something else in that ancient gaze now. Not just hunger, but ... anticipation.

Everything happened at once.

Hans' men opened fire, their blasts illuminating the chamber in strobing flashes. The kaegar moved with impossible speed, its massive form flowing between shots like water through stone. Three mercenaries went down before they could scream as claws found chinks in modern armor.

Markus grabbed Aylin's arm, dragging her toward the platform's edge. His blood felt like fire in his veins, responding to unseen powers. The stone's light intensified, casting wild shadows that seemed to move with purpose.

"The tunnel!" Aylin pointed toward a gap barely visible behind fallen debris. "If we can ..."

A blast caught stone inches from her head. Hans advanced through the chaos, his weapon never wavering as the kaegar tore through his remaining men. "Nobody leaves," he snarled. "Not until ..."

The platform *ignited*.

Markus felt something tear through him—power that resonated in his cursed blood. The kaegar's roar became something else—recognition of its own kind, awakening after centuries of slumber.

The chamber's floor cracked. Not from any weapon,

but from something rising from below— darkness given form, shadow made solid. Hans stumbled back, his careful control finally shattering.

"Run!" Markus didn't recognize his own voice. Power surged through him, making his scar pulse with light that matched the stone at Aylin's throat. Together they bolted for the tunnel's mouth, pursued by otherworldly sounds.

Dawn was breaking somewhere above, but in the mountain's depths, older shadows stirred. The hunt was changing, becoming something else, a convergence of powers that would reshape everything they thought they knew.

* * *

The chase had only begun.

The sky smoldered in hues of ember and ash as they stumbled from the mountain's depths. Markus' blood still burned from whatever power had awakened below, but survival instincts took over as they sprinted through the trees. Behind them, Hans' remaining men regrouped with mechanical efficiency while that other, more terrible presence pursued.

"There!" Ditta's voice cut through the morning air. An aerglide waited in a natural hollow, partially concealed by fallen logs. The vehicle was older than their previous ride, its turbines bearing the wear of countless storms, but it purred to life at Markus' touch.

They piled in as the first blaster shots scorched tree bark around them. Nix returned fire from the back seat while Aylin's fingers flew across the control panel, bypassing security protocols. The engine's whine built to a fevered pitch.

"Hold on!" Markus yanked the controls, sending them shooting between tree trunks. Their pursuers weren't far behind—he caught glimpses of two vehicles in his mirrors, Hans himself visible in the lead car. But it was the third presence that made his scar burn—the kaegar moving through the forest with malicious purpose, gaining ground with each stride.

The aerglide's turbines screamed as Markus pushed them beyond safe limits. Tree branches whipped past close enough to tear paint, while morning mist made the ground below a treacherous blur. Behind them, Hans' vehicles fanned out, trying to flank their position.

"We've got company!" Ditta called from the back. A laser blast caught their rear stabilizer, sending them into a spin that Markus barely controlled. The smell of burnt circuitry filled the cabin.

"The primary turbine's failing," Aylin reported, her hands steady on the diagnostic panel. "We need to ..."

The impact came from nowhere. The kaegar burst through the trees like a force of nature, its giant form slamming into their vehicle's side. Metal screamed as claws scraped for a hold on their hull. Those burning eyes fixed on Markus through the windscreen, carrying recognition that made his cursed blood ring with answering power.

Markus threw them into a desperate dive, scraping the creature off against a massive trunk. The kaegar fell away, but the damage was done—their port stabilizer was gone, leaving them limping.

"The ridge road!" Nix pointed toward where the forest

thinned, revealing a maintenance track carved into the mountainside. "It leads to Duniduiir!"

Hans' vehicles were closing in fast, their weapons finding range again. But the kaegar's roar shook the morning air. It wasn't just hunting them now. It was driving them, herding them toward something that pulled at Markus' blood like a lodestone drawing iron.

The aerglide shuddered as Markus pushed the failing turbines harder. Whatever power had awakened in those ancient tunnels, it wasn't finished with them yet.

The chase had become something else—an intersection of modern ambition and ancient purpose, racing toward a destiny none of them could fully understand. The ridge road beckoned ahead, its path threading between cliff and sky while morning mist swallowed the forest below.

They flew toward dawn's reckoning, pursued by forces both human and inhuman, while somewhere ahead lay answers to questions they hadn't dared to ask.

* * *

The ridge road narrowed treacherously, stone walls meeting empty air. Markus fought the dying turbines as another impact rocked their vehicle. The kaegar had caught them again, somehow keeping pace despite the impossible terrain. Those granite-like claws tore at their hull, struggling for a grip, while burning eyes fixed themselves on Markus with menacing recognition.

"The spears!" Ditta's voice cracked through the chaos. He grabbed one of the black-tipped weapons Yewwa had handed them days ago—*family relics*, or so they'd thought. Weapons from forgotten hunts, meant for beasts no one truly believed in anymore.

He hesitated just a second. Then drove it through a seam in the hull—into the Kaegar's shoulder.

The impact didn't just pierce—it *reverberated*.

The Kaegar's roar shifted—not in pain, but in something deeper. Recognition. Memory. Rage.

It let go. Dark fluid leaked where no wound had ever shown before.

The black metal sang through it—not just pain, but memory awakened. Something it had not felt in centuries. Its cape coiled protectively, and in its eyes, for the first time... hesitation.

"Impossible," Aylin breathed.

Markus didn't speak—but the scar on his side burned. He felt the spear's impact inside himself, as if something old had been stirred—*and seen.*

The creature reeled, but its cape coiled around the wound like a living shroud—shielding it, absorbing the dark fluid. For a breathless moment, it stared—not in pain, but in uncanny familiarity.

The kaegar recovered almost instantly, its burning eyes now carrying something beyond mere hunting instinct. Whatever that black metal was, it had awakened something in the creature— A mirrored fury lit in both beast and man.

Their vehicle screamed around another bend with the failing turbines pushed beyond their limits. Hans' cars were closer now, their weapons finding range again. But the kaegar's pursuit had changed—more cautious now, yet somehow more purposeful.

The chase continued toward dawn's reckoning, but

something fundamental had shifted. In that brief moment of vulnerability, ancient powers had recognized their own kind, and nothing would be the same.

* * *

Light streaked across the morning sky as the damaged craft finally broke free of pursuit. Dark clouds gathered on the northern horizon, heavy with winter's promise. The air carried that metallic taste of approaching snow, while wind-torn clouds raced above like harbingers of the storm to come. Markus guided them into a secluded ravine, the dying turbines giving one last whine before falling silent. For a moment, only their breathing disturbed the dawn.

Through the cracked windscreen, sunlight painted the world in shades of gold and shadow. Markus' hand found the half-pendant at his throat, fingers closing around it like an anchor against the chaos. Beside him, Aylin watched silently, seeing not the scarred fighter or failed recruit, but something else—someone who had chosen to stay despite every reason to run.

Miles away, in the governor's crowded office, Xara stood amid a storm of voices and motion. Mercury's presence beside her carried the weight of his new authority as Prefect, while Yewwa observed the proceedings from the shadows. But her thoughts were elsewhere—her fingers finding her own half of the pendant, pressing it briefly to her lips as she closed her eyes. The gesture spoke of promise. They had survived Vesper's shadows together. They would survive this.

"You understand what you're asking?" Governor

Tarnsford's voice cut through her thoughts. He stood at the window, watching dawn paint his domain in deceptive peace. "Contact the Capitol? You'll bring the entire kingdom down on our heads."

"Your Sentinels have already failed," said Mercury with a ring of command. "Your oath to the crown demands action."

"My oath?" Tarnsford's laugh was bitter. "While you lecture me about oaths, Hans Lumen hunts our princess through my lands. Give me time to marshal our own forces ..."

"Time?" Xara's voice was quiet but incisive. "Like the time you bought with spice shipments through Duniduiir?" The room fell silent. "How many crowns has that silence cost, Governor?"

Tarnsford's face hardened. "You dare ..."

"I dare everything for family," Xara cut him off. Her eyes never left his face. "The question is: What do you dare for yours? How many more lives are worth your secrets?"

The governor's hands tightened on his chair. Dawn light caught his face, revealing the war between duty and self-preservation. "The generals will tear this island apart," he said finally. "Everything I've built ... will mean nothing if Hans succeeds."

Mercury stepped forward. "You know what powers he's awakened, what ancient forces now walk these lands."

Silence stretched between them, heavy with choices.

Xara's fingers found the pendant again, thinking of her brother somewhere in the vast wilderness. They had always survived together, watching each other's backs. Now fate had forced them apart, but their bond remained—two halves of the same whole, each protecting what mattered most.

"Very well," said Tarnsford, in a tone of surrender. He reached for his transmitter with hands that trembled slightly. The glow of the communicator lit his face—not with resolve, but resignation. "May the gods forgive us all."

Xara turned to the window, watching storm clouds gather over the distant peaks. Her brother was out there somewhere, along with Ditta and Nix—all of them racing against time and winter's fury. Mercury's wounds had stopped him from protecting his princess, while she stood helpless, unable to watch her brother's back. They had set greater forces in motion, but the cost of waiting gnawed at them all.

"The generals will come," Mercury said quietly, his immortal composure easing just slightly. "But the storm ..."

Mercury's words hung in the air, but Yewwa didn't answer at once.

He turned slightly, his hand brushing the cloth bundle at his hip—fingers curling briefly around the spearhead within. A familiar weight. A question left unanswered.

He'd seen something in the boy. Something he didn't yet name. But the spearhead had responded. That much, he felt.

"The storm," he said finally, eyes still on the horizon, "will not wait for armies."

"Will not wait for armies," Yewwa finished, eyes fixed on the darkening horizon. Wind rattled the windows, carrying the first bitter touch of winter's rage.

Morning's hush carried the power of choice, the land-scape caught between the silver of waning night and the gilded promise of day.

In a ravine far from civilization, Markus guided their battered vehicle back onto hidden paths, while Aylin's aether stone trembled with purpose. And in a crowded office, Xara stood witness as the governor chose duty over pride, knowing they could do nothing now but trust in bonds stronger than blood.

The pieces were in motion now. There would be no turning back.

CHAPTER TWENTY-ONE

The tundra stretched endlessly before him, a stark canvas of whites and grays, a far cry from Moorwood's sheltering wood. Until now, Markus hadn't noticed the landscape's transformation as his thoughts had been consumed by Xara's absence, a hollow space beside him where his sister should have been. The half-pendant at his throat felt heavier than ever.

His shoulder throbbed where the kaegar's claws had sunk in, but physical pain was easier to bear than separation. For the first time since that night in Vesper's alleys when an eleven-year-old girl had dragged him home, he faced the darkness alone.

Through the cracked windscreen, he caught glimpses of Ditta and Nix in the back seat, their youthful faces grim with understanding beyond their years. Beside him, Aylin sat in uncharacteristic silence, her fingers absently tracing the patterns of Liyzia's shawl—the last piece of home he had to give.

The vehicle's diagnostics panel flashed warnings he tried to ignore. Half a tank of fuel remained, the port stabilizer was failing, and behind them, Hans' forces were regrouping. But it was the other presence he felt—that ancient hunter whose blood seemed to recognize something in his own—that made his scar burn with warning.

*** * ***

Markus gradually eased the brakes and initiated the breaking turbines from below, slowing down the vehicle to study his surroundings. In the far distance to the north along the horizon, lay the faint outline of a plateau marking the base of the dormant volcano and its crater.

It wasn't much to go on. Looking around, left to right, his eyes scanned the panorama until he noticed a patch of distant vegetation and the remnants of a rock structure behind it. He turned the vehicle in that direction and punched the accelerator, speeding across the barren landscape that offered no visible shelter or hiding place from their pursuers.

Within moments, the vehicle had reached the base of the mountain, and Markus spotted the outline of a rock structure pressed against the vast wall and cliffs. A triad of three massive, rectangular sheets of granite appeared to have collapsed long ago, perhaps during the volcano's active days. Now, the structures lay at just the right angle to form a potential hiding spot barely big enough to back the vehicle into—if Markus could pull it off.

Struggling and swerving, bobbing and nearly tipping, Markus managed to back the levitating vehicle beneath the shadow of the prehistoric granite sheets. The vehicle fit snugly in with barely an inch to spare, its nose tucked just beneath the shadows cast by the imposing stone slabs.

And just in time too.

In the distance, he spotted his pursuers approaching. His chest tightened as he wondered if they had seen him in time to track his location. But, to his relief, the group began wandering aimlessly, veering off in scattered directions in the serene but unforgiving landscape.

Markus slumped back into his seat, reaching for his shoulder and grunting against the ache that ran through his body.

"Are we safe?" Aylin's voice was soft but strained.

"Oh, they'll find us soon enough," Markus muttered, pointing to the dashboard. "It's only a matter of time."

"The Immortals you speak of," she asked hesitantly. "Where would they be?"

"Up top. At the rim of the crater," he said grimly.

Her brows furrowed. "You mean for us to climb?"

"There's a path," he explained in a voice tight with exhaustion. "A steady trail for the last leg of the ascent. Somewhere around here. Two distinct rock formations above the plateau—the 'Narrow Gates'—you can't miss it."

Her eyes rested on his shoulder. "You're hurt."

"I'll live."

"What's next?" she asked, though her tone suggested she already dreaded the answer.

Markus didn't reply immediately. Instead, he stared straight ahead with racing thoughts. The group of aerglides and cycles began to hover back and forth in front of the rock structure's opening. Their headlights and high beams shone directly into the tiny gap, where the front bumper and hood of his vehicle were exposed. Gunmen on driftcycles raised their blasters and rifles, taking aim.

His heart pounded as he weighed their options. There was only one choice that made any sense—desperate, dangerous, and almost certainly suicidal. His mouth was dry, and his hands trembled slightly as he checked the charge left in the cartridge of his pistol.

"Here. Use mine," Aylin offered, holding out her weapon. Her hands shook as she extended it to him, though she tried to hide the fear beneath her regal composure.

Markus gently closed her fingers around the weapon and paused, his own nerves fraying under the gravity of what he was about to do. He turned to Ditta and Nix. The two brave hunters exchanged grim looks with him, their weapons ready, their grips tight. Markus tried to muster a reassuring smile, but it felt hollow.

"Look," he said, his voice firm but low, "I'll lure them away. You three get out. I'll floor this thing as far and fast as I can. They'll follow me."

"Are you sure?" Ditta asked skeptically.

"Trust me," Markus replied. "I've pissed this man off so much by now, he'll probably kill me just to make a point."

Aylin grabbed his arm, with trembling fingers. "That's not funny! This is suicide! We need to stay together."

"If we all try to break out, none of us will make it," Markus reasoned. "This is the only way. I'll lead them away, and give you a head start to climb the plateau. Let's finish what we started."

"I forbid this!" Aylin's voice cracked with desperation.

Her fiery gaze locked on him, and for a moment, her royal authority was replaced by raw, vulnerable pleading.

Markus exhaled heavily, certain she hadn't yet grasped the scope of their situation—or the depth of the sacrifices that might be required. He reached behind his belt, untying the native shawl given to him by Liyzia. He unraveled it briefly, staring at the fabric that had started him on this path, the relic of her lineage, a symbol of his adoption into her kin.

He pressed it into Aylin's hand, closing her fingers around it. "Make sure they see this," he said. "They'll know where it came from. That I helped you."

She clutched it tightly, her eyes welling with tears as she whispered, "Markus ..."

"This is the only way," he repeated, his voice steady but edged with pain. "Go! Get a head start! And don't look back!"

Ditta handed Markus a black sharpened spearhead, whose smooth surface gleamed faintly in the dim light. He waited until Markus looked him in the eye. "Fight on," he said. "And don't give up."

Markus nodded as the hunters eased out of the vehicle's passenger side, carefully sticking to the shadows cast by the granite walls. Aylin hesitated, her gaze lingering on Markus before she turned away, following the others.

In the shadows, the trio interlocked arms, Aylin in the middle. The winds from the vehicle's turbines whipped around them, carrying the rumble of a machine on the brink.

Ignoring the pain in his shoulder, Markus strapped himself in, narrowing his focus on the task ahead. His pursuers were waiting, patient but ready to strike. He took a deep breath, flipped on his high beams, and slammed the accelerator.

The vehicle burst from its hiding spot in a blur of motion. The sudden flash of light and violence overwhelmed the pursuers before they could react. A cacophony of metal, aluminum, and machinery erupted into flames. Markus rammed through the group of vehicles like a cannonball, his aerglide hurling debris and bodies in its fiery wake. He soared across the tundra landscape, the wreckage shrinking in his rearview mirror.

But from the surging black smoke, three remaining aerglides emerged, shooting toward him with alarming speed. Markus pushed the throttle to its limit, but the engine began to sputter, sparks flying. His heart sank as he realized the vehicle was failing. The throttle wouldn't respond, the cyclic control was sluggish, and even the emergency braking system refused to engage.

The pursuing crafts rammed into him, pinning his vehicle. Markus fought for control, but the machine spun out, hurtling toward the cliffs. His aerglide collided with the rock face in a cataclysmic crash, breaking apart in a spray of debris and fire. It skidded to a halt, smoking and battered, as silence fell over the plateau.

* * *

The world around Markus spun wildly as he struggled to piece things together. His back, pressed against what was once the ceiling of his overturned vehicle, ached with a throbbing pain. The harsh smell of burning fuel and the sting of thick, gray smoke filled his lungs, forcing him to cough.

Suddenly, the shattering of glass cut through the chaos. He barely registered the sound before he felt the rough hands grabbing him, dragging him out of the wreckage.

The first blow was a brutal impact to his stomach that knocked the wind out of him. Before he could recover from doubling over in pain, another punch smashed into his ribs. He was held up by strong arms and forced to endure the onslaught as fists rained down on him from every direction. His mind reeled in agony as the barrage continued.

A vicious punch landed squarely in his face, nearly snapping his neck back. He felt the agonizing nose break, a sickening crunch followed by a flash of pain. Blood poured from his nostrils as he collapsed to the ground. His body crumpled like a rag doll.

Barely clinging to consciousness from the brutality of the beating, his vision was a blurry mess. He could barely make out the shapes of boots surrounding him as they backed away slowly, leaving him in a broken heap.

The world steadied slowly as Markus turned over. He caught a glimpse of Hans watching with calculated interest—not the rage of a thwarted enemy, but the careful study of a man trying to solve a puzzle.

"Curious," Hans said finally, his cultured voice carrying that same unsettling warmth. He knelt beside Markus, just out of reach. "You keep appearing at the most ... inconvenient moments. The alley, the port, the festival, and now this." His head titled slightly. "Tell me, how does a failed watchman end up at the center of events that will reshape kingdoms?"

"Maybe it's destiny."

"Ah, yes. Your newfound sense of purpose." Hans studied him with genuine curiosity. "The same determination that's drawn the attention of my colleague's 'hunter.' I wonder—what does it see in you that we can't see?" The question hung in the arctic air between them, weightier than mere interrogation.

"Toss him in the trunk."

Rathmar stepped forward from the rear of the group. "We should leave him!" he demanded, boldly confronting Hans. "Taking him is a mistake."

"Wrong, Mr. Rathmar. He's bait. For luring her back in. She won't survive in this coming blizzard!"

"He carries something." Rathmar whispered harshly. "Something odd. Something ancient stirring inside of him ..."

"Mr. Rathmar—dispense with the cryptic tales and get to your point!"

"He distracts the kaegar every time he is near. Can't you see? As if he were some sort of ... prey"

"We're pressed for time." Hans explained, "We need all the bait we can afford. Besides, the last word I received was that three hydro cruisers have already left the mainland."

Hans glanced over his shoulder at the mercenaries surrounding them, then back to Rathmar.

"I forewarned the captain," he uttered softly. "He's taking the cruiser to the northern port to pick us up. Time is not on our side."

The Dromelan finally relented with a nod and walked away.

But as Hans signaled to the group, a sound cut through

the gathering darkness—a low, haunting howl that made everyone freeze.

The brash and overly confident mercenaries suddenly faltered as their attention was drawn to something moving in the distance. Out of the west, over the grainy and snow-covered landscape, a dark shape emerged, moving steadily towards them. A massive creature prowling on all fours. And as it drew nearer, the details came into focus, revealing the last beast you'd ever want to encounter in the wild.

Pointy ears broke through the haze, along with the finer details of its thick coat with changing hues of black to gray to bluish bristling against the icy wind. The fur rippled with each powerful stride as it came further into view. Yellow eyes were focused and unblinking, glowing like embers against the cold backdrop, above a long wolverine snout.

The most fearsome and infamous features that distinguished this beast from all others finally came into full view: two oversized canine teeth, three inches long, jutting from its upper jaw. Sharp and glistening, clearly meant for tearing the flesh off its next meal.

"A bloody saber wolf!" one of the men exclaimed, as if the rest of them needed any further clarity.

Slowly, the rest of the pack emerged from the mist. At least a dozen of them—wolves of varying shades of gray, blue and black that blended into the bleak landscape. Even two small, newborn pups stumbled alongside a mother wolf, dwarfed by the larger, battle-thirsty leaders of the pack.

One by one, they joined in a chorus of low growls, grunts and sharp barks echoing across the tundra waste. The men instinctively raised their weapons as they retreated, slowly and deliberately—not taking their eyes off the pack, nor turning their backs.

Suddenly Hans noticed that Markus was missing. Though he urged them to search for them, the men were already scrambling for the vehicles, rifles raised as they half-heartedly scanned the wreckage while back-pedaling.

As the thrusters and powerful turbines lifted the vehicles out of reach, the pack turned their attention to Markus, who somehow found the strength to slither away in the direction of the plateau's base canyon. As Hans wrestled with the decision, these seasoned bandits were hell bent on not tangling with these predators. And with a wave of his finger, he strapped himself in as they took off.

From over his shoulder, Markus' blurred vision barely made out the three shiny bullet shapes zipping away in the distant winter light. But not far from the black, simmering smoky wreckage still burning behind him, the growls, snarls and grunts grew louder. The wolf pack came into view.

He turned over onto his back, and counted a dozen adult saber wolves, teeth bared, dripping and salivating. Behind the larger wolves' legs, two small pups darted and weaved, staying close to what appeared to be their mother, a silvery female whose watchful gaze never left Markus. The blood trail he'd left might as well be a dinner bell, marking his path clear as day.

What he would give for an armed weapon right now— even just a pistol with a little charge left. A few shots would have kept them at bay. Yet all he had was Nikel's dagger and Xara's gauntlet—if he dared to mess with these wild creatures.

A dislocated shoulder, broken nose, bloodied face—and God knows what else—was all that was wrong with his body.

Markus stumbled to his feet, holding out the dagger, stepping backwards and limping in his hip. Never turning his back to the group, he surveyed his surroundings. There was no way out. Nothing but the wreckage behind them, the mountains and crater behind him, and the vastness of shrubs and lichen as far as he could see.

Slow. Steady. No sudden moves. Still backpedaling. Farther and farther. They kept their pace. And their distance.

Out of the corner of his eye, the plateau's rocky and mossy green structure grew closer and closer.

Slowly, one of the wolves drifted away from the pack, inching closer to Markus. This one was larger than the others, not by much, but its bulk was evident in the powerful, muscular frame beneath its matted fur.

The alpha advanced slowly, while the silver female drew her pups back with a quiet growl, positioning herself between them and the potential threat. The pups pressed against her legs, their earlier curiosity replaced by instinctive obedience. The rest of the pack spread out in a drilled formation that spoke of countless hunts.

Markus felt his heart race as the alpha wolf advanced. He backpedaled carefully, gaze locked on the beast. He couldn't afford to look away, not even for a second.

Palms slick and sweaty, brow wet with perspiration and blood loss, his thumping heart grew louder with the reality that this could be his final moment.

CHAPTER TWENTY-ONE

Fearing the worst, Markus prepared to make a last stand.

The beast reared his mouth back to reveal a formidable weapon: a pair of retractable canine teeth with fangs that protruded like giant curved fingers alongside the front row of teeth. Its yellow eyes frowned and glowed, nostrils flaring.

He could practically feel the beast's hot breath mere feet away, more intimidating than anyone he'd ever tangled with in the roughest harbor towns.

Markus raised the dagger, muscles coiled in exhausted defiance. The beast snarled, poised to strike. Then his foot missed the edge.

And he fell.

Tumbling down the slope, he crashed against jagged rock, pain shattering through his body like glass.

The beast descended along the canyon's slope. The rest of the pack stayed back, watching from the top as spectators waiting to be enthralled.

His dagger? Where was it? Markus finally located it— grabbing it from among the pile of bones. Bones?

Yes, bones! Everywhere! Fibulas. Scapulas. Hips. Femurs. Big. Small. Even what appeared to be another predator's skull. The grimmest, grimiest, and grayest atmosphere that reeked of decay and despair could be a grave foreshadowing of his own impending fate.

The saber wolf moved closer. Markus scrambled, his body toppling, rattling, slithering and slipping across the litter, between the broken and scattered pieces. Struggling, sliding and kicking, he tried to get away.

The beast lunged. And struck.

It was like lighting pulsating through his body,

striking every last nerve in him, unleashing an unimaginable pain for the first moments. Anguish and rage riled up from within him, like a caged animal unleashed. The massive wolf's teeth ripped through his fatigues into his thigh. Its claws scratched at his legs, digging with nails that stung, pierced, and pinched, ready to tear more flesh away.

He shook his leg violently, pounding the ground. Squirming. The wolf's head bobbled back and forth with every spasm and gesture holding on.

In his rage, Markus slashed repeatedly with his dagger. First, awkwardly, in a panic at the air around its head, missing repeatedly. He finally grabbed the beast by the ear and pummeled the blade into its face. Then he dropped the weapon and went on the assault. First, a jab. Then a hook. Another right hook until the beast released its violent grip. Now multiple kicks with his right boot to the face knocked the beast further back.

The beast rebounded with bloody teeth, lunging in for another bite. But Markus was quick, hurling the heavy pieces of bones directly at its head, long enough to grab the dagger, aiming once again for its head. The beast backed off, snapping and grunting, its mouth covered in blood, salivating and licking it off.

Markus continued skidding backward, painfully and awkwardly over the uncomfortable bones and against the dry, chalky canyon wall until his arms reached a hollow space. What first felt like a narrow crack turned out to be a shallow den, barely wide enough to crawl into.

He didn't hesitate. His hand found the three-inch flashlight on Cael's belt. Holding the dagger in one hand, the light in his teeth, Markus cast a shaky beam into the cavity.

He dragged himself inside. Every inch deeper, the air grew colder. Even with light behind him, the shadows pressed inward, closing around him.

Outside, the wolves snarled. Prowled. But none entered.

Not fear. Not hesitation.

Something else.

A stillness between them—unspoken, unknowable. It held them just beyond reach. And him, just beyond understanding.

Markus seized a jagged branch and carved it to a crude point, then tied a makeshift tourniquet with fumbling fingers. The bleeding slowed, but the chill crept in.

Sleep pulled at him like undertow.

He flicked off the flashlight. The den swallowed the light.

He still had Nikel's dagger. And Ditta's black spear-head—cold and silent in his hand.

"Stay awake," he muttered. "Just... stay awake."

But the weapon sagged. His eyes closed.

And outside, the wolves waited—silent. Still. Watching.

CHAPTER TWENTY-TWO

The damp chill of the wolf den seeped into his bones, reminding him of that night he found himself in the drainage pipe years ago when he ran away. Then as now, as the darkness pressed against him, the same metallic taste of fear was on his tongue. Even the rough stone at his back mirrored the corroded metal that had once gripped him with that initial wave of claustrophobia and anxiety.

The tension of waiting was palpable. His rapid heartbeat, sweating, and trembling soon began to trigger those memories again—the same tremors felt by that eleven-year-old from his childhood, who had been hiding that night, the last time he ran away from another orphanage.

He had fled the authorities down the dark alley, so terrified that he had taken a chance to hide in the shadows. A rusty drainage pipe jutting out from the alley wall was barely wide enough to crawl through, and he had dived in.

As young Markus had curled himself up as small as possible in the darkness with the stale, pungent, damp air pressing in on him, he held his breath. Then he noticed the first beam of light. A thin, yellowish streak had cut through the darkness, sweeping across the ground and walls of the alley just outside his hiding place.

The light had been searching and probing, casting fleeting, distorted shadows across the weathered bricks. As the footsteps grew louder and closed in on the area around the drainage pipe, the flashlight beams had crisscrossed inches from the pipe's opening, not quite reaching the inside. He had prayed they wouldn't look in, that they would pass by without noticing the narrow hiding place. The voices had been low and menacing, muttering and cursing among themselves with threats and insults.

Then the lights had shifted away, until he was alone once more in the darkness. He exhaled for a moment until a blinding light flooded the pipe, searing into his eyes, shocking him into stillness.

In that moment, he had panicked, and before he could react, a pair of strong adult arms had reached in and pulled him out into the harsh light of the alley.

With four deputies surrounding the boy, their high beam flashlights flooding the decrepit alley, his hopes had sunk as he fearfully waited for the unknown. A fifth man had broken through the group, yanking him up by his collar. He hadn't recognized the man's voice and could barely register his face. But the man had been strong, and the lawmen had struggled to tear the defenseless child from his grasp in the face of his manic aggression.

"That's him! That's the little freak who killed my boy!"

"He didn't kill anybody! Let him go!"

"He 'infected' him, didn't he?"

He had been pulled apart like a ragged doll between the lawmen and the traumatized father. And all he could think about was running—if he could only get away from them.

One of the lawmen had torn the boy away and held him as the rest of the group continued to wrestle with the father. But the boy had slipped through the lawman's arm and slid back into the drainage pipe, knowing they wouldn't be able to follow him.

"Come back here, you little freak!"

The boy had crawled and splashed through the unpleasant and unsanitary drainage, his senses overwhelmed by the pungent odor. He was like a rat, fleeing for his life in the dark cesspools of the harbor town's back alleys, pitch black and cramped, his only sense of direction being the occasional grates that appeared overhead, where the streetlamps had peered through.

When he saw an opening to his left, he had taken a chance and tumbled out of it into a pile of garbage in a neglected conveyor bin, partially concealed in the shadows of an abandoned building's backlot.

As the boy cautiously peered around the corner of the alley, his eyes had traced the distant figures of pedestrians passing under the boardwalks and the dim glow of the harbor's shady taverns. He had picked himself up from the ground, his clothes soaked and smelly, his spirit heavy with dejection. Alone once more, he had wandered through the partially lit shadows, homeless and adrift, surrounded by piles of old, ravaged furnishings, worn crates, and charred debris.

Then, something caught his eye. A cracked, standing mirror, layered in thick, tangled cobwebs, reflecting the light of a nearby lantern. Any other night, he would have walked past it, indifferent to the sight of his unkempt, ragged features. But that night, the man's words had still echoed in his mind, pulling him back to the mirror. He had paused, staring at his reflection for the first time in a long while.

His eyes, red and strained, traced the tear stains on his dirt-smeared cheeks. His gaze had lingered on the hideous, blackened scar that streaked down the right side of his face. In the deep loneliness that gripped him, he had forced himself to look—really look—into the pale face staring back at him, into those dark, soulful eyes that seemed far too deep for someone so young.

Then, something shifted. He was no longer simply recalling it—he was watching. As though the memory had become a stage and he, its distant witness. Slowly, as if stepping into a distant dream, Markus had moved forward and looked upon his younger self from the past. His throat tightened unexpectedly at the sight of the small, frightened boy—so vulnerable yet somehow surviving. He leaned in beside the boy's reflection, their features aligning in the cracked glass—similar faces, the same scar marring their right temples.

Young Markus now glanced up, eyes widening in surprise as he recognized the older version of himself—looking into the future. In that surreal moment, the child's expression had softened, the despair lifting ever so slightly, replaced by a glimmer of hope. The boy's face softened. And to Markus' disbelief, he smiled.

Markus watched, caught between fear and wonder.

He couldn't remember ever smiling or laughing as a child, and seeing himself like this was both unnerving and encouraging. For so long, he had believed the cruel names and taunts—'Scarface,' 'freak'—words that had shattered his self-image and fueled his hatred. But now, in that moment of quiet reflection, he began to see himself in a new light. He saw beyond the scar, to the strength it represented.

In that instant, Markus began to accept his past, his identity. He understood that the boy he was and the man he had become were not defined by the scars or the words of others. They were defined by the resilience to endure, to survive, and to find hope even in the darkest of hours.

* * *

Fever dreams and blood loss blurred the borders of reality. He should have been unconscious by now, should have succumbed to the lethal combination of hypothermia and shock. The rational part of his mind knew that—knew no one survived this kind of trauma in these temperatures without proper medical care. But something else burned in his veins now—a time-honored fire that refused to let him slip away.

The dehydration was almost as bad as the blood loss. His tongue felt like sandpaper; his lips were cracked in the arctic air. Each breath sent icy daggers into his lungs. But that same force that kept him alive seemed to feed on the pain, transforming it into fuel for whatever change was taking hold.

In the darkness, time had lost all meaning. It felt like

an eternity before the first faint light of dawn began to creep into the den. He opened his eyes slowly, half-expecting to find himself frozen solid. But to his surprise, he was still alive—barely.

Then, he heard it. A soft, rhythmic sound—something breathing. His heart leapt, and he gripped the sharpened branch with trembling hands, scanning the den for the source. His eyes widened in shock when he saw them—the two small wolf pups, curled up beside him, their tiny bodies pressed close to his for warmth.

A wave of relief washed over him. But it was short-lived. The realization that where there were pups, there was a mother, sent a jolt of fear through him. He turned his head slowly, every muscle tensed. And there she was, the large, gray saber wolf, lying just inside the entrance of the den, her golden eyes locked onto him with an intensity that froze his blood. A low growl rumbled deep in her throat, a warning.

Her gaze alternated between him and her pups, who seemed content by his side, as though unaware of any danger. Her mouth opened for a moment, and within seconds, her retractable canines were already extending—but then, they slowly retracted. A clear warning.

Markus' heart pounded, while clutching the makeshift spear in his hands. Slowly he began to nudge the sleeping pups away from him. His movements were careful and deliberate so as not to trigger the mother. Finally, the pups awakened and, sensing their mother's presence, began stirring about and scuttling over to her.

* * *

Still feeling the tension, he locked eyes with her, and though her pups were near, she let out another growl. Slowly, as Markus laid the sharpened limb behind him out of sight, her growls and aggression began to soften. He let out a shaky breath and relaxed when she turned her attention fully to her pups, nuzzling them gently. She raised her eyes to him in quiet acknowledgment as he watched in stunned silence, still trying to process the surreal turn of events. As the first rays of morning light filtered into the den, he realized that he had survived the night somehow through a fragile connection with one of these creatures he had feared.

The mother wolf's golden eyes studied him carefully with primal curiosity. For a moment, it reminded him of someone else's ancient wisdom that looked at him the same way as though they both seem to recognize something in him that he was just becoming aware of himself.

The cold had numbed the worst of the pain, but that was its own kind of danger. His thoughts kept slipping sideways, the blood loss making it harder to focus. Each time he blinked, it took longer to open his eyes again.

Fever made the world swim in and out of focus. The rational part of his mind knew he needed water, needed to clean the wound properly, needed real medical attention. But out here, with a storm approaching survival meant making impossible choices.

His hands were shaking so badly he could barely tie the crude tourniquet. Xara would have done this in seconds—always the steady one, the one who could think clearly when everything went awry. "You're doing it wrong," he could almost hear her say in that familiar mix of exasperation and concern. "Tighter, or you'll bleed out before you can do anything heroically stupid."

The ghost of her voice steadied him enough to finish the job, but the silence that followed felt heavier than before.

* * *

As he emerged into the frosty, arctic air, he faltered, his strength failing him. His knees buckled, and he crashed into the hardened surface, gasping in pain. The world spun sickeningly as fever and blood loss took their toll.

Through blurred vision, he noticed something strange—the blood trail leading to the den had transformed overnight. Each drop had crystallized into something black and unnatural; the surface gleaming like polished obsidian in the pale morning light. The realization hit him like a physical blow—this was his blood, his curse made solid.

Following the trail back to where he'd fought the alpha, Markus found the massive wolf's body. His breath caught as he saw the creature's blackened teeth, as if burned by acid. The truth he'd been running from for so long lay bare before him. His blood wasn't just different: it was *lethal*.

Movement drew his attention. The rest of the pack had emerged—at least ten wolves of various sizes watching from a safe distance. Their eyes held a mix of fury, fear, and something deeper— recognition. They knew what he was now, what his blood could do. Their low growls carried warning rather than threat.

The luna wolf appeared at the den's entrance, positioning herself between Markus and the pack. Her presence commanded attention, though whether she meant to protect him, or the others remained unclear. When she snapped at several younger wolves that ventured too close, Markus realized the pack's hierarchy was shifting around him.

He tried to stand again but his injured leg gave out. The world tilted as the fever spiked through him. How could he protect Aylin, help the others, face what was coming, when he could barely stay conscious? The thought of them in danger while he lay here useless made his chest tight with familiar guilt.

But as darkness crept in at the edges of his vision, Markus knew he had no choice. Like that night in the drainage pipe, survival meant accepting his helplessness before he could find his strength. First, he needed shelter. Fire. Food. The basics of staying alive.

The wolves watched as he crawled back toward the den, their golden eyes reflecting judgment or understanding—he was too weak to tell which. The luna wolf's gaze followed him, carrying that same innate wisdom he'd seen in Liyzia's eyes.

Night would come again soon, bringing bitter cold and darker threats. But, for now, Markus had no choice but to surrender to his body's demands. Real strength, he was learning, sometimes meant knowing when to wait.

* * *

The canyon offered little comfort, but at least its walls blocked the bitter wind. Markus dragged himself through the scattered bones and debris, gathering any-thing that might burn. Each movement sent fresh jolts of pain through his leg, while fever made his hands shake as he attempted to build a fire pit.

His survival training from the evolution kicked in mechanically—gather tinder, arrange kindling, create a wind break. But his thoughts kept slipping sideways, drawn back to the dead alpha. Its massive form lay like an accusation in the morning light, yet also offered his best chance at survival.

The strike of his match echoed in the canyon's silence. The small flame caught the tinder, growing steadily as he fed it smaller sticks. The wolves watched from above, their forms dark against the pale sky as smoke curled upward. He could feel their eyes on him as he worked— some hostile, others curious, all wary.

Using his knife was agony, but hunger drove him to butcher what he could from the alpha's carcass. The liver would provide the most nutrients, he knew, though the thought of eating it made his stomach turn. But beggars couldn't be choosers, and he'd survived on worse in street alleys.

As he worked, snowflakes began to fall, small at first, then thicker. The storm was coming sooner than expected. The fire's warmth barely reached him as he huddled closer, his body shaking with fever and cold. Above, the wolves paced restlessly, their forms becom-ing ghostlike in the growing snowfall.

A sound made him turn—the luna wolf had descended into the canyon, her pups close behind. She kept her distance but settled near enough to share the fire's heat. Her golden eyes studied him as he speared pieces of liver on a sharpened stick, holding them over the flames. The smell of cooking meat drew her pups closer, their small forms trembling with either cold or eagerness.

"Hungry?" he asked hoarsely, surprised at the roughness of his own voice. The pups' ears perked up at his words, though their mother's quiet growl kept them from approaching further. Markus tore off a piece of the cooked liver and tossed it carefully in their direction.

The pups fell on the meat eagerly while their mother watched. Something shifted in her gaze— not quite trust, but perhaps understanding. She recognized an offering when she saw one. As darkness crept into the canyon and snow continued to fall, Markus found himself sharing his meager meal with creatures that should have been his enemies.

The fire painted shadows on the canyon walls as night descended fully. His fever made the darkness move strangely—at least, that's what he wanted to blame it on. The shadows seemed to take shape, flowing against the natural light like water upstream. For a moment, he could have sworn he saw figures moving in that darkness as he blinked and rubbed his blurring eyes, fighting to separate hallucination from reality.

Was it his imagination? He swore these were actual beings—both there and not there, as if caught between worlds.

The luna wolf's head snapped up, her eyes tracking something he could barely perceive. A shape that might have been human, might have been something else entirely, wavered at the periphery of his vision before dissolving like smoke. The wolf's low growl confirmed what his mind wanted to dismiss. He wasn't just seeing things.

"Tell me you saw that!" he uttered. The wolf and Markus glanced at each other, then back. Her ears perked, while her fangs partially extended, her eyes glowing brighter while assessing the threat.

His blood drummed with recognition, as if it had always known these things existed, had always been able to see them. He remembered Liyzia's quiet warnings about those who walked between worlds. Shadow Walkers, she had called them once in a whisper he wasn't meant to hear— ancient powers stirring from sleep. Was this what she meant? These glimpses of something beyond normal sight?

He recalled his first night, hearing Nikel's stories by the evening hearth, while he dramatized his adventures with his own shadow dancing across the wall. He remembered glimpsing a shape before the dinner firelight at camp in Nenevuiim when eating alone. Then there were the eerie shapes that played on his fears in Moorwood, moments before they parted, making way for the kaegar.

He tentatively lifted his hand, then paused—almost as if attempting to reach out—but to whom or what? Cautiously, he pulled back. Perhaps some enigmas were better left alone.

Nearby, the wolf's teeth slowly retracted, her glowing eyes dimming. She made a gentle huff, followed by a soft, trilling whine, tilting her head in curiosity.

When he turned his head to look directly at the shadows, they resumed their normal patterns.

Likewise, the luna wolf's gaze remained fixed on that

empty space, though he noticed how she instinctively had moved a bit closer to him. Her presence felt protective now, as if she understood exactly what he was beginning to see.

The fever made his thoughts drift again, but now he wondered if it wasn't just burning away his old limitations, teaching his eyes to see what had always been there. The kaegar's burning eyes haunted his memory—though differently now. Had it recognized this emerging sight in him, this ability to perceive what others couldn't?

He fed another branch to the flames, watching sparks spiral up into darkness. The shadows continued their strange dance, but he forced himself to focus on immediate concerns: survival, healing, preparation. Whatever was awakening in him would come in its own time. For now, the night was long, and he had work to do.

The wound in his leg throbbed, reminding him that infection could kill as surely as any predator.

He needed to cauterize it. But first, he needed to gather more firewood. The storm was deepening, and the night would be long.

* * *

The pile of gathered wood looked pitifully small against the deepening night. Markus fed another branch to the flames, watching sparks spiral up into the falling snow. The wound in his leg had worsened from throbbing to a deeper, more dangerous kind of pain. He'd seen enough infected wounds in Vesper to know what that meant.

His knife lay heating in the fire, gradually turning orange. The sight made his mouth go dry. He'd watched others do this—street doctors in back alleys, battlefield medics in training—but watching and doing were very different things. His hands shook as he cut a strip of leather from his belt to bite down on.

The luna wolf lifted her head, perhaps sensing his distress. Her pups had curled up near the fire's warmth, but she remained alert, watching him with those knowing eyes. Other members of the pack had drawn closer as night deepened, though they kept to the shadows beyond the firelight. Their forms shifted like spirits in the falling snow.

"Don't suppose any of you know how to work a needle and thread?" A hollow attempt at humor! The knife's blade glowed brighter, almost ready.

Taking a deep breath, he positioned himself with his back against the stone, leg extended toward the fire. The strip of leather felt rough between his teeth. One more breath. Just do it fast, like pulling off a bandage. Except this bandage was searing metal against open flesh.

The first touch of hot steel sent lightning through his body. His scream echoed off canyon walls, muffled by the leather but still raw. The wolves started at the sound, some retreating into darkness while others lifted their heads in instinctive response. Then, as his cry faded into ragged breathing, something extraordinary happened.

The luna wolf threw back her head and howled—a sound of such pure, mournful beauty it seemed to pierce the very night. One by one, other wolves joined her until the canyon rang with their voices. The sound wrapped around Markus' pain like a living thing, carrying it up into the storm-dark sky.

When he could think again, could breathe past the agony, he found himself laughing weakly. "That's one way ... to start a choir." His voice cracked on the words. Sweat ran down his face despite the cold, and the smell of burned flesh made his stomach turn. But the wound was sealed —yes, ugly and crude—but sealed.

The luna wolf padded closer, her nose twitching at the scent of charred meat and blood. To his surprise, she settled beside him, close enough so he could feel her warmth. Her pups, encouraged by their mother's boldness, crept forward to investigate. One sniffed curiously at his bandaged leg while the other curled against his side.

"Guess we're all full of surprises," he murmured. The wolf's only response was to rest her head on her paws, as a kind of acceptance. Or perhaps she simply recognized another creature's attempt to survive, to rise above pain and fear.

The fire crackled, sending more sparks to dance with falling snow. Markus leaned back against the stone, exhaustion dragging at him. His leg still burned, but differently now—a clean pain, cauterized like the wound itself. Above, through breaks in the storm clouds, stars wheeled in ancient patterns. Somewhere out there, Aylin and the others were counting on him. But for now, surrounded by creatures that should have been enemies, he let himself drift toward uneasy sleep.

The night had only begun, and tomorrow would bring its own trials. But he had survived the first test, marked by fire and blood. Whatever came next would find him changed—not just by pain, but by the strange communion of this night.

* * *

He woke to gray dawn with relief that he hadn't frozen to death. The fire had burned low, but somehow, he was warm. The luna wolf and her pups still pressed against him, their shared heat having kept the worst of the cold at bay. Beyond the den's entrance, snow had blanketed the canyon floor, muffling the world in white silence.

The fever hadn't broken, but it had changed. Instead of the chaotic burning that had threatened to consume him, now it felt more even, as if his blood itself was transforming. Each heartbeat sent pulses of strange warmth through his veins, neither entirely painful nor pleasant. His curse, his burden, was becoming something else.

Moving carefully to avoid disturbing the sleeping wolves, Markus examined his leg. The cauterized wound was ugly but clean, the flesh sealed, black as obsidian. Like the crystallized drops of his blood that still dotted the canyon floor, the scar tissue had an almost metallic quality. He touched it gingerly, feeling heat radiate from the darkness there.

A sound drew his attention—more wolves had descended into the canyon during the night. They lay in scattered groups around the dying embers, having drawn closer to the fire's warmth as the storm intensified. Their golden eyes watched him with cautious recognition rather than the previous day's hostility. Not quite acceptance, but no longer pure threat.

His stomach cramped with hunger. The remaining

liver meat had frozen solid, and the thought of eating it cold made him shudder. But as he reached to rebuild the fire, his hand brushed something that felt wrong among the scattered bones—too smooth, too regular. Brushing away snow and debris revealed a spearhead, ancient but perfectly preserved. Its black surface caught the dawn light like frozen blood.

"Your people's work?" he asked the luna wolf, who had lifted her head to watch him. The weapon's craftsmanship reminded him of Ditta's spear—the one that had actually wounded the kaegar. An idea began to form, born of fever and desperate need.

Near the den's entrance, more of his blood had crystallized into dark formations. The surfaces were strange—neither metal nor stone, but something between. Like the spearhead, they caught the light oddly, as if holding shadows within. His fingers traced their edges, finding places where the material had naturally formed into sharp points.

The luna wolf's pups stirred, watching curiously as he gathered scattered branches. His hands worked with fevered intent now, mind racing ahead to what he needed. A bow could be fashioned from fire-hardened wood. His belt would provide leather for binding. And these black crystals of his own blood ...

"Time to make something useful of this curse," he murmured. The wolves watched as he rebuilt the fire that would help forge a new kind of weapon. Above, the storm continued to howl, but Markus barely heard it now. He had work to do.

* * *

The work became a kind of meditation. Each step required total focus, keeping darker thoughts at bay— worry for Aylin, fear for Xara, the kaegar's burning eyes. His hands moved with careful precision despite their shaking, testing each branch for the right combination of strength and flexibility.

The fire spoke in pops and whispers as he heated the chosen sapling, bending it incrementally against his knee. The luna wolf watched his every movement, her head tilted in a way that reminded him of Liyzia studying her herbs. Her pups had grown bolder, dragging small branches to the fire to mimic his gathering.

"Thanks," he told them seriously, adding their offerings to his pile. "Though I'm not sure pinecones will help much." The larger pup wagged its tail, proud of its contribution, while its mother's eyes held something almost like amusement.

The crystallized blood proved harder to work than he'd expected. Normal knapping techniques would shatter the material, but he found that heating it slightly made it more malleable. Each piece had to be shaped carefully, its edges refined against smooth river stones. Some formations had naturally taken on arrow-like points.

His fingers bled occasionally from the sharp edges, dark drops falling onto snow. He watched with feverish fascination as each drop slowly transformed, the liquid becoming solid, holding whatever shape it landed in. Why had he feared this power, when all along it had been trying to show him its true nature?

The other wolves drifted closer throughout the day, drawn perhaps by curiosity or boredom. One grizzled male with a scarred muzzle settled nearby, watching the arrow-crafting with particular interest. His presence seemed to ease the others' wariness, though they still maintained a careful distance.

"Not exactly standard issue," Markus said, holding up a finished arrowhead. "But I guess neither am I." At his voice, the scarred wolf's ears twitched, but his golden eyes remained fixed on the weapon with almost tactical assessment.

By the time darkness fell again, his quiver held six arrows. Not many, but each one felt like a promise. Like his blood itself, they were both beautiful and deadly—a reminder that every curse could become a gift, if you survived long enough to understand it.

The luna wolf's warmth pressed against his side as night deepened, her presence now as familiar as his own shadow. Her pups had claimed his lap, their small bodies radiating heat against the bitter cold. Other wolves had drawn closer to the fire, forming a loose circle that felt almost like protection.

Markus worked by firelight, his hands steady now despite exhaustion. Each arrow he crafted felt more natural than the last, as if he were remembering a skill rather than learning it. Or perhaps his blood itself was guiding him, showing him how to transform curse into capability, weakness into strength.

Tomorrow would bring its own battles. But tonight, surrounded by creatures that should have been enemies, he allowed himself to feel something like peace. As his fingers found the half-pendant at his throat, he thought of Xara, of all the times she'd believed in him when he couldn't believe in himself.

"Rest," he told himself softly. "Then we hunt."

The wolves' ears pricked at that last word, as if they understood perfectly what came next. The luna wolf's tail thumped once against stone—not quite agreement, but something close. Above, the stars wheeled in timeless patterns, while below, a man who was perhaps becoming something more than he knew, worked through the night, preparing for whatever dawn would bring.

* * *

Sleep came in waves, broken by fever dreams and bitter cold. Each time consciousness returned, the fire had burned lower but, somehow, he was still warm. More wolves had drawn closer during the night, forming a living barrier against the storm. The luna wolf remained closest, her breath creating small puffs in the frozen air.

He woke fully to pre-dawn silence and a strange sensation. The fever had finally broken, leaving behind something different—a clarity that felt almost primal. His blood no longer burned but hummed, as if recognizing its own power at last. The wound in his leg had healed impossibly fast, the blackened flesh now smooth.

The pups were the first to notice his stirring, their small forms wriggling with excitement. The luna wolf lifted her head, studying him with those soulful eyes. Beyond the fire's dying embers, other wolves rose and stretched, frost falling from their fur.

"Time to move," he told them softly, though his body protested as he stood. The wolves watched him gather his makeshift weapons—the bow, the arrows tipped with his crystallized blood, Ditta's black spearhead now mounted on a fire-hardened shaft. Each piece felt like an extension of himself, transformed by the same power that ran through his veins.

The grizzled male with the scarred muzzle approached first, no longer content to watch from afar. Markus held perfectly still as the wolf sniffed his hand, recognizing the moment's importance. When he tentatively touched the wolf's head, then stroked coarse fur beneath his fingers, something shifted in the pack's dynamic. One by one, other wolves came forward, each acknowledging him in their own way.

The luna wolf watched it all with what looked like satisfaction, her tail sweeping the ground slowly. Her pups tumbled around his feet, play-fighting over who got to be closest. They felt like family now—not quite pack, not quite human, but something in between. Like him.

The rising sun gilded the canyon walls in molten gold, stretching long shadows where Markus and the wolves moved as one, as if they had been hunting together for years. His weapons felt natural in his hands, his steps sure despite the lingering weakness. More storm clouds gathered on the horizon, but for now the sky burned clear and bright.

The luna wolf padded to his side, her presence steady as a rock. Other wolves spread out in a hunting formation that spoke of primordial instinct, reading each other's movements with fluid grace. They were ready. He was ready.

Markus touched the half-pendant at his throat one last time, thinking of Xara, of Aylin, of all that waited beyond this moment of transformation. His blood—no longer a curse to fear but a power to wield—sang with new purpose. Whatever came next would find him changed—not just by survival and repurpose, but by the communion of those three days and nights.

The wolves waited, their golden eyes fixed on him with something between respect and expectation. The hunt was about to begin, but this time he wasn't the prey. This time, he was the head of the pack.

* * *

The canyon awakened beneath streaks of golden light as Markus took his first steps toward whatever lay beyond. The wolves moved with him, their paws silent on frozen ground as they ascended the winding path. Each breath of arctic air felt sharp and clean in his lungs, carrying scents his newly awakened senses could finally understand.

Sounds caught his attention—voices carrying on the wind. The wolves tensed, hackles rising, but Markus recognized the cadence of human speech. He signaled the pack to hold position as he crept forward, bow ready.

Through gaps in the rocks, he spotted them—Cypran and Luc, two fellow recruits he'd sailed with from Vesper. They were huddled atop a boulder outcrop, surrounded by snarling wolves. The same two pups that had first approached him now darted around the boulder's base, their movements more confident, though they stayed within their mother's reach. The silver female—the luna wolf—maintained her position with quiet authority, controlling her pups' enthusiasm with subtle growls.

"I don't believe it! It's Markus!" cried Cypran in equal parts of relief and disbelief.

"Markus, quick! Get up here!" Luc waved frantically. "Before they strike!"

The wolves circled the boulder with predatory interest, the pups mimicking their elders' movements in a display that would have been almost comical if not for the deadly precision of the adults. Yet something in their movements felt more cautious than hungry. They remembered his blood's power, even if they didn't understand it.

Markus limped forward, watching his newfound allies' reaction. A few wolves approached him, sniffing his hands to confirm his scent before turning their aggression back toward the recruits.

"What is this?" Cypran asked, eyes wide.

"They seem to like him better than us!" Luc remarked.

"Are they your pets, Markus?" Cypran added nervously. "If so, you don't suppose you could call them off?" His words tumbled out. "And where have you been? You didn't come back from the trail that day they dropped you. And now you show up hoping to finish the evolution?"

Markus studied their dirty but intact fatigues. Their appearance was weathered but far better than his own blood-stained features. "Are you two headed toward the Narrow Gates?" he asked, ignoring the barrage of questions.

"We were—until your furry friends chased us up here!" Cypran shot back. "We're lucky! The other two trainees ..." and he drew a line across his throat.

"Finishing this evolution is the last thing on our

minds right now," Cypran added. "We just want to get out alive!"

"Listen to me," Markus said, his voice carrying new authority as he gestured to the wolves around him. The luna wolf had drawn close, allowing him to rest his hand on her enormous head. "They won't touch you now. But there are worse things than wolves ahead. If you want to live, stay close and stay quiet."

The recruits exchanged glances, clearly wondering what had changed in their former companion. The man who stood before them seemed to carry himself differently—a man who had faced death and emerged stronger, who spoke the language of deep-seated powers.

"You know the way to the Narrow Gates?" Markus asked.

"Due northwest," Cypran replied, pulling out his compass. "We have until sunrise tomorrow to reach them."

Markus checked his battered field watch—a quarter past one in the afternoon. Time was growing short, but now he had allies, both human and wild.

"Just lead the way," he said quietly. "We'll take it one step at a time."

The two recruits trudged ahead, guided by their compasses across the unforgiving expanse of tundra. Markus followed closely, eyes glancing back every few steps at the wolfpack, who shadowed them at a distance, yet never strayed too far. The cold bit through their layers, each breath crystallizing in the frigid air as they pressed forward. The wasteland itself seemed endless—an unyielding stretch of white where the horizon bled into the sky, and every step felt like a battle.

His hand found the bow crafted from his blood, fingers tracing the black arrowheads that had transformed his curse into strength. The luna wolf padded silently beside him, her presence as natural now as his own shadow. Behind them, the rest of the pack moved like spirits through the gathering storm, their golden eyes reflecting a wisdom as timeless as the land itself.

Somewhere ahead lay the Narrow Gates, and beyond them, Aylin and the others who needed him. The kaegar still hunted, carrying that same recognition that Markus seemed to understand. Hans and his mercenaries would also be waiting. And above it all, winter itself gathered its fury, promising to transform the tundra into an arena where only the strongest—or perhaps the most desperate—would survive.

Unconsciously, Markus touched his half-pendant, thinking of Xara, of all the times she'd protected him before he learned to embrace what he truly was. Now it was his turn. Whatever waited beyond the storm would find him changed—no longer running from his nature but transformed by it.

The wolves moved with him as one, their forms blending with the swirling snow that signaled the storm's approach. Together they pressed forward into the gathering darkness, toward a reckoning that would test not just strength and courage, but the very essence of what it meant to be human, beast—or something in between.

The hunt was about to begin.

CHAPTER TWENTY-THREE

High on the mountainous crater's frozen slope, Ditta and Nix huddled behind massive snow-covered slabs of granite. Their bodies trembled despite the shelter of a shallow depression carved into the rock. The bitter cold had long since penetrated their layers of clothing, turning each breath into crystals. Both hunters kept their sharp eyes fixed on the distant glow of firelight far below—a tempting beacon of warmth that might as well have been from another world.

Their makeshift camp, if it could be called that, was little more than a hollow scraped beneath the lee of the rock. It was partially protected by two feet of fresh powder that muffled every sound to an eerie whisper. The younger hunter, Nix, pressed his fingers to his mouth, blowing desperate warmth into hands that had long since lost feeling. Beside him, Ditta fought to keep his teeth from chattering as he maintained his vigil with bow ready despite numbed fingers.

"She's getting worse," Nix whispered over the wind's low moan.

At the base of a towering aspen, concealed beneath

a crude shelter of branches and moss, the princess lay curled into herself. Her face had taken on the waxy paleness of extreme cold, broken only by the alarming pink of her wind-burned cheeks. Dark circles beneath her eyes spoke of exhaustion beyond mere physical fatigue. They had tried to let her rest, but true sleep was a luxury they couldn't risk—not when the cold might claim her forever.

Ditta crawled to her side, his movements careful to preserve what little warmth their shelter retained. "My Lady," he murmured, gently shaking her shoulder. "You must stay awake."

Aylin's eyes fluttered open, though the usual sharp intelligence in her gaze had dulled to something distant and confused. "Markus?" she asked softly, her words slurring slightly.

"No, my Lady. Not yet." Ditta began rubbing her hands between his own, trying to stimulate circulation. "But he will find us. You must hold on."

A sound caught Nix's attention—not quite a whisper, not quite a sigh—something that made the hair on the back of his neck rise. The Shadowvein trees around them had begun to stir, with their streaks emanating a faint blue light despite the lack of wind. He and his brother were practically raised in the forests and learned their ways at his father's knee—but this was something else entirely.

"Brother," he motioned softly, "look at the trees."

Ditta's head snapped up, his hands cautioning Aylin's. The light rippled through the Shadowveins, spreading outward as if in response to some presence they couldn't perceive. In the distance, a stand of Songbarks began to resonate in low tones—like a mourning, or a warning.

Against Aylin's throat, the aether stone shimmered with a gentle rhythm, almost like a second heartbeat. Each wave of light made the stone glow—not the harsh flare that warned of the kaegar's presence, but something softer, more resonant. She touched it uncertainly, feeling its warm ebb and flow in time with the forest's stirring.

"The forest knows something approaches," Ditta breathed, unconsciously drawing closer to Aylin's lying form.

"We cannot stay here," Nix said, though they all knew the bitter truth—in her condition, Aylin could not travel far. The storm had forced them to shelter here, but now that same decision might prove fatal.

A sound carried on the wind—not the howl of the storm, but something deeper. The Shadowveins' light intensified briefly before fading to darkness, as if recoiling from whatever approached.

The hunters exchanged glances, reading the weight of their situation in each other's eyes. They had sworn to protect her, and had promised Markus they would keep her safe. But as the forest awakened around them and unknown powers gathered in the darkness, they felt the true magnitude of that oath settle over them.

The storm was no longer their only enemy. And the night was far from over.

* * *

The campfire cast restless shadows across Hans Lumen's face as he studied the tactical display projected from his wrist unit. Seven red dots marked his remaining men's positions around the perimeter of their small camp, while topographical lines traced the crater's treacherous slope above them. Modern technology was making the pristine wilderness manageable—or so he told himself.

But something about the forest tonight made his skin crawl. The shadows seemed to move against the firelight, while the wind carried sounds that set his teeth on edge. His men felt it too—he could see it in the way they gripped their weapons too tightly, the way they startled at every crack of frost-split wood.

"The storm is approaching." Rathmar's voice carried from the darkness beyond the fire's reach. The Dromelan emerged like a shadow, frost coating his dark robes. "But that is not what troubles you, Senator."

Hans' hand tightened on his flask of brandy. "Where is your pet? The kaegar should have found them by now."

"Arrakos is ... distracted." Something in Rathmar's tone made Hans look up sharply. The Dromelan's yellow eyes reflected firelight like a predator. "He senses something. Something that calls to his ancient blood."

"Speak plainly," Hans snapped, though his voice lacked its usual authority. "We're running out of time. The naval vessels ..."

"That will not matter if you continue to ignore what awakens in these mountains," said Rathmar, moving closer to the fire, with inhuman grace. "The young man you thought you'd killed: Kane. Did you never wonder why Arrakos was drawn to him? Why the forest itself seems to recognize his passage?"

Just then one of the men called out—a sharp warning cut suddenly silent. Hans rose, weapon drawn, but Rathmar's raised hand stopped him. Through the swirling snow, they watched the kaegar emerge from the trees. Its burning eyes were fixed on the northern slope with terrible intent.

The creature's massive chest rose and fell with breaths that stirred the snow at its feet. But something was wrong. Instead of the mechanical precision Hans had come to expect, its movements now carried a strange tension—like a compass needle straining toward true north.

"What's wrong with it?" Hans demanded, noting how his men had instinctively drawn back from the fire, seeking shadows.

"Wrong?" Rathmar's laugh held no humor. "No, Senator. For the first time since its awakening, something is very right. It senses one of its own kind."

"Impossible. You said the kaegars were ..."

"I said many things." Rathmar's eyes never left his creation. "But some bloodlines run deeper than kingdoms. Some powers refuse to die, no matter how ruthlessly they are hunted."

The kaegar's head snapped up, nostrils flaring. A sound emerged from its throat—not quite a growl, not quite speech, but something that made the very air vibrate with recognition. Above them, the Shadowveins' striations quivered with answering light.

"The young watchman," Hans breathed, realization dawning. "All this time ..."

"Is beginning to awaken to his true nature." Rathmar's smile was sharp as frost. "The question is,

Senator ... what matters more? Your political games, or the ancient powers you've helped stir from sleep?"

Hans' reply was lost in a sudden gust of wind that scattered the fire's embers. The kaegar's burning eyes remained fixed on the northern slope, where something old and fearsome called to its blood. The hunt was about to change—becoming something far more olden and dangerous than mere pursuit.

The storm was coming. And with it, powers that cared nothing for human ambition.

* * *

The wolf pack moved like shadows through the deepening snow, padding silently in the treacherous terrain. Markus followed in their wake with a new fluidity that belied his recent injuries. The black-crystallized blood that had sealed his wounds now quivered faintly beneath his skin in rhythm to some deeper force that seemed to flow through the mountain itself.

The luna wolf paused, lifting her enormous head as she tested the wind. Her pups pressed close to Markus' legs, their little forms trembling, not from cold but from something they too sensed in the air. Around them, the Shadowveins quivered.

Markus pressed on through the deepening snow, as his transformed blood brimmed with a strange awareness. Not just tracks or signs, but something deeper, a pull he couldn't explain. Like the way the wolf pack had sensed their prey, he could feel the same traces in the frozen air.

Then everything seemed to still. The storm's howl

faded to silence. Even the crunch of snow beneath his boots grew distant, replaced by a rhythm that seemed to reverberate through the very earth. It was the same subtle cadence he'd sensed in those quiet moments with Aylin but never understood until now.

Somewhere ahead, through darkness and storm, that rhythm called to him.

The world slowly returned—first the whisper of wind through branches, then the soft padding of wolf paws in snow. Suddenly Markus drew a breath, the frozen air sharp in his lungs, grounding him back in the present moment.

A sound shattered the night's careful silence—a low, rattling hiss that made the wolves' hackles rise. The kaegar's presence pressed against his consciousness like a storm front, ancient blood calling to ancient blood. But now, instead of fear, Markus felt something else stir in response—a power that had always lived in his veins, waiting to be understood.

The luna wolf's growl harmonized with the Songbarks' deepening tone as more trees joined the chorus. The sound rippled through the forest like a living thing, carrying warning or welcome—Markus couldn't tell which. His own blood seemed to sing in answer, the crystallized wounds on his leg throbbing with inner light.

"Find them," he told the pack, with an authority that felt both foreign and natural. The wolves moved with fluid grace, understanding his intent without the need for human words. They were more than allies now—they were extensions of his awakening nature, bridges between what he had been and what he was becoming.

The storm's fury began to build, but Markus barely felt the cold. Something older than winter drove him forward, each step carrying him closer to both salvation and confrontation. The forest itself seemed to bend around his passage.

He was no longer simply following tracks or hunting signs. The mountain's very essence spoke to his transformed blood, showing him paths hidden from ordinary sight. Somewhere above, Aylin's aether stone called to powers rising in his veins, while below, the kaegar's burning eyes tracked his movement with awful recognition.

For the first time since this chase began, Markus felt neither prey nor pursuer. He had become something else entirely, something that both hunted and protected, that bridged worlds as naturally as breath. The hunt was changing into something that spoke of powers forgotten by contemporary minds but remembered in blood and bone and the very earth beneath their feet.

Dawn was coming. And with it, a reckoning that would shake the foundations of everything they thought they knew.

* * *

A loud huff shattered the pre-dawn silence. Hans' men reached for their weapons. But Rathmar's raised hand held them in check as the kaegar emerged from the treeline. Snow caked its dark purple hide and cloak, but something else had changed in its bearing—a new tension, as if caught between competing forces.

The creature's burning eyes weren't focused on them,

or even its Dromelan master. Instead, its gaze fixed on something uphill, nostrils flaring as they tested the wind. A low sound emerged from its throat— not quite a growl, not quite speech—that made the air vibrate.

"What is it?" Hans demanded, noting how the beast's attention seemed torn between two distant points. "What's wrong with it?"

"Silence," Rathmar hissed, moving closer to his charge. He spoke in that forbidden tongue, his words carrying strange harmonics. "What do you sense, Arrakos?"

The kaegar's response came in snarls and guttural sounds. Beneath the bestial noise was meaning that only Rathmar could understand. The ancient stone called to powers older than kingdoms, while something else—something that shared the kaegar's own nature pulled at its consciousness.

"The stone," Rathmar breathed, understanding dawning. "She's close. The aether stone reveals her."

The kaegar's head kept turning between that call and another source, torn between competing instincts. Its burning eyes fixed briefly on the eastern slope, where something pulled that spoke to its ancient blood.

"No!" Rathmar's command cracked like winter ice. He spoke again in that terrible tongue, his words carrying such authority that made even Hans flinch. "The girl. Find her. The stone is what matters."

For a moment, the kaegar's form seemed to waver, caught between obedience and something deeper. Then with a roar that shook snow from branches, it surged uphill, each massive stride taking ground with dreadful purpose.

"Move!" Hans ordered, already in motion. "Four of you, with me. The rest spread out below." His tactical training took over as he assessed the terrain. "They'll head for the crater's rim. We can cut them off if we ..."

"Wait." Rathmar's voice carried that same innate recognition as the beast. "Something else is approaching. Something that requires ... personal attention." His yellow eyes fixed on the eastern slope, where the kaegar had been drawn. "Take your men. The girl is what matters. I will deal with this ... distraction."

Hans studied the Dromelan's face, reading something there that made him hesitate. But the storm was building, and time was short. With a sharp gesture to his chosen men, he set off after the kaegar's trail, leaving Rathmar to whatever dark purpose gleamed in those inhuman eyes.

High above, Ditta caught the first rumbles of the kaegar's roar. The sound galvanized them into desperate motion, despite Aylin's weakened state. They half-carried, half-dragged her between them as they climbed through deepening snow, noting how the aether stone pulsed stronger with each passing moment.

"They're coming," Aylin whispered in both terror and strange certainty. The stone at her throat cast wild shadows across the snow, its light now impossible to conceal. "It knows. It senses ..."

"Save your strength," Nix urged, though his own voice shook. Behind them, sounds of pursuit grew closer—the thunder of the kaegar's stride, the sharp commands of Hans' men trying to coordinate their advance.

Dawn crept toward the mountain's rim, stirring ancient powers from sleep. The hunt was changing, moving into a clash of kingdoms. And somewhere below, moving like a shadow through the storm, Markus approached with allies of his own.

The night's final showdown was about to begin.

* * *

The three gunmen found Luc and Cypran huddled beneath their meager cover of snow and dead leaves, easily located by their shivering forms. Frost coated their fatigues as they were roughly hauled to their feet, their breath clouding in the pre-dawn air.

"Check the freak's tracks," one of the men ordered, gesturing to footprints barely visible in the fresh powder. "He can't be far."

From the shadows between aged trunks, Markus watched with predatory focus. The wolves had melted into darkness at his signal, understanding his intent without the need for words. His transformed blood vibrated with strange awareness, every sense heightened beyond human limits. Not only could he could hear the gunmen's heartbeats, he could smell their sweat-soaked nervousness beneath their winter gear.

An arrow from his makeshift bow would be the cleanest. But the sound might draw others. The black-crystallized arrowheads gleamed with deadly purpose in the dimming starlight, but he forced himself to wait. Patience. Like the wolves had taught him.

The first man died without a sound. Markus emerged from shadow like winter itself as Ditta's black spearhead pierced the gap between armor plates. Before the body hit the snow, he was moving again, flowing between trees with an alacrity that felt both foreign and natural.

The second gunman had time to turn, eyes widening at the sight of Markus. Transformed blood that should have frozen in these temperatures ran black as pitch down the front of his fatigues, crystallizing where it fell. His last breath carried a question he never had a chance to voice.

The third mercenary turned slowly, a cruel smile playing across his weathered face as he studied the two recruits. His blaster remained holstered as he drew a wicked-looking blade, its edge catching starlight.

"Well now," he drawled, circling them with predatory motions. "What've we got here? Two little boys playing soldier?"

Luc and Cypran exchanged glances, as fear challenged their training. Then Cypran, in what might have been the bravest or stupidest moment of his life, charged forward with a wild yell. The mercenary sidestepped easily, but Luc seized the moment to tackle the man's legs.

What followed was more farce than fight. The two recruits scrambled and flailed, their academy training forgotten in desperate survival thrusts. The mercenary toyed with them, his blade drawing shallow cuts that spoke of skill held carefully in check. He could have killed them a dozen times, but something held him back—perhaps memory of his own youth, or simple distaste for slaughtering boys.

"Come on then," he taunted, dancing between their uncoordinated attacks. "Show me what they teach at that fancy evolution of yours. Come on, boys! My grandmother fights better than this!"

Markus watched from shadow, knowing he should act but sensing Rathmar's approach. The Dromelan's presence was growing stronger, old power radiating like cold through the trees. The choice was being stripped away—Rathmar or the recruits. He had to decide now.

The decision was made for him as Rathmar emerged from the storm like a shadow taking form. The Dromelan's yellow eyes fixed on Markus with ancient recognition, ignoring the desperate scuffle nearby as if it were beneath his notice.

"Your blood sings with old power," Rathmar said softly, his voice carrying harmonics that made the Shadowveins ripple with answering light. "I felt it that first day in Cenovira. So did Arrakos."

Markus drew his bow in one sweeping motion, the crystallized arrowhead gleaming with inner darkness. "What do you know about my blood?"

"More than you can imagine." Rathmar moved like liquid, closing distance faster than seemed possible. His first blow sent the bow spinning into shadows while the second caught Markus in the ribs, driving breath from his lungs.

With Rathmar's next blow, Markus rolled, his transformed blood lending him speed he'd never known. But the Dromelan's skill was beyond human, each strike precisely calculated to wear him down. When Markus tried to counter, Rathmar seemed to flow around the attacks like water around stone.

"You could be so much more," Rathmar said, his words punctuated by brutal strikes. "Join us. Learn what you truly are."

"I know what I am," Markus snarled, though his

body screamed with pain. His hand found Ditta's black spearhead.

The Dromelan's laugh held no humor. "Do you? Do you know why Arrakos hunts you? Why the very forest bends around your passing?" His next blow sent Markus stumbling backward into a Shadowvein trunk. "You're still playing at being human when you could be something far greater."

A cry of pain drew Markus' attention.

The mercenary nearby had tired of his game; this time, his blade opened a deeper cut across Cypran's arm. The recruit fell to one knee while Luc stood frozen, survival instinct warring with loyalty.

"Time to end this farce," the mercenary growled, raising his blade for the kill.

Rathmar seized Markus' throat with inhuman strength, pinning him against the tree. "Last chance," he hissed. "Choose power. Choose ..."

Shadows darted at the edge of darkness.

Two small forms burst from the brush, yipping with absurd bravery. The mercenary actually laughed, blade hovering inches from Cypran's throat as he watched the wolf pups bounce and snap.

But Markus saw his chance. With Rathmar's attention split for that crucial second, he drove his crystallized arrowhead deep into the Dromelan's side. Rathmar howled—not in death, but in rage and pain. His yellow eyes blazed as he struck back, sending them both tumbling into the snow.

They rolled through the freezing slush, wrestling for control. Markus' transformed blood sang with ancient power as he fought, each movement carrying the wisdom of everything he'd learned. This wasn't survival anymore: it was claiming his own destiny.

The luna wolf erupted from the snow-laden bushes like winter's judgment, but she didn't immediately attack. Instead, she circled, her golden eyes reading the fight with predatory intelligence.

Rathmar's hands found Markus' throat, but the Dromelan's strength was fading as black blood seeped from the wound in his side. "You could have been so much more," he snarled.

"I already am," Markus growled. With desperate strength, he twisted, breaking Rathmar's grip. The arrowhead found its mark again—this time in the Dromelan's chest.

Rathmar's roar shook snow from branches. With inhuman speed, he slammed his forehead into Markus' face. The impact sent Markus sprawling, consciousness wavering as blood filled his mouth. Through blurred vision, he saw Rathmar lurch toward him, yellow eyes burning with fury.

Only then did the pack move. The luna wolf's fangs closed on Rathmar's throat, her attack carrying swift and terrible purpose, while the rest of the pack descended on the mercenary with coordinated fury, while the pups yipped excitedly, proud of their part in the victory.

As the Dromelan's life ebbed, his yellow eyes found Markus one final time.

"You can't escape what's awakened," Rathmar gasped, blood staining his lips. His final laugh held no humor, a sound that might have been triumph or despair.

When silence fell again, Markus rose unsteadily,

tasting copper in his mouth. Every breath sent daggers through his ribs where Rathmar's blows had landed. But something else burned in his blood now—not just pain, but awakening power. The Dromelan's final words echoed in his mind, carrying a truth he was only just beginning to understand.

CHAPTER TWENTY-FOUR

Markus exhaled deeply. Relief washed over him as he assured himself that his comrades, Cypran and Luc, were alive and in one piece—remarkably, in better shape than he was. Their faces were etched with trauma, the 'Trial by Fire' they'd been thrust into, far more harrowing than any evolution tests.

As the wolf pack roamed around them, circling the mangled remains of the enemy, Markus pulled the shell-shocked youth to their feet. His hands trembled slightly as he instructed them to gather branches and twigs. The adrenaline still coursed through his veins with such intensity that even simple tasks felt strange and distant. First though, he stripped the thick coats from the dead men, draping them over his comrades for warmth, trying not to look at the faces of those he'd killed.

The two young men huddled by the growing fire, relief spreading over their faces as the first light of dawn began to push through the orange sky. The snowstorm finally eased. Markus knelt by the campfire, allowing himself a rare moment of respite, though with an underlying anxiety he couldn't quite suppress. The dancing yellow and red flames provided temporary warmth, both physical and emotional, that he desperately needed. He hoped that Cypran and Luc would respect his need for silence. The crackling of the fire, surrounded by the hush of the snow-covered forest, was the only sound he wanted to hear—a peace he knew wouldn't last.

At his legs, he felt the playful nudges of the wolf pups, their young coats dusted with snow. His battered hand reached out, trembling slightly, to pet each one before finally resting on the luna wolf holding guard nearby. Her golden eyes met his, carrying an instinctual wisdom that seemed to see right through his carefully maintained composure. She could sense his fear—the terror of what waited up that valley, the weight of more deaths that would surely come. Words weren't necessary; the unspoken bond between them said it all. They had saved his life, and the gratitude he felt was immeasurable.

"What's next?" Cypran finally asked, breaking the silence.

Markus swallowed hard, forcing steel into his voice that he didn't quite feel. "A reckoning."

He gazed at them for a moment, then tossed a second blaster at their feet, along with two pocketknives. The luna wolf stepped forward, but Markus placed a firm hand on her head, gently pushing her back. "No," he whispered. "Not this time." Her eyes held his for a long moment, and she understood. This was his path to walk alone.

Without another word, he turned and dashed through

the valley, up the path, disappearing swiftly from sight, leaving behind both his human and wild allies as he moved toward whatever fate awaited him above.

* * *

Draven stared into the fire, whose reflection danced across his armor plating. Behind him, tents fluttered in the bitter wind though the storm was easing.

Now, the camp stirred. Dalton, Kratz, and Viktor pulled on gauntlets and reconnected neural sync-links to their shoulder ports, their half-bared torsos steaming against the morning chill. Azlo stood silently nearby, already fully robed and masked; his soulsteel cloak trailed faint sparks with each step.

Draven rose slowly and deliberately. His armor hissed softly as it adjusted to his frame, and the familiar buzz of integrated weaponry reinitialized. With Azlo at his side, they turned toward the ridge.

The storm had passed. But the reckoning had not.

"What in the world was that sound that woke us earlier?" Dalton asked in a gruff voice. Sounded like a wounded beast caught in a trap."

"Beyond the saber wolves? I can't imagine," Draven replied.

"Let's leave this place," Viktor said, shaking off the cold. "Surely there are no survivors."

"He's right," Dalton agreed. "Who was left? Luc, Graigs, and Cypran? Not the bravest or strongest to survive the storm or the predators."

"Pity about Markus dropping out," Viktor added. "Had my money on him."

Draven glanced at Azlo while sipping his black coffee. The knight folded his arms, shaking his head.

"What?" Draven asked. "He disappeared after running the trail? It's called 'quitting.'"

"You did not exactly have faith in him now—did you?"

"I didn't give him a second thought. He was a bit rough around the edges, not exactly a team player. He failed, Azlo. Deal with it."

Azlo poured himself a cup of the hot brew. "Very well. But we'd better find him before we leave these lands."

"I didn't promise anyone his safety," Draven retorted.

"Do you not remember how Nikel's wife looked at you? Sharp enough to cut you! She has special powers, you know?"

"I'm not responsible for him. Quit pulling my leg!"

"Don't come crawling to me if she haunts you in your sleep, my friend."

Draven choked on his coffee, nearly burning his lips. Beside him, Azlo went suddenly still, his cup slipping into the snow. A change came over the knight's features—subtle but profound—slightly dilated pupils taking on an almost bluish sheen. Draven had seen this transformation before, when his friend's bonded spirit stirred within him.

Azlo now moved stealthily to the camp's edge, each step deliberate as a stalking predator. The Shadowvein trees around him seemed to tremble at his presence. He knelt, pressing one hand to the frozen earth while the other traced patterns in the air that seemed to catch the morning light.

"The forest knows something approaches," he said,

his voice carrying harmonics that made the flames dart. "Three heartbeats drawing near. Two who move like hunters born to these lands." His head tilted, reading signs invisible to normal senses. "And one ... one whose presence makes even the spirit beasts restless."

Draven set aside pragmatic doubts, having learned to trust his friend's mystical perceptions. Azlo's ancient bond often revealed what technology missed. "Survivors from below?"

"No." Azlo's eyes remained fever-bright. "Something more. The very air trembles with purpose I've not felt since crossing the Frigid Mountains." His fingers curled against the earth, as if catching whispers that traveled through root and stone. "They bring warning ... and hunger follows in their wake."

The wind had picked up, bringing with it a bitter chill that even these hardened warriors couldn't ignore. Ice crystals stung exposed skin, while their breath frosted in clouds thick enough to obscure vision. Even Viktor, who had boasted of his tolerance to the cold, pulled his thermal gear closer.

Draven signaled to the others while pulling out his binoculars and eye scope, trying to cut through the foggy, almost whiteout conditions. Azlo swiftly took off, heading south. Draven warned the others to arm themselves, and then followed the knight into the misty landscape.

He caught up with Azlo, and it wasn't long before they spotted figures in the distance—tiny specks growing larger as they approached. Draven drew his blaster, but Azlo lowered it.

Two young men, clad in tattered eastern hides,

staggered into view, carrying a woman. They exchanged a Nevrish plea with Azlo, who rushed forward to take the barely conscious woman, from their arms. Moments later, the two men collapsed at the campsite. Not long after, a rekindled fire and warm food revived them, along with the woman, who they'd covered in a blanket.

Aylin finally revealed her necklace—a golden seal from the last monarchy, the aether stone. Around her waist was a strange native garment that made both Draven and Azlo's eyes widen.

"Where'd you get this?" Draven asked.

"Kane," she whispered. "Markus—one of your recruits."

"You know him?"

"He saved us ... for the moment."

Through numbed lips and chattering teeth, she thanked them for the warm food. The warriors gathered around her, their earlier bravado replaced by growing concern.

Kratz, the eldest, respectfully acknowledged her. "Your Highness, you have your father's eyes. And his seal on that necklace—it will be yours upon coronation. But where is Cael, the prefect in charge of your protection?"

She shook her head, her voice trembling. "Only Mercury is left—protecting the others."

"Protecting them from what?" Draven asked.

"Are you not aware of what's been unleashed upon this land?" Nixa, one of the young hunters, spoke up, his voice carrying a desperate edge despite his exhaustion.

"No one has alerted us to any trouble," Draven

pressed. "What's been unleashed? And how do you know her majesty?"

Before Nix could answer, Azlo's head snapped up sharply. The knight's earlier certainty shifted to something else—a tension that made the air itself feel heavy. His bluish eyes fixed on the southern horizon where storm clouds gathered.

"Something else approaches," he said cautioned above a whisper. The Shadowvein trees around them had gone eerily still, their striations dimming as if recoiling from some unseen presence. "Something that walks between worlds."

"He's right," Kratz added, instinctively reaching for his weapon as he tested the air. "Something's coming."

Ditta and Nixa, now strengthened from the meal and fire, tossed off their blankets and grabbed their spears, the black crystalline tips gleaming in the dim light. Aylin rose, retreating as the two warriors flanked her. The Immortals moved with practiced efficiency, their obsidian-hued tactical armor coming alive as power coursed through the poly-alloy plates.

Snap. Clunk. Pull. Click. The familiar rhythm of weapons being primed echoed across the camp. Kratz shouldered his Thunderlord Carbine, its kinetic core drumming to life, while Viktor and Dalton checked their Black Viper Repeaters—the serpentine recoil systems sliding into place with deadly precision. Each weapon bore the crimson sigil of the throne.

Draven's nanotech armor seemed to ripple as its stealth systems engaged. Azlo stood apart from him— his soulsteel armor catching the firelight like liquid mercury, while the spirit mask he wore obscured all emotion. The Zylvan knight inhaled deeply, his usual centered calm giving way to something closer to ancient dread. His hand rested on his sword hilt, though the weapon remained sheathed.

Draven stepped forward, raising his tactical scope to scan the perimeter. Through its enhanced optics, he detected movement at the edge of the storm ...

Zooming in, he saw nothing at a hundred yards. Nothing at one hundred and twenty. Then, at one hundred and fifty yards, he caught sight of a figure in the snowy white haze—a tall apparition, a bipedal, resembling a man covered in heavy winter gear. But each step revealed more details that made Draven doubt his senses.

This was no man in winter attire, nor fur, nor armor. It was a chiseled, grayish-blue mass of a beast, with arms and hands larger than any man's and trunk-like legs that surged forward. Glowing red eyes locked onto Draven from seventy yards away, as the distance closed fast.

"What the hell is that?"

"Some sort of demon?"

Draven lowered the scope, joining the others and drawing his blaster. "Stop right there!" he shouted.

The kaegar lumbered forward, snorting and growling. Dalton and Viktor raised their pistols. Kratz steadied his rifle.

"That's far enough!" Dalton yelled.

Azlo grabbed Draven's shoulder, his movements swift but controlled. "Stay focused, my friend! This is no ordinary being." His eyes blazed with fire as he assessed the threat, reading the battlefield as only an eastern knight could.

Draven nodded and raised his blaster. Aylin stumbled back behind Ditta and Nixa, the young hunters instinctively forming a protective wall before her. On cue, the Immortals unleashed a barrage of laser blasts. The air crackled as the shots punched into the humanoid, dropping it onto the ground.

They paused, letting the smoke clear. A charred smell. The giant body motionless in the snow. Then, a leg moved. Followed by an arm. The humanoid slowly rose to its feet, dark blue smears covering its rocky torso—charred but unharmed.

With a hiss, it bared its teeth, locking eyes with each of them before focusing on the younger Nevrans at the rear. Aylin cowered behind them, barely visible.

The stone attached to her necklace suddenly glowed stronger—radiating in the eye of the swirling snow and winds.

"It's come for her!" Azlo whispered to Draven.

The kaegar took a step forward. Viktor opened fire, and the others followed, pounding the creature with more blasts. This time, it roared, fighting to stay on its feet beneath the bright, burning strikes. It raised its arms, trying to fend off the attacks.

They quickly reloaded, taking turns firing upon the giant—Draven, then Kratz, then Dalton. But the relentless barrage seemed to have no effect.

* * *

Nearly a kilometer away, Hans and the last three gunmen crept forward over the snow-peaked crater, as the thunderous sound of laser fire and lightning cut through the arctic air. Through his binoculars the vague forms of armored silhouettes came into view.

"We're exposed!"

"No!" Hans yelled, "They're doing exactly what we want! They won't last much longer! Stay out of their line of sight. We'll circle around and see if we can find her."

They kept low, moving in single file, relying on stealth and the element of surprise. They inched forward, rifles ready, hoping to blend in beneath the haze.

The laser blasts grew louder—like the sound of sparks and lightning. They snuck closer. The angry roars and growls of the carnivorous humanoid made their hands shake with fear and adrenaline. The terrifying howls continued as they moved through the shadows of scattered pines and frost-covered rocks.

A massive whiteout swept over the area. Aylin dropped to the ground, covering her head as laser blasts tore through the air. Nix was hit in the leg, collapsing under the searing pain. Ditta detected in the storm silhouettes darting in and out of view. He spotted a figure in the distance—a man in western winter attire, but not his brother. An Earthen.

He hurled his spear, piercing the man's shoulder and sending him down. But before he could react, a massive hand closed around him, smothering his cries. The kaegar's grip tightened, but the violent winds tore them apart, sweeping both man and monster into the blinding storm.

Markus dropped to his knees. Snow whipped across his face, forcing him to shield his eyes from the blinding whiteness. The violent gusts hissed as tiny ice crystals scraped against each other and amplified in his ears, sporadic, coming and going—making it impossible to hear anyone around him.

The kaegar lay motionless among the scattered pines, its massive form deceptively still in the pre-dawn darkness. Kratz moved first, his Thunderlord Carbine raised, each step calculated. The weapon's kinetic core throbbed with stored energy, ready to unleash devastating concussive force.

"Careful, Kratz! It might not be dead!" Dalton called out, his Black Viper's serpentine recoil system humming as he kept the weapon trained on the fallen creature.

"It might not be human either," Kratz muttered, leaning in closer to examine the kaegar's stone-like features. "What in God's name are you?"

As he examined the kaegar's granite-like skin, movement caught his eye in the distance—figures approaching through the storm. His nanotech armor's sensors triggered an immediate warning. Without hesitation, he raised his carbine.

Suddenly the kaegar's burning eyes snapped open.

Before Kratz could react, a massive hand shot out, wrapping around his neck with crushing force. His trigger finger squeezed reflexively, but the shots went wide, the carbine's kinetic discharge sending shockwaves through the air. Dalton and Viktor charged forward, their soulsteel blades singing as they drew them, and struck.

Hans, who had been watching from afar, dived into the snow as stray laser blasts whizzed past. His gunmen scattered, dropping to their knees. Hans barked orders, and they opened fire on the Immortals.

The last Immortal backpedaled, his armor's stealth systems glinting as he tried to disappear into the storm. But the kaegar moved like shadow itself, its burning eyes tracking him unerringly through the swirling white. The warrior's armor, designed to withstand the deadliest modern weapons, barely slowed the ancient horror's assault.

* * *

Azlo stood alone now, his soulsteel armor shimmering like quicksilver. Through his spirit mask's glowing lenses, he saw what the others couldn't—an aura of ancient malice surrounding the kaegar, its presence a tear in the fabric of the natural world. His bonded spirit stirred within him, recognizing power that predated kingdoms and crowns.

"Brother, stay back!" he called to Draven, his voice carrying harmonics that made the very air vibrate. But his friend, trusting in tactical armor and modern weapons, had already charged.

The kaegar's attack left Draven broken in the snow, his advanced gear useless against forces older than technology itself. Azlo's hand moved to his final weapon—not with a warrior's desperation, but with the solemn acceptance of one who knew what price such power demanded.

From his blade's sheath came a sound like wind through ancient temples. The sword, crafted in the forges of Niri and blessed by eastern mystics, responded to his touch. With practiced reverence, he drew the blade across its fuel chamber while striking the ignition crystal. Blue flame erupted along its length, the color of spirit-fire, burning with heat that belonged to no natural flame.

The kaegar paused, its burning eyes fixing on this new threat. For the first time, something like recognition sparked in those ancient depths. Azlo moved with liquid stealth, his soulsteel armor flowing like water as he assumed the stance of Final Judgment—a form not seen since the Third Zylvan War.

The blue-flamed sword cut through the storm's fury, its light casting wild shadows as Azlo struck. Not with the brute force of modern combat, but with the precision of one who understood that true power flowed from spirit, not steel. For a brief moment, his blade found its mark where others had failed, the metal burning with supernatural heat as it scored the kaegar's hide.

The kaegar recoiled from the blue flame's touch with a sound like preternatural rage rumbling from its chest. But its momentary retreat was merely a prelude to greater fury. It moved with impossible speed, its gigantic form streaking through the storm like living shadow. Even Azlo's spiritual awareness couldn't track its full motion—the creature existed partially in realms his bonded spirit could barely perceive.

Azlo's blade traced patterns of blue fire through the darkness, each strike guided by generations of eastern wisdom. The kaegar's stone-like flesh sizzled where the supernatural flame made contact, but the wounds sealed almost instantly, as if the creature's very nature rejected modern weapons, no matter how mystically enhanced.

"Fall back!" Azlo called to Draven, who had struggled to his knees, his tactical armor's systems blinking as they tried to compensate for massive damage. "This is not a battle that technology can win!"

The storm itself seemed to respond to the clash of ancient powers. The wind rose with unnatural fury, while the temperature plummeted. Snow whirled between them with increasing violence, transforming the battlefield into a sea of blinding white.

The kaegar's burning eyes pierced the growing whiteness, fixing on something beyond their position—some presence that called to its soul. With terrible purpose, it turned from their battle, its massive form disappearing into the storm like a nightmare fading into dawn.

Azlo's blade dimmed, the blue flames guttering in the arctic wind. His soulsteel armor bore deep gouges where the kaegar's claws had found its mark, while exhaustion from channeling such powerful mystical energies left him barely standing. But they had survived—bloodied but alive, when so many others had fallen.

Through the thickening snow, he caught glimpses of movement—Aylin's cloaked form, Hans' men closing in, and beyond them all, Markus' silhouette dark against the white. The storm's fury grew stronger, as if nature itself sought to separate these forces until their final, inevitable showdown.

"We have to reach them!" Draven shouted, his voice nearly lost in the wind.

But the whiteout descended fully now, turning the world into a realm of blinding chaos. The storm had become a living thing, driving them apart, ensuring that what came next would be decided not by armies or weapons, but by choices made in darkness and desperation.

* * *

Markus dropped to his knees as shards of ice sliced his face. The metallic taste in his mouth grew stronger, his transformed blood resonating with an ancient presence he could sense but barely see in the blinding white. Behind him, through swirling snow, he caught the faint murmur of Aylin's aether stone.

The kaegar's massive form appeared again through the storm's fury. Its first strike came from nowhere—a backhand that sent Markus flying through the air, his body crashing into frozen ground with a bone-shattering force that would have killed any normal person. But his blood, black as pitch now, crystallized where it fell, sustaining him even with cracked ribs and bruised organs.

He tried to rise, squinting through the white wall of snow. The wind shifted, revealing nothing but swirling shadows. The kaegar was there waiting, its burning eyes the only clear thing in the storm. Another of its devastating blows sent him reeling. The creature's massive hand closed around his throat, lifting him like a child's toy, and studying him with uncanny intelligence as it sensed how his blood refused to yield to death.

Markus clawed desperately at the granite flesh, his own blood leaving black streaks that sizzled against the kaegar's skin. The ancient hunter released him with a snarl—the first sign that it could be hurt at all. But any triumph was short-lived. The next impact drove him into the snow, and the taste of copper flooded his mouth, a sign of internal damage.

Suddenly, through the whiteout's fury, Markus caught a glimpse of his bow half-buried in powder. The crystallized arrowheads brimmed with dark energy, but the howling wind made any shot nearly impossible. He fired into white nothingness, the arrow disappearing into the storm—only to hear the kaegar's snarl of pain from an unexpected direction.

The predator emerged again from the white like a ghost, its granite skin now bearing a crystallized wound. But before Markus could react, the storm swallowed them both again. He spun desperately, trying to track movement through the blinding snow, knowing the kaegar could appear from any direction.

"What are you?" The words weren't spoken, but somehow Markus heard them—felt them—in his blood. The kaegar circled him now, its movements carrying a stalker's patience ... no longer hunting, but investigating.

Markus' arrow struck true, the black tip piercing where other weapons had failed. Dark fluid seeped from the wound, crystallizing in the frozen air. The kaegar's roar carried something beyond pain—recognition of its own essence turned against it.

But the victory was momentary. The creature moved like quicksilver, faster than anything its size should allow. Markus felt his ribs shatter as it slammed him into the ground. Each breath became agony as the kaegar methodically tried to break him, perhaps trying to understand how he still could live.

Through the haze of pain, Markus' blood sang with ancient memory. Images flooded his mind—battles fought before civilization, powers that could bridge worlds. The kaegar wasn't just hunting him now. It was testing him, pushing him toward some awful awakening.

Markus' hand closed around Ditta's spearhead—his final weapon. The kaegar's massive form loomed over him, those burning eyes carrying almost curious recognition. Blood dripped from Markus' mouth, each drop turning into black crystals where it fell.

Time seemed to slow. His body was broken and pushed far beyond human limits. But his blood—his curse—had become something else. Power older than kingdoms charged through his veins as he drove the spearhead up with all his remaining strength.

The black crystal pierced deep. The kaegar's roar shook snow from distant peaks, its colossal form convulsing as ancient blood bowed to ancient blood. It collapsed forward, its weight driving Markus deeper into the frozen ground.

The kaegar's body slumped forward, its weight crushing Markus into the snow. His ribs screamed. He couldn't breathe. Every nerve in his body begged for unconsciousness.

Then came the voice.

"Still alive," Hans muttered, stepping into the fraying storm.

Markus barely lifted his head. Blurred through the snow, Hans approached, face bruised, eyes hollow, something metallic glinting beneath his coat.

"Did all the hard work for me," he said, circling the

kaegar's carcass. "One monster kills the other. And you—you just don't know when to die."

Hans drew a long, narrow blade—not crude, not standard Guild issue. Something sleeker. Custom-made. Modified. It crackled faintly with energy across its edge.

Markus tried to rise. Failed. Blood soaked his side where the kaegar had crushed him.

Hans stepped closer, crouching to eye level.

"And yet," he said, "you keep crawling back. Vesper. The festival. My men. My deals. You should have stayed in the gutter."

He lunged.

Markus rolled, barely dodging the blade's first swing. The next cut grazed his arm, burning hot. He bit back a scream. Snow kicked up as he staggered to his feet—barely upright.

They circled each other. Wind howled through the crater's ridge.

"You're nothing without that sister of yours," Hans growled. "Without her, you're just a scar and a story."

Markus's hand tightened around a shard of spear shaft still sheathed at his side.

Then Hans lunged again—fast, trained, and fueled by desperation.

They collided in a tangle of limbs, fists, and bone-jarring impact. Markus ducked the blade. Punched low. Hans twisted, slammed his fist into Markus's gut, then reached—and ripped something from his neck.

Markus froze.

The half-pendant and necklace flew. It skidded across the ice—*spinning, sliding*—until it stopped just inches from the edge of the cliff.

CHAPTER TWENTY-FOUR

Hans smirked. "That belonged to her, didn't it?"

Markus didn't answer. His eyes locked on the pendant—on the sliver of silver resting over nothingness.

Then Hans's hand came up, blade gleaming again. He pressed it to Markus's neck—just beside the scar.

"Funny how it always ends in the snow."

Time slowed.

Wind ripped across the cliff. The sky vanished in white.

And beyond Hans's shoulder, Markus saw her—not in body, but in memory.

Xara. Standing in a cracked mirror. Eleven years old. Smiling with defiant eyes.

He remembered the alley. The pipe. The flashlight. The first time anyone ever reached for him—not to hurt him, but to pull him out.

Hans sneered. "Say something, freak."

Markus's eyes flicked.

The pendant was right there. At the edge.

He moved.

One hand shot past Hans—grabbed the chain.

In one brutal motion, Markus yanked the pendant from the cliff's edge—looped the chain around Hans's throat—and pulled.

Hans gagged.

The blade dropped.

Markus twisted. Drove Hans backward—snow scraping beneath their boots—until the man slammed into the jagged ridge.

They fought for breath. For control.

But Markus *held* the chain tight—his whole body trembling from the effort.

"That's for Xara," he said, voice hoarse with frost and fury.

Hans thrashed once. Twice. Then stilled.

Markus let go.

Hans collapsed to the snow—eyes open, unseeing.

Silence returned. A different kind.

The storm still raged, but it no longer touched him.

The broken chain lay twisted in the snow, glinting faintly. He collapsed beside it.

Markus's fingers closed around the pendant, a ragged breath slipping through cracked lips.

He'd nearly lost it. Nearly lost *her*.

But it was still here.

So was he.

The worst had passed. The storm began to break, clouds lifting as the sky paled to a faint blue. Wind still howled across the cliffs, but it carried no more screams.

A voice cut the wind.

"Markus!"

Aylin. Staggering toward him.

He turned, just barely. Her figure blurred in the snow, but her eyes were clear.

She dropped beside him, hands at his chest.

She took the pendant from his fingers and pressed it to her lips, then laid it gently just above his heart.

"Stay with me," she whispered. "Please..."

She crawled across the frozen ground, her breath coming in ragged gasps, her legs trembling from exhaustion. Her fingers closed around the edge of the heavy, weathered crimson cloak—once worn by the relentless kaegar. She dragged it across the snow, straining under its weight, determined to shield Markus from the bitter cold. Her hands clenched at the sight of his motionless body and face pale beneath the blood and grime.

She sank beside him, hands trembling as she gently lifted his head into her lap, pulling the cloak over him. His torn fatigues were soaked in blood, and the faint rise and fall of his chest told her how close he was to slipping away. His eyes fluttered open, the faintest glimmer of life still in them.

She wiped the dried blood from his face before her fingers rested on his skin. She'd seen what his blood could do to others, but now it had crystallized into harmless black streaks, like war paint across his weathered features.

"Hey ... 'Stranger,'" he whispered, his voice hoarse but tinged with that familiar, reckless spirit.

A choked laugh escaped her, mingled with stifled sobs. She brushed a matted strand of his hair away from his forehead, her fingertips lingering on the scarred skin. "You're late, you know," she murmured, trying to hold back her tears. "Thought you were going to stand me up."

He managed the faintest of smiles with lips cracked and bloodied. "And miss ... all this fun?"

Her laughter was shaky, her heart ached. "We're just in time for the sunrise," she whispered, glancing at the sky. "Looks like you're an 'Immortal' now."

He coughed, weak and strained. "Well ... this'll be ... the shortest career ever."

"No," she whispered fiercely, her voice breaking. "Don't you dare. Don't you dare leave me, Markus."

She could feel the life slipping from him, each breath a struggle. Desperately, she wrapped the cloak tighter around his broken body, pulling him closer to her, trying to shield him from the cold that was stealing him away. Her fingers, icy from the wind, brushed the dry blood and dirt from his face, tracing the line of his scar, and warming his skin with her touch.

"The monsters are gone," she whispered, trembling. "Do you hear me? They're all dead now. We made it!"

His eyes fluttered open, barely. A breath escaped—ragged and low.

"Not all of them," he murmured.

Her lips trembled. "Don't say that."

"It's true," he said, a faint smile ghosting across his face. "Some monsters wear your face."

"You're not ..." She pressed her forehead to his, fierce and trembling. "You're not that."

He said nothing more. His strength was fading.

She pulled the cloak tighter. "There's a new story to tell," she whispered, voice soft and unsure. "One with a new hero."

His breath hitched, a ghost of laughter. "No..." he rasped. "Not me."

"Then who?" she whispered, leaning in.

His eyes opened just enough to meet hers. A beat passed.

"The one who believed in me," he said.

She waited for more—but he said nothing else. His eyelids slipped shut, and his head grew heavy against her shoulder.

Tears slid down her cheeks, as she cradled his head in her hands. She pressed a gentle kiss to his forehead, her lips lingering there, as if she could seal him to this world with that touch alone. His breath was faint, but steady, and she clung to it—the small, fragile sign that he was still with her.

As the first light of day chased away the remnants of the night, she held him close, her heart swelling with both pain and hope. The world around them began to thaw, the snow melting under the gentle warmth of the sun, and for the first time in what felt like forever, she allowed herself to believe in a future.

And as the sun climbed higher in the sky, she held him tighter, refusing to let go.

CHAPTER TWENTY-FIVE

Dawn painted the northern harbor in shades of steel and silver as naval vessels cut through the morning mist. Their sleek hulls dwarfed the scattered smuggling ships, many already abandoned by their crews. Xara stood at the edge of the dock, her fingers finding her half-pendant as she scanned the steady stream of stretchers being carried down from the crater.

Beside her, Mercury maintained his stoic vigilance, though exhaustion showed in the stoop of his shoulders. Yewwa moved between the wounded with quiet purpose, while his sons helped wherever they could. The old hunter's herbs had saved more than one life in the bitter night.

When they brought Markus down, Xara's careful composure cracked. Her brother lay frighteningly still, his skin nearly as pale as the snow that still clung to his torn fatigues. But his chest rose and fell with steady breaths, and when she took his hand, his fingers tightened weakly around hers.

Her eyes caught the pendant lying loosely atop his chest, crusted with frost. For one awful moment, she realized how close she had come to losing both halves of what mattered most.

"Still watching my back?" he said in a hoarse whisper.

"Someone has to." She pressed her forehead to his.

A shout shattered the moment. "Saber wolf!"

The massive silver form emerged from the tree line, her shoulders nearly level with a man's waist. The dockyard erupted into disarray—soldiers moving into defensive positions while civilians scrambled for the safety of waiting ships. Weapons raised, their bearers tried to steady hands at the sight of such ancient power.

Behind her, two pups, already rivaling hunting dogs in size, bounded through the snow. Their presence made the soldiers hesitate—no one wanted to fire on a mother protecting her young. The luna wolf stood perfectly still, her golden eyes taking in the scene with predatory intelligence. There was something mournful in her gaze as she watched the humans gather closer to their vessels, as if accepting that their worlds must remain forever separate.

With a grunt at her pups, she turned towards the tree line. But as the magnificent beast prepared to head back into the wild—she paused, her gaze searching one last time among the humans clearing the docks.

Amidst the rocking motion of medics lifting his stretcher, Markus weakly squeezed Xara's wrist sensing something. Through the flurry of physicians and soldiers around him, he caught the movement. His body screamed in protest as he turned his head, fighting to focus through his one good eye. The wolf's form wavered in his blurred vision, and their eyes met across the distance, carrying recognition that transcended natural order.

His charred lips moved, forming a single word that barely carried on the winter wind: "Come."

The pups moved first, tumbling over each other in their eagerness to reach him. Their mother followed with fluid composure, navigating the forest of raised weapons with purpose. Each step radiated power that made even the trained soldiers step back, but her focus remained solely on Markus.

"Hold your fire!" Yewwa's voice carried quiet authority. The old hunter's eyes held recognition as he studied the great wolf's approach. "Stay calm. Let her come."

When she reached Markus, her head lowered to his level. Her breath stirred his hair as she pressed her muzzle gently against his temple, where his black scar responded in recognition.

Xara watched the great predator settle protectively near her brother's stretcher, the pups already jumping into his lap. Her street instincts battled with what she witnessed—but she knew that this wasn't just an animal accepting a human; it was ancient powers acknowledging their own kind.

"They're part of him now," she said quietly, understanding, as she studied the wolf's posture—so like her own instincts to guard her brother. "Just as I am."

* * *

The sun dipped low, painting the North Sea in shades of gold and shadow. Naval vessels cut through the evening swells, their sleek hulls gleaming as they carried their precious cargo home. Above them, migrating birds traced patterns across the steel-blue sky, their calls a reminder that winter's bite wasn't far behind.

On the lead ship's deck, Markus lay wrapped in bandages, his broken body still bearing the marks of his transformation. The luna wolf's warmth pressed steady against his side, while her pups slept curled against him. Through fever-bright eyes, he watched the horizon, each breath a reminder of survival. Xara maintained her vigil nearby, her fingers absently touching the half-pendant at her throat.

Through the gathering dusk, Orwein waited—and with it, the beginning of whatever was to come.

* * *

In the village of Orwein, Nikel stood at his window, watching the distant dust cloud of riders wind through the country roads. The murmur of anticipation spread through the house as servants gathered, hope and uncertainty on their faces. When armed soldiers bearing the insignia of the Central Kingdom began to surround his estate, Nikel's hand tightened on his cane.

The great doors opened, and the hall filled with a moment of profound silence before the whirl of homecoming. Draven and Azlo entered first, battle-worn but standing tall. When Markus and Xara appeared in the doorway, something in Nikel's stance changed to a mixture of relief and pride that transcended words. The young man's black uniform hung loosely on his battered and bandaged frame, but the gold flames gleaming beneath his nameplate told a story of transformation no one had expected. Despite supporting each other's weight, the siblings carried themselves with a quiet dignity that spoke of trials they'd survived together.

The room seemed to hold its breath as Princess Aylin stepped through the door, her velvet cloak sweeping the floor. When she drew back her hood, revealing her face for the first time in a decade, Nikel recognized the child he'd once known in the woman who stood before him. The royal seal gleamed at her throat, catching morning light from the high windows.

Only then did the sound of movement draw all eyes toward the entrance once more. The luna wolf's massive form filled the doorway, her silver coat catching the light as her pups tumbled at her feet. The household staff drew back instinctively, but the wolf moved with deliberate poise to Markus' side, her presence demonstrating in him—not just a warrior now, but something bridging realms that had long been separate.

Before anyone could speak, Aylin stepped forward, the aether stone at her throat pulsing gently as she approached Nikel. From her palm, she lifted the pendulum that had guided them through darkness, its ribbon catching morning light as she raised it. Nikel bowed his head to receive it, the simple movement carrying decades of service and loyalty. As the pendulum settled against his chest, the years seemed to fall away—revealing the warrior who had once stood beside her father, who had seen something worth saving in a scarred boy from Vesper's streets.

His eyes met Markus' across the hall, carrying understanding that needed no words. The mission was complete. The circle closed. Yet something in how the pendulum caught the light, how it swayed ever so slightly without a breeze, suggested their story was far from over.

Amid the quiet reunion, Markus' eyes searched the gathered faces, not finding the one he sought. With a subtle gesture to the luna wolf, who responded with a low rumble of acknowledgment, he slipped away from the gathering celebrations. His feet carried him through familiar halls toward the back of the house, where morning light painted the farmstead in shades of gold and shadow.

Morning light spilled across Nikel's farmstead, the frost-covered fields sparkling like scattered stars. Markus found her kneeling in her garden, the space around her holding that familiar ethereal quality—as if reality itself bent slightly in her presence. The decaying plants of winter should have been brown and brittle, yet somehow the air felt alive with possibility.

Liyzia didn't turn as he approached, her fingers nimbly working in the frozen soil. The luna wolf, who had followed at a respectful distance, settled at the garden's edge, a silent guardian as her pups played in the frost.

Markus stood for a moment with the shawl draped across his outstretched hands—an offering carried through battle and transformation. Only then did Liyzia turn. Her eyes found his with that same mysterious warmth he remembered from their first meeting. As she rose, something caught the dawn light in her palm—a lumidawn flower that should have been impossible in winter's grip, its spiral petals faintly pulsing with gentle luminescence.

Her gaze lingered on his face, tracing the black scar

that carved down his temple. What had once burned like a brand now brimmed with a different rhythm—no longer a mark of isolation and pain, but a testament to survival and transformation. Her fingers reached up, hovering near but not quite touching the darkened tissue, while her eyes held a knowingness that made him wonder how much she had foreseen his journey.

They exchanged no words as she accepted the shawl, her fingers brushing his in a way that stirred his transformed blood. The connection between them transcended language—the abandoned boy and the mysterious guardian, bound by threads woven long before either understood their significance.

He offered his elbow, a gesture that bridged worlds— the street orphan he'd been, the warrior he'd become, and whatever destiny was still to unfold. Liyzia tucked the glowing lumidawn into her sleeve and took his arm, her presence steady as starlight. Together they turned toward the house, where their new family waited.

Behind them, in the frozen earth where Liyzia had knelt, a faint pulse of light remained. The soil around it had thawed in a perfect circle, revealing the impossible bloom of another lumidawn, its spiral petals opening toward the winter sun. With each gentle burst of light, the frost receded further, as if spring itself had awakened in this single spot—a promise of renewal. Or perhaps a warning of ancient powers stirring once more?

THE END

Aerial chart of Central Aerias and its Northern territories during the time of Markus Kane's emergence

AFTERWORD

A Glimpse into Aerias

This section is for the curious. A quiet guide for those still lingering by the firelight, wondering what echoes beyond the page. The world of Aerias is wide—steeped in myth, veined with technology, and shadowed by forgotten powers. What follows is a glimpse into the shape of that world, and a thread leading toward what comes next.

🌐 The World of Aerias

Aerias is a planet of contradiction.

Ancient ruins sit beside floating markets. Rituals and codes of honor clash with syndicates and senators. At its core are three forces:

The Kingdoms – Political bodies like the Nevran Realms and the Dromelan Empire, steeped in tradition, driven by legacy.

The Guilds – Corporate-tech cartels that regulate everything from weapons to transport to communication. They hold power not by crowns, but contracts.

The Old Powers – Fading legends. Prophetic symbols. Lost artifacts. And perhaps ... beings who were never truly gone.

🏙 Places That Matter

Vesper - A neon-lit maze where steam and circuitry mix. Streets run by bribes, backdoor deals, and Watchmen who uphold justice in their own way.

Orwein - A rural village steeped in tradition, nestled against the Canivere Forest. It's here that visions still stir, and old stories walk in silence.

Canivere Forest - A veil between worlds. Strange winds, whispering trees, and places where time seems to bend. Some say seers still walk its paths.

🤝 The Groups that Shape Aerias

The Watchmen - Semi-legal enforcers like Markus, often found in lawless zones. They live in the cracks between order and chaos.

The Guild - Technology monopolies that blur the boundaries of science and sorcery. Want to travel? Communicate? Fight? You'll need their license.

Senators and Nobles - Like Hans Lumen, many hide corruption behind charm and fine words. But some still seek to protect the realm.

The Lorekeepers—Keepers of truth and myth. They guard what most forget—and record what even history fears.

The Ilyrians - Ancient beings tied to prophecy and nature. Many believe them to be extinct. Others say they only sleep.

⚔ Tech and Magic

In Aerias, science is enchanted—and magic often comes with circuitry.

Pulse Pistols - Standard Guild issue. Semi-magical weapons powered by crystal cores.

Aerglides – Personal hovercrafts. Sleek, fast, and expensive to maintain legally.

Whispershot – A rare, silent weapon used by Xara. Lethal and almost undetectable.

Guild Enhancements – From weapon mods to encrypted ID papers, the Guild's tech fuses mysticism with math.

Old Powers – These are not spells—but deeper forces. Intuition. Foresight. Echoes of ancient design. Often subtle. Always watching.

🧬 Bloodlines and Secrets

Markus Kane is more than a name.

His blood corrodes lab equipment. His scar pulses with unnatural energy. No one knows why. Not even him.

Some say his name is a trigger, others, a warning. But one truth echoes across time: He was never meant just to survive. He was born to become something else.

In Aerias, identity isn't inherited: it's chosen.

❄ Myth and Memory

The Great Sundering – A cataclysm that shattered the balance between technology and magic. Aerias never fully recovered.

The Seer Shawls – Worn by prophet-women like Liyzia. Said to hold memories in their threads.

The Lumidawn – A rare, glowing bloom. Appears only in winter—or in moments touched by grace.

The Kaegars – Whispered horrors. Once believed to be legend. Once ...

🧠 Themes to Remember

Duality – Light and shadow. Magic and machine. Rich and poor. Old world vs. new age.

Found Family – Markus and Xara are bound not by blood, but by choice. That makes it stronger.

Prophecy vs. Free Will – Visions may guide—but they do not decide. In Aerias, choice still matters.

Power and Corruption – Every institution has its rot. Every hero their price.

→▣ Want to Go Deeper?

Explore maps, timelines, languages, species, and artifacts at: markuskane.com/appendix

Or scan the QR code at the back of the book to enter the full world of Aerias.

What you've seen is just the beginning.

🕊 Curious about the winged symbol above each chapter?

It's no coincidence. Some myths are just waiting to awaken.

For those curious how this world came to be, I've shared a personal note on the next page.

AUTHOR'S NOTES

This world lived in my imagination for nearly twenty years. I never thought I'd be brave enough to share it—but here it is. A story born from silence, refined in solitude, and shaped by grief, hope, and resilience.

Markus Kane: Dawn of Shadows is the first step into the world of Aerias—a world I've carried quietly through notebooks, sketches, memories, and the long nights in between. It came from a personal place, but I wrote it hoping someone else might recognize something familiar in the silence, in the struggle, or in the strength it takes to keep going.

If this story moved you in any way, I invite you to explore more at **markuskane.com**. There, you'll find expanded lore, character insights, artwork, and updates as this journey continues—because this is only the beginning.

Thank you for walking with me this far.

See you in the shadows.

—Isaiah Burch Jr.

SILVERSMITH
PRESS

Serves new and emerging authors
to help them write, publish, and promote their books.
Are you ready to share your story?

Visit us!
www.silversmithpress.com